"Ms. Jocks's poignant novel reminds us all that love is love, no matter who or why or where. Four Stars!"
—*Romantic Times* on *The Rancher's Daughters: Behaving Herself*

THE CHOICE

"It is true that Papa dislikes sheep," she admitted, wincing slightly at the understatement. "And it's true that if he sees you only as a sheep farmer, his . . . bias . . . might cause difficulty. But if he knew you as a person first, as the responsible, worthy man I do, then perhaps. . . ."

"Mariah," he whispered, as if inhaling her name off her hair. He wanted to marry her, she reminded herself through the tingling warmth of his embrace.

"Perhaps you can introduce yourself after church this Sunday," she suggested, closing her eyes. . . . Her words seemed to blur in her mouth, unfocused by the solidity of Stuart's chest at her back and head, his breath on her cheek. "You could . . . you could say hello on the street, if you see him."

"He would not answer."

She feared he was right. Papa did not waste words. "You never know until you try. Please, Stuart. For me. Please let me ease the idea of you—of us—onto him before you ask to marry me. If you ask too soon he'll say no, and once Papa makes a decision he hardly ever takes it back. And to go against him . . . please don't make me do that."

Stuart stood very still behind her. Then he said, "But you would? Go against him?"

Other *Leisure* books by Yvonne Jocks:
THE RANCHER'S DAUGHTERS:
BEHAVING HERSELF

THE RANCHER'S DAUGHTERS: Forgetting Herself

YVONNE JOCKS

LEISURE BOOKS NEW YORK CITY

A LEISURE BOOK®

August 2000

Published by

Dorchester Publishing Co., Inc.
276 Fifth Avenue
New York, NY 10001

ISBN 0-8439-4763-2

The name "Leisure Books" and the stylized "L" with design are trademarks of Dorchester Publishing Co., Inc.

Printed in the United States of America.

For this book in particular, I owe a debt
of gratitude to my critiquing friends:
Pam, for making me question things
Kayli, the Continuity Queen
Cheryl, for loving Jacob as much as I do
(even if she can't have him)
and Toni, who gave up a weekend to make sure I
remembered to eat and to count the periods in my
ellipses, and who knows where to put the hyphen
(and, of course, to Paige and Chris)
Much obliged!

But I'm dedicating it to my big brothers.

Forgetting Herself

Prologue

Wyoming, early 1890s

Stuart MacCallum expected the worst when he met Mariah Garrison beneath the Kissing Bridge.

"Well, I am here," he announced on a puff of frozen breath, his fisted hands stuffed deep into his patched coat pockets. "I got your note, and I am here."

He did not know how to talk to ladies, but he would not start worrying the matter with such as her.

When Mariah's eyes widened at his arrival, though, he could not help but notice, up close and alone like this, how very pretty she'd become. He guessed she must be about fourteen now—the same age as his sister Emily, three years younger than him—but she did not look anywhere near as gangly as Emily did. Her hair, swept into neat curls down her back, glinted pure gold even in the dingy shadows of the bridge. Her dark blue coat boasted a fur collar that framed her fine, oval face. The fur was no mere squirrel or rabbit either, like Stuart's sisters or mother might wear. He thought perhaps it was mink.

Against his better judgment, he found himself wondering which would be softer to the touch, the collar, the hair, or the pretty face. Even now, she did not look like a girl who would lure boys to the Kissing Bridge—or into an ambush. But the note, read and reread since he had found it in his school desk after lunch, crackled its reminder in his pocketed fist.

He scowled down at the snow-dusted mud beneath his boots rather than gawk at her. He would go to hell before he would deign touch the likes of her.

"Why . . ." Her voice fell away, strangely hesitant considering where they were. Traitorously, Stuart's gaze crept back up from the snow, over her expensive coat to her fine, fine face. He saw that her eyes were light gray, like the predawn sky. "Why are you so angry?" she asked him.

Because even if this is not an ambush, my folks raised me better than to trifle with game-playing girls like . . . like . . .

But until today, as far as he had ever noticed, she had *not* seemed that kind of a girl. She had seemed like a proper young lady, even from across the schoolroom—across the infinite prejudices between her family and his.

He guessed it did anger him at that, to think otherwise.

"You left me a note and I am here," he repeated again, stubborn.

"I can see that," she said, her voice so soft and unsure it was almost a whisper. "Thank you."

Stuart did not bid her welcome. As surely as the bridge sheltered the two of them, it blocked the rest of the world from their sight, too. Even now, any number of her cowboy friends could be creeping up, listening for him to say something they could hold against him, waiting for their chance to teach the oldest MacCallum boy why sheep farmers oughtn't take liberties with a cattle rancher's daughter. Well he was here. He would not let them call him a coward. But they would have to invent any further accusations.

Not that their like would hesitate to do so. Just this year, the cattlemen responsible for the nearby Johnson County range war—massacre, more like it—had gone free without trial because not twelve impartial jurors could be found.

Not twelve men who would dare side against Wyoming's cattle interests . . .

Stuart would dare, were he old enough—but for a worthy reason. Not merely to be with a girl, especially not one forward enough to leave notes in boys' desks.

He stood there in the muddy snow, his breath misting, and watched Miss Mariah Garrison stand on the bare ground, in the shelter further under the bridge. He had never dared to look at her this closely before. Forgetting his upbringing with a girl this pretty, this delicate, this fancy . . . it would almost be worth a beating.

If only she were not the one who had lured him here.

She lowered those large, fine eyes of hers, as if unused to such attentions, and the pink in her cheeks looked to be from more than the cold.

"There is work I could be doing," Stuart prompted. "If you have nothing to say to me, I had best get home."

"I'm sorry. I've never . . ." A fur-mittened hand drifted up to her pink cheek, uncertain, and brushed a golden curl back. Soft, he thought again. "We—my sisters and I—we found . . . I mean . . ."

She shook her head, made an intriguingly human noise of frustration deep in her throat, then simply turned to retrieve something off the ground behind her. A picnic basket? He had not seen it past her skirts, at first. Now that he did, Stuart did not understand it, any more than he understood Mariah Garrison—*the* Mariah Garrison—

leaving notes in his desk. She did not mean to offer charity, did she? She could not have planned a picnic. This was November!

Setting the basket between them, the girl knelt and opened the wicker cover. A white, woolly head popped out, bright-eyed and incautious, to sniff the air.

An autumn lamb!

Stunned, Stuart dropped to one knee in the dusting of snow and lifted the lamb with experienced hands, turned it, examined it. Three weeks old, at most. Something had mauled it, but the wounds had been tended. The beastie did not even seem to notice, wriggled only once, then tried to suckle hungrily at his thumb.

"He's been very good," assured the girl who had made this fantastic delivery, as if he might fault the lamb's behavior. Then she did something even more amazing. She reached a hand across the space between them and stroked the lamb's head, near his own bare hand. She did not seem to think she would soil her fineries by touching such an animal. When the lamb nuzzled the fur of her mitten, searching for food, she laughed as if it tickled.

Stuart looked up from the soft, delicate creature in his hands to the soft, delicate creature just across the picnic basket from him, and something deep in his gut shifted, as subtly as a heartbeat, as dramatically as an earthquake.

By all that was holy. If this was neither ambush nor tryst, Miss Mariah Garrison had suddenly risen to his highest esteem.

"He hasn't made a sound, hardly," assured Mariah, her nervousness such that she had to fill this awkward silence with something, anything, even babbling. "We found him yesterday, when we were out riding, and he had blood on him. My sister Laurel said perhaps he was stolen from his mother by some animal that we frightened away."

More's the pity, Laurel had also said, but Mariah would not repeat that. Neither would she admit that little Audra had not even known what the dear creature was, at first. And oh, the lamb was dear. Watching it decline her glove and go back to suckling at Stuart MacCallum's callused thumb, she wondered yet again how such an innocent animal could do such dreadful damage to the open range originally settled by the cattle ranchers. How could *this* inspire such anger in good men like her father and his colleagues?

"Likely a bobcat," agreed Stuart, and for the first time since he had descended the creekbank to join her under the bridge, he didn't sound angry. He squinted up at her through a fall of hair the color of dark wheat, and she thought him surprisingly handsome, now that his mouth no longer pulled into that dreadful scowl. "Maybe a coyote. A wolf or cougar would have killed him faster."

She rather liked his eyes—a rich brown, like tilled soil in a garden. She hadn't noticed before now how very tall he had grown, either; even kneeling, he seemed tall and solid. The Garrisons and the MacCallums might attend the same school, the same church, but they did not move in the same circles. She'd never before had cause to note Stuart's height.

Now she could not stop noticing. He seemed so . . . solid.

"We couldn't leave him to freeze to death," she hurried to add, to fill the silence, and wished her voice would not sound so frivolous and silly, wished her stomach were not so unsteady. "We brought him home, hid him. And we fed him with a rag dipped in milk. Cow's milk. I hope that's all right."

Stuart's eyes darkened with a seriousness she sensed more than understood. "Why bother?" he asked. "For a sheep?"

Which was what Laurel had said—but Mariah suspected that to be mere posturing on her sister's part. Laurel had known full well the other girls would outvote her.

"He is yours, isn't he?" she asked, rather than deign

answer his question. It was hard to speak self-righteously about caring for all God's creatures, what with the sick suspicion that her beloved father might well have let the lamb die—or helped it out of its misery. Papa would never approve of this exchange, should he ever find out. That must be why her heart was pounding so dramatically, why her throat felt so tight. She felt guilty to be doing something Papa would so clearly forbid.

"There are few sheep ranches around here," Stuart reminded her, which made her feel guilty in a whole different way, made her look down. "Yes, he is likely one of ours."

"Then you take him." All that mingling guilt roiled around in her chest in a most disturbing way, and she lashed out against it and against the closest source of it. Standing, still not looking at him, she said, "Try to do a better job at keeping the bobcats and the coyotes away."

Then she turned away and waited for him to leave. So much for doing a good deed.

"You . . ." After an awkward pause, Stuart MacCallum also stood, and tried again. "Do not forget your basket."

"You may take it," said Mariah.

"No need," insisted Stuart, somewhat more sharply, and curiosity drew her to glance over her shoulder back at him. He had tucked the lamb under his rough but clean coat, so that the baby would stay warm against his chest. His chest, too, was broader than she had remembered. Like so many of the older boys, Stuart only attended school in the winter, and then only when weather permitted.

Mariah retrieved the now lightweight basket, held it with both hands. She hoped her father would not see her sneaking it back into their town house.

"Mariah," said Stuart suddenly, which surprised her—the attention, more than the name. Apparently it surprised him, too. His eyes flared at his own boldness, and he looked quickly down at the shadowed ground between them. "That is . . . Miss Garrison."

"You may call me Mariah," she assured him. "Your sisters and I are . . . acquaintances." Now she felt guilty about that, too—why were they no more than simple acquaintances? Was she such a snob?

Stuart scowled again, still at the ground. "Thank you for doing this," he said, awkward. "I have been less than . . . than gracious. My apologies, but I feared . . ."

She cocked her head. Stuart MacCallum, who several years ago had faced down three full-grown cowboys in the street, and them armed, and him not? Stuart MacCallum fear *anything?* She would as soon believe her father could be frightened.

"I suspected less than proper intentions," he blurted. She was not sure, but he might even be blushing.

"Goodness—what intentions could possibly be less proper than giving a sheep back to a sheep farmer?" she asked him, even more intrigued. She had known as soon as she and her sisters secreted the lamb home, then up to her and Laurel's bedroom where her father was least likely to intrude, that she had left appropriate behavior far behind.

He widened his eyes at her, but since he hadn't looked fully up, his hair was falling across his face again, which made him appear far more endearing than reproachful.

Endearing? Oh, yes, very. Proud and stubborn. Tall and strong and solid. And remarkably, amazingly endearing.

Since he wasn't saying anything, she dipped her own head, eyed him at a slant, and risked the slightest teasing smile. "You might as well tell me, Stuart MacCallum, because now I am determined to find out."

"This—" He swallowed hard. Now he *was* blushing! She had not realized that men blushed. "This bridge."

"It's the bridge closest to our house," she noted, impatient to understand.

He quickly looked away, then back, jaw set. His eyes were just as wide, but now they were reproachful. "You ought not be let out of the house," he told her, testy.

"What?"

And then, to her everlasting surprise, the quiet Stuart MacCallum lost his temper with her. "This is the *Kissing Bridge,* Mariah!" he exclaimed. "It is where the boys bring their best girls to *kiss!* If I caught a fellow meeting with my sister here, I would thrash him within an inch of his life and never let her out again! You should *not* come here, certainly not invite boys to meet you here. People will think . . ."

Then, stumbling to silence, he just stood there like a rock and smoldered helplessly down at her.

"They . . . will think . . ." he tried again.

She stared back up at him, flushed with embarrassment to realize what he had thought of her, guilt-ridden to have betrayed her family even more thoroughly than she had meant to. And along with the horror, she felt voiceless with fury that he would dare chide her about it as if he had any right to do so, as if she did not realize the magnitude of her mistake as soon as he had explained it to her. The *Kissing Bridge?* Her town had a Kissing Bridge?

And amidst all that, she felt confused—so very confused by how beautiful his brown eyes struck her, crackling with a passion she had never suspected in anyone from Sheridan, Wyoming . . . much less a MacCallum.

She swallowed hard herself, anchoring herself on the nearness of his gaze so that she could stay focused through all that confusing, overwhelming distress. He had eyes one could find a great deal of steadiness in, despite their passionate intensity.

Suddenly, like a balm, she realized she was glad he would dare chide her. It seemed to mean something important, something she didn't wholly understand yet, but was not about to ignore. As if perhaps, just perhaps, he cared about her.

Not a MacCallum for a Garrison. Something far more personal than that. Stuart. For Mariah.

"What," she whispered back up to him, a dare, "would people think?"

Even though they both knew.

Then, to her delight, Stuart MacCallum leaned across those extra few inches and kissed her. On the lips! It was a quick kiss, not so long as the ones she sometimes caught her parents sharing when they thought they were alone, but it felt nice. Very nice. Something about him doing that—leaning close and kissing her like that—warmed her like sunshine, like firelight, like summertime. He bumped her with the lump in his coat that was the lamb, and knocked the basket she held against her knees, but the feel of his lips sang through her nevertheless.

Then he took a quick step back, his brown eyes stubborn, his lips pressed tightly together.

After a moment's consideration, Mariah smiled at him.

He swallowed, looked down, then scowled back up. "I ought not have done that."

"Neither should I," she agreed. It was hard to feel guilty, though, with her whole body warm and summery. She should not be here in the first place. What she *did* here hardly seemed more significant, propriety-wise. "But . . . I'm glad we did. Aren't you?"

"My folks raised me better than that," he pointed out, which seemed a very rude thing for someone who had just kissed her to say.

"My parents have done a perfectly good job raising me, too!" she had to point out.

"Well then, if I am going to be kissing you, it should not be under a bridge! I should be courting you, outright."

Courting? Not that he'd said he would *like* to court her . . . but perhaps he had enjoyed the kiss after all, to even consider such a thing. Such a marvelous, impossible thing.

Their annoyance at each other faded to dismay. Mariah put their dilemma into words. "Papa would never allow that."

"Not a sheep farmer," agreed Stuart.

"Not a sheep farmer," echoed Mariah, then caught a fleeting hope. "I don't suppose you've considered other—"

But his stubborn expression silenced her, and she felt guilty again.

Stuart seemed angry, but she no longer thought he was angry at her. "Thank you for the lamb, Mariah. And . . . I apologize for compromising you."

"You didn't compromise me, Stuart. You . . . I liked it. Can't . . . can't we see each other? Again?"

He made a groaning noise and turned away, stepped out from under the bridge. "Do not forget who you are," he reminded her bitterly over his shoulder. "Do not forget who I am, either."

Halfway up the bank, he paused long enough to reach down a gentlemanly hand—the one not holding the lamb to his chest—and guided her all the way up. She liked how strong his hand felt, closing protectively around her mitten. But as soon as she reached level land, he released it and climbed to the top himself, nodded at her, and again turned away.

He paused when she said, "I won't forget who you are."

But then he walked on.

Mariah raised a fur-mittened hand to her lips, closed her eyes, thought about being kissed. Kissed by Stuart MacCallum.

Maybe she *was* the oldest daughter of one of the most respected cattle ranchers in northern Wyoming. And maybe he *was* the oldest son of one of the greatest pariahs of the grasslands, her father's dire enemy: a sheep farmer. But he had kissed her, and it had not seemed sinful at all.

So that, thought Mariah in wonder, is who I am going to marry.

And then she thought: *Poor Papa!*

Chapter One

October, four years later

Poor Garrison, thought Stuart MacCallum from where he leaned against the wall of the red train depot, half hidden on its shadowed platform.

Of course, he meant that sarcastically. Jacob Garrison owned maybe the biggest spread in northeastern Wyoming. Stuart had heard talk of him refusing requests to run for senator, for governor, probably for God. The rancher likely thought himself above such jobs. He was above everything and everybody else.

Stuart watched the man rein in his surrey team across the street from the depot, farther from the track. That put it beside the exclusive, multigabled Sheridan Inn. A hotel porter hurried out to help him hitch his horses. What seemed like half the town had come up for Miss Mariah Garrison's homecoming, yet at the appearance of her father, folks fell quiet enough that Stuart could hear the porter ask, "Here for the eleven-fifteen, boss?"

"Yep," said Garrison. He finished the hitching himself, then turned toward the depot. Stocky, his hair and beard streaked white, he moved like the old cowboy he was.

He is not even tall, noted Stuart. But cattle barons did not need height. They had power.

The stationmaster himself crossed the platform to meet him. "Your oldest girl gets home today, boss?"

Beneath the shadow of his black Stetson, Garrison stared at the railroad man for a long moment. Why else would he be wearing his Sunday go-to-meeting coat on a Thursday? "Yep."

Stuart wore his cleanest work clothes today, the best he could do besides getting away from his claim at all. Mariah, he firmly hoped, would not mind. To the parasoled ladies strolling the Inn grounds across the way, his simple duds made him near about invisible—and probably just as well. But Mariah never seemed to place importance on such things. It was one of the things that made him wonder at her bloodline.

Garrison's fierce brows furrowed into a scowl. He stared down the tracks as if he could bring the train by force of will.

Likely thinks he can, decided Stuart. But he knew a truth that Old Man Garrison himself did not.

Stuart meant to marry Garrison's eldest daughter.

You enjoy everyone calling you boss, he thought at his future father-in-law's rigid back. *Enjoy it while you can.*

Stuart would do a great deal for Mariah, including stooping to subterfuge. But he would not call a cattleman "boss."

He'd meant what he'd told Mariah under the bridge that first time: If he was to kiss her, he should call on her openly. Since a sheep farmer courting a rancher's daughter would never end up healthy for the sheep man, nor come to anything real and lasting, he had determined to forget about her.

But Mariah proved impossible to forget. Every time

their gazes had touched in church that winter; every time she stood to recite a lesson at school; every time he heard her laughter, something twisted inside Stuart's chest. Something deep-rooted and incontrovertible warmed him at the very thought of her. Miracles seemed possible with Mariah . . . someday. And in the meantime, subterfuge had won out. He and Mariah secretly met, again and again. And they'd kissed, again and again . . . and again. . . .

Standing on the platform of Sheridan's two-story depot, Stuart felt a flush of shame at that. If ever some fellow took such advantage of one of his sisters, much less a daughter, Stuart might well kill the son-of-a-dog.

But it's his own fault, he thought darkly at the cattle baron's back. *Neither of us would have behaved so badly if we could have had a proper chaperone—if not for him.*

Kisses still fresh on his mind, he caught his breath at the distant wail of the train approaching from the south.

Garrison's hat came up, alert. Impatient to have his daughter back under his rein, was he? Well, things were about to change. In the time since Mariah's parents had sent her to Europe, Stuart had turned twenty-one and filed claim on his own quarter section of government land. He could ask her to marry him outright now. Proving up a claim would be hard work, even with his brother helping. But Mariah had never failed to surprise Stuart yet, and they would be working together. At eighteen, she knew her own mind. She'd said as much in the letters she'd secreted to him through a friend and his sister Emily.

The train bore down on them. With a great gusting of steam and clanging of bells, the locomotive chugged to an ungainly stop beside the depot. Stuart took several steps nearer the first-class passenger car, searching its fancy windows—then hesitated.

The first man off the train felt like danger.

He wore a conspicuous gunbelt, unusual attire on a

passenger train even without the tooled leather and pearl handle. He walked cocky, too. But most damning, Stuart realized, was how the gunman's gaze paused knowingly on Old Man Garrison before he nodded and stepped out of the way.

The rancher's head turned to follow the gunman's progress and Stuart thought, with a shudder: *It's starting again.*

Stuart could remember when his and several other sheep families first moved to Wyoming territory on the promise of a homestead and free range. Cattlemen, it turned out, had a different definition of the word "free." Their beef cattle were too dainty to drink water "tainted" by sheep, too stupid to tear off grass that had been eaten as short as sheep ate it. The Wyoming Stock Grower's Association—whose definition of "stock" proved equally narrow—publicly took what action they could in the Territorial government. Privately, they turned the Wyoming range into sheer hell. Gunnysackers, their faces hidden, rode out of the night to kill sheep, dogs, even herders. Rim-rockers chased panicked bands of sheep over the edges of cliffs with cowboy precision. The warring factions finally called truce, accepting a "deadline" on the range that neither party was to cross, only after a massacre of homesteaders in nearby Johnson County caused a public outcry the ranchers dared not challenge.

Then.

By then, only a few sheep farmers remained in Sheridan County. Others had run—not MacCallums. *Never* MacCallums. But to see a hired gunman and a cattleman together added a deadly chill to the November afternoon. . . .

Suddenly, with a sunlit swoop of pale blue cloak, Mariah Garrison herself flew down the iron steps onto the platform and launched herself, wide-armed—

At her father.

From his spot to the side and slightly behind the

reunion, Stuart forgot to breathe. She was so beautiful! He had always known that, of course, but . . . now! He understood neither fashion nor hairstyling—as his sisters would surely agree—but on a gut level he recognized that Miss Garrison's golden curls and traveling coat must be the height of style. She looked so neatly put together; so clean, and polished, and *worldly!*

She looked as far from his world of fleece worms and hoof rot as . . . as Europe and posh hotels.

Her father put his hands on her shoulders and looked her over. "Well ain't that fine behavior for a lady."

Mariah smiled as if he'd complimented instead of chided her, kissed his bearded cheek, then hugged him again.

Then, over Garrison's shoulder, she saw Stuart.

Barely breathing even yet, he nodded a silent hello.

She stared, her gray eyes warming with the delight of recognition. But when Stuart, emboldened, took a step closer, those same eyes widened.

He paused, immediately wary.

She looked quickly away, before her father might notice anything amiss. Another passenger—a tall, light-haired gentleman with a young lady of the same complexion on his arm—approached Mariah as if he belonged with her. Looking everywhere but back to Stuart, Mariah touched the man's arm, smiled a welcome to him. He looked familiar.

Did he belong with her? Stuart watched Garrison nod at her introductions, watched the rancher touch his hat brim at the lady and firmly shake hands with the gentleman.

During this, Mariah lifted her contrite gaze back to Stuart's. She raised a gloved hand to her hair, wrapped a golden curl around a finger—the old signal asking him to meet her later, at their bridge. With her eyes she begged him to understand. Even he, no master of silent communication, could read those fine eyes of hers.

He moved his attention, almost angrily, to the light-haired man who did not need secret trysts for her attention, her touch.

Mariah widened her eyes back at him, clearly distressed.

Stuart reluctantly nodded—but the light-haired lady had said something and Mariah spun to respond, to mask her distraction. If she saw Stuart's agreement, she gave no sign of it.

She smiled at the light-haired man—who *was* he?—as well.

Too soon, their party turned to leave. Suddenly, Stuart found himself locking gazes with eyes the identical shade of gray as Mariah's, but as cold in the shadow of a black Stetson as hers had been warm beneath a jaunty blue bonnet. Jacob Garrison, cattle baron and town founder, had just caught a sheep farmer staring at his eldest daughter.

Stuart stared right back. He might only have a quarter section of land, and barely four hundred head of livestock—and yes, they were sheep. He might not have a surrey or two fine houses. But he was a full-grown man with his own land and a good name. He would rot in hell before he would lower his eyes before a cattle rancher.

Likely Garrison felt equal hatred. He wasn't lowering his eyes either.

"MacCallum!" The voice at his ear startled Stuart into looking away—at the stationmaster who had called him. Damnation! When Stuart glanced back, the Garrison party was already leaving the platform. All four of them.

The light-haired man, the one Mariah had touched, was splitting from the party in the direction of the cocky, narrow-eyed gunman.

"You here to fetch something?" The stationmaster meant that this was not downtown; he did not want people loitering at his depot without business to conduct.

Especially not sheep men.

"No," said Stuart, after one last glance at the only

woman he'd ever considered worthwhile. "Not yet, I guess."

And he strode angrily away.

Stuart had met the train!

Never had Mariah felt so grateful for Papa's steadying arm; it kept her from crumpling into a surprised heap. She knew how much work Stuart's claim demanded of him and his brother; hadn't he told her so in his letters? She knew how difficult it was for him to get into town. She had never dreamed, not in the midst of her most shocking fancies, that Stuart would meet a Thursday-morning train just to see her, much less that he would be so bold as to approach her—

And in front of her father!

Just as well that, when she dared peek back at the depot for another glimpse of him, she could not find him. Papa might see, and Stuart had risked so much already.

But she searched the platform twice more, just to be sure.

She barely noticed the heartwarming reception several of the townspeople were giving her, though she did try, gratefully taking people's hands and promising to pay visits. She went through the mere motions of bidding farewell and thank you to Alice and Alden Wright; six months with Alice had proved several too many, and after only a day Alden made her nervous with his barely concealed staring. She would not let them soil her homecoming.

Here she stood on her beloved father's arm, the Bighorn Mountains dominating the western horizon, Wyoming air sharp and clean in her lungs, and she was home, home, *home!*

And Stuart MacCallum had met the train—would, she fervently hoped, meet her at their bridge. Tall, broad-shouldered, stubborn-eyed Stuart. Summer had darkened his skin, lightened the ends of his hair, weighted his eyelids to give him a sleepy, serious look. And something else had darkened his brown eyes as he had squinted at her across the platform.

Mariah liked it, for years had liked it, when his eyes went dark. It made her shiver inside, with a warm excitement she did not fully understand. Yes, he would meet her at their bridge.

Why care any longer what Alice Wright thought?

"Primed for a longer tour, are you," teased Papa under the wail of the train whistle, after directing her trunks to the surrey. His gruff, low drawl could cut through anything. Mother sometimes said that was because he was a force of nature, "half German and all Jacob."

If not for his reticence at public affection, Mariah would have hugged him again. "You would need to force me away at gunpoint!"

As if to emphasize her determination, the train began to huff and puff and then, with one last wail, to chug northwards toward Montana—without her.

"Reckon you'll stay a spell, then." She could see from the gleam in his shadowed eyes that he approved. He helped her onto a curbside step provided by the Inn, then into the surrey.

"I suppose I will," she agreed, heartfelt, as he unhitched the team and climbed up beside her. "Poor Papa! You simply can't get away from all of us heifers, can you?"

He clucked to the horses. "I'll endure."

From her closemouthed father that was high enthusiasm, and Mariah returned it by taking his arm while he drove, supremely comforted by his familiar silence. Papa did not, she knew, play favorites amongst his six daughters—she doubted a fair-minded man like him would know how! But that had never stopped her, his oldest girl, from sometimes savoring her storybook life as if he were some kind of cowboy king and she his crown princess.

And oh, Mariah thought her life even better than the

most glorious storybooks. Whether wolves howled outside the walls of their old log cabin, or Indians rode up to their ranch well, she knew Papa would protect her mother, her sisters, and herself. Their fine homes, on the ranch and in town, were due to his hard work and determination. Mother made sure the family never forgot their blessings, encouraging what charity work was proper for young ladies and teaching them to see beyond their own lives—one of the many things that had annoyed Alice Wright in Europe.

But never had Mariah felt so blessed as now, luxuriating in Papa's effortless security as surely as in the crisp October air, the familiar houses along Scott Street, and the expectation of seeing her family—and Stuart—again.

"I'm so glad to be home!"

"I did notice." They drove another block of the mile between the depot and their town house. Then her father asked, "They mistreat you, over there?"

He did not look at her but when she turned to study his weathered profile, she detected a furrow between his brows. Oh dear, had she shown too much excitement? Papa did not, of course, know that she was in love. He could not possibly understand the extra undercurrent of excitement that had built in her from the time she stepped foot on the steamship from Italy to return. It had increased with each passing day, with each milestone—arrival in New York City, the train West, changing onto the Burlington line—until now she could hardly breathe through it, Wyoming air or not.

For the best part of her storybook life had become Stuart.

She felt safe with Stuart too, of course—safe from Indians or wolves—but perhaps not from something feverish, deep inside herself, that seemed to threaten whenever she saw him and his stubborn eyes. Competent and wonderful though he was, Stuart represented his own delicious risk. Especially when his eyes went dark.

No, she could not explain that to her father. Not yet.

"No sir," she assured him instead, leaning her cheek against his shoulder. "Alice's parents took good care of us. I had a glorious time . . . I'm just glad to be home again."

Papa considered that, then nodded, his gaze speculative. For a moment a great, hollow foreboding opened up in Mariah's chest. Did he know? Had he guessed? She had to swallow, hard, before managing the words, "Is something wrong?"

But all he said was a gruff, "Learn these horses poor habits, findin' their own way home." So she respectfully loosened her hold on his arm while he drove, and split her attention between her beloved hometown, her father's silent companionship . . . and thoughts of Stuart.

In the summers Mariah's family still lived out on their Circle-T Ranch, in the foothills of the Bighorn Mountain Range. But in the autumn they moved into town so that the girls could attend school. Mariah loved their three-story brick town house with its wraparound veranda and gazebo, its gables and sparkling windows, its fine lawn. Now she studied it with new eyes while Papa circled toward the carriage house behind. Even compared to houses in Europe, it was beautiful. The perfect place to begin happily-ever-afters.

Her stomach did a nervous flip-flop as she again slanted her gaze up at her father's stern profile. Before she could have her happily-ever-after, she must tell him about Stuart once and for all. Papa would no doubt disapprove at first, which had made it disturbingly easy for her to keep secrets. But he did love her, did want her to be happy; she never doubted that. And Stuart *was* a good man—honest, hardworking, churchgoing.

Handsome. Forbidden. Meeting her in secret . . .

"Ho," ordered her father, pulling the team to a halt and then setting the brake and swinging down from the driver's seat. The horses stood with charmed obedience as he came around and lifted Mariah down to the brick walkway.

"Best go kiss your mother," he ordered her, in much the same tone. He would see to the rig, to her bags. He always managed things like that for his girls.

Mariah gave him one more hug, which this time, in the privacy of their own trees and carriage house, he returned.

"I love you, Papa," she said earnestly. He had to understand that, no matter who she meant to marry. She would never, ever stop loving her family.

He exhaled deeply into the embrace, almost a sigh. Then he let her go. "Get on with you."

Affection, solid and enduring, warmed his gray eyes behind the usual scowl. Mariah wondered how she had stayed away from her favorite men in the world for so long.

With a last kiss on his whiskered cheek, she spun and all but raced up the walkway to the back porch, the kitchen, and her mother. Ladies did not, of course, run. And with the thought of Stuart's darkened eyes still fresh, Mariah remembered far too much unladylike behavior she had to make up for.

She shivered happily at the very idea.

Chapter Two

Mariah's younger sisters hurried home from school for their midday meal, to welcome her in a gratifying cluster of squeals and hugs. As they settled around the kitchen table, she had the satisfying sensation of never having left—not in any way that counted.

Papa sometimes called himself a *mädchenvater,* or father of girls. While that wasn't strictly true—his son Thaddeas, by his first wife, would be home for supper tonight—he and Mother did have six daughters. Mariah sat in the place that had always been hers, at Papa's immediate right, across from dark-haired, sixteen-year-old Laurel. Fourteen-year-old Victoria, beside Mariah, plied her with questions while seven-year-old Kitty kept quiet as ever at the far end. On the other side of the table, thirteen-year-old Audra behaved herself between Laurel and four-year-old Elise. Mother, of course, sat at the opposite end of the table from their father, where she could best deal with the baby of the family—not that Elise was a baby anymore.

As always, Papa still commanded silence to say grace, the same simple words he'd used since Mariah had memory. Mother divided her attention between her husband and their daughters until the "Amen." Then she passed platters of meat and bowls of vegetables around the table so that everyone except the very youngest children could serve themselves.

Other mothers waited on their families, Mariah knew, but hers was not like other mothers. Younger than Papa—still brown-haired and pretty—Mother was a progressive. Even now, she teased Mariah by asking, "So were you wooed by any handsome noblemen abroad?"

Papa stopped chewing to stare at her, and Mama winked—*winked!*—back at him.

"No, ma'am," assured Mariah, trying not to blush. She had, after all, been wooed, in a simple, earnest way. But it had been in writing, and in secret—and by Stuart MacCallum.

Laurel asked, "By any ugly noblemen?" When Mariah huffed in protest, Laurel grinned her same old, sassy grin. "I'm just joshing! You'd be loco to have truck with any fancy-pants shorthorn, less'n he was ornamental."

"Watch yer language," warned Papa drily—as always. Hardly a meal had ever gone by without him chiding Laurel for something.

"Cowboys say pants," challenged Laurel, also as usual.

"You ain't no cowboy," noted Papa right back, and he held Laurel's rebellious gaze until she finally capitulated.

"Yessir." But Laurel's capitulations lost no sass, even if she wore long skirts now.

Victoria, dark-haired like Laurel, filled her usual role by asking endless questions—Did Mariah meet any noblemen at all? Noblewomen? Did she ride in a gondola? Mother called Victoria the eyes and ears of the family, because of her penchant for gathering information. When she took inappropriate measures to do so, Papa called her the nose of the family.

Mariah answered as best she could, between bites of pot roast—far tastier than any of the remarkable things the French had thought to cook up. But her anecdotes felt increasingly unreal, even as she related them. What did gondolas and Alps signify when she had true happiness right here in Wyoming, around this table?

And, perhaps, waiting at the bridge . . .

She ate a little faster.

Audra, who was fair-haired and well-mannered like Mariah, sat as quietly as ever, happy to just listen. Occasionally Mariah smiled at her, and Audra smiled back.

Kitty, small and frail for her seven years, squinted at her plate with unnecessary concentration. Kitty was the dreamer of the family.

And Elise . . . of course, Elise had grown a great deal from the three-year-old baby Mariah had last seen to the four-year-old child she was now, but even she seemed the same. The family beauty, Elise had golden curls, blue eyes, Mother's pert face and features . . . and since infancy, she had grasped her special position. Today she bounced in her chair, kicked the table leg, pushed at her food—and once even interrupted the conversation—until Papa made her walk around the table to stand beside him.

"Behave," he ordered. She nodded with such big-eyed repentance that he lifted her onto his lap to finish the meal there, where he could keep tighter rein on her. Of course she behaved perfectly then. She'd gotten what she wanted, and everyone at the table—except maybe Papa—knew it.

Home, thought Mariah, luxuriating in the familiarity of it all. *I have come home.*

And even now, Stuart MacCallum might be waiting for her at the Kissing Bridge.

Perhaps a good daughter would pretend to forget their tryst, stay home and help her mother, cling to the security of her homecoming a little longer. But a good *person* did not leave friends waiting. The need to extend her homecoming to Stuart resonated far too deeply.

Besides, now that she was eighteen and Stuart had his claim, they could finally speak of the future. Surely loving him did not make her less of a proper daughter. Mother would understand. So would Papa, even, if she just presented it correctly.

Everything would be fine. She knew it would.

"May I go along to the schoolhouse?" she asked, as they bundled her sisters up for their afternoon classes. It only hurt a little, that fib . . .

Papa said, "You ain't walkin' home alone," just as she expected he would; proper young ladies did not roam the downtown streets on their own.

So Mariah asked, "May I walk them as far as the bridge, then?" which felt better, more honest. To her relief, Papa—distracted by Elise—nodded curtly. The bridge was not halfway to the school, before they would even reach Main Street.

A flurry of hugs and kisses followed. Mother made happy "Mmmm" sounds with every tight embrace and Papa, with Elise on one arm, touched a steady hand to each daughter's shoulder in turn, warning Laurel in particular to "Behave." Mariah collected her hugs last—first from her pretty mother, with her visible love and subtle strength, and then from her solid father, with his visible strength and subtle love. Just like always.

Papa did not, she noticed, warn her to behave. That, more than anything else, made her stomach cramp with sudden guilt.

But not nearly guilt enough to keep her home.

Hidden in the shadows of the bridge over the rushing Goose Creek, Stuart realized he was clenching his jaw. He made himself stop doing that. But how did one react to such a strange, discomforting sensation as the doubt that had eaten at him since the train depot?

He refused to borrow trouble regarding the gunman,

without more knowledge. So why could he not stay as calm about Mariah?

Waiting out the time it would surely take for her to escape her parents—assuming she escaped at all—he settled into a comfortable crouch and reread her last letter to him. Her neat hand reassured him that she was making the best of her tour, which pleased him—his own sisters would never get such a chance, nor would she have such opportunities after their long-presumed marriage. As long as they'd had to wait, why should she not enjoy herself?

He easily found his place in the worn letter, read of her adventures, her discomfort over the Wrights' apathy in the midst of European unrest—and her desperately missing him. He hadn't imagined that. Just because she didn't want to upset her homecoming with her father, and just because she'd smiled at that strangely familiar greenhorn at the depot. . . .

Stuart stood and stuffed the letter back into his pocket, impatient again. This business of lurking under bridges had been bad enough in his youth. Now he had adult responsibilities—ewes to breed, hay to cut for winter. The sooner he spoke for Mariah, the better.

Unless her father really did kill him for it. That seemed extreme, even for Garrison.

Unless he hired in an outside man to do it.

Stuart heard the Garrison girls before they reached the bridge, even over the rushing water. ". . . at the Inn, to welcome you home *and* for my birthday. The whole town is invited!"

"Surely not the whole town." That voice he knew, after months' absence, and even in his impatience Stuart felt his shoulders lighten at the sweetness of it.

Mariah was with them.

"Just about," noted the voice he knew as Laurel's. "You know Mama."

Their footsteps tapped across the wood over Stuart's

head. Careful not to move, he felt guilt at the forced eavesdropping. The sooner this secrecy stopped, the better. The sooner he and Mariah made their courtship honest . . .

He tried not to picture how that fellow at the depot had taken her arm, tried not to remember the expensive cut of the man's suit.

"You can't go any farther," insisted a smaller voice. "Papa said."

"Telltale," scolded Laurel.

"I am not a telltale!"

"Do-gooder."

"No, Audra's right," insisted Mariah, quieting their tempers as simply as that—Stuart heard a shuffling of feet and the occasional kiss. "I'll see you after school."

For what seemed like a small eternity, Stuart listened to the sounds of the sisters moving on—the called good-byes and I-love-yous, even one set of footsteps hurrying back for one more hug. "Welcome home," said a young voice, and Mariah said, "Thank you, Kitty."

Stuart was not the only one grateful for Mariah's return.

He was, however, the only one hiding under a bridge.

The creek continued to rush past him; a flock of geese honked overhead. His jaw began to ache. This bridge was relatively sheltered by trees, thus its reputation. How long could it take before the girls were out of sight?

Then Stuart heard the crack of a twig and looked up to see Mariah's kid shoes descending the creek bank; her shapely, button-lined ankle—

He ought not be staring at her ankle. He seemed to have lost his ability to control himself, though, and stared anyway.

Her skirt, the edge of her cloak—and then Mariah herself peeked under the shadow of the bridge, as if unsure what she would find there.

Stuart swept his hat from his head. By all that was holy, she was beautiful. He had always thought her pretty, but her time overseas gave her the air of a world traveler, a princess, someone he never would have imagined could want a simple man like him.

Yet here she stood, against all the rules, peering at him where he stood in the dirt under a bridge.

Stuart swallowed, hard, then nodded. "Miss Garrison." His voice did not crack. Since that did not seem sufficient, he added, "Welcome home."

She took a step closer to him, he took a step closer to her—and then somehow, like so many times before, they were in each other's arms. Her soft, warm body pressed against his, filled his embrace even as her fingers dug furrows into the back of his coat. Her exquisite face turned up to his, her sweet lips meeting his own.

"Oh, Stuart," she breathed into his mouth, and he inhaled his own name, continued to kiss her in a way that was downright sinful—a way that he could not seem to stop, no matter what.

Since he could not stop himself from devouring her kisses, could not fight the way his hands slowly slid down her back toward more dangerous territory, Stuart did the next best thing. "We're old enough, now," he gasped. "I have land, sheep. Marry me."

He barely formed those basic words—not even managing a "please"—before one of his hands dipped onto the roundness of, well, of a place he ought not be touching before they made their vows. He managed, through sheer force of will, to fist that treacherous hand and drag it up to the small of her back again, but that did not undo his indiscretion.

Mariah laughed sheer pleasure against his cheek—he assumed at his proposal, not the indiscretion. "Yes," she whispered, lacing her words with little kisses up and down his jaw. "Yes, yes, yes. There has never been another man for me, Stuart MacCallum. Never. You know that."

And he did. Any lingering memories of the light-haired fop at the depot vanished.

The years of waiting no longer mattered. The hiding no longer mattered. Mariah was home and in his arms, for good, and Stuart had life by the tail with a downhill pull.

Then he said, "I'll call on your father this afternoon," and her lips faltered against his.

"This afternoon?" she whispered.

Life yanked free of Stuart's hold and sent him tumbling.

"This afternoon?" Mariah repeated, a sudden hesitance warring with the excitement that had made her so reckless in Stuart's arms.

Picturing her father at the same time that she was tasting Stuart's salty skin hardly helped. She could imagine Papa's reaction, if he knew what she was doing right now, much less with whom. He would be furious—worse, disappointed in her.

And rightly so. She had always assumed she would have time to ease him into the idea.

She drew back from Stuart's embrace. To his credit, he let her go. "So soon?" she asked.

Even as she said it, she recognized her mistake. Stuart's jaw set. His eyes, already dangerously dark, narrowed. "I am in town," he pointed out with terse logic. "And so is he."

"Well yes, of course! But Stuart—" How could she make him understand? "I only just got back. How can I surprise my family with something like this, and me not home for a day?"

"He'll be no more receptive to the idea a year from now, and you know it."

"I know no such thing! Nor do I mean to wait a year, but—"

"What we just did—" He spread his hand at the ground between them, the ground where she had risen onto her toes, pressed herself against the broadness of his chest, kissed him until she felt so dizzy that only his tight, tight hold on her had kept her from crumpling.

Mariah blushed.

"I thought—have always thought—I behaved so with my intended," Stuart finished.

His meaning stunned her. "*So did I!*"

Stuart scowled a silent challenge to her words.

Well! Unsure whether she felt more hurt or anger—both roared louder than the creek in her ears, tightened at her throat—Mariah reverted to propriety. If only she had remembered herself long before now. "If you mean to insult me, Mr. MacCallum, you have succeeded."

Her lips still tingled, cooling as they dried, and her face burned all the hotter to notice that. He had compromised her honor in more ways than one—but oh, so had she.

Stuart's scowl wavered, but he said nothing.

Mariah turned away, determined not to cry in front of him. "How is it insult to ask your father for your hand, even should he refuse?" His words sounded sullen, but at least he had spoken them. "If we truly are intended, he must know it. Would you have us elope?"

She took a deep breath, soothed by their shared distaste for elopements. Neither of them wanted to do the wrong thing; they had that in common. Perhaps they could discuss this after all. "It isn't. And I wouldn't. But to surprise Papa so soon . . ."

"Would waiting help? Your father hates sheep farmers worse even than nesters. He will hate me sight unseen, no matter when he finds out."

She could not keep her back to him, not through that bitter confession. When she turned, he looked as stubborn and resentful—hurt, really—as she had feared. "You can't know that, Stuart! Papa doesn't hate anyone, especially not you. He doesn't even know you."

"He sees me and mine in church every Sunday."

And he hadn't behaved hatefully once. When Mariah reached both hands for him, to her bone-deep relief, Stuart took them, steadied her. She also felt relief that he did not use the grip to draw her back against him right away, because she would not have been able to resist if he had.

Relief, and a naughty whisper of disappointment.

"It is true that Papa dislikes sheep," she admitted, wincing slightly at the understatement. Papa might not hate people, but like other ranchers, he did despise what he called *them hooved locusts.* "And it's true that if he sees you only as a sheep farmer, his . . . bias . . . might cause difficulty. But if he knew you as a person first, as the responsible, worthy man I do, then perhaps . . ."

Stuart stared at her, incredulous.

"Do not underestimate my father's intelligence," insisted Mariah, drawing herself up.

Stuart opened his mouth—then shut it, seemingly unable to frame the right response to that. Finally he took a chance on, "And just how do you intend we familiarize your father with my finer qualities?"

"Don't tease me!" She snatched her hands from his, turned away, but—as she had more than half hoped—Stuart's arms encircled her from behind and he drew her back against him.

"Mariah . . ." he whispered, as if inhaling her name off her hair. He wanted to marry her, she reminded herself through the tingling warmth of his embrace. She had assumed as much for years, of course, but this time he had actually asked. Her storybook life just kept getting better.

"Perhaps you can introduce yourself after church this Sunday," she suggested, closing her eyes . . . her words seemed to blur in her mouth, unfocused by the solidity of Stuart's chest at her back and head, his breath on her cheek. "You could . . . you could say hello on the street, if you see him."

"He would not answer."

She feared he was right. Papa did not waste words. "You never know until you try. Please, Stuart. For me.

Please let me ease the idea of you—of us—onto him before you ask to marry me. If you ask too soon he'll just say no, and once Papa makes a decision he hardly ever takes it back. And to go against him . . . Please don't make me do that."

Stuart stood very still behind her. Then he said, "But you would? Go against him?"

The possibility stuck in her chest so that she could barely breathe. Unlike her mother, Mariah never wanted to be progressive. She loved her father, and took pride in her reputation. . . .

Except with Stuart. She rarely ever remembered her family or reputation, rarely ever behaved properly with Stuart. Him officially asking for her hand would be the first proper thing they had ever done. But if he did not succeed . . .

Mariah nodded. For him, and how she felt with him, she would even go against her father. But she should not, would not have to. Everything would be fine—somehow.

Stuart kissed her temple. Mmm. She tipped her head toward her opposite shoulder, allowing him better access to her throat, and he kissed the sensitive skin beneath her earlobe. She sank weakly back against him, her strength draining from her at the ecstasy of his lovemaking. As sweet as his kisses was the certainty that she had won her bid for more time. Stuart would do anything for her, and so would Papa. If she just approached them right.

And in the meantime—they were now secretly engaged.

"I canna be with you like this," Stuart murmured into her shoulder, his work-thick arms tightening around her waist and ribs, scandalously close to her bosom. She shivered at the tickle of his words, at how he slipped into the faint brogue of his kinfolk when truly overcome. "I canna be this close to you and not . . . It will ruin the both of us."

He spoke the truth. They were behaving—rather, *mis-*

behaving—reprehensibly. And she loved it. In Stuart's arms, beneath his kisses and the feverish need to be with him in ways she did not even understand, she had little or no self-control. Apparently, neither did he.

Or so she would have thought, until suddenly he had her arms in his grip, instead of her waist, and was stepping determinedly back from her.

Trust Stuart to act in her best interests, even now.

Relief warred with a real ache of disappointment that he would not forget himself, even with her. Mariah turned to face him, the man she would marry, to memorize him again. How solid he was, strong and proud. She did love him, even the sense of propriety that left her cold and somehow unfulfilled. All they need do was show her father Stuart's finer points, persuade him to accept their engagement, and in less than a year she could kiss this man, hold him, know him in mysterious, connubial ways without any sin at all.

"I'll ease Papa into the idea," she promised breathlessly while Stuart backed away from her, seemingly unable to trust himself to get near again. "I'll find a way to make him see. I will."

He nodded curtly, then retrieved his hat from the ground, where it had somehow fallen from his fingers. He hesitated, looked down, then met her with that steady, solemn gaze of his. "Who was that man, Mariah? At the depot?"

A lock of wheat-brown hair had fallen over his face and oh, but he was handsome. "Alden Wright?" she countered, staring especially at Stuart's small, firm mouth. "Alice's brother, back from college. He escorted us from St. Louis."

Who would think that imagining someone's mouth on her skin could make her feel so warm and wicked, so . . .

She blushed again.

Stuart raised his chin. "You will marry me, then?"

"I said I would," she reminded him, secretly glad it mattered that much to him.

He nodded. "Aye. That you did." And, even as a quiet smile crinkled his heavy-lidded eyes, brightened his intent gaze, he backed another step away from her for safety's sake.

Then she remembered. "Stuart!"

His eyes flared, as if she presented a danger by stepping closer to him, drawing her treasure from her cloak pocket.

"This is for you! I brought it all the way from Scotland. . . ." And she handed him the woolen muffler.

He looked down at it, drew his hand across the dark blue and gray plaid.

"It's the MacCallum tartan," Mariah admitted, suddenly shy. "I asked . . ."

Stuart continued to stare at the muffler in his hands, then raised his gaze to hers. The admiration that heated his brown eyes thrilled her as surely as any of his kisses ever had.

"Thank you, Mariah," he said, his words thick with emotion.

"You are welcome, Stuart." The automatic answer felt strange in her own mouth, as well, especially when she longed to say so much more. She wanted to tell him about Scotland and Europe, about how seriously the Wrights took their social standing, about how glad she was to be home . . . to him. She felt cold, standing separate from him.

He was right. They had to admit their interest—their engagement—soon, or they would explode from their need of each other. If he felt anything close to what she did when near him . . .

She wanted to kiss him again. She wanted to lean into his strength, drink in his love for her. He was correct; they had no right to any of that until they followed the proper steps. They needed the chaperones that a proper engagement would provide. But she did want it.

With one last, longing glance in Stuart's direction, Mariah spun and scrambled up the bank of the creek to level ground, before he could even assist her.

After all, they meant to do this properly!

Chapter Three

Evangeline Taylor's feet were cold. That alone would not concern her so much—fourteen-year-old Evangeline's life held worse hardships than going without shoes. But as she trailed the Garrison sisters home from school, she feared her bare feet would embarrass them. Victoria, Audra, and Kitty wore fine leather shoes with gleaming buttons up the side, and clean cotton stockings. Laurel, at sixteen, had taken advantage of her mature, longer skirts to wear cowboy boots again. But that was Laurel.

Evangeline tried to hang back, so that the others could pretend she was not with them. But Victoria, ever observant, turned and extended a welcoming hand. "Hurry! Mariah said we could help her unpack!"

So Evangeline ran to catch up, cold feet forgotten. Victoria squeezed her hand and smiled at her. Evangeline would have smiled back, except that she was afraid of breaking the spell. And it did, indeed, feel like magic.

Her life transformed every Tuesday and Thursday afternoon.

A month ago, Mrs. Garrison of the Circle-T Ranch had asked Evangeline—as the best speller in Victoria's level—to tutor her daughter; in her joy at writing wonderful, exciting essays, Victoria rarely considered details like spelling. When Evangeline protested actual cash wages, Mrs. Garrison offered payment in piano lessons. Evangeline had never imagined herself doing anything so cultured as playing a piano! But the chance to visit the mansion on Elizabeth Street twice a week—on Tuesdays to help Victoria, and on Thursdays for music lessons like real ladies took—proved too tempting. Until now, she had only seen the mansion once a year for Victoria's birthday parties, and felt grateful for even that peek into another world. Most of her classmates did not extend even annual invitations. But now Evangeline followed the Misses Garrison home not once but twice a week!

She had offered to skip today. After all, Victoria's oldest sister had returned from Europe! But Victoria would not hear of it. Even Audra, who normally shied away from the slightest of misdoing, agreed. "Mama told us to remember you," she said.

So here Evangeline was, walking up the brick walk to the wide verandah, as far from her mother's little house in the unseemly section of town as she could get.

Heaven.

She wiped her bare feet very carefully before crossing the threshold, uncomfortable even after three and a half weeks to be using the gleaming, glass-paned front door. But she was following the others, and they used the front door. Once inside, she gave herself up to the sense of magic that overcame her every time she visited. The floors were never dirty here. It always smelled good—today, like cookies. They had gas power, and never hesitated to light lamps if the afternoon was gloomy or heat their home against the cold, so it was always bright and comfortable here. Family called to one another from room to room—like Mrs. Garrison even now: "Come back here for some buttermilk, girls!"—and today Evangeline heard faint hammering from behind the house, likely a workman making sure nothing fell out of repair. The house was very modern; along with the lighting, they had a kitchen pump, an icebox, even an indoor privy! Evangeline had never dared venture into that—she was always careful not to drink much, on days she would be visiting the mansion—but she marveled at the very idea.

Here was a world where everyone loved each other, where nobody screamed or hit, where girls who got good lunches still had cookies and milk upon arriving home instead of going all day with their stomachs pinched—and where, incredibly, nobody seemed to recognize just how far beneath them Evangeline Taylor really was.

She sat carefully at the kitchen table with the other girls, including little Elise, not because she assumed any right to their afternoon treat but because she had already learned the futility of protest. Though a small woman, Mrs. Garrison was determined. And to please her, Evangeline would willingly swallow bugs, much less milk—buttermilk!—and cookies.

She noticed that she was given one more cookie than the other girls took on her pretty china plate—Mrs. Garrison always deliberately served her, or Evangeline would not have eaten—and she hesitated. She hated to interrupt the others' conversation, much less to accuse anyone of a mistake, but it wasn't fair for her to get more. When she ventured to look toward where the girls' mother was wiping dishes and humming, hoping Mrs. Garrison might recognize her mistake without Evangeline having to say anything, Mrs. Garrison simply winked at her.

Winked! As if they had a secret between them! Evangeline took an obedient bite of the best cookie she had ever tasted and thought maybe Mrs. Garrison did not realize what her own mother did for a living. Maybe she had not yet heard that Evangeline had never had a father of her own, to build a house or buy proper clothes—to keep her respectable. Maybe Mrs. Garrison did not understand the social risk of welcoming someone like Evangeline Taylor into her home.

But no, that would mean questioning Mrs. Garrison's intelligence. Mrs. Garrison was surely the prettiest, smartest, kindest, bravest, best-smelling woman in town.

Then Evangeline heard light footsteps on the back stairs, the ones that opened directly into the kitchen, and looked up to see a challenger for that position—at least, in the "prettiest" category. She recognized Miss Mariah from the days when the oldest Garrison daughter still attended school, before she had grown up. But the grown-up Mariah was twice as lovely as anything she remembered. She wore a work dress of blue calico, nicer than anything Evangeline owned, even from out of the charity barrel. Over that Mariah wore a starched apron. Her golden hair, pulled back from her face, glowed. Her posture was perfect, her movements graceful. And when her large, gray eyes fell on Evangeline, she only blinked once before smiling polite welcome and even remembering her name, as if they could ever have been friends.

"Evangeline Taylor! How pleasant to see you again. Have you been well?"

Evangeline swallowed, hard, and managed the word "Yes." Not that she had done so well in the last year, but she would not repay this family's kindness by mentioning her own or her mother's troubles. Nobody in this household would ever behave so badly as Evangeline's mother did. That, she felt sure, was why their home life was so perfect and hers . . . not.

That, and their respectable father.

As usual, all the girls except Kitty talked at once. Victoria explained her mother's tutoring arrangement. Audra announced her examination grades. Elise decided that her paper dolls needed winter clothes from Paris. And Laurel, gulping her milk too quickly, asked to go to the stables before doing her schoolwork. Miss Mariah sat down beside Evangeline, with one cookie and a tumbler of buttermilk. She even smelled beautiful, like flowers. Like a princess.

Not for the first time, Evangeline wondered why Mariah Garrison had no beaus. There was a time, several years ago, when she suspected feelings between the oldest Garrison girl and Stuart MacCallum—but of course Evangeline had been mistaken. The MacCallums were a good family, their name in many ways as respectable as hers was not, but they raised sheep. A MacCallum had as little chance of being welcomed into this family as . . . as a Taylor!

Her feet tingled as they warmed up, and the rich buttermilk filled the hollow hunger she had felt since midday. The otherworldliness of this place made Evangeline sleepy and content, fascinated by everything about these people.

Even now, conversation had turned to Miss Mariah's friends from her European tour, the Wrights, who were staying at the Sheridan Inn. Perhaps, thought Evangeline, Mr. Alden Wright was now Mariah's beau. That would make sense. Mrs. Garrison suggested telephoning them about Saturday's party, which led to showing Mariah their newest gadget—she had been gone for the arrival of Sheridan's independent telephone company. Few people used it yet—the Inn and a few of the Main Street businesses, a handful of the better homes. But to even *have* telephones spoke well of their town.

Then Mrs. Garrison added, "You'll be at the party on Saturday, won't you Evangeline?" And Evangeline nearly choked on her cookie.

Miss Mariah patted her gently on the back.

"Of course she'll come," said Victoria, as if she could not imagine why the Taylor girl would not be welcome amidst the cream of Sheridan society. "It's for my birthday as much as Mariah's homecoming. Evangeline always comes to my birthdays."

Miss Mariah said, "In fact, the whole town is invited—isn't that right, Mother?" But she said it in an odd way, slowly, as if tasting more undercurrents to the words than others knew of.

"The whole town," agreed Mrs. Garrison firmly.

When Evangeline dared peek at the young woman beside her, Miss Mariah was biting her lower lip, her eyes bright as she nodded. Years of being on the edge of conversations, all but invisible, had developed in Evangeline an instinct for noticing things other people might not. She had no idea what Miss Mariah meant when she agreed with her mother, but felt sure it meant something weightier than anyone else realized.

But why? The Wrights were already invited!

Before she could puzzle the subject out further, the back door opened; the outside hammering had stopped. But when she looked up expecting a workman, Evangeline froze.

It was Mr. Jacob Garrison. The girls' father.

She wanted to sink into her chair, perhaps as far as under the table, so that the old-time cattle baron would not see her. But it was too late; even if she could have commanded her frozen body to move, Evangeline had waited too long. In glancing approvingly across his daughters, Mr. Garrison's gaze fell upon her—and stayed there.

For a moment he seemed confused, as if trying to place her from amidst the other girls he had seen in town. Then his steely eyes narrowed.

He, she felt certain, knew exactly what her mother did for a living

Mariah clearly saw that Papa had not known about Evangeline Taylor's lessons. Her delicious, newly formed daydream of dancing in Stuart's arms faltered.

"Have some buttermilk, Jacob," invited Mother, purposefully ignoring how stiffly Papa stood. "You know

Evangeline Taylor, don't you? She's the tutor I told you about."

Papa turned his stern gaze from poor Evangeline, who had gone white at his appearance, to Mother. "A minute of your time," he drawled, iron command beneath the invitation.

"I always have time for you, dear," assured Mother, just as much grit beneath her loving reply, and took the forgotten hammer out of his dusty hand to put on the counter. "As soon as you finish your cookies, girls, start on your homework," she instructed. "And Evangeline, I expect to hear you playing your scales before I return."

Poor Evangeline said nothing at all as Papa led Mother upstairs toward the privacy of their own room.

Mariah stood to assume her mother's duties. Her sisters, falling back into innocent conversation, finished their snack, but Evangeline simply sat there, shoulders hunched and head down, until the others had moved to the dining room to start on their schoolwork. Then, alone with Mariah, Evangeline whispered, "I should go."

Mariah looked more closely at the town outcast. Evangeline had grown almost a foot taller since Mariah had last seen her, revealing too much bare leg under her old dress to be at all proper. Although she seemed clean enough, the girl's thin, pale hair would not stay in its single braid, giving her a messy look. And her posture! It all but invited people to abuse her.

Not only that but Evangeline Taylor was a bastard. And her mother—well, her mother did unspeakable things that Mariah was not supposed to have heard about, on the upper floors of Sheridan's less reputable saloons.

Of course Mother would defy social censure to welcome such a child into their home, as easily as Mariah would to fall in love with Stuart MacCallum. But Papa . . .

Would Papa have taken equal affront at finding one of Stuart's sisters sitting here?

Despite her sudden disappointment, Mariah said, "You will do no such thing. My mother owes you a piano lesson; you don't want to insult her by not accepting it, do you?"

Evangeline raised wide eyes and shook her head, face pinched. Mother could have resisted her no more than Mariah and her sisters had resisted that lost lamb, years ago.

"Why don't you start practicing," she suggested, putting a reassuring hand on the girl's bony shoulder. "I'll clean up in here."

Evangeline nodded, but hesitated. When Mariah waited long enough, the girl dared a horrified whisper. "He won't beat her, will he?"

It took a long moment for Mariah to even realize what she meant. Papa? Hit any woman, much less Mother? The idea was ridiculous. . . . So why had Evangeline thought to ask it?

"No," Mariah answered simply, watching relief ease some of the tension from the girl's face. When Evangeline slipped noiselessly out toward the parlor, the first thing Mariah did was wrap her remaining cookies—plus several more for good measure—in an old napkin for the girl to take home. As she poured hot water from the stove's reservoir into the sink, cleaning plates and tumblers, scales began to sound through the house with the precision of someone who took her practice seriously. But neither Papa nor Mother reappeared.

By the time Mariah put the dishes away, she'd begun to daydream about dancing with Stuart again. She *had* to hope. . . . If only she knew what was being said upstairs!

She went to the parlor, set Evangeline's cookies beside the girl, then paced restlessly back through the dining room where Audra and Kitty bent over their own books. Elise played happily with her paper dolls beside them. Laurel would be in the stable. . . .

And Victoria was nowhere to be seen.

Oh!

Mariah climbed the stairs quietly enough that Victoria, crouched beside their parents' closed door, did not even hear her until discovery. When the younger girl looked up, face flushed at being caught, Mariah simply leaned closer.

"Who's winning?" If anyone would know, it would be the nose of the family.

Victoria blinked surprise at Mariah's acceptance, but did not question it. "I'm not sure," she whispered back. "It all depends on whether Evangeline's visits are part of our social lives or our moral upbringing."

Their social lives were Mother's responsibility, along with clothing and education. But Papa took his own duties—their safety and moral raising—very seriously. Mariah wondered which category Stuart fell under. Mother would accept him far more easily than her father would.

Victoria, with a confused shrug, went back to listening at the door for her friend's fate. Mariah stood near her—though closer to the safety of the back stairwell—and held her stomach, only in part to keep her hands from shaking. Behind the door, she could hear their mother's voice. Her father's only sounded once or twice, but that was normal. What were they saying?!

Victoria must have read her concern, because she beckoned her sister closer again. "Mother says Evangeline is less likely to follow in her mother's footsteps if she sees another side of life, so she's our moral duty. Papa isn't saying anything."

Mariah nodded, wondering where their mother had gotten these extraordinary ideas but glad she had them. Victoria leaned nearer the door again. Then, grinning, she scrambled away.

"What?" demanded Mariah as her younger sister pulled her into the stairwell. She noticed, as they clutched close and something bumped her hip, that Victoria carried her shoes.

It was almost frightening, how good Victoria was at this. "Papa said that he saw someone at the depot."

Normally, Mariah would recognize that for the triumph Victoria did. Papa would not change the subject unless he considered further protest useless. But . . .

Had he seen Stuart? "Who?" she asked, even more uneasy.

Victoria said, "I don't know. It was none of my business."

But at least Mother had won. Papa had resigned himself to a less restrictive guest list. And that meant the MacCallums were included in "the whole town!"

"Did he sound angry?" she asked her sister, just in case.

"No. Just tired. Mama asked him if she was pretty—the person he saw at the depot—and then she made that 'Mmm' sound she does when she kisses him, so everything should be fine."

Mariah tried not to blush, to think of her parents kissing—in the middle of the afternoon!

Victoria certainly did know an awful lot, for fourteen.

"Have you . . ." Mariah hesitated as they reached the empty kitchen. Then she thought of Stuart, and his kisses—and their secret engagement—and forged on. "Have you ever overheard Papa's views on the homesteaders? He's so careful not to talk business around us. . . ."

Victoria cocked her head, a little too observant. "Well, the depression has been very hard on beef. And Papa took President McKinley's election badly. He thinks that's why homesteaders have become so thick, thinking they can find a better life out West without working for it. He's losing more head than ever, some to rustlers, but a lot is probably the nesters, too. . . ."

It was a general policy among the big ranchers to look the other way when they found a hungry family had slaughtered one of their cows—"slow elk," they called it, to distinguish from animals rustled for monetary profit.

"What about the homesteaders who've been here awhile, who've always worked hard?" prompted Mariah. "Like . . . the sheep farmers?"

Victoria rolled her eyes. "Sheep!"

"Sheep farmers," Mariah clarified, afraid she had given away too much. "Or any of the smaller ranchers who have moved in over the last, oh . . . ten years?"

"Well, they *did* wait until men like Papa and Uncle Benj did the hard part," Victoria reminded her. "Facing down Indians, putting in towns. So it irks them when men move in now and overgraze the range. But at least the smaller ranchers are still raising cattle. *Sheep* . . . "

She shuddered. They both knew how sheep ate all the grass in front of them and killed all the grass behind them. But as long as the sheep stayed away from the cattle . . .

Mariah wondered if, with the crowded range, ranchers might resent even the little bit that the sheep used. Surely Papa could see past that once he got to know Stuart. He had to.

Victoria continued to watch her, speculative. Mariah's own failure as a responsible older sister came upon her belatedly. What Victoria—she and Victoria—had done was wrong.

In retrospect, anyway.

"You know, you ought not eavesdrop," she pointed out now, low. "We ought not, I mean. Our parents deserve their privacy."

Especially if they would be kissing each other. People should have privacy, for kisses. Especially married couples.

The very thought made her flush.

"How else can I know what's going on?" challenged Victoria, and she snitched a cookie on her way into the dining room to do her schoolwork.

Mariah stared after her for a moment.

Then she firmly set aside her concerns for her sister's moral character, her fears that Papa had noted Stuart's presence at the depot, even her worries that Papa might prove even more stubborn about her beau—her betrothed—than she'd been willing to believe. Such fatalistic thinking would get her nowhere.

Instead, she started planning what kind of an invitation she would write to Emily MacCallum and, through her, her older brother Stuart.

Chapter Four

Stuart thought the party a bad idea as soon as the two oldest of his sisters rode out to his claim, thrilled at their personal invitation. By Saturday night he had not changed his mind. Mariah did not want him approaching her father in private—so instead she invited them to the finest hotel between Chicago and San Francisco? It made no sense.

But to judge from Emily and Bonny's excitement, girls valued sense less, and parties more, than did men. Saturday found Stuart driving them into town in Da's spring wagon, dressed in their Sunday clothes. Perhaps he could have disappointed his sisters—for their own good, of course. But he could not bear to disappoint Mariah. And who knew? A MacCallum had never been invited *anywhere* by a Garrison before—except maybe invited to leave the state. Perhaps Mariah's optimism wasn't as desperately misplaced as he often feared.

Besides, foolish or not, Stuart ached to see his intended again.

And see her he did.

When he escorted Emily and Bonny guardedly into the Inn's main dining hall, bright as daytime from their touted electric lights, the sight of Mariah stopped Stuart cold. For a moment he stood in the wide doorway, a sister on each arm, unable to breathe.

What was she wearing?

"Oh," sighed Emily softly. "It's a *ball gown!*"

And sixteen-year-old Bonny whispered, "Do you think it's from France?" That, thought Stuart numbly, would explain a great deal.

The dress was made of some shiny blue fabric that oozed wealth. Nobody had scrimped in measuring out the puffy sleeves, nor the skirt that flared from Mariah's slim waist into a wide sweep at the floor. Only in the collar had the dressmaker apparently found material too dear. Mariah's hair, piled into a high, golden mass of curls, revealed a sinfully bare throat, much of her shoulders . . . even a hint of her collarbone!

"We're leaving," declared Stuart, stopping his sisters. But Em turned willful on him.

"We are *not* leaving," the redhead hissed, pulling loose of him. "We only just arrived."

"Even if we are underdressed," murmured Bonny, raising a tentative hand to her own neat, black braids. When Stuart followed her hungry gaze, he found himself trapped by the sight of Mariah—this shocking, home-from-Europe Mariah—yet again. Underdressed? His sisters' frocks buttoned sensibly up to their chins, but Mariah's. . . .

What kind of logic made a girl wear gloves up past her elbows, but not cover her shoulders?

"Someday," sighed Emily, "I want a gown like that."

"Ma would rather see you in your grave," warned Stuart, torn. He disapproved, of course . . . and yet, the elegant picture Mariah made, all bouncy hair and luminous skin and liquid gown, drew him in a way more powerful than his disapproval. If only she were not presenting the same picture to near about everyone in town.

And why shouldn't Emily, the same age as Mariah, want similar things? "I could die happy," she said.

"It's indecent, Em!"

Bonny said, "It's the fashion, Stuart. Look, Emily! Is that Lady Cooper?"

Stu recognized the British "Lady" Cooper, an elegant woman whose ruby neckline plunged even lower than Mariah's. *She,* however, wore an intricate necklace that drew the eye up from her . . .

From where no man should be looking, except perhaps her husband. And her husband, Stu remembered, was Jacob Garrison's partner in the Circle-T Ranch. Both cattlemen stood talking with Colonel Wright of the Triple-Bar spread. In fact, this party crawled with cattlemen and cowboys both, like maggots on carrion. More than one cast distasteful looks in the MacCallums' direction.

From a man as powerful as Garrison, even the briefest of distasteful looks carried threat.

So much for optimism.

"We ought not be here," Stuart said again. On top of everything else, cowboys were eyeing his sisters. And everyone knew that cowboys were wild. They drank too much, used foul language, associated with bad women. . . .

"Hush, Stuart," chided Bonny. "Here comes Mariah. Don't you dare be rude to her!"

Emily smiled at that—Em, who'd helped disguise their correspondence over the last half-year, seemed to think Stuart's affection for Mariah forbade any rudeness on his part.

But as he watched Mariah approach to welcome her guests, Stuart almost wanted to be rude to her—his intended. Her extravagant beauty hurt in his throat, because even in a year he'd not likely earn enough to buy her even one such dress. Not that he would.

Much less let her wear it in public.

"Emily!" greeted Mariah, extending a gloved hand to the one of Stuart's sisters, then the other. "Bonny! What a pleasure to see you again! And you brought your brother."

The secret gaze she slanted upward shared her pleasure at seeing him again, too—and in a public for once! Stuart could hardly breathe. Were things different, he would ask her to dance, all brightly lit skin and shiny hair, hope-filled eyes and silk.

"Miss Garrison." But he moved his gaze carefully past her too-nearly-bare shoulder—this time noting more than one pair of suspicious cowboy eyes. Men outnumbered women, out here on the frontier, as surely as the cattle interests outnumbered the homesteaders.

"I . . . I hope the drive was not too strenuous." Mariah's voice wavered with her attempt at chitchat.

Wondering how many of these men were armed, overly conscious of his younger sisters beside him, Stuart wondered again how Mariah had imagined this to be a good idea.

It was Emily who said, "Oh, no. It's a beautiful evening. And we've never seen the Inn at night, before! Thank you for inviting us."

The violin music seemed particularly loud in the silence that followed. Even without looking at Mariah, Stuart could still smell her—soap and lilacs. He swallowed, hard.

Bonny added, "Your dress is beautiful, Miss Garrison."

"Thank you," said Mariah, her voice uneven now. "If I had hair as pretty as either of you, I would not need bother with such fancy clothing."

Stuart ached with the effort not to look at her, memorize her—give himself up to the richness of the moment. For both their sakes, Emily and Bonny's too, he must not dare. Whatever the girls said next, he barely heard over the need to publicly claim Mariah at last—and the even more desperate need not to. He had not gotten permission from her father to keep company with her, much less marry her. They were outnumbered here.

And yet, when she finally left to greet another arrival, he missed her voice, her scent, like a hunger.

Only then did Emily say, "How dare you, Stuart! She was nice enough to invite us, and you all but ignored her. And after you—"

Stuart's scowl stopped her just in time. Nobody else in the family knew about his and Mariah's letters.

It did nothing for his temper to notice that the pair Mariah now spoke with was the same that had accompanied her on the train. Alden and Alice Wright, heirs to the second-largest ranch in the area. No wonder he'd not recognized them, upon their arrival. The family spent more time in Cheyenne and Denver than in Sheridan.

Alice Wright's gown bore a striking resemblance to Mariah's—and, to be fair, many other women's throughout the room—though Stuart suspected girls would notice a dozen differences. And Alden! His sleek frock coat showed rich facing at the lapels. His trousers bore a stripe down each side, and he even wore *spats.* Not boots, but shoes with spats!

Some milksop wearing spats was leading Mariah toward the center of the room to dance, one hand on her elbow.

She glanced once over her shoulder at Stuart, bewildered, and he made himself look away from how softly her springy curls bounced against the bare back of her neck.

Emily thought his silence was rude? What would be rude would be Stuart's yanking off his own go-to-meeting coat, wrapping Mariah in it, and bundling her away from this ridiculous party, revealing his claim on her once and for all.

What would be unforgivably rude would be his behavior once he got her alone . . . and looking like that. Engaged was not married. Secretly engaged began to feel no different from secretly in love.

This, Stuart thought again, was a very bad idea.

Mariah had hoped for so much more from this party.

Oh, it had all the requirements for a storybook ball. The elegant, four-year-old Inn sparkled with light and music. The food tasted delicious. And everyone Mariah loved was here: her parents, her sisters, her older brother, and even "Uncle" Benj Cooper and his family.

And Stuart, shoulders almost too broad for his good coat, hair slicked darkly back to hide its length, looked more handsome than possible. Stuart, the man she loved, was here.

But Stuart seemed angry with her, and she did not know why.

She'd thought that, if only their families got to know each other socially, it would smooth the way for their plans. But his parents had not come, nor the younger MacCallums. Stuart himself hung back on the fringes of the party, guarding his sisters and not looking at Mariah.

But sometimes she felt his eyes on her . . . and she felt everyone else's eyes on them.

"Aren't those the sheep farmers?" asked Alden Wright, after roping her into a dance. "Who invited them?"

Mariah said, "I did."

Alden lifted an eyebrow. "How very charitable of you."

Later, his sister Alice Wright giggled and said, "Look at those dresses. I believe they meant to attend Sunday school!"

"I think they look fine," said Mariah, all the more annoyed because they stood beside Alice's parents, whom Mother was welcoming back to Wyoming. "And their behavior is charming." *Unlike some other people's,* she thought darkly.

Alice sighed. "Oh Mariah, did Europe teach you *nothing?*"

At least her father the Colonel tutted at her in genteel reprimand. "I, for one, admire Miss Mariah's sense of *noblesse oblige.* It was a singular experience, Mrs. Garrison, viewing the splendors of the Old World through your daughter's . . . altruistic . . . eyes."

As she had in Europe, more than once, Alice pulled a face at Mariah's "altruism."

Mariah wanted to believe the Wrights to be a snobbish exception, but nobody else approached the MacCallums, either. When she danced with Papa—and oh, Mariah usually loved dancing safe in her proud father's arms—she said, "Thank you for the party, Papa. It's wonderful, to have the whole town here."

But Papa only looked at her for a long minute, then toward the too-quiet corner where folks like the MacCallums and Evangeline Taylor stood, then slanted a glare toward his wife.

"Welcome," he drawled, without enthusiasm.

Mariah checked back on her guests as often as seemed appropriate, insisting they taste the punch, trying to engage them in conversation, but felt increasingly helpless—especially when Stuart continued to ignore her and to glare darkly at any men who might have approached his sisters. She recruited Victoria and Audra to help, when her own hostess duties drew her elsewhere, but they could only do so much.

Then the second time Stuart led Emily onto the far corner of the floor himself, dancing with the requisite discomfort of a dutiful older brother, Mariah remembered her own brother.

"I'm not surprised," said Thaddeas when she reported the MacCallum girls' exclusion. "Folks do feel strongly about sheep."

"They don't have any sheep with them right now!" she

insisted. It was not as if Thaddeas, a lawyer, was active in the cattle business himself.

Her upset amused Thad, that quirk of a smile setting him apart from their father as much as his brown eyes and absence of whiskers. "Wise decision, leaving them at home."

Mariah took a deep breath, unwilling to accept the ruin of all her lovely plans. "I invited the MacCallums personally," she explained, desperate. "And they are being all but shunned, at my own party. *Please,* Thad . . ."

When Thaddeas sighed—the long-suffering sigh of a too-indulgent big brother—she knew she'd won him over. "One dance," he agreed, perhaps in part because his own girl was visiting in San Francisco. "For you."

"With Emily and Bonny both?"

When he nodded, she hugged him, accepted his kiss on her hair. *Yes!* If she could win Thad over to the MacCallums' side, surely the rest of her family would eventually follow.

Even if Thad did have an especially soft spot for her. . . .

She watched, hopeful, as he approached the trio and spoke to them. Emily brightened visibly as she accepted his gallantly offered hand.

Stuart turned and widened his eyes at Mariah, less clearly pleased. She smiled. *See, Stuart? Our families can mix!*

He opened his mouth, as if they stood close enough for him to make comment. Then he closed his mouth, shook his head, and glowered toward Thad and his sister.

In the meantime, Emily and then Bonny seemed to enjoy their dances. Once Thad left the second MacCallum sister some cowboys, perhaps encouraged by the Garrison heir's example, approached them with their typical mix of abashment and feigned bravado. Mariah, feeling expansive, noted that Thaddeas even asked Evangeline Taylor to dance, after that. The skinny blonde, who seemed as out of place as the MacCallums despite wearing one of Victoria's nicer party dresses, glowed with shy pleasure.

Perhaps now Stuart would put his concerns to rest. Perhaps now, finally, he would ask her to dance too. Mariah savored the thought of being in his protective arms, his big hand on her waist. She kindly declined one, then another, then a third invitation from other gentlemen so that she would be free for Stuart.

Finally Stuart did turn and deliberately looked at her again, intent. For a moment, Mariah thought he'd read her mind—that the power of their love had carried her thoughts to him.

Instead, with a grim shake of his head, her prince turned and left through one of the pairs of double doors that flanked the ballroom, out onto the Inn's wide verandah.

Mariah had to school her expression into something more pleasant than a scowl herself as she moved to the refreshment table, ladled some punch into a glass for little Elise, made sure Kitty was enjoying herself. After delaying several minutes, for discretion's sake, she then slipped through a different set of double doors to go find him.

She'd never known Stuart to be cowardly or rude.

Something must be wrong.

"Are you angry with me?"

At the familiar voice, Stuart spun. Faced with Mariah up close—all that skin milky in the moonlight—he swallowed, hard.

She'd asked him a question? He could barely think past the shocking need to pull her to him, cover her bared skin with . . . with himself.

He gritted his teeth and tried to think of hoof rot.

"Or are you being rude for no reason?" she prompted, which drew his gaze to her pretty face, to the uncharacteristic little line between her finely shaped brows.

Stuart forgot hoof rot. If one more person called him rude tonight . . .

"It's not the MacCallums' behavior that lacks," he assured her. "My sisters stood ignored for half the night until you made your brother dance with them. And the only men who've asked since are likely after more than dancing."

Her gray eyes widened. "Someone insulted your sisters? Here?"

Her blindness to it was so typically Mariah that his own irritation—with her, anyway—softened. She so rarely saw the worst in people, even with it right under her pretty nose.

"Nobody has done enough to merit calling him out," he reassured her grudgingly. Good women were sacred out here—even sheepherder's daughters. The cowboys' disrespect lay more in the proprietary way they seemed to hold his sisters while dancing, the way they sneaked looks toward the front of the girls' dresses. Nobody ought to be looking at his sisters that way.

Mariah let out an impatient sigh, with enough fervor that Stuart's gaze landed in exactly the same territory he'd wanted to kill the cowboys for surveying.

He shut his eyes. Hoof rot. Bloat. Sheep dip.

"Then what is wrong?" she demanded, innocent as a lamb.

"We do not belong here," he said, eyes still shut. "It helps nothing, for us to have come."

"You've hardly made an effort!" she protested, as if he were at fault. "You haven't said a thing to my parents, not even to thank them for the invitation."

"They did not invite us," he pointed out, opening his eyes again.

"But they gave the party."

Paid for it, you mean, thought Stuart, jaw tight. Her father's riches had paid for the ridiculously dainty food, the small orchestra, the rental of the hall, *and* that dress.

Frowning with obstinacy, Mariah folded her arms in front of her to hug herself against the chill night air. The posture plumped her bodice enticingly.

"Go inside," Stuart said, looking away, toward the mountains. Distant snowcaps caught and reflected moonlight. "You'll catch your death, without a wrap."

"Come inside with me and introduce yourself to Papa. We have to start somewhere."

He almost choked. "In a room crowded with cattlemen?"

"Well it seemed less obvious than inviting you to tea," she pointed out. "And they aren't all cattlemen. Some are storekeeps and . . . and bankers. . . ."

All of whom earned far more off the cattle barons than they ever would off sheep farmers. "I won't test their loyalties with my sisters here."

"You're talking as if you expect trouble!" Now he had to look at her again, to truly believe her innocence. Of course. Mariah could no more imagine her family or friends turning on Stuart than she could imagine them turning on her.

Her illusions made him ache in a completely different way than did her revealing dress. *What was he asking of her?*

"You ought not be out here," he chided softly, again. "It's not proper."

"Yes," said Mariah—without making a move to go in.

Was it any worse to let the woman he loved catch a chill than to meet her without her family knowing? Defeated, Stuart put a hand on the silkiness of Mariah's gloved elbow and drew her off the wide porch, into the shadows beyond, where he felt safe enough to shrug off his Sunday coat and drape it over her too-bare shoulders. *There*. Now she seemed more like *his* Mariah, neither shivering in the cold nor luring him toward forgetting himself.

"Perhaps there will be no trouble, at that," he supposed, trying with words what he'd done with his coat. He wished he had half the confidence she clearly did, but perhaps it was just as well he did not. One of them ought to remain pragmatic, even wary. Best that it be him.

Her gaze gentled at that, dawn-gray eyes filling with moonlight and hope.

"But I'll not risk my sisters by challenging your father's authority here," Stuart continued. "Nor will I risk you. You are too important to me."

She smiled then, no longer so set against him, even though he had not given in.

"Will you at least thank my parents before you go?" she asked softly. "Will you do that for me?"

Knowing she'd wanted so much more from this party—how could he deny her yet again? Besides, he did owe her parents. Without them, he should not know this fine woman.

Surely a thank-you could not annoy even the most hostile of cattlemen. And if it did . . .

"Yes, Mariah," he agreed, taking her hands despite his best intentions. Her silk-gloved fingers felt fragile, cold beneath his big, working hands. "I will do that."

"Thank you." She tipped her face up toward him, and the love in her gaze made his throat hurt with gratitude.

"You . . ." He felt her shiver, through the link of their hands. "You'd best go inside."

Inside, where he would not feel so compelled to kiss her. Stepping onto the verandah together was not quite so scandalous as meeting at the Kissing Bridge, but . . .

"Not yet," she protested. "There's so much to talk about! I've missed you, and I see you so rarely."

Then let me court you formally. But he had agreed to wait. So he looked at her, admiring her, and the longer he did, the more he wondered if perhaps she was right. Perhaps he was being too careful.

Then, with the metallic "chink" of spurs on the

wooden verandah behind them, the ugly truth arrived to speak for itself.

"If you're MacCallum," drawled the intruder, "you're dumber than I figured."

Stu turned, instinctively drawing Mariah behind him—and recognized the gunman from the depot earlier that week. The one who'd nodded knowingly to her father. The one who'd smelled of danger.

Trouble had found them at last.

Chapter Five

Everything inside Stuart went deathly still.

"Mariah," he said quietly. "Go inside."

But Mariah did not move from where she stood behind him, lightly holding his left arm. He should have realized that a girl who would go against her father's wishes would be unlikely to obey her—

Her what? He had no official claim on her for the gunman to observe, so why should she?

"You're MacCallum, ain't you?" demanded the stranger. "The sheep lover?" His tone made a particularly nasty implication of that last word.

Stuart grasped at a careful stillness inside him, used it as a shield against the ugliness this man taunted from him: the insult, the injustice . . . and yes, some healthy fear. Plenty of men wore guns—but not at parties. This one had tied down his holster for a faster draw.

And here stood Mariah, too close to the line of fire. For the first time ever, Stuart felt tempted to deny his identity, if only for her safety.

The temptation passed. "I am," he agreed. Then he growled, toward her, "*Inside.*"

Mariah said, "No," and stepped out from behind Stuart. "We haven't met, Mr . . . ?"

Stuart put a hand on her arm, but felt no trembling. Did she not understand the full threat here? Women might be sacred—but accidents happened! "I will handle this," he murmured.

Meanwhile the gunman studied her, his eyes shadowed. He did not tip his hat.

"Johnson," he said finally. "The name's Johnson." He did not call her "ma'am"—but neither did he insult her outright. Her rich gown, visible beneath Stuart's Sunday coat, probably had him suspecting her class and its implicit, extra protection.

Much as Stuart resented the gulf between his and Mariah's worlds, he found himself counting on it now. *Don't trifle with her, Johnson. Even if I cannot destroy you for it, the rest of the town will.*

Mariah said, "You're not from around here, Mr. Johnson."

"I hail from Idaho." Now the gunman, perhaps noting her cultured speech, added, "ma'am."

But he was squinting from Mariah to Stuart, calculating.

"I do not know how such things are done in Idaho, but here in Wyoming—"

"Here in Wyoming," interrupted Johnson, "folks hate sheep. And sheepers."

Now Stuart pulled Mariah bodily behind him. It was the first time he'd ever overpowered her for any reason, and he did not like doing it—even before her eyes flared startled accusation at him. But he did.

Johnson added, "And those what keep company with sheepers."

Stuart said, "You came looking for me, Idaho. Say your piece."

It might already be too late. Folks attracted by the confrontation drifted onto the verandah. Most, being cowboys, set themselves just behind Johnson. A few, recognizing Mariah Garrison under Stu's coat, stayed neutral.

Johnson said, "I got a message for you from the local ranchers, sheeper."

The last time Stuart had gotten a "message" from cattlemen, the bruises had lasted almost a month. He lifted his chin and waited—and sorely wished Mariah were not here. He could take Johnson, were the man not armed. But the men behind him . . .

To his surprise, this message consisted only of words. "Your kind ain't welcome on this range anymore," drawled Johnson. *Anymore?* "Herding them hooved locusts south of Montana is fixing to get . . . unhealthy."

It's happening again. Stuart wondered just who had sent this particular threat. Was it Irvine, or Wright . . . or Garrison? Maybe the three of them together, splitting this man's salary?

Or maybe the whole Wyoming Stock Grower's Association. Again.

But Mariah's nearness still warmed his shirt back. He would not risk unmasking her father in front of her. Some illusions were best left intact—better she learn that truth for herself, if ever. And from the source.

Stuart said, "My stock has the same right to the grasslands as anyone's, Idaho."

Behind Johnson, several cowboys muttered protests at that. One even swore.

Johnson said, "Plenty of folks 'round here would disagree."

Stuart said, "They'd be wrong."

Johnson took a threatening step closer. "I'm thinking you'll change your mind."

Stuart set himself for whatever meant to happen. "No," he said steadily. "I will not."

"Stuart," whispered Mariah. "Don't . . ."

Johnson's shoulders seemed to be tensing, and Stuart knew he meant to argue with more than words. "Could be I'll change it for you."

Stuart set his heels. "Could be you'll try."

"Stop it!" To his horror, Mariah darted in front of him again, between the two men. "Stop it right now!"

Johnson took a startled step back. Stuart reached automatically to again sweep Mariah out of harm's way—

One of the cowboys snarled, "Keep your oily hands off her, you son of a bitch!" And the night shattered.

Someone yanked Mariah safely away while cowboys surged forward. Stuart lowered his head and met their charge. He bowled at least one man over, hit two more and took a blow to the jaw himself. He barely felt it, just kept swinging. They might outnumber him, but he would damned well hurt as many of them as he could before—

A pistol exploded, too close. Stuart and everyone else went completely still.

Every instinct in him wanted to stay still—moving animals drew predators, after all—but concern for Mariah overrode it. Stuart turned to seek her out, fearing, praying. . . .

She stood, wide-eyed, with her gloved hands covering her mouth. At some point in the scuffle she'd lost his coat, and her nearly bare shoulders in the cold night added to her fragility. But she did not appear hurt.

Too bone-deep relieved to fear his own safety now, Stuart sought out the source of the gunshot—and faced the rancher himself.

Old Man Garrison stood beside Johnson, smoking six-gun in hand. As always, he'd gotten folks' attention.

"Best get now," the cattle baron drawled to all and sundry. His stern gaze settled on Stuart as he added, dangerous, "You boys just wore out your welcome."

As if they'd heard from God Himself, the cowboys started to collect their scattered hats and back away.

"Papa—" started Mariah, but Garrison silenced her with a glare.

Johnson said, "Nobody touches my gun, mister," and Stuart saw that the stranger's holster hung, snug and empty, against his thigh.

Garrison looked at the revolver in his hand, then lifted his gaze back to Johnson. *Someone,* said his impassive expression, *just did.*

Stuart looked at Mariah again, at her stricken expression. He took a step toward her—

Only to be stopped by her father's low drawl. "You heard me."

Stuart met the cattle baron's steely glare with his own. Maybe Old Man Garrison hadn't seen Mariah wearing his coat, hadn't yet put the pieces together, but other folks had. Would it even be days before the questions started, the whispering . . . the very scandal he and Mariah had hoped to avoid?

Time had come to speak, whether they were ready for it or not.

Emily arrived beside him, then Bonny, each clinging to one of his arms as if they'd feared him dead—or feared he'd get himself killed, if they weren't hobbling him. "Let's go home, Stuart," whispered Bonny. "Please. You were right. Let's go home."

Stuart looked from her desperation to Mariah's, feeling the weight of her father's glare on him as he did. He could still smell the gunsmoke from the pistol in Garrison's hand. His jaw hurt.

"Tomorrow," he promised, low.

Mariah nodded, miserable.

Only with effort did Stuart drop his gaze from hers and scan the ground for his once-good coat, now trodden into the dust. He reclaimed it before collecting his sisters again.

But despite the girls' hurried tugs, Stuart walked slowly, his head high. And he stopped beside Jacob Garrison and Idaho Johnson—the cattleman's hired gun—one more time, just to prove he wasn't running.

"Thank you for the hospitality," Stuart said evenly.

Garrison's eyes sharpened at the perceived sarcasm, and Johnson's lip curled, but Stuart continued toward the buckboard, a sister on each side and Mariah's anxious gaze burning a spot between his shoulder blades.

Stuart, at least, kept his promises.

Mariah said, "Papa, that Mr. Johnson is the one who—"

But her father glared her into silence. There was a time and a place to talk to him, of course. The verandah of the Sheridan Inn, surrounded by half the town, was neither.

At least Papa's partner, Uncle Benj, showed up to smooth the waters. "There you go callin' attention to yourself again, Jacob," he chided jokingly. "How about you let me take that Johnson fellow's hog's-leg to the sheriff. Seein' as he's the only feller ought to be carrying one at this shindig anyhow?" Sheridan did have firearms regulations, after all.

Even once Benj took the gun, folks made way for Papa as he stepped back onto the verandah. He stopped just inside the double doors. "Mariah," he commanded without turning around. "Victoria."

Only then did Mariah notice her younger sister amidst the cluster of bystanders, clutching the hand of a wide-eyed Evangeline Taylor. She knew now who had alerted her family to the confrontation outside—and wasn't sure whether to resent the interference or appreciate it.

How much danger had Stuart been in?

And how much of it was because of her?

After driving the family home, Papa had words with Mariah in his den. But his disapproval stemmed from her endangering herself, not from going onto the verandah with a MacCallum. He did not know, then, and Mariah should be the one to tell him. She should tell him a lot of things before tomorrow.

And oh, she did try. "Stuart MacCallum didn't do anything wrong, Papa. Mr. Johnson just walked right up to him—"

To us . . .

Her father stared at her with disbelief, having just *told* her not to interfere in men's doings. "Get on to bed, Mariah Lynn."

"But Papa . . ."

He waited, arms folded, his most forbidding.

To her dismay, Mariah could not force the words out her throat. She tried. She even opened her mouth. *I love Stuart MacCallum,* would be too direct, too shocking. *We mean to marry* stuck in her throat as well. Perhaps she should ease him into the idea of her wanting to keep company with anybody at all, before she told him who . . .

Papa scowled and looked away. "Weren't nobody hurt," he reassured her awkwardly, voice rough. "Just remember yourself, in the future."

Mariah tried to swallow, but her throat hurt too badly from all those unsaid words.

Papa's gaze slid back to her, then veered away. "You get on to bed, now," he repeated.

And Mariah, defeated, said, "Yessir." She kissed his whiskered cheek, loving him so much that she ached with it. Stuart had been right all along.

Papa was not going to take this well.

She closed the den door behind her, to give him his privacy, then paused in the foyer at the sight of Victoria sitting on the stairs.

"Stuart MacCallum?" Victoria whispered, somehow as informed as ever.

Mariah nodded.

She would have felt more relief if Victoria had not winced at the very idea.

* * *

The next morning did not go any better. Getting ready for church rarely went smoothly, with six girls bustling about and Papa trying not to catch sight of anybody not fully dressed. In what seemed like a quiet moment, downstairs in the foyer, Mariah took her father's arm and said, "Papa, I'm eighteen now."

He frowned down at her, baffled. He knew her age.

"It's time . . . time I started thinking of the future."

"Future takes care of itself," he said, then turned his attention to his second daughter, descending the stairs. "Proper shoes, Laurel Lee. *Now.*"

And by the time Laurel had clumped back upstairs to change out of her cowboy boots, Kitty and Audra and Elise had descended into the foyer and the moment had passed. Especially when Mariah ended up bundled in the back of the surrey, instead of up front.

During services, she glanced occasionally over her shoulder toward Stuart. Sometimes he raised his intense gaze to meet hers, the curve of his jaw bruised . . . and once, he nodded.

Tomorrow, he'd said. That meant today.

Victoria kicked Mariah's ankle then, and inclined her dark head in a different direction. Mariah noted Alice Wright watching them, eyes gleaming. Quickly, Mariah turned her gaze back to the minister. Were other members of the congregation watching, too, judging as they sang and prayed and followed their respective families from the church?

We are engaged to be married! Mariah wanted to shout at them, but of course her parents—especially her father—should know first.

She tried yet again, once they got home. Her sisters settled in to read or draw or play piano—quiet activities, appropriate for the Sabbath—and even Papa sat in the parlor with Elise on his lap, squinting at the newspaper he read to her.

"Papa," said Mariah—at least she'd managed the voice for that—and he looked up expectantly.

"What's *that* letter?" asked Elise, pointing to a bit of type, but Papa guided her little hand firmly out of the way; she knew better than to interrupt.

"Papa, about last night," Mariah forged ahead.

He waited.

"I . . ." No, that wasn't right. "When I went outside, Papa, I wasn't alone. I was . . ." That wasn't right either. She swallowed. Hard. Then she tried, "I never meant to disappoint you."

Papa said, "Yesterday's done with, Mariah."

He didn't understand! "But Papa—"

Then a knock sounded at the door—so firm as to be defiant—and Laurel, first to look out the bay window, said "It's the sheep farmer!"

Mariah had just run out of time.

Chapter Six

Well, he was here.

Nothing in Stuart MacCallum's life had taken so much courage as walking up the brick path to the Garrison mansion and defiling their fine front door by drumming his knuckles on it.

Facing Mariah's home up close, for the first time, did little to clarify why she would want to marry him. One corner of the verandah rounded out into a gazebo with a porch swing. Everything from the snug, arch-roofed sheep-wagon where Stuart lived could fit within the railings of that gazebo. Yet here he stood, fixing to ask her father for the right to resign Mariah to such a home as that.

Stuart knew full well the answer would be "No." The only question was how violent that "no" would be. But at least they would have asked.

If worse came to worst, they did not need her father's blessing to legally marry.

But for themselves, they needed to have asked.

Stuart knocked on the door again, harder. It opened, and he stood face-to-face with Jacob Garrison at last.

The rancher blocked the threshold to his home as surely as the door had. Although Stuart stood taller, Garrison exuded authority. Even in a go-to-meeting suit, his white head bare, Garrison's posture bespoke power.

Which changed nothing.

"My name is Stuart MacCallum," said Stuart, just in case the cattle baron had never bothered to peg a name to him.

Garrison said, "I know it."

"It is time I spoke with you." Stuart swallowed, hard, and managed to add, "sir."

Mariah *was* this man's daughter, after all.

"I don't talk business on the Sabbath." Garrison began to close the door in Stuart's face.

Stuart shouldered into the closing space. "This is not business."

Garrison looked Stuart up and down, unimpressed.

"But it is important," Stuart added—and that, too, was the truth. He'd never had a more important appointment . . . next to filing his claim.

Maybe not even that.

For a moment, he feared the cattleman would not allow him in. *Afraid I'll stink up your mansion?* Then the older man moved out of the way in silent, begrudging invitation. Taking off his hat, Stuart stepped over the threshold and into Mariah's world.

A lush green rug brightened the front foyer, the kind that a clumsy footprint of mud or manure would likely ruin. Autumn flowers fanned out of a glass vase on a table, poised to be bumped to the floor with a misplaced elbow. Gas lamps hung from the ceiling, complete with crystal droplets to catch the sunlight, and the stairway boasted a sturdy, carved banister that Stuart could not imagine keeping his younger siblings off, should they ever live in such a place.

But his family did not live in such a place. Likely they never would.

Off to one side of the foyer sat an open parlor and six neatly dressed girls, some more familiar than others, staring at Stuart with frank curiosity. The only one who mattered, though, was Mariah, still wearing her fine Sunday dress. Wide-eyed, obviously unsure about this, she took a determined step toward him—

Even as Stuart began to raise his hand to signal her back—she could not help with what he had to say—she hesitated. He realized that her father had made the same gesture first.

Garrison led the way into a room with a huge desk and overstuffed furniture, an eight-foot pair of longhorns arched over the main chair. More framed pictures hung on the paneled wall than Stuart had ever seen outside of a photographer's studio, but he did not get the chance to study them, only caught a glimpse of faces, many of them Mariah's. Even after pulling the door shut, Garrison neither sat nor offered a seat to Stuart. He folded his arms and waited.

Stuart said, "I am here to ask for your daughter's hand in marriage."

Garrison stared, his expression so blank that he either had not heard or could not grasp the meaning of the words.

"Your daughter Mariah," Stuart qualified, since the man did have six. "I have a legal claim northeast of town and mean to prove up in four years. I have a home—a wagon, but it will keep her warm enough until I can build a house. My flock is small, but it will grow. Wool will always be needed."

Garrison continued to stare.

Stuart said, "I do not drink, or gamble, or consort with

loose women. I attend church regularly. My wife and children will never go hungry, nor will I never raise my hand to them. And I intend to have your daughter Mariah as my wife."

Only when Garrison blinked did Stuart realize that, for most of his speech, the rancher had not even done that.

"I am no man for pranks, MacCallum," drawled the rancher.

"This is no prank. I mean to call on your daughter Mariah, and I am here to do you the courtesy of saying so. My intentions are honorable."

For a moment, humor lit Garrison's shadowed gaze—that, more than anything else, prodded awake the sullen hostility that coiled deep in Stuart's gut. "What makes you think any of my girls would have you?"

Because she said so. Because of how she looks at me, kisses me. But those reasons were for Mariah, if they should be spoken at all. "I believe she will consider it," Stuart hedged.

Perhaps even that was too much information. Garrison had not become one of the most powerful ranchers in the territory through stupidity, after all. His gaze sharpened as he obviously figured out the only sane reason Stuart would hold such a belief: through previous acquaintance with Mariah.

"Get," said the rancher, barely a whisper but deadly as the hiss of a viper. "Now."

Stuart said, "It is your house," and turned to leave. Even lacking an answer, he'd done what he meant to.

But Garrison said, "Ain't stopped you before," and Stuart hesitated. He looked, curious—and faced hatred.

He wondered, with a moment of discomfort, where Garrison kept his firearms.

"I have never been in your house." That much, at least, Stuart could say. He was not proud of his and Mariah's secrecy, much less their behavior, but they'd never violated the sanctity of her father's home.

"My grass," clarified Garrison. "My water. *My range.*"

He wasn't talking to Stuart at all. He was talking to a nameless, faceless sheepherder. Well he and the other cattlemen may have arrived first, but Wyoming had *free* range nevertheless. Free water. Free grass.

So much for showing respect. "Not anymore," said Stuart quietly.

Jacob Garrison, steel eyes glittering, said, "*My daughter.*"

Not anymore. But that was Mariah's decision to make now, not Stuart's.

"Good day," Stuart said instead, and turned his back on this man's fury, walked into the foyer. Mariah stood waiting at the foot of the stairs, one hand clutching the banister tight enough to turn her knuckles as white as her stricken face.

Stuart's heart ached, to see her distress. Had she thought her father would say yes? Was her love truly as blind as that?

But of course it was. Mariah's faith in human nature was only one of her many fine qualities. Likely he was taking advantage of that gentle blindness, to marry her away from this.

But he stared at her, and he knew that he would do almost anything to have her with him—if only she still agreed.

If only she could bear the troubles that faced them.

Stuart heard Garrison's boot-step behind him and wrenched his gaze away from Mariah to look back at the man who now thoroughly hated him—the man he meant to make his father-in-law. Garrison was not looking at him, though. Garrison was looking at his daughter.

Questions burned in his gaze. Then a moment of betrayal. Then fury.

"Mariah Lynn," drawled the rancher, voice gravelly and thick. "You got somethin' to tell me?"

Mariah's fine, gray gaze fluttered from her father to

Stuart and back, helpless and hurting. How could she possibly go against her father, her family . . . her storybook world?

She parted her lips, but no sound came out.

It was asking too much. Stuart should have known all along. Perhaps he had.

He inclined his head slightly, but not so much that he had to wrench his gaze off of the sight she made. This might be the last he got to see her for some time. He would need to remember. "Miss Garrison," he said, low. "Good day."

She stared, stricken, but said nothing. So be it.

Stuart turned to leave, the spot between his shoulder blades feeling more like a target than ever. Garrison would not likely forgive this insolence. Stuart had been a fool.

But at least he'd been a fool for the finest woman he could ever have shared dreams with. . . .

He opened the glass-paneled door himself, stepped out onto the verandah, reached the brick pathway.

Then he heard soft footsteps—and turned to see Mariah rushing after him. "Stuart!"

He stopped and she caught up to him, caught his hands with hers before he could even take off his hat. "*Yes!* Of course I will marry you! That is . . ." She lowered her gaze, suddenly shy after having announced herself to the neighborhood. "If you still want me. I've been such a coward. But I *do* mean to marry you, if . . . if that's what you want."

Stuart held her hands, so small and delicate, tightly in his own and he felt dizzy with surprise. Relief. Joy.

With love.

Perhaps he was not such a fool, at that.

"I would be honored," he assured her, surprising them both with a shudder of nervous laughter to his words. *She's said yes—openly!* "How could I not?"

She laughed with him, despite tears glittering in her

soft eyes, and she clutched to his hands as if for strength. The nervousness beneath her joy drew Stuart's gaze upward from her to the dark form looming on the porch behind her.

Jacob Garrison's bearded face held a fury so potent it seemed to paralyze him—and it focused, full force, on the man with his daughter.

Stuart knew better than to assume that paralysis would last. "How can I call on you?" he asked quickly, while he still could. He doubted he would be welcome through the doors of the Garrison house again! "May I walk you home after services on Sunday?"

"Next week?" asked Mariah.

Stuart felt his mouth stretch into an uncharacteristic grin. "Aye, next week. When else?"

"I—of course I will! But won't I see you before then? We have so much to talk about!"

Several of Mariah's sisters crowded the front doorway, letting out the heat, listening to them. Stuart saw Mrs. Garrison join her husband on the verandah, take hold of his arm. She was not a large woman. He doubted she could hold the rancher back for long.

"We'll talk on Sunday," Stuart assured her, and squeezed her hands before releasing them, backing up, belatedly thumbing his hat brim. Then a horrible thought came to him, and again he raised his gaze to her father's silent fury. It still burned specifically at him, but . . . "You'll be all right until then, won't you?"

She followed his gaze, spun back to face him. "*Me?* Of course I will! I'll—I'll make Papa understand. . . ."

Papa growled.

Stuart continued to back away. Better her try to make the cattleman understand than him—as long as she was safe.

Only when he reached the tree-lined street and his old riding horse, and swung into its used saddle, did Stuart face the fancy Garrison home again. Despite its gazebo, its turret, its gables and bay windows, the finest part about it was the beautiful young woman lingering in front of it—and, behind her, the rancher who hated him.

But who hadn't moved to kill him. Yet.

Dizzy with warring emotions, Stuart chose hope—in honor of Mariah—and rode wisely away.

"I will see him dead first!"

Watching Stuart's broad shoulders as he rode off, still damp-eyed from her confusion of fear and guilt and joy, Mariah froze at her father's pronouncement.

He did not mean it, of course. He was just angry. Shocked, even, and that was her fault. She should have let him know before now.

But Papa could not mean to harm Stuart!

Mother said, quiet and firm, "We can discuss this inside."

Mariah finally wrenched her gaze from Stuart to look back at her parents then, and her sisters behind them. Mother seemed perhaps too calm—set for a crisis—and Papa . . .

The infuriated questions in Papa's eyes made Mariah's stomach ache.

"Nothin' to discuss," he said—but he could not mean that, either. He was her father, not some villainous guardian in one of Victoria's dime novels. Once he recovered from the surprise, surely he would see reason.

Wouldn't he?

Mariah looked quickly down the street once more, for reassurance, ignoring several shocked neighbors to watch Stuart ride across their bridge. For a fleeting moment, she wished he were waiting under it instead, wished she could sneak away to meet him, to find shelter in his strong arms, to lose herself in his embrace.

But they were courting properly now. With the intention of marriage. That had to be better than meeting in secret . . . once everyone understood.

Returning to the verandah, Mariah faced her father. "I wanted to tell you before now, Papa," she insisted. "And I tried . . ."

He glared at her, silently demanding more from her than she even understood.

Mama took a deep, shuddering breath and said, "Oh, Mariah."

And Laurel said, "Not a MacCallum!"

Papa turned and stalked inside. The younger girls scattered backward to make room.

Mama slid her arm around Mariah's waist—oh, how wonderful that gentle show of support felt—and followed him, closing the door behind them. "Girls, go upstairs," she said to the others. "Jacob, don't you think we had best hear her out?"

Papa said, "Nope."

Elise, squirming as Audra and Victoria herded her up the stairs, stuck her face between the posts to ask, "Is Mariah getting married?"

Again, Papa said, "Nope."

As if that, at least, were not her decision to make! Mariah raised her chin and said, "Yes."

Papa spun on her, then. "How do you know that man?"

The intensity of his question frightened her. "He . . . I first met Stuart at school."

The half-truth sounded too much like a lie, and Papa nodded suspiciously, eyes burning. He did not believe her—which made her memory of those secret meetings under the bridge, those longing looks across the church, feel even more damning.

But she *had* first met him at school!

Mama said, "Upstairs," one more time—in the quiet voice that they never disobeyed—and then Mariah stood alone in the foyer with her parents.

"Stuart wanted to talk to you from the start," she insisted, looking from one to the other, searching for the acceptance she'd never been without. "*I'm* the one who thought he shouldn't, who said we should keep our feelings secret until he had his claim. I can see now how wrong that was, but—but if you're angry at anyone, be angry at me."

"He took liberties with you," Papa reckoned.

"*No!*" But that was also a lie—at least, too close to a lie to be defended—and he seemed to know it. He turned sharply away, as if from an image too horrible to envision.

Mariah's face burned. "Stuart MacCallum has always been a gentleman with me! Any . . . any liberties he might have taken . . . I offered freely."

Papa said again, his voice strange and raspy, "I will see him dead."

Mother said, "Jacob."

And finally, horribly, Mariah wondered if he might actually mean it.

"No! We've done nothing that would shame you! Just kisses—Papa, it's only been kisses. I love him, and he loves me. We've had honorable intentions from the very start." She grasped her father's arm, wanting him to face her again—

To her shock, he recoiled from her touch.

Mother said, "That's enough! Mariah, you join your sisters upstairs. Jacob—"

But Papa was already stalking toward the back of the house. Mother went after him, and Mariah followed her mother.

"Where are you going?" Mother demanded.

Papa said, "Out."

"You are not to do anything rash. Do you hear me?"

Papa continued out the backdoor toward the stables.

Mama turned and pointed at Mariah. "Stay here."

Confusing cowardice and common sense now, Mariah let her own footsteps falter while her mother continued after her father—

An angrier father than she'd ever, ever seen.

He could not really want Stuart dead. The mere possibility made Mariah's head swim. If anything happened to Stuart because of this, it would be her fault. Her fault for loving him, and for keeping it secret for so long. Her fault for the family she came from. . . .

But no, such thoughts were inconceivable. Her father—even angry—was a good, decent man. Like Stuart. She had to trust that.

What else could she do but trust it?

That, and pray.

Riding toward his family's ranch, where they would soon have Sunday dinner, Stuart felt good. He'd braved the lion's den and emerged with the greatest of prizes.

Mariah loved him—loved him even more than she loved her family. She still meant to marry him, despite her father's protests.

Leaning his head back, Stuart let out a foolish, exuberant whoop. What man wouldn't want to crow, with a woman like Mariah Garrison promising herself to him? He felt guilty for having doubted her devotion.

Although really, seeing that house . . .

Rather than dwell on the riches Mariah would forsake for him, Stuart turned his thoughts forward. He had a great deal to do, in the next week, and plans to make. Few proper engagements lasted under six months. Despite his impatience, Stuart knew that the folks of Sheridan would be watching for any hint of scandal in their courtship. A short engagement would lead to rumors that they'd only married from necessity, and he would not stand for that slur on Mariah's reputation or his own.

Spring would come soon enough, with all the work ahead of them. In the meantime, she must have an engagement ring. Stuart's mother had promised him his granny's. That meant letting his own family know his plans. Though Stuart felt confident of a better reception than he'd received at the Garrisons', he had some explaining to do as well.

And then there was—

The spray of dirt from the road in front of Stuart's horse surprised him almost as much as the gunshot that echoed it. A second followed the first, then another, each throwing up dirt, until Pooka reared back and almost unhorsed him.

Stuart leaned forward in the saddle, drew his frightened horse in a tight circle and searched the horizon of the wide, rolling grasslands as he did. Johnson? he thought. Or . . .

He had a shotgun on his saddle, more for unexpected hunting opportunities than safety. But without seeing where the gunman hid, it did him no good to draw the blasted thing. Especially at a distance.

To Stuart's relief, no more shots sounded. Pooka tossed his head and snorted, frightened even without having seen Garrison's murderous fury.

The back of his neck itchy, a shudder building deep in him, Stuart nevertheless took a long, deep breath of qualified relief. He nudged the gelding into a trot, then a canter, to better escape this stretch of road before the gunman decided to sight a little better.

He could almost hear Mariah's likely protests: Perhaps someone was hunting antelope. Perhaps the gunshots weren't meant for him at all.

Ah, Mariah . . .

The shots were meant for Stuart, all right. But the farther he rode unharmed, leaning over Pooka's neck at full gallop, the more he knew them for a warning. Repeating rifles held up to fifteen, sixteen, even seventeen cartridges. If someone had wanted to kill him, surely they wouldn't have stopped.

He wondered if that eliminated Mariah's father from the list of suspects.

Her father, Stuart thought darkly, would keep shooting.

Chapter Seven

"I don't want Mariah to bake anymore," announced little Elise on Tuesday, putting down the cookie she'd just nibbled.

"Then you don't get cookies," countered Mrs. Garrison smoothly, touching Mariah's arm before her oldest daughter, pretty cheek streaked with flour, could argue with her youngest.

Evangeline Taylor took another polite nibble of her own cookie. It tasted a little burnt, but still . . . it was a cookie! Had she dared speak up, she would praise it. But she would never be heard over the others, not on Elizabeth Street, not as the Garrison girls were vehemently debating the perils of courtship.

The impossible had proven true: Mariah Garrison meant to marry a sheep farmer.

"She has to learn wife skills," Laurel told Elise, and not very nicely.

"I can cook," argued Mariah, as if saying the words would make them even more true.

Laurel muttered something that sounded like, "For a sheep farmer?"

"Enough," chided Mrs. Garrison. "We have company."

Victoria said, "Evangeline knows, Mama. Everyone at school is talking about it."

Mariah, mixing something in a bowl, tried to look nonchalant. "What are they saying?"

Mrs. Garrison said, "Elise, eat your cookie or go to your room."

Elise contemplated her cookie as if weighing her choices.

"Mollie Gregory said it's because you never kept company with proper men," reported Victoria, as thrilled to share her copious knowledge as ever.

"Proper?" Mariah stopped stirring.

"She meant—" started Audra, then realized that nobody needed further explanation. "Oh."

Victoria nodded. "She said if Papa could get someone like Alden Wright to woo you, maybe you would come to your senses."

Mariah and Laurel exclaimed, "Alden Wright!" and then blinked at each other, startled by their momentary agreement. Evangeline did not understand their objection. Alden Wright was considered one of the best catches in town, second only to Thaddeas Garrison.

The older girls looked deliberately away from each other and Laurel added, "At least his family runs cattle. Me, I'll only keep company with cowboys."

Mrs. Garrison said, "Just have them talk to your father first, Laurel. Then they can sit with you in the parlor some evening. . . ." On the excuse of checking Mariah's progress, she dusted the flour off her oldest daughter's smudged cheek. "Or walk you home from church."

Evangeline wondered if a gentleman would ever want to call on someone like herself, with neither a father nor a parlor. She took another nibble of cookie.

With a snort, Laurel fell back in her chair, folded her arms, and scowled. "What kind of cowboy would want to do something tedious like that?"

Audra said, "A well-behaved one."

"You'll be amazed what a man will endure to spend time with a girl he's sweet on," their mother insisted, smiling at Mariah.

Victoria resumed her report. "Sophronia Pierce's mother says if Papa made you choose between a roof over your head and a sheep farmer, you'd come to your senses fast enough."

Elise said, "May I go to my room?"

"Eat your cookie!" snapped Mariah.

Elise began to pout. Evangeline would gladly eat the cookie for her, if that could help.

"Mercy James thinks that Stuart MacCallum just wants your inheritance," added Victoria. "Do we get an inheritance, Mama?"

Laurel said, "Not if we marry sheep farmers."

Mariah said, "Stop calling him a sheep farmer!"

"If he'd stop farming sheep, maybe I would." Laurel considered it. "But probably not."

"Laurel," warned their mother, "that is enough. Kitty, you haven't touched your cookie. Does your stomach hurt? Would you like some bread and jam?"

Kitty shook her head.

"I want bread and jam please," piped up Elise.

Mrs. Garrison said, "The cookies are not that bad, Elise!"

"Not that bad?" Mariah's pretty mouth fell open.

Evangeline took a deep breath. "I like—"

But Victoria was reporting again "Then Carrie Benton said she fears Mariah might be in a family way, and Laurel—"

"Vic!" warned Laurel, while Evangeline gasped. Victoria hushed, but too late.

Mariah blushed deeper than Evangeline had ever seen anybody blush. "Oh!"

Mrs. Garrison, eyebrows high, said, "Audra, please take your younger sisters upstairs."

Blushing herself, Audra said, "Yes, ma'am."

"In *our* family's way?" asked Elise, following Audra. "Or the *MacMallumses?*"

As soon as they'd gone, Victoria said, "I'm sorry, Mama. I forgot who was listening."

"Mmm." Mrs. Garrison folded her arms. "Laurel, finish Victoria's story, please."

Scowling, Laurel obeyed. " 'And Laurel got Carrie Benton to take it back.' That's all."

"How?" demanded their mother.

"I didn't touch her!" insisted Laurel. "All I did was tell her what I would do if she spread such vulgar lies about my sister again, so she stopped."

In fact, Carrie had burst into tears, but Evangeline hoped nobody said so. Laurel always stood up for the smaller children at school. She once kicked Cotton James for pulling Evangeline's hair.

Mrs. Garrison said, "I'm going to get a visit from Mrs. Benton, aren't I?"

Scowling down at her plate, Laurel admitted, "You might."

Victoria said, "But you might not. Sophronia Pierce said no respectable person in this town will have anything to do with us as long as Mariah persists in this dreadful perversion."

Mariah slammed her mixing bowl down onto the table. "perversion!"

Mrs. Garrison said, "Sophronia Pierce would not know what 'this town' intends if they wrote a declaration in India ink on her—" She stopped, though it seemed to take effort. "On her face," she finished. "But we all know not to take gossip to heart, now don't we?"

That surprised Evangeline almost as much as did the answering nods. But perhaps Mrs. Garrison had never known the suspicion and scorn that grew from the seeds of such slander.

Should she warn them? But Mrs. Garrison excused herself upstairs, and the kitchen fell silent behind her. The stark contrast to previous afternoons made Evangeline's heart ache.

Even when Mariah said softly to Laurel, "Thank you for standing up for me."

"I didn't do it for you," her dark-haired sister insisted, standing. "I did it for the family honor. Something *you* seem to have forgotten!" And she stalked out the back-door, her footsteps loud and clumping because she'd worn cowboy boots under her skirts again.

Evangeline whispered, "I will go get our books," and escaped the kitchen to the front hallway. But Victoria did not follow.

Behind her, she heard Mariah ask, "Are things as bad for Stuart's brothers and sisters?"

Evangeline decided to practice her piano lesson, even if it wasn't Thursday. Playing scales, she need not hear Victoria's answer. None of this made sense. Why would Mariah or Stuart cause their families such grief? If Evangeline ever had such a home, she would never . . .

But not even a MacCallum would deign ask for Evangeline's hand. So she concentrated on her practice, wondering if she would ever have the talent to play a piece of dance music that had haunted her dreams since Saturday night. . . .

Thaddeas Garrison was not, to Stuart's surprise, among the three cowboys who rode toward him and his flock Tuesday afternoon. He knew he wouldn't see the rancher himself so far east of town, where the range got dry. A benefit of age and power was the avoidance of this kind of dirty work. But he'd expected the man's son, Mariah's half-brother or not.

He did not think the lawyer's absence bode well.

Still, there was nothing Stuart could do but stand and await the approaching trio—and to gesture toward his two black border collies, Beauty and Buster, to stay with the flock. Sheep, when spooked, were more likely to bunch up than to scatter, which made them easy targets. The dogs' job, among other things, was to keep them from spooking.

Best that Stuart let himself draw the attention. So he did not hike back to Pooka to collect his shotgun or, God forbid, to ride away. He walked in the direction of the riders, more to put himself farther from the sheep than out of any frontier courtesy—and he waited.

The men from the Circle-T rode cow ponies, small and shaggy with winter coats. They wore the dusters, neckerchiefs, leather gauntlets, and Stetson hats of their trade. Coils of rope and rifles in scabbards hung from their saddles. Only one, the man in the middle, looked to have any age on him. The two backing him up were no older than Stuart.

Their youth didn't bode well, either. But Stuart took a certain comfort in the fact that he had no dignified choice but to wait. At least it gave him the chance to show them that he was not afraid of cattlemen. Not enough to matter, anyhow.

The younger cowboys sneered at the flock behind him—as if they owned anything more than their saddles and their clothes, much less over four hundred head of good Merino stock. Even their ponies likely belonged to their outfit—the Circle-T Ranch, of course. Their brands said so.

Their leader, a blond man with bleached eyebrows and a face like leather, drew his pony to a halt not five feet from Stuart. His associates followed suit.

"You're the oldest MacCallum boy," he announced.

Though no longer a boy, if the range wars had ever allowed him a real childhood at all, Stuart said, "I am."

The blond man nodded and swung easily from his horse, shrugged his shoulders to readjust to standing on the ground. The other two men stayed on horseback.

"Hear tell you've been taking liberties with a certain rancher's daughter," said the older cowboy, squinting at the unpleasantness of the words—and what would surely follow them. Garrison had figured everything out, all right.

Stuart might've argued that he had to meet Mariah in secret, or she'd been too inviting to resist, or that they planned to marry. But the truth was, he *had* taken liberties with her.

The fact that a lowdown cowboy was saying it did not change that.

So Stuart, trying to take a deep breath in such a way that the cowboys would not notice, said, "Yes, that's right."

Their leader shook his head. When a younger cowboy said, "You son-of-a—" Stuart tensed. Nobody insulted his mother, whether they outnumbered him or not. But the older cowboy raised one hand, and that was enough to command silence.

"That weren't real smart," he said then, and Stuart had no answer. He hadn't met with Mariah to be smart. He'd kept seeing her, kissing her, because . . . well, because she was Mariah. He needed her like he needed water to drink and air to breathe. And she'd been worth it, was still worth it, even knowing what he faced.

Stripping off one leather glove, then the other, the older cowboy asked, "We gonna need to hold you down?"

Stuart just shook his head. But he did ask, "What's your name?"

"Schmidt," answered the blond man. "The Boss is my uncle. We gonna have trouble with those dogs?"

Stuart looked over his shoulder, saw Beauty and Buster watching him with their usual alertness. He whistled the command he'd only gestured before: Watch the sheep. The dogs' bright eyes stayed on him, their ears up, but they would obey.

He turned back to Schmidt, not unaware of the real bias here. "Leave the flock alone and they'll stay where they are."

Schmidt said, "I don't give a damn about your stinkin' woollybacks."

Then he slammed a fist into Stuart's gut.

"I don't get it," said Dougie, Stuart's seventeen-year-old partner and brother. "After all that, you honestly think Old Man Garrison will stand by and watch you court his oldest girl?"

"Nope," said Stuart from where he sat at his pull-out table, and he wiped more blacking onto his boot. After four days, the worst of the pain from his beating had faded . . . though it helped to sit inside at night, with the heat of the stove at his back.

Dougie, who prided himself on his ability to sleep on the ground in any weather, often proclaimed his independence from walls and foundations—not that Stuart's home, a caravan-style sheep-wagon with an arched canvas roof and Dutch door, had a foundation. But that did not keep him from stretching across the wagon's single bed that Saturday night. "Then why are you slickin' yourself up for church?"

"Because I mean to court her anyway."

His redheaded brother laughed. "You hold your life cheaply then, do you?"

"Even Garrison won't come armed to church." He hoped. And as for what might happen after . . .

Well, he'd taken one beating and was still standing. More or less. The knowledge that he would do the same to any man who secretly kissed one of his sisters discomforted Stuart even more than the ugly purple bruises across his gut, his ribs. Since he intended to keep his dealings with Mariah aboveboard from here on out, any further violence would cross the kind of deadline you couldn't mark in the dirt. But whether or not Garrison crossed it . . .

Focusing on what he could control, Stuart began to buff his boots with hard, short swipes. That only hurt a little.

"Could be she won't be there," added Dougie, as if Stuart hadn't considered the same thing. "Could be he'll lock her in her room or send her off to a convent."

The Garrisons were no more Catholic than the MacCallums, but his brother's predictions held a grain of truth. So Stuart said, "He might."

"You do know that Garrison could ruin you, or worse, and get away with it."

Putting down his boots and turning to open a cabinet, Stuart paused mid-wince to stare at his brother. Then he shook his head and considered the package of paper collars that Montgomery Ward had sent him free, last time he ordered suspenders. Mariah deserved to be courted proper. He'd always believed that.

Dougie shook his head. "She's really worth this?"

"Yup." Stuart need not even think to answer. It seemed Mariah was always dancing through some piece of his thoughts or his dreams, smiling or laughing or looking at something in that eager, delighted way of hers. . . .

Trouble was, Stuart wanted more than dreams of her. He'd wanted it for years. No number of beatings would change that.

"And she thinks you're worth it?" Which sometimes did seem odd, but . . .

"Apparently." Stuart decided on the paper collar. It was better than no collar at all, even if he had no proper paper cuffs to match.

Dougie looked around him, at the confines of Stuart's home. "And the lass knows you live in a wagon?"

"She's nae daft, Douglas." He'd told Mariah about the

wagon as soon as he bought it, a year previous. Most herders, like Dougie, made do with tents and bedrolls. But Stuart meant not merely to herd sheep but to own them. And unlike Dougie, Stuart had meant to marry even then. Had Mariah realized the leap of faith buying this wagon, instead of more sheep, had taken? It would be better than starting out in a mining camp tent, a nester's dugout or soddie, or his folks' place. Some newlyweds barely managed *that.*

"She's not daft," he said again, annoyed by the lingering pain in his ribs. Mariah knew what he had and, blacked boots and paper collars aside, it would do him no good to start questioning his worth now.

Her father and the town would sure enough do it for them.

Mariah's nervousness, arriving at church that Sunday, had little to do with her appearance and everything to do with her father's continued censure.

"I never meant to hurt you," she whispered desperately up at him, clutching at the sleeve of his great coat after he helped her down from their surrey. "Not you or anybody else."

"Then don't," said Papa curtly, turning away. It was one of the few times he'd spoken to her all week.

When Kitty slipped her mittened hand into her older sister's, Mariah smiled her best reassurance for the little girl—and, she supposed, for herself. Everything would be fine. She'd never known her father to be less than loving or fair, even at his most stern. Never! She had to believe that he thought himself fair, even loving, in this as well.

But as she followed her mother and sisters out of the cold and into church, conscious of the townspeople's undue interest, Mariah also knew her father was mistaken. The thought felt blasphemous. But she need not peek toward Stuart, already seated in back with his own family, to accept its truth. In this one thing, Mariah's father was wrong.

As she passed the MacCallums, she peeked anyway.

Stuart's gaze met her own, determined—and he nodded at her. "Miss Garrison," he murmured in greeting, low but sure.

In that moment, Mariah forgot the weight of everyone's scrutiny, Papa's disapproval, her sisters' anxiety. She smiled, nodded back. Everything *would* be fine.

Then Stuart's gaze shifted, sharpened—and Papa's hand settled against the small of Mariah's back. She obediently resumed following her family. But oh, he was mistaken. Sooner or later, her father would realize as much. And until then . . .

Until then, Mariah meant to remember her duty as his daughter in every way that did not require forsaking Stuart. She owed him that. As she sat between Kitty and Audra, on the pew that had been her family's since the church was built, she decided that would surely keep peace until everyone came to their senses.

It had to! And for a prize as wonderful as Stuart, she could endure until then.

After services, when the family usually talked amongst their friends, Elise and Audra tried to tug Mariah toward the surrey by both hands, as if fearing the confrontation to come. But Mariah, looking for Stuart, set her heels. She found his family. Though never formally introduced, she easily recognized his lank, mustached father and prim, severe mother, and of course she knew the older of his siblings from her schooldays. When she smiled a shy greeting to them, her cheer felt more artificial than ever, even before they stared solemnly back. Was everyone watching her? And where . . . ?

Fingers brushed her coated shoulder, more tentative than her father's, and Mariah spun to face Stuart MacCallum directly. Here in the wintery sunlight. In front of God, her father, and everybody.

She smiled.

Stuart quickly moved his hand, but he did not step back from her. Instead, hat in hand, he offered his arm.

Mariah noted his shined boots and proper collar, flattered by the effort he'd obviously made. She noted, too, how the wind ruffled through his thick hair, wheat-brown; noted the cleft in his chin, the curve of his clean-shaven jaw in the sunlight. She noted the very real breadth of his chest, the set of his stocky shoulders as he proffered his arm.

But mostly, Mariah noted the stubborn certainty in Stuart's solemn brown eyes and oh, she felt glad for his tenaciousness! He had always meant to court her. . . .

Taking his arm, which felt as solid as a stone or a tree and just as enduring, Mariah allowed him to keep his word.

Then someone cleared his throat in an ominous growl—and together they turned to face her father.

Chapter Eight

Even the solidity of Stuart's arm under her mittened hand could not soften Mariah's unease at so blatantly defying her father. Her entire life, this man had stood unflinchingly between her and bears, marauders, even cold and hunger. Mistaken or not, he deserved her respect—hers and Stuart's both. If only he would accept it.

"I mean to walk my fiancée home," announced Stuart, low but clear, before Papa could even speak. "The weather is fair, and we will stay in plain sight. I'll let nothing happen to her."

Which was all respectful enough—except for the not-asking-permission part. So why did it sound uncomfortably like a dare?

Papa continued to stare at them both, eyes bright but unreadable in the shadow of his black hat. When he shifted that formidable gaze to Mariah, it was all she could do not to squirm beneath his silent condemnation. Never had she or any of her sisters ever disobeyed him so blatantly, even in private. Not even Laurel! Now here she stood, in full view of the town . . .

Her throat burned as her need to speak battled her inability to form words. She could not apologize for her boldness without seeming to apologize for Stuart, which she would not do. She could not plead for his blessing without giving him yet another opportunity to deny it, this time in public. So Mariah grasped at the only thing she hoped might sway him: sincerity.

"He's a good man, Papa. Really!"

Only her father's quick blink indicated that this, he'd not expected. Mariah reached for his sleeve, bridging the two men she loved with her two hands.

"If only you got to know him, you would understand! Stuart's a decent man, Papa, honorable and hardworking like you, and—"

Papa lowered his gaze to her touch. Was he listening? Finally?

Then he abruptly turned away, strode away to the surrey, to his wife and daughters.

The daughters who did not defy him.

The only thing that kept Mariah's heart from cracking was Stuart's unwavering presence at her side. At least Papa had left her standing with Stuart. Not, she suddenly saw, that he had accepted defeat just yet.

Hoisting himself into the driver's seat of the surrey, Papa glanced purposefully across the street—at a cowboy.

Mariah recognized the young man slouched against the hitching post. Young Dawson rode for the Circle-T. Like most cowboys he had not, she thought, attended services. So the only reason he would be in this part of town on a Sunday morning was if he were courting, or if his boss had sent him here. And he had not dressed as if he were courting.

As Papa drove away, Dawson swung into the saddle of a waiting cow pony. Then he tipped his Stetson toward

Mariah, raised his eyebrows almost comically at Stuart, and waited.

"A guard," muttered Stuart, arm rigid beneath her hand. He sounded like he had an ugly taste in his mouth. "Him."

"A chaperone," clarified Mariah anxiously, turning to watch Stuart's profile. Normally his face seemed so gentle, his jaw rounded and lips soft, even his eyes with an innocuous, heavy-lidded slant. But his expression took on a hardness she'd not seen in him before. "Just like we wanted, remember?"

Of course Stuart would know the difference. Only certain people could be chaperones—parents, brothers, respected matrons. Cowboys were the kind of men chaperones protected young ladies *from.* And yet . . .

She and Stuart did have to start somewhere to earn her father's trust, didn't they?

Stuart angled his brown gaze down at her, annoyed enough that his brows had leveled out. "A chaperone," he challenged, low.

Mariah nodded hopefully. "So that we don't cause a scandal."

To her relief, Stuart smiled then—a quiet, close-mouthed smile that nevertheless crinkled up into his eyes.

"Mustn't cause a scandal," he agreed gently. His gaze flicked away from her for a moment, toward the dozens of faces pretending not to watch them and further. Mariah saw the MacCallum wagon already departing toward the north before Stuart's attention returned to her, serious and somehow resolved. "May I escort you home, Miss Garrison?" he asked formally.

"I would be honored, Mr. MacCallum," agreed Mariah, so very glad to smile again. "Assuming your intentions are honorable"

Now, when Stuart glanced down at the frozen ground, his brief smile even revealed a dimple. "Well . . . I intend to marry you, if that's what you mean," he murmured, very low. "I canna speak for the rest of it."

"Stuart MacCallum!" Mariah had to whisper her protest, lest their guard—rather, their chaperone—misconstrue. Or construe correctly. "You are too bold, sir."

For some reason, Stuart's gaze crept back to where Dawson waited, watching their exchange, and hardened there. "If I have to be," he said.

But she was too busy fighting a blush to ask what he meant by that.

The November air smelled sharply of snow, and their footsteps sounded a kind of joint heartbeat on the wooden sidewalk. For years, Stuart had longed for the day when he would walk openly through the middle of Sheridan with Mariah Garrison on his arm. Now here they were.

But never had he imagined a guard following on horseback, much less a cowboy who had overseen his thrashing not a week earlier. The growing injustice of it burned in his chest, framed by the ache of lingering bruises, and did nothing to improve his ease with words. He and Mariah had spoken together countless times before, but that had been in secret, under the bridge. That was before it had mattered to anybody but them.

Now townsfolk watched—from carriages and the opposite sidewalk, from windows and stairways. More than ever before, Stuart meant to prove the town wrong by remembering his manners.

Since Mariah seemed occupied dividing her attention between the gray sky and sneaking shy peeks at him, up from beneath her fancy oversized hat, Stuart shouldered his responsibility as best he could. "I . . . enjoyed the sermon." When he hadn't been busy glaring at nosy parkers who could not keep their attention on the minister, anyway.

Mariah smiled perhaps too brightly. "Oh yes! I've always liked Reverend Adams's viewpoint. Although I admired Dr. Terrence's thoughts as well, when he visited last spring"

Then she looked down and her hat hid her face again.

"He had interesting things to say," agreed Stuart quickly, hoping she would not ask him about any of them. This felt nothing like their conversations beneath the bridge.

Mariah tilted her head back to look at him more directly—and, he thought, a little more honestly. Not that she'd been lying before! "Does this feel . . . awkward to you, Stuart?"

She felt awkward? Was it his fault that she felt awkward?

He would rather blame the cowpoke riding several lengths behind them.

"Yes," Stuart admitted, wishing he knew how to fix their discomfort. If only he could whittle a good conversation with a jackknife, or build one from stones.

To his surprise, Mariah squeezed his arm in one of her impulsive gestures, and much of the awkwardness faded on its own. "Thank goodness it's not just me! Not that I'm uncomfortable being with *you* of course. Or even people knowing about it. But . . ."

"But they're watching for us to make a mistake." Stuart glared briefly toward a cluster of boys who stood across the street, hoops hanging useless in their hands as they stared. "Judging us. They've made up their minds already. I've lived with it all my life. It helps to keep your head up. Don't let them think they're better than you."

It wasn't until he'd finished speaking that he heard the unintended vehemence in his words—and realized just how many he'd spoken.

Mariah's up-tilted hat revealed her wide gray eyes and pretty face, pinker in the cheeks than the November wind merited. "I mean . . . going against Papa."

Oh. Now Stuart looked off toward the gray sky. When Mariah asked, "Have people really stared and judged you your whole life?" he said, "Never mind. You get used to it."

He had. But would she?

After that they walked in silence for a good block or two. At least Mariah's warmth beside him did not feel uncomfortable, even if the silence did.

Then she said, "Papa really is a good man," as if he wanted to hear about her father's finer qualities. "I can't remember him ever behaving so rudely. I'm sure once he adjusts to the idea of . . . well, of us . . ."

"He won't," predicted Stuart, gently but firmly.

He might as well not have spoken. "Of course he will! Papa just wants what is best for me, is all. . . ."

And it clearly was not Stuart? He remembered the blow of Schmidt's fist against his ribs, the effort of not crying out. What was best for her?

". . . old bias against sheep, but they aren't sharing the same range anyway, are they? Perhaps you could explain that to him yourself, and then he'll see. . . ."

Stuart's leg still ached from where a rock dug into his shin when he finally dropped, kneeling, glaring impotent murder at those damned cowboys.

". . . perhaps even become friends," insisted Mariah cheerfully.

Stuart blinked away the memory of lying crumpled on the range—on his land—and the sound of cow ponies riding away. Breathing had felt precarious, swallowing an agony. He'd struggled for God knew how long before he could even whistle Beauty over, roll onto his back with his dog licking worriedly at his face. At the time, despite how the pain jolted through him on every heartbeat, Stuart had felt relief to be left alive.

He had worse memories than that though, if he thought back far enough. Every single one of them was connected to cattlemen.

"We won't ever be friends," he told Mariah now. He felt surprised to see that they'd almost reached their bridge, and more annoyed than ever by the cowboy still following them.

"You've seen him at his worst," she insisted—which was truer than she realized. She did not know about the thugs sent to rough him up, likely did not understand the truth about who had hired Idaho Johnson. Mariah thought her father was decent and honorable. *Like him!*

Stuart doubted he would ever fully understand the world Mariah saw through those earnest, predawn eyes of hers. But as her affianced husband, he meant to protect it as best he could.

As they began to cross their bridge, footsteps harmonizing again like on the sidewalk, he stopped her and fumbled at his breast pocket.

"Here," he said, and pressed his granny's ring into her mittened hand. "For you."

Mariah's eyes widened as she stared at the aged gold ring, an amethyst chip mounted atop a tiny thistle design. His mother had given it up grudgingly, complaining that Miss Mariah Garrison probably owned ear-bobs of more worth. But his sister Emily had secretly polished it for him, so at least it shone.

If Mariah had ear-bobs worth more, she did not let on. Instead she said, "Oh! Here—hold it while I get my mitten off!"

He took the ring back while Mariah fumbled at the mitten on her left hand. She finally used her teeth to remove it, then tried to say something and, in doing so, spit out the mitten. She stepped on it quickly, so that it would not blow off the bridge, but did not stoop to retrieve it. Instead she peered at the ring Stuart held.

"Oh Stuart. It's *beautiful*."

Her approval relieved Stuart considerably, eased a tightness in his gut that he'd mistakenly attributed to bruising. He so very much did not want to start their official engagement by disappointing her.

"For you, lass," he insisted again. Likely a man from

Europe—or Cheyenne or Denver—would say something fancier than that, but he did not. "So that nobody doubts our intentions."

"Put it on me?" she pleaded, with an excited bounce. Glad for so simple a means to please her, Stuart clumsily slid the ring onto her soft, ladylike hand.

When she raised her shining gaze to his, he did wish he was someone who'd even been as far as Cheyenne. Then maybe he could tell her what she meant to him, what he would gladly endure to be with her, how proud she made him by accepting his suit and his grandmother's ring. But even if he could wrap his ungainly thoughts around such ideas, his mouth would never have kept up; he would only embarrass them both. So Stuart just stood there and held her soft, bare hand in his while, together, they admired the ring, tipping their heads comfortably—but not too improperly—close.

They had done it. After years of secrecy, they were truly engaged to marry.

The air smelled of snow. The creek rushed endlessly past beneath them, as it had during all of their trysts, all of their kisses. But now they stood above the bridge, in plain sight of neighbors . . . and their "chaperone." The air and the water were the same. They had changed.

"I had best get you home," Stuart said finally, crouching to retrieve her fallen mitten for her. "Before your father comes gunning for me."

"He won't come gunning for you, Stuart," Mariah laughed. "He's an honorable— Are you all right?" For someone who could not see the truth about Wyoming's beef empire, she had no problem noticing his slight wince at the effort of standing again, and then straightening up.

"I'm fine." But his words came out a touch more guttural than he'd meant.

Mariah held his arm. "Does your tummy hurt? Mama makes a peppermint tea . . ."

As if he would be allowed to drink her mother's tea! "I am fine," he started to insist, but her hand on his chest, so gentle that his still-bruised ribs did not twinge, distracted him in a different way. He raised his face to hers, even if he was still wincing. The wince did not last long. Her honest worry caught and held him

The Goose Creek, which had serenaded every kiss they'd ever shared, swirled noisily past. And they were engaged now! How could they not lean nearer each other? Mariah's wide, fine eyes held Stuart's gaze with a visible adoration, a trust he could only pray he would someday earn. Somehow her concerned fingers touched him more deeply than just his coat. Her full, sweet lips parted in soundless invitation. Past the chill smell of snow he tasted the warm scent of lavender and soap off her as he closed the distance between them, accepted her invitation. . . .

Then straightened, angrier than ever, when hoofbeats drummed the bridge.

"Somethin' wrong, Miss Garrison? This sheepherder of yourn ain't sick, is he?" From his superior perch in the saddle, the cowboy's eyes laughed knowingly at Stuart's stiff posture.

"Everything is fine, Mr. Dawson." Mariah pointed firmly back behind them. "Now leave us alone."

Touching his hat, Dawson wheeled his horse around right there on the bridge and rode away perhaps a quarter block . . . then resumed his watch, visibly amused. Were Stuart a swearing man, he would have sworn then, and loudly.

Instead he muttered, "An honorable man would do his own 'chaperoning.' "

Mariah patted his arm as she took it again, more innocently. "But that would mean condoning our relationship, and Papa's not ready to do that. Yet. He will."

Stuart stared down at her, incredulous, as they began to walk again. "He wants me dead."

"Papa?" As if he'd meant Dawson, the lackey. "Oh no, Stuart! True, Papa said some things he didn't mean after you left last week." He could only imagine what. "But if he wanted you dead, he certainly would not hide it."

They rounded the corner onto Elizabeth Street.

There stood the subject of their conversation at the foot of the walk, waiting for them. Old Man Garrison could easily have been a marshal standing off the outlaws. This time, the rancher wore his gun—and he'd tied down his holster.

Mariah's tone held less confidence as she challenged, "See?"

It would certainly help her courtship, thought Mariah, if her father and her beau did not bristle like rival bulls every time they caught wind of each other. But since she could not possibly understand the depths of their animosity, all she could do to diffuse it was to ignore it as best she could.

"Papa, look what Stuart gave me." As soon as they got close enough, she extended her exposed hand. It *was* an amazingly beautiful ring—nicer, in truth, than she'd expect a homesteader could manage. Perhaps it would ease Papa's worries.

But Papa just said, "Get inside, Mariah Lynn." And he glared at Stuart as he said it.

"Then come inside with me." Giving Stuart's hand a final squeeze—still wishing she could kiss him instead—Mariah stepped onto Garrison property and took her father's gun arm.

His gaze, when it lowered briefly to hers, told her she had not fooled him. "Get," he repeated, more low than soft.

When she glanced back at Stuart, he looked none too pleased by her interference himself. As if anything between these two men were not her doing and thus her concern.

"Promise not to argue," she instructed, and now both men stared at her, their expressions mutually unbelieving.

"Then I'm not going anywhere," she declared with feigned confidence. She tried not to remember the time Papa bodily carried Laurel away from a roundup she refused to leave. In front of Stuart, such a thing would be mortifying.

"I'll go," declared Stuart. "For now. Anything your father has to say to me, Mariah, he knows where to send his messengers."

His messengers? Mariah did not understand—but she understood how the two men glared at each other well enough

"Stay out of my way, MacCallum," warned Papa, more dangerous than Mariah had ever heard him . . . before he'd met Stuart, anyway.

"Stay off my land, Garrison," countered her betrothed.

"What?" Mariah looked from one man to the other. Papa had been on Stuart's land?

"Stay away from my daughter," insisted her father.

And Stuart said, "No."

It did not soften the answer that he added, "Not unless she tells me to."

"What is it you want?" Her father's arm remained steely beneath her grasp. Mariah knew that if he really wanted to shrug her off, he could. "Money? Grazing rights?"

"*Papa!*" she protested, unsure whether to feel more insulted for Stuart or for herself.

Stuart said, "Good day, Miss Garrison," and turned away, not deigning to answer.

"You'd take her today," challenged Papa, obviously unconvinced. "With just the clothes on her back."

"I'd take her to my folks' ranch for a respectable engagement," Stuart countered, unable to resist the bait. "None of your kind will say we did not behave ourselves."

"Stuart!"

"Too late for that," accused her father, and Mariah gave up. Perhaps her presence merely egged them on.

"Thank you for the walk and the beautiful ring, Mr. MacCallum," she told him, her tone nowhere near as dulcet as a lady's should be when saying that. "I hope to see you soon."

"After church next week," Stuart offered—or dared. "Send for me if you need anything sooner."

"I look forward to it. Papa?"

When her father did not turn to walk her in, Mariah took a deep breath and went on her own. Papa wouldn't *really* shoot Stuart—she would stake her life on it.

In fact, reaching the verandah, she peeked back with less confidence than she liked. As deeply as she loved Stuart, she *was* staking her life on it. Worse, she was staking his.

If either her father or her beau said anything else, it was too low and too terse for Mariah to see. In only a moment, Stuart had turned to walk away, in the direction of the church, where he had left his saddle horse. Her father watched him go until he vanished around the corner, then said something to Dawson and turned to follow Mariah in. He hesitated only a moment when he saw her on the verandah, then continued toward her, his usual, silent, force-of-nature self.

His hand when he gripped her shoulder, to herd her inside, felt particularly disapproving.

Mariah's sisters had of course been watching—some clustered on the stairway by the door, while others peered in from the parlor. But when Papa said, "Get," they—unlike Mariah—got.

Unlike Mariah—and her mother, who stood quietly in the hallway from the kitchen. Apparently he'd meant her as well, to judge from his glare, but Mama just lifted her chin, folded her arms, and waited. So Papa ignored her and asked what he'd meant to ask.

"Why are you doin' this?"

Despite the raw undercurrent of his voice, Mariah took hope. For a week, her father had barely spoken to her, much less allowed her to explain.

"Because I love him, Papa! I understand that you're angry at us, so you don't see it yet, but once you get to know Stuart, you'll understand! He's good and decent and hardworking and honorable—"

"Like me." So he'd been listening outside of church after all. But he parroted back her words with sarcasm.

"Yes, like you. I know you hate that he's a sheep farmer, but as long as he stays on his part of the range, why should that bother you? At least it's honest work. He's such a good man, Papa. *Truly!* And . . ."

Papa did not look to be softening—nor did his grip.

"And I do love him," she repeated, faltering. "I would never, never defy you like this if I were not certain of it. I have loved Stuart for years."

For a moment, just a moment, she took hope from his silence. But his next, low words came out more accusation than question.

"Just how'd you manage that, Mariah Lynn?"

Which did complicate things. How much of his anger rested on Stuart's vocation, and how much on their secrecy?

"I regret that we went behind your back, Papa," she admitted again, her heart aching. "But I was so certain you would disapprove. I was correct about that, wasn't I?"

He stared at her as if he had never really seen her before and did not like what he saw. The difference between the self she saw reflected in his steely eyes, and that happy girl she'd seen reflected in Stuart's earlier, felt humbling.

Then his gaze fell to her engagement ring, and he released her shoulder. "Still are."

And he walked away, stiffly circling her mother as if she, too, held blame, and out the back of the house. He would ride to the ranch again, Mariah knew. Papa always rode back to the ranch when he felt upset. On purpose or not, Mariah had been sending him there a lot lately.

Her shoulder seemed cold now. Her whole body felt cold, and not just because of the November chill.

Swallowing around her disappointment, she extended her left hand toward her mother. But instead of the joyful announcement it should have been, her words only strained out.

"Stuart gave me a ring."

Chapter Nine

Before he got to see Mariah again the next Sunday, Stuart stayed up with his brother three nights while the dogs warned of something that never quite showed itself. He found a dead antelope on his land—gutted by human hands. And he lost credit at almost every store in town.

At least nobody beat him up again. But he'd rather take another beating than learn that his father's credit had fallen under equal suspicion. Stuart spent all day Thursday in town, going from store to store, arguing for equal treatment. "We just paid off everything we owed with our fall lambs—and we'll do it again after spring shearing! The ranchers and farmers won't make any more payments until harvest!"

Most storekeeps dismissed him with the cryptic, "Let's not have trouble, MacCallum."

Only Crazy Pete of the Big Goose Hardware store, who had incurred his own trouble through pro-granger politics, dared confirm what Stuart had already guessed.

"Word is, Old Man Garrison's been asking questions about your resources. It's scared a lot of folks."

"And you?" challenged Stuart through gritted teeth.

Pete grinned gap-toothed and said, "Hell, boy, bring 'em on."

So at least as long as Pete held fast, the MacCallums had credit through the winter.

And still Stuart shined his boots and pressed his good shirt Saturday night, and Sunday he met with Mariah after church to walk her home. Everyone still watched them—including their mounted guard—but Stuart could hardly blame them. He liked watching Mariah, too. She chatted about what she would plant in her garden once they married, and what color material Stuart liked for shirts, and dozens of other little, personal things that made her eyes shine as she strolled, bold as ever, holding his arm. Snow fell, and she tried to catch snowflakes on her tongue but caught them on her lashes instead, laughing her joy up at him. He wanted to kiss her then. . . .

But cowboy Dawson rode behind them, and Old Man Garrison waited for them down the street. Though he hated to admit it, Stuart had a limit to his courage.

He'd already lost some dignity and a great deal of credit. So instead of kissing Mariah, he just held her arm and said, "I wish it were spring."

She glowed at him as if he'd kissed her anyway. "I do too."

But in the meantime, at least *she* wasn't dealing with beatings, threats, and lost business.

At least one of them was all right.

Before Mariah got to see Stuart, the Sunday after that, she was snubbed by two school friends at the millinery, received an insultingly fatty cut of pork at the butcher's, and sat up two nights with her little sister. Kitty was sleeping badly and throwing up every other meal. Mariah took turns with her exhausted mother, playing nursemaid.

The doctor could find nothing wrong, as the eight-year-old was neither feverish nor in pain. But Mother had limited confidence in the medical profession, and her apprehension proved contagious.

Then on Friday evening, while Mariah sat in the younger girls' bedroom with both Kitty and a bowl of chicken broth balanced on her lap, their father knocked softly.

"Your mother says you're still feelin' poorly, Kathryn May," he offered, standing uncomfortably in the doorway. Papa had never seemed quite so at ease in the fine town house as he did at the ranch, much less in his daughters' frilly bedrooms. His presence there just wasn't proper, in his view; he preferred to kiss the girls good night in the hallway. But even *he* would risk impropriety for the sake of a sick daughter. He always had.

Still, with his effort not to look at Mariah while facing the daughter in Mariah's arms, he'd clearly taken on extra discomfort.

"I'm better, really," insisted Kitty—as she had all week. But there was truth when she added, "I haven't thrown up today."

"Well that's fine." Papa hesitated. "Is there aught I can do for you?"

To Mariah's surprise, Kitty asked, "Would you please read to us?"

Papa nodded, then scanned the room for a book, which Kitty slid off Mariah's lap to fetch. In a few moments, she was happily cuddled on her father's lap, readying for another chapter of *Little Women* and giggling softly because his clothes and hands and whiskers were still cold—he'd come straight up after arriving home from the ranch.

Remembering that kind of attention, Mariah tried not to feel jealous as she collected the soup tray and readied to leave. Then Kitty said, "Don't go, Mariah, please? Stay and listen!"

Mariah hesitated in the doorway. Papa avoided her nowadays, except at family meals. Even then he seemed to talk to her sisters, but not her. Still, Kitty *had* been worrisomely ill. . . .

"May I?" she asked warily.

Carefully not looking at her, Papa drawled, "Ain't disowned you yet."

So Mariah put down the tray, draped an extra blanket over Kitty's shoulders, and settled at her father's booted feet to hear him read a story he clearly would not have chosen on his own. As he continued, Elise and Audra came by to check on Kitty. Since it was their room too, they stayed, Elise crawling into Mariah's lap. Victoria crept in, then even Laurel, though she pretended boredom. Soon Mother was standing in the doorway, leaning against the doorjamb and hugging herself as she watched everyone, and Kitty had fallen asleep.

Papa finished the chapter he'd been reading, then quietly cleared his throat with something like embarrassment and put the book down. "Reckon it's past dinnertime," he announced to the girls with his gravelly version of a whisper.

"Dinner's keeping just fine," assured Mother. "But everyone should wash their hands." And she herded the other girls from the room, leaving Papa and Mariah to put Kitty to bed.

Mariah liked watching her father tuck Kitty in so carefully, brushing back her fine, little-girl hair with his big, outdoorsy hands. Stuart, she thought, had hands remarkably like that.

Papa eyed her warily as he straightened. "You got something on your mind?"

Foolishly, she told him. "I was just hoping Stuart will be as good a father as you are."

As Papa's expression chilled, she realized her mistake. Bad enough to mention Stuart to him—but to mention having children by Stuart?

"Not if I've got say in it." And he strode past her.

"Papa! I didn't mean—it's just that you're so good with us, even if you are really an old cowboy at heart, and—"

But when she grabbed at his arm, he just kept walking, so she had to let go. "Papa?"

Behind her, Kitty made a whimpering sound—and threw up. And it was Mariah's fault.

And still, by Sunday morning, Mariah rolled her hair and tightened her corset and chose her best dress and boots for walking in the melting slush. When Stuart came to stand beside her after church, she took firm hold of his arm. Her mother had insisted on being the one to stay home with Kitty, saying "Either you see this through, or you don't."

And it wasn't as if Mariah did not want to be with Stuart!

In fact, Stuart seemed so constant and solid, in contrast to the upheaval she'd helped create at home, she wished she could hold onto his sturdy arm for more than just the walk from church. He listened to her concerns about upsetting the household, his head bowed in thought and his eyes as warm a brown as ever, and after she'd finished he asked, "Are you thinking to leave, then?"

"Leave? Where would I go?"

"You can live with my folks," he said—not the first time he'd made the offer. "It would get you out of that house, maybe take our courtship off your folks' minds some. I could come by for dinners, some nights. You could get to know my family."

Mariah did want to formally meet his family. And she wanted to sit in a parlor with him, take a meal with him . . . behave as other engaged couples were allowed to behave.

But to leave her home again, after being away all summer? She shook her head. "I'm sorry, Stuart."

"It was just an idea," he assured her.

"I *do* want to spend more time with you, truly, but—"

"Mariah." He stopped, brushed her cheek with his fingers. "Just know that you have someplace to go."

And she nodded, and oh she loved him, and as his strong fingers slid away, she wished more than anything at that moment that he would kiss her.

Behind them, Dawson called, "Whoa there, you old nag. Whoa." When Mariah peeked over her shoulder, his horse had done nothing more unruly than turn in several tight circles, and that was because he was turning her.

Mariah ducked her head to think that Dawson could see her unladylike feelings about Stuart. "I wish it were spring," she whispered, slipping her arm through her beau's yet again.

"And I," Stuart sighed.

But in the meantime, at least *he* was living on his own, without his family's daily disapproval. At least he need not worry about upsetting his family with their engagement, or being snubbed by former friends he'd thought more highly of. And thank goodness for that.

At least one of them was all right.

"Do you ken of something called wolf fencing?" asked Stuart's father from the seat of his spring wagon, as he drove the family to church the next Sunday.

Stuart, flanking the wagon astride Pooka, felt everything in him go still. "Fencing?"

He'd thought courting a rancher's daughter put his life in jeopardy, but *fencing?*

Ma, seated beside Da with little Rose on her lap and six-year-old Ian bundled between them, said, "No business on the Sabbath, Mr. MacCallum."

Da said, "We've not reached the church yet, Maggie."

When Ma scowled, she looked even less like a "Maggie" than usual. "Church doesna make the Sabbath, Mr. MacCallum."

And Da said, "Well there you have me." But the way he slanted his hat-shadowed gaze toward Stuart, his droopy moustache twitching, promised a return to the topic at her next distraction. And they had plenty of offspring to do the distracting. Besides Ian and Rose, up front, six more—Emily, Bonny, Jenny, Kevin, Anna, and Caroline—huddled under blankets in back. Spring wagons did not give a particularly pleasant ride anyway. With the snow gone, frozen patches of mud added to its jolts, and thawed mud splashed up to spoil Sunday clothes.

Like Da's Basque herders, Dougie had stayed behind to stand guard. Earlier in the week they'd come across some longhorn cattle grazing on their side of the deadline. Of course they'd chased the beasties back to their own range, but their very appearance concerned Stuart.

The weather had not gone cold enough for cattle to range this far from the foothills of the Bighorn range—not on their own. But someone could have driven them across the deadline to start trouble. And he'd not missed that at least two of the rangy cows bore the Circle-T brand.

Bonny let out a screech, and Kevin laughed at her, and Da turned back to Stuart.

"They've been trying wolf fencing down Texas way," he said. "It's wire, but the way this fellow told it, it's woven, meshlike, so that the stock canna get out—and fewer predators get in."

"And cattle?" challenged Stuart. As little sympathy as he had for cattlemen, he knew why they so hated fencing. Unlike sheep, cows roamed the range wild. Faced with a big blowup, they outwalked the worst of it . . . unless they tangled into a fence and froze to death.

"Are you so worried about cows now, Stuart MacCallum?" asked his mother, finished with the malcontents in the wagon bed. "This lass you're chasing has you putting the interest of those hulking great beasts over that of good, honest sheep now?"

Da said, "Don't forget it's the Sabbath, Maggie."

"And I'm not speaking of business, Mr. MacCallum,

I'm questioning your son's loyalty, and high time someone did!"

"I'm a good sheep man, Ma, and you know it."

"Then marry a lass from a herding family. The Wallaces over the Montana line have a daughter just turned sixteen. Why not court her?"

One reason was that he'd only met the girl once or twice. Another was that he had loved Mariah since he'd been old enough to love any woman at all. "I mean to marry Mariah Garrison."

"Or a granger. At least a farmer's daughter would know hard work. Sheep farming would be a step up from plow-chasing."

Stuart suspected even a nester's daughter would question the social advancement of wedding a sheep farmer. And in any case, "I'll marry Mariah Garrison, Ma."

"If she doesna get you killed outright, you'll starve or freeze to death, her being accustomed to servants and gas heat and the like."

"If you mean to see your grandchildren, Ma, you'll speak of my bride with a civil tongue or not at all."

For a long moment, the only sounds were chains, creaking wood, and the squelch of mud under hooves and wheels. Da said nothing. Once Stuart filed for his own claim and moved out, that gave him the right to say his own piece . . . as long as he was not rude about it, of course.

Ma backed down first. "The good Lord knows you'll need somebody who can keep bairns alive out here."

Stuart said, "I'm sure Mariah will appreciate your wisdom, Ma." As far as fibs went, it did not feel so bad as some he'd told. At least it gave his mother a graceful way out.

Da said, "I didna mean to fence off the range, lad. But I'm of a mind to start penning the beasties at night. It could mean better sleep for all of us, including the dogs."

Ma said, "No business on the Sabbath, Mr. MacCallum."

Da said, "Yes, Maggie, my love."

And Stuart decided not to force a proper introduction today after all. As ever, after church, his folks loaded the children into the spring wagon while he found Mariah. As he did, she spotted someone else she knew leaving the services.

She stood on her toes and waved. "Gerta! Hello!"

But the round-cheeked woman and her friend did not even look in their direction.

Mariah's arm sank slowly—and Stuart cleared his throat. "Lass?"

When she turned to him, it was with an expression of determined cheer. "She must not have seen me," she supposed, slipping her arm through his. "I haven't talked with her since the party . . . but she normally doesn't come into town. She must have been distracted."

Stuart looked after the departing woman, her head bent to her companion's in clear discussion, and he hated that woman enough to say, "She saw you."

"No, not *her,*" insisted Mariah—had others done the same thing? "That's Gerta Schmidt, and her husband is very close to my family. She wouldn't snub me."

Stuart stared down at her, unblinking. "Schmidt?"

He remembered the first blow all over again. And the second. And the third . . .

Though the bruises had near to vanished, even off his ribs, he remembered the whole afternoon of his beating all too clearly.

Mariah nodded. Schmidt.

"Your cousin," remembered Stuart, gut clenching.

"Not exactly. Hank is Thad's—my brother's—cousin, actually. Through Papa's first wife, who died." She cocked her head. "I'm surprised you knew our families were related."

Stuart saw his mistake then—briefly, as they started walking, he considered a lie. But Mariah gazed up at him with her fine gray eyes, holding his arm as if she trusted him for countless things he may never achieve. If he were to lie to anybody, it would not be to Mariah.

"We had words," he admitted, and hoped that would be enough. "But it's done with."

"Oh." Considering, Mariah asked, "Over sheep? Sheep and cattle, I mean?"

"It's done with," repeated Stuart, but apparently she saw that as the denial it truly was.

Her eyes widened, and her lips, forming an "o." "Over *me?*"

"Mariah," insisted Stuart, wishing he'd said nothing. "It's done with."

"You didn't even mention it!"

" 'Twas between him and me, not you. I'll not be telling you everything that passes between me and other menfolk. Not even once we marry."

Mariah made a sound that reminded Stuart of a snort. "Well I don't see what business Hank should have with you anyway. He usually only does what my father tells him to."

Stuart said nothing at all, that time.

They walked on in a rather thick silence; he noted that, somehow, the mud had not yet spattered her coat. That somehow fit her. She lived in so charmed a world, after all.

He said, "Look. Those boys are playing catch instead of following us." Not as many people watched them from windows, either. Mariah should see *something* cheerful in that.

Instead she stopped. Rather than pull her along, Stuart stopped too. "Is aught—?"

From the furrow between her brows, something certainly seemed wrong.

"*Was* Hank doing what Papa told him to do, Stuart?"

she demanded. "Was he giving you a message from my father?"

When Stuart admitted nothing, she asked, "But what could Papa possibly have Hank tell you that he could not tell you himself?"

"Will you please leave it be?"

"It concerns me too, doesn't it? Doesn't it concern me too, Stuart?

It was clearly too late for her to leave it be.

But he would rot in hell before he was the one to tell her.

Chapter Ten

Over the last two weeks, Papa had taken to waiting for Mariah on the verandah instead of at the street. He still wore his gun, but Mariah had hoped it meant he trusted her at least a little more now, to stand back as she bid Stuart good-bye for another week.

They still knew better than to dare a kiss or embrace.

Now she wondered if instead, his bias against sheep-herders ran so deep, he did not want to even hear or smell one. But no, of course Papa had good reason for staying on the verandah. And he surely had good reason to send some kind of message, via Hank Schmidt, to Stuart. Papa always had good reasons for what he did, even if he was sometimes mistaken in them.

Stuart's refusal to tell her more still worried her, deep inside where worries hid. She loved his nearness, how he held and released her hands as he promised to see her the following week, then stepped reluctantly back. She loved his height, his breadth, how safe he made her feel. She wished they need not wait another entire week.

But when she turned away from him, Mariah all but ran up the walk to where her father stood scowling at both the street and at Stuart.

"Don't know what you're plannin' for January," he drawled, opening the door for her. If he would let her invite Stuart inside, they would not have to worry about the weather in January. But Mariah had other concerns at the moment, concerns that would not wait for her to get inside.

"Papa, why did you send Hank Schmidt to see Stuart?"

Was it her imagination, or did Papa stiffen at that? "What's your sheeper say about it?"

Mariah followed his gaze to where Stuart was already striding away, back toward the church where he'd left his horse. Dawson was riding around back, to stable his mare and come by the kitchen for always-hot coffee. "He won't tell me," she admitted, still hurt about that.

"Then why should I?" Papa put a firm hand on her shoulder and guided her inside, following her. No reason to chill the others, just because she wanted to talk.

But she very much did want to talk. "I thought you had nothing in common with Stuart," she challenged, surprised by her own boldness, as he closed the door.

Perhaps she'd surprised Papa, too. "Well Mariah Lynn, you just think on it a minute. What generally happens when a fellow takes liberties with a man's daughter?"

For a long moment—long enough that Papa left her for his den, conversation over—Mariah did not understand. Rather . . . part of her mind understood, of course, but another part of her did not want to face it. If someone took liberties with a young woman who had no male relatives—like Evangeline Taylor—she had nobody to seek out that young man and . . .

And make it right.

No. What Mariah was starting to think had nothing to do with Stuart. Stuart was strong and proud . . . almost invincible! Besides, a young man made things right by marrying the girl he had compromised, and nobody had known about Mariah and Stuart until *after* Stuart proposed.

And yet . . .

Nobody seemed to want her marrying Stuart. Worse, Mariah remembered how stiffly he'd held himself, the first Sunday he walked her home. As if his tummy hurt.

Her fears were ridiculous, of course! And yet . . .

She trailed her father into his den like she had so often during her childhood, so that he could tell her the blizzard would end, the wolves couldn't get in, the Indians were peaceful. "Papa! Hank didn't . . . He wouldn't have *hurt* Stuart. Would he?"

Now he could tell her not to be silly, and she could breathe again. She just wanted to breathe again.

But Papa stood still, his back to her, and sighed—and said nothing.

He was supposed to say something, to make it right!

"If Hank did, you would fire him. Wouldn't you? Even if he is your nephew?"

"Not likely," said Papa. But he still did not confirm that anything had really been done.

Perhaps he didn't know for sure. Why would he? A fair man like her father . . .

"But that wouldn't be fair! Stuart did nothing that I didn't do," she reminded him, her voice oddly thin in her building panic. As bad as the thought of Stuart being hurt over her was, something even worse lurked at the edge of her realization, waiting to strike. "Wouldn't you fire Hank if he hurt *me?* No matter *what* I did?"

"That's just foolish," scoffed Papa to the opposite wall.

"Why? What's sauce for the goose is sauce for the gander, Mother always says."

"Leave it be," Papa warned. But then he added, under his breath, "Hear tell the boy took it fine, anyhow."

Took it? Stuart *took it?* "Took *what?*"

And why would Papa know so much about it?

Behind Mariah, her mother's voice cooly asked, "Yes, Jacob. What did he take?"

When Papa turned to face them, he looked angry and defensive both. "Less than he had coming to him."

Mariah once saw a cowboy struck by a rattlesnake—lightning fast, deadly poison. When she finally understood Papa's defense of Hank, it felt like she'd just been bit. She felt the cold shock of disbelief more than anything else—but with a slow realization that she was about to start hurting . . . and that part of her might even die.

Her father had really told Hank to hurt Stuart?

Mama said, "Oh Jacob . . ."

But Mariah didn't hear anymore, because she had to escape her father's den, his house. Barely thinking, she grabbed her coat from its hook and pushed out the front door and ran. She did not know what to do, even what to think, except for one overwhelming truth.

She had to find Stuart in order to do it or think it.

Mud sucked at Mariah's boots, tried to pull her down, but she fought it to run in the direction Stuart had taken, back toward the church. Surely she could catch up to him before he reached his horse. She could catch up to him and . . . and . . .

And oh, she could apologize!

She needed to apologize for her father, and for her step-cousin, and for causing Stuart such trouble in the first place. She needed to apologize for not believing him when he'd warned her of her father's bigotry. She needed to apologize for . . .

For being her. Somehow she needed to apologize for being herself—and a cattleman's daughter—most of all, because *that* was what hurt him. And to do that, she needed to find him!

When she caught sight of him several blocks up, walking steadily away with his hat tugged low against the cold, she could have sobbed with relief.

"Stuart!" she tried to yell—but her breath was tearing through her throat so, his name came out a mere croak. She stumbled to a stop and clutched the corner post of the Sanford family's white fence to steady herself, gasping for air, and tried again. *"Stuart!"*

He stopped, turned—and immediately started back to her. *Stuart's here,* she told herself, over and over, to quiet the drumming in her head. *Everything will be fine. Stuart's here.*

A door opened and Mrs. Sanford stepped onto her porch, wiping her hands on her apron. "Mariah Garrison. What in the world—!"

Unable to wait, or to listen to any more talk of propriety, Mariah ignored her to run again.

Stuart ran the last few feet to her, too, and when he caught her to him, wrapped her protectively in his arms, he sounded ironically like Mrs. Sanford. "What in the world . . . ?"

But now that she'd reached him, she wasn't sure she could force the words out. All she wanted to do was hold him—and cry.

"Mariah? What's wrong?" Stuart's usually low voice rose slightly with concern. "You must be freezing, lass! For mercy's sake, at least put on your coat!"

Only then, as he guided first one arm and then the other into her coat sleeves, did she realize that she had grabbed it but not put it on.

With the practiced ease of a man with younger siblings, Stuart buttoned her coat, then checked her pockets for mittens and put them on her, too. He kept asking questions. "What is it? Does your family know you're out?"

"I'm sorry," she managed finally, her teeth chattering. "Stuart, I'm so sorry. I didn't believe you, but Papa said . . . Did they hurt you, Stuart? And was it really him? Why didn't you tell me? I'm so sorry. . . ."

When she looked up at him, he was scowling down at

her. His scowl looked blurry, and she realized she was crying after all.

Well, why shouldn't she cry?

How could her father do *such a thing?*

"You truly do not listen," Stuart finally chided her, gruff. Still scowling, he wiped his thumbs over her cheeks. "I didna speak of it because it was between your menfolk and me, and because it's done with. I told you that. More than once."

"But it's not over!"

Only when he shrugged out of his own great coat and draped it, cloaklike, over her shoulders, did she realize she was still shivering. But it wasn't from cold—not the temperature, anyway. The cold that seeped deeper and deeper into her, like spreading poison, was the horror that too much of her storybook life may have been a lie. The one man she'd trusted beyond all others, perhaps even beyond Stuart . . .

"It's *not* over," she insisted. "I didn't know he could do something like that. It's not fair."

"I did take liberties, Mariah," Stuart reminded her, as if that made it all right. He'd promised to marry her, too!

She sniffed. "I thought you were wrong about people. But you were right." Stuart put his arms around the bundle of coats she'd become, held her tightly against him so that her nose smooshed into the warmth and weave of his chambray-shirted shoulder, and he said, "I'm sorry, lass."

She was sorry, too. Turning her head to lean her cheek against his broad, hard chest, her tears stinging her eyes in the cold air, Mariah felt sorrier than she had in a long, long time.

When someone called, "Mariah Garrison!" she barely saw old Mr. Parker, halfway down his own walk. "What are you thinking? Does your family mean nothing to you, girl?"

He was just a neighbor—one of several who had

appeared on their porches. Once, she would have thought they were watching out *for* her. Now it seemed they were just watching, and with far less benevolent intentions.

Stuart eased her away from him, despite her mew of protest. "I am Stuart MacCallum," he called, since even folks who'd heard of the scandal might not recognize a lowly sheep farmer. "Mariah Garrison is my fiancée, and I am taking her home to her family right now."

Mr. Parker made a "hrmph!" sound, perhaps in part because when Stuart offered Mariah his arm, she cuddled back into the crevice between his arm and his chest instead.

"Mariah!" he protested, low—but held her. "People are watching."

"I don't care. I don't want to worry about what they think anymore!"

Stuart's voice somehow smiled when he murmured, "Well you may not, lass, but I've hardly recovered from the consequences of our last indiscretions."

As if Mariah could laugh at something like that.

"Stuart," she said, as he eased her into a walk. "I don't want to go home. I want to come live with you."

He stopped and stood still—almost as still as she felt inside, to have said something so very weighty as that. But how could she not prefer living with Stuart now? They meant to marry anyway. If they just went ahead and did it, everyone's protests would become moot. People would have to accept them.

In any case, how could she go on living in luxury provided by a man who had hurt him—on purpose? A man who'd threatened all along to do more than hurt him!

Her own father . . .

"Live with my family, you mean?" Stuart prompted with strained nonchalance, easing her homeward again even as he asked.

"With *you* Stuart. Let's marry, right away, before anybody can stop us."

He sighed, hard enough that she felt his body shift with it. "I'll not do that to you, Mariah. Nor to us. You know full well what people would say."

"They would say that we had to marry but . . . but phooey on them! Some are already saying it anyway."

"Bad enough that. But they might also say that only *you* had to marry, lass—and that I was the only man desperate enough to take you in such circumstances."

She looked up at him, appalled. How could anyone think something so terrible as that?

But she'd underestimated Stuart's grasp of people before, all too recently. And she *had* just returned from a long trip, where nobody in town could really say what she had been doing . . . nobody except the Wrights, and she certainly would not count on them to speak on her behalf.

"And then," Stuart added, "I would have to go find anyone who would speak so against you and beat them senseless, and you would be just as angry with me as you are with your father. Where would we be then?"

She had not fallen in love with Stuart for his marginal sense of humor—why did he have to attempt jokes about such horrible things as this?

"I'm not simply angry with my father," admitted Mariah, suddenly bone-tired. World-tired. "It's worse than that. I'm . . ."

Disillusioned. Betrayed. Adrift.

"I always thought he was one of the good guys, Stuart." Her voice thickened and the world blurred around her, even as she said it. "I thought we *deserved* to live like a storybook!"

"Don't go making me defend your father," protested Stuart softly, into her hair. Never had they walked so close. Their hips bumped every few steps. "No matter how dearly I love you, or how much it pains me to see you hurting, I'll not defend a cattle baron."

"You can't," Mariah insisted dully. "Not anymore."

Stuart said nothing at all.

"If we mustn't marry yet . . . may I come live with your parents, then?" she asked. Part of her hated the idea of leaving her home and family again, and so soon. But it wasn't the home she'd thought it was anyway . . . was it? "Will they be willing to take me?"

"You're my future bride," Stuart reminded her. "That makes you family. Of course they will be willing."

"Can we go there now?"

He squeezed her shoulders once, tight. But he said, "I'll not be accused of abducting you, nor will I see you accused of running away."

Thank goodness she had Stuart to think of such dark possibilities—and plan against them. "No," she agreed, if without enthusiasm. "Of course not."

"Tomorrow or the day after will be soon enough, won't it?"

No. Of course not. She wanted to leave now—with her father's betrayal as fresh motivation, before she had to face her sisters' disappointment. But that would be cowardly. Stuart did not deserve to marry a coward.

Somehow, Mariah would wait.

Two days later, Mariah's mother drove her and her trunk toward the MacCallums' ranch. Looking out across the seemingly endless, snow-dusted plains northeast of town, holding a sleeping Elise close to her side, Mariah wondered if they had yet crossed the unmarked "deadline" that divided cattle country from sheep land.

At the moment, all she saw was a distant herd of antelope, bounding away over yet another rise on the wavy sea of winter grass. With the mountains behind her, it felt like riding into a rolling, gray-skied nothingness.

"He doesn't want you to go," Mrs. Garrison told her oldest daughter, handling the traces with practiced ease. Her cheeks glowed in the November wind. "Just because he won't say anything doesn't mean he approves. I want you to know that."

"Papa's approval no longer matters to me." Mariah hoped that saying it could make it finally true, but instead the words made her sound petulant.

"I don't agree with men using violence to solve problems either," her mother said "And I understand why you're angry. But your father clearly thought he was doing the right thing. He thinks he's protecting your future—and your reputation—by rejecting this engagement."

"Neither Stuart nor I did anything truly bad," Mariah insisted. "We fell in love."

"Behind our backs," noted Mother, only her gentle tone keeping the words from cutting.

"If I'd fallen in love with Alden Wright without telling you, met with Alden Wright in secret, would Papa have hurt *him?*"

"I wouldn't be surprised," cautioned her mother. "But I'll admit, your father has an unattractive prejudice when it comes to sheep. In fact, I'll tell you a secret. They scare him."

Then she clucked exasperated reassurance to their buggy horse, who'd nervously tossed his head and pranced several steps. "Come on, Rue; it's just a dust devil."

Mariah ignored the dust devil, staring at her mother over Elise's tucked head instead. *Papa?* Afraid of *anything?*

"Oh, men have fears too," said Mother, reading Mariah's expression too well. "But they aren't to show it. Since it has to go somewhere, they get angry instead. Your father has put his entire life into cattle. His family raised them before the War. After that, he worked as a trail boss until the railroads threatened to put him out of business. He and Benj Cooper risked their lives driving enough head north to start the Circle-T when this area was a wilderness, while most of the country were still cowering back East at the memory of the battle of . . . of Custer's last stand. Everything your father has, he's fought for. Because of the homesteaders, the small-time ranchers—and the sheep—he's afraid of losing it. And the more he has to fear, the angrier he gets."

"That doesn't excuse him," Mariah insisted. "He shouldn't have sent men to hurt Stuart."

"No. But Stuart threatened to take something even more precious than your father's land or cattle—and now he has."

Mariah hesitated to think of it that way. She was going to live with Stuart's family now—where she could see Stuart more often, learn to love his mother and sisters as she loved her own, focus on her joyous future. She must not start questioning her decisions now.

"Just try to be tolerant until everything works itself out," insisted Mother. "I went through more than you can imagine to keep your father in your life, early in our marriage. I don't intend to sit by while the two of you ruin that."

But Mariah was no longer fully listening. Instead, she said, "Oh!"

Their buggy had just topped another rise and come into sight, her first sight, of the MacCallums' ranch house.

Elise, waking, sleepily asked, "Does Mariah have to live there?"

Mariah sternly shushed her younger sister.

But for the briefest moment—shameful and guilt-ridden though it felt—she found herself wondering the same thing.

Chapter Eleven

Stuart sneaked furtive glances across the table at Mariah as they ate his mother's mutton stew. Sometimes she peeked up through her lashes at the same time, and their gazes met.

Acknowledging. Accepting. Appreciating.

Then one of his younger brothers or sisters would giggle, or whisper, or kick him under the table, and he would look back down at his tin dinner plate.

Even without visual proof, Stuart took comfort in Mariah's presence. If the MacCallum home had proved too spare for her refined sensibilities, surely she would have bolted already. In moments of shameful uncertainty, he'd wondered if she would truly leave her storybook life for the honest hardship he could offer. But upon her arrival, Mariah had not flinched from the sight of the U-shaped homestead, its main log cabin flanked by two cut-lumber additions, low-roof covered in sod for better insulation against the winter cold. She'd complimented his mother on the curtains, cooed over the old family dog,

Bruce. She'd even seemed pleased that she would share a room with Stuart's six sisters. "I won't be lonely that way!" she'd said.

But that was Mariah, cheerful to the end. Stuart still would not have wanted to gamble, as he rode back for dinner three nights later, on what he would find. He felt more uneasy than he'd expected with the burden of taking the woman he loved away from luxuries she deserved.

But when he sneaked another glance and caught her watching him, she did not look sad at all. Her golden hair did not curl much tonight—she had drawn it back into a simple ponytail, and wore a plainer work dress than those she had for church. Her only jewelry was the engagement ring, winking in the dull light of the kerosene lantern. But her gray eyes shone at him. She'd never looked so pretty as here amidst the family he loved, across from him—where she belonged.

Stuart smiled, a silent attempt to tell her that, and after she smiled back she hesitated, parted her lips. Then his mother cleared her throat, and they both looked quickly back to their respectably silent dinners.

As soon as they'd finished, though, and the girls stood to clear the table, Stuart caught Mariah's soft hand and drew her firmly out of the main bustle. He did not release her hand, either. "All's well with you then?"

He hadn't had a chance to ask before dinner, because almost as soon as he crossed the threshold, his mother had the family seated and speaking grace. Even if his parents did not disapprove of conversation during the meal—not unwise, considering the chaos that could ensue otherwise—Stuart would not have asked this in front of the others.

"Of course it is," Mariah assured him, lowering her free hand to four-year-old Rose's carrot-colored curls when the child attached herself to Mariah's skirts. "I'm hoping to learn from your mother how to be a good sheep farmer's wife."

He'd never smiled so easily as around her. "And I *am* a good sheep farmer," he teased.

She laughed up at him. "I should hope so. Only the best sheep farmer will do for me."

Twelve-year-old Kevin crowded in on their right, making smoochy noises. Stuart covered the boy's freckled face with one big hand to push him away. "Ma's not asking too much of you?"

"On the contrary! In fact . . ." She glanced over her shoulder, to where Emily was pouring water into the wash pot on the stove.

For the briefest moment, Stuart had—a feeling. Nothing more than that, just an unsettled sensation deep inside him that all wasn't as happy as he'd thought. Hoped.

He narrowed his eyes, studying her more closely.

"A minute of your time, son," called Da from by the fireplace, where he liked to enjoy his after-dinner pipe. Six-year-old Ian caught Stuart's free hand and began to plead for a ride.

"We have company, Ian," Stuart chided, waiting for Mariah to turn back. When she did, he saw uncertainty in her eyes—but no dishonesty. Not Mariah.

"I am *not* company," she reminded him. "So I should help with the dishes. Go ahead."

Stuart squeezed her hand before releasing her, as pleased to see her pitching in as to be able to touch her without fearing for his life. Surely he'd imagined that unsettled feeling.

Mariah ducked her head and blushed so prettily that he watched her walk to the stove—Rose still attached to her swaying skirts—then watched her wipe her first dish, before he even noticed Kevin resuming the smoochy sounds.

In fact, the boy had the right of it. How many weeks

had passed since their last secret meeting, under their bridge? Stuart longed to kiss his fiancée with an almost physical ache, and now he intended to. He intended to kiss her every time he came for dinner, and every time they got back from church together. He doubted kisses would completely sate his years-old need for her . . . but they'd certainly make a start of it.

"Jealous, are you?" he teased Kevin, knowing full well the insult a twelve-year-old would take that as. Then he scooped a squealing Ian up under one arm and gave him a ride as he went to see what Da had to say. He crouched and scratched old Bruce behind his near-deaf ears.

Then, when Da said, "That Johnson fellow's been threatening more sheepherders," Stuart felt just as glad that Mariah was across the room.

Whatever the latest trouble was, he would prefer she not have to worry about it.

Mariah would prefer Stuart not have to worry about how homesick she felt. So she did everything she could not to feel homesick.

"Ma says you needn't help with the chores," protested Bonny, not for the first time, but Mariah stood firm.

"And what if I want to?" she asked, hoping her smile carried more cheer than challenge. "Think of how much faster the work will go, with all of us helping!"

Almost reluctantly, Bonny handed her a corner of the flour-sack towel she was using and Mariah began to help dry the tin plates, conscious all the while of Mrs. MacCallum's silent gaze.

Surely Mariah imagined any censure she saw there. Stuart's mother was a plain, angular woman, sober to the extreme. But she'd been kind enough to take Mariah in and had at no point spoken sharply to her, not even as sharply as she spoke to her own daughters. In fact, Mrs. MacCallum consistently treated Mariah as a pampered guest. Not once had she asked Mariah to lift a finger around the homestead. And yet, when Mariah's sense of fairness compelled her to help anyway, Mrs. MacCallum's protests carried with them an edge of . . . well, of disapproval.

Was Mariah imagining it?

"I shouldn't want you to spoil your soft hands," Mrs. MacCallum would say. Or, "You're not likely used to carrying water."

"I'd best get used to it," Mariah would reply cheerfully, unwilling to take offense to such indulgences lest nothing snide was meant. But that continued sense of uselessness, of a difference between herself and the others, unsettled her more than any of the hardships here at the MacCallum ranch. Yes, she did miss having a pump in the kitchen! She missed her mother's big, beautiful iron stove with two ovens and a cistern for heating wash water. The gloomy light of kerosene lamps hurt her eyes and gave her headaches, and the outhouse remained an unpleasant necessity. But such incidentals could easily be endured in cheerful silence, especially on nights when she knew Stuart would visit.

The sense that she was walking on eggshells, however, only one step from proving some unpleasant truth about herself which Mrs. MacCallum knew even better than she, was making Mariah as skittish as a bit-up foal in fly time.

"Dinner was delicious," she said now, determined not to seem standoffish.

"You like mutton, then?" asked Stuart's mother, wiping Anna's face.

"Yes, ma'am." Mariah did not admit that she'd never had it before this week—but somehow, Mrs. MacCallum stared at her as if she knew.

Then Emily drew her mother's disapproval by saying, "You won't after a few months!"

"You'll be grateful for any food the good Lord sends us, Miss Emily!"

Emily said, "Yes, ma'am."

But as soon as her mother drew Rose away, to put her, Caroline, and Anna to bed, Emily whispered, "But I surely do hope Da or Stuart shoots a goose or antelope sometime soon!"

Grateful for the familiarity, Mariah whispered, "I felt the same way about beef, when I was younger."

Jenny looked aghast. "About *beef?*"

"Do you miss it?" asked Bonny.

Yes, Mariah missed beef too—especially the way her mother fixed it. She missed lively conversations at the dinner table. She missed laughter and songs. She missed Laurel's obstinacy and Victoria's nosiness and Audra's determined good behavior. She wondered daily about Kitty's continued health, Elise's continued temperament, and whether Papa had come to terms with her engagement, at last. And yet . . .

Mariah glanced across the main room to where Stuart stood near his father, one booted foot hitched up on the bench by the fireplace hearth, in serious conversation. His suspenders somehow emphasized the taper from his broad, working shoulders to his narrow waist and hips. He'd rolled up his shirtsleeves, revealing soft, light-brown hair dusting his forearms. He looked solid, and real . . . and here.

Tonight made twice that they'd dined together. They really *were* engaged; really were to be married. And that was why she willingly forewent everything else.

Did she miss beef? She smiled at Bonny and said, "Likely I will after a few months!"

When she and the others smiled together, it felt almost as good as laughing with her own sisters. In spring they *would* be her sisters. And by spring, surely Papa would have mended the rift between them and she would have her own sisters back as well.

Then she could be happy without trying so hard.

By lamplight, spring seemed forever away. But Stuart's presence brought it closer.

As if drawn, Stuart turned his head and caught her gaze, smiled that quiet, heavy-lidded half-smile of his. Then, with a few more words to his father and to Kevin—who scurried quickly out the door—he straightened and strode back toward her. Almost every man in Mariah's life was a cowboy, and cowboys had notoriously awkward walks. Stuart walked with easy grace.

His walk made Mariah go warm all over, like sunshine on an August afternoon, despite the cold wind that shook the MacCallums' windows.

"I'd best be going soon," he admitted as he reached them. "The sky's clouding. I'll want for moonlight as I ride home, if I'm not careful."

"You don't want to ride home in the dark," agreed Mariah faintly, caught by the nearness of him. He seemed more confident here than he ever had in town, her Stuart—and he'd not lacked there. She liked the strength his confidence implied.

"Pooka could likely find the way blindfolded," he reassured her, hooking a thumb in his pants pocket. "But just the same . . ."

"Just the same . . ." Mariah repeated.

Behind her, Emily or Bonny giggled. Stuart's eyes gleamed at her as he offered his free hand. "Will you see me out, lass?"

She began to feel even hotter than sunshine on an August afternoon—and not, she suspected, because of the close proximity of the pot-bellied stove. The sensation intrigued and somehow alarmed her . . . but as long as she was with Stuart, she felt safe enough to welcome the discomfort. She put her hand in his, marveled at how soft his strong hand was—from the lanolin, she knew—as his fingers closed around hers and he drew her toward the door.

His easy, confident walk looked even better when she was closely following him.

"Take a lantern and stay on the stoop," warned Mr. MacCallum around his pipe, which made Mariah blush. "Don't forget that you're both from respectable families."

Emily and Bonny giggled again, and Mariah flushed even worse than when she'd been helping with the dishes. Did *everyone* realize that she and Stuart were going outside to kiss?

As Stuart shrugged on his coat, then helped her into her own, she stole a peek over her collar and realized from the brown-eyed stares that, indeed, everyone did. Even Stuart's mother watched from the girl's room, her expression unreadable and yet still, somehow, disapproving. It reminded Mariah of the inscrutable look her father got when he objected to what he was seeing.

Papa would most certainly disapprove of her going out onto the stoop to kiss Stuart—even if they took a lantern and stayed within view of the MacCallums' front window. Even if they were engaged. More than anything else, that knowledge unbalanced her while Stuart shouldered open the door and drew her outside into the cold night, hung the lantern as agreed. *Papa would not approve.*

Then again, she did not approve of some of Papa's behavior either. . . .

Pooka greeted them with a whinny from the yard and Kevin greeted them with more smooching sounds. "Ready to go, Stu," he said, looping the reins around a post by the stoop.

"Thank you," said Stuart absently, staring down at Mariah. "Now go inside."

"So that you can kiss your sweetheart?"

Stuart said, "So that I can kiss my sweetheart?"

Kevin made a gagging noise, but went inside, only to reappear in the window, freckled nose mashed against the glass.

Stuart said, "It's the best we'll manage until springtime."

I wish it were springtime, she meant to say. And oh, she did want that. Surely, by the time spring came, the ill feelings between their families, between herself and her father, would have somehow been resolved. She longed for that day. She should tell Stuart that.

But he brushed his knuckles lightly over her cheek, gazed solemnly into her eyes, began to lean nearer her—and Mariah instead said, "I don't think your mother likes me."

Stuart stopped, blinked. "My mother?" He straightened again as he said that. "Why not?"

"I don't know. I just . . ."

"Shall we go ask her?" suggested Stuart, brows leveling into a frown.

"No! I mean . . ." To question Mrs. MacCallum would seem unforgivably rude, after everything the woman had done. "I'm sure I'm imagining it."

After all, she was a different kind of woman than Mariah's outspoken, affectionate mother. Not everyone could or should be Elizabeth Garrison.

"Has she been uncivil to you?"

"No, of course she hasn't. I'm sorry, Stuart. I ought not have mentioned it."

He searched her face. "You're sure all's well with you, then?"

She nodded, increasingly aware of his hand holding hers. "This is what courting should be like," she said, by way of changing the subject. Except that they should be on *her* parent's stoop, not his. . . .

"You have the right of it there," agreed Stuart thickly, leaning nearer her again.

She half expected cowboy Dawson to ride out of the shadows and challenge them, so much so that when Stuart's lips brushed hers, the easy completion of his kiss startled her. Then, as she adjusted to the reality of it, to the way warmth spilled through her at his touch, Stuart was already straightening, squinting at her. "Something's wrong."

Mariah quickly looked down at her feet, blushed. Here she stood, alone in the night with her beau, and she could not concentrate on his kiss? Something must be wrong, were that so!

"I'm just . . . just not used to being allowed to do this," she admitted shyly to her feet. "Papa would disapprove . . ."

"He disapproves of our engagement as well," Stuart reminded her, and now he sounded annoyed. Her shoulders tensed defensively—but she quickly reminded herself that Stuart was the one who'd taken a beating on her behalf. If anybody had the right to be annoyed . . .

"I'm sorry," she said again, and laid a hand on the lapel of his coat. "Don't go yet."

His warm, brown gaze lifted from her touch to caress her face. "I've no intention of going yet," he murmured, seeming pleased.

"You haven't?" Mariah felt flushed, despite how the wind tugged at her hair. They both knew what he'd do if he did not leave. . . .

Then Stuart closed the distance between them and did just that.

This time as his lips pressed to hers, Stuart parted them slightly so that they caught hers, held her captive as surely as the arms that encircled her. He sighed, as if at the sheer heaven of the sensation. The warmth of his breath all but scalded her. Melting under his kiss, Mariah sank into him, trusting him to hold her up. Then his arms tightened around her, and his lips grazed across hers, and the little flames that Stuart's lovemaking somehow ignited in her shivered into deeper places than she knew she had, made her ache for . . . for *something,* something more, something even hotter. . . .

He kissed down her jaw, his strong arms holding her

tight against him so that even if she'd wanted to, she could not have escaped him without effort. Mariah wondered if she were a wanton for not desiring escape. On the contrary, trembling as if with fever, she pressed herself eagerly against him, but that didn't cool her at all. His lips on her throat made her squirm happily. Before she knew what she was doing Mariah was kissing the side of Stuart's throat in return, sandpapery and salty and wonderful, and she was all but burning up. . . .

Something—a noise—tried to distract her, but Mariah was too busy seeking Stuart's lips again. His mouth fastened onto hers, open now, and they drew at each other, clutched at each other. . . .

The distraction got louder, more insistent. With a gasp, Stuart pulled back, stepped back, then quickly drew his hand across his mouth, either to wipe away the trail of her lips or to muffle something that sounded suspiciously like a bad word. But Stuart never swore.

The insistent distraction, Mariah realized, was the sound of Mr. MacCallum knocking on the window. She tucked her head quickly against Stuart's chest to hide her face, mortified to have been seen forgetting herself so thoroughly as she and Stuart . . .

As they . . .

Mortified.

Stuart kissed the top of her head, far more gentlemanly. "The benefit of chaperones," he suggested in a low voice.

"How can I face him?" she whispered into his lapel.

"By remembering the ring on your finger." Stuart caught her chin, gently lifted it so that she faced him—his pride in her, his affection.

"I love you, Stuart MacCallum," she told him earnestly. And oh, she did. Her love for him seemed to thrum through her entire body, like joy on a cloudless spring day. Surely, with a love like theirs, everything would work out fine.

"And I love you, Mariah," he assured her.

By spring, she would be a MacCallum as well.

So why did she find herself wishing he'd called her Mariah Garrison?

Chapter Twelve

Evangeline Taylor sat very, very small on the edge of her pew as the Garrison family filed into the church. Though the generous greetings from Victoria and Mrs. Garrison flattered her, it would not do to be noticed again by Victoria's father! So she hunched her shoulders and focused her attention on her lap, her bare and carefully scrubbed hands clenched tightly, until the cattle baron's firm boot-tread passed her as he herded his family toward their pew up front.

Up where the respectable folks sat.

Only then did Evangeline dare peek at the rancher's retreating back, his shoulders set under a dark frock coat, his distinguished white hair, the way he held his black hat in one hand. He looked disapproving and unapproachable even from behind, and not just because of Mariah's desertion last week. Mr. Jacob Garrison, one of the town founders, always looked that way.

Not for the first time, Evangeline wished he were *her* father.

Of course, for that to be true, the distinguished cattle rancher would need to have lain with Evangeline's mother. That was impossible. Jacob Garrison did not sin. *Mrs.* Garrison occasionally caused a stir, with her newfangled ideas and outspoken ways, but the rancher had so high a moral standing, folks tended to dismiss even his wife's brushes with recklessness.

"The Boss will straighten her out," they would say, leaving the wife's character to her husband's capable hands. They said the same thing when Laurel got into a fight at school, or when Kitty did poorly in class, or little Elise caused a fuss at the store. "Garrison will see to it."

The few times Evangeline had even been suspected of wrongdoing, folks said, "It's no surprise," and "What do you expect from a Taylor?"

Evangeline did not even know who her father was. She could imagine nothing better than a father who would speak for her, care for her, keep her in line. It made Mariah Garrison's abdication even harder for Evangeline to understand.

When the MacCallums arrived, they made their way to a pew only a few benches ahead of where Evangeline sat—well in front of the repentant gamblers and whores, but behind even the farmers. Stuart and Mariah followed them, a surprisingly handsome couple.

Mariah held Stuart's arm as if drawing strength from it, and he led her to the bench behind his large family and stood until she sat. Then he settled himself beside her, solid and steady, his hat in his hands and his hands between his knees.

Mariah touched his arm with gloved fingers. Stuart turned his head to look at her. From where she sat, Evangeline could see his expression soften, see them exchange a glance full of . . .

Of yearning. Of hope. Of promise.

Mariah and Stuart were clearly sweet on each other. But when Evangeline peeked back toward the front of the church and Jacob Garrison's dark, stiff back, she still could not understand. Stuart MacCallum was a fine enough man, for a sheep farmer—better than Evangeline could ever merit. Despite cruel rumors about town that Mariah had been disowned, or was living on Stuart's claim instead of rooming with his family, most folks accepted that the MacCallums were near about as principled as Garrison himself.

Except for raising sheep, of course.

But Mariah could have any number of fine men to marry, men with money, men her father would approve of. Surely she could learn to like one of them too, if only to have her father and brother to speak for her, protect her, keep her in line. If only to guarantee that protection for her own future daughters. Instead, she was spurning a safe place in society that Evangeline could only dream of.

Could love blind someone to reality so thoroughly as that?

The congregation stood to sing their first hymn. Halfway through the song, Evangeline felt a rush of cold air through her thin, knitted shawl. She glanced toward the open door—

And froze in a completely different way when Thaddeas Garrison, closing the door, momentarily caught her gaze and winced embarrassment at his tardiness.

Before Evangeline could even blink, the cattle baron's only son had gone ahead to his family's pew, borne the look of dark censure his father cast at his late arrival, taken his place beside Victoria.

Evangeline could no longer breathe deeply enough to finish the hymn. In fact, her heart beat so quickly that she barely remembered to sit when the singing stopped.

He'd looked at her! Not in any special way, of course—unlike Mariah, Evangeline had eyes long adapted to reality. But that he had met her gaze instead of avoiding it, had clearly recognized her, warmed her more thoroughly than her charity-barrel shawl. Thaddeas Garrison was a lawyer, college-educated and respected, with almost as clean a reputation as his father . . .

Which of course made any doings between him and Evangeline as unlikely as doings between his father and her mother.

Impossible. More than impossible—insulting, to entertain even the wisp of a dream. Evangeline looked back down at her clean, bare hands and wished she were the sort of lady who could wear fine gloves to church.

Then she thought to look at Mariah Garrison again, sitting beside Stuart MacCallum and watching her brother's set shoulders and straight back. When Stuart turned his attention to her, Mariah bowed her head as if in thought or prayer.

Stuart looked toward the Garrisons, his jaw tight.

Evangeline's stomach cramped as she watched them. She still did not agree. But for a forbidden glance into an inappropriate man's eyes . . . Perhaps she could understand the temptation to pretend away reality after all.

To Stuart's relief, Mariah's family did not shun her after services. He stood back while her sisters clustered around her, giving her hugs and vying for her attention. Her brother draped an arm over her shoulder and kissed her cheek before strolling past her to where her father stood glowering behind the others, waiting. And her mother not only spoke to Mariah—but to him.

"Stuart MacCallum," she greeted. Of course they'd been introduced when she brought Mariah to his family's home; now he scrambled to remember his manners, take her hand.

"Mrs. Garrison." But his gaze crept over her shoulder toward her husband's obvious displeasure. His mother would never do something his father so clearly disapproved of.

"I'm down here," confided Mrs. Garrison, startling his attention back to her. "That's better. I love my husband dearly, but I speak for myself. And speaking as myself, I miss my oldest daughter and would like to invite you both to lunch."

Mariah gasped with pleasure. "Lunch? At . . . at home?"

The difference between the hope that glowed from her at the idea of going "home" and her stoic good cheer about his family's hospitality couldn't be more apparent to Stuart. The reality that his family could not so easily replace hers bothered him almost as much as the disappointment on her earnest face when her mother dashed those hopes, too.

"No, honey. I'm sorry. Your father still disapproves of your fiancé. I thought to take you both to eat at the restaurant in the Helvey Hotel."

The hotel, while not as fine as the Sheridan Inn, boasted an opera house on its third floor. Nobody in Stuart's family had ever eaten there, not even flush with shearing profits.

"I cannot afford restaurant lunches just now," Stuart admitted sharply. Especially not after most of the stores in town had cancelled his credit! Before Mrs. Garrison could protest, he added, "and I'll not eat on a cattleman's tab, though I thank you for the offer."

"Despite rumors to the contrary, I do have my own money," said Mrs. Garrison. "Your acceptance need hold no political implications whatsoever."

Even as Stuart wondered if that could in fact be true, Mariah put a tentative hand on his arm. "Could we, Stuart? Mother and I have so much to talk about and I'd love for you to get to know each other better!"

By allowing a rancher's wife to pay for his meal? Stuart thought of everything the ranchers had said, done, been to him over the years and he could not do it, not even for Mariah. Especially not with her father still glowering at them both from the road, much less with his own family waiting by their wagon. "Perhaps after shearing," he suggested, uncomfortable with disappointing two women at once. "I could treat the both of you . . ."

Mariah's face fell. Her mother's, however, seemed more calculating than downcast—as if she had expected as much and had more than enough arguments. But all she said was, "I should like that very much, Mr. MacCallum. Shearing time is spring, isn't it?"

Stuart nodded stubbornly—but could not ignore Mariah's dejection. It weighed on him, like a responsibility unmet. She'd given up so much for him already.

His brothers and sisters were in the wagon bed, waiting for her. . . .

"Perhaps Mariah could stay for lunch on her own," he suggested then, reluctantly. "Even had we both stayed, we would have needed a chaperone back to Da's place. Could you . . . ?"

"We would be happy to see her safely back to you, Mr. MacCallum," promised Mariah's mother—at least, he hoped it was a promise. Even as the suggestion left his lips, he'd wondered if he would ever get Mariah back.

That possibility scared him more than he would like to admit, and he turned quickly to Mariah to remind himself of the way she looked at him, the fact that she wore his ring. . . .

She'd glanced toward his family's wagon, conflicted.

"Mariah?" her mother prompted. "It's your decision."

But it was Stuart Mariah turned to, his arm she pressed her delicate hand against. "Are you sure your mother won't take offense? I won't be there to help with Sunday dinner."

Considering that his mother never asked her to help anyway, he couldn't see why that would be a problem. "Visit with your family," he insisted, trying to sound more confident than he felt. "You saw me once a week before now; why not give your family the same courtesy?"

Mariah bit her lip, considering, and Stuart risked a little more honesty. "Just tell me you'll be back before nightfall, lass. Or I'll come looking for you."

At that, she smiled up at him, a smile worth ten times the uncertainty he felt at this turn of events. "Wild horses couldn't keep me away, Stuart MacCallum!"

He nodded, pleased to have managed to win that smile, much less the woman who wielded it. To his surprise, she even stood on her toes and kissed him on the cheek, right there in front of the church and her parents. "I love you, Stuart," she whispered in his ear.

His face felt warm as he nodded again, unable to find the voice to repeat the sentiment. Especially not in front of her mother!

Instead he said, after a confused moment, "My family's waiting."

"Go on then," insisted Mrs. Garrison. "We'll bring her back to you safe and sound."

But Stuart backed away, instead of turning his back on the squeals and hugs of Mariah rejoining her sisters, telling them she'd be visiting for the afternoon. She would have left them when he married her anyway, he reminded himself. Girls grew up and left home all the time.

But he was scowling when he finally reached his family and made her excuses for her.

Stuart was the one Papa would not allow under his roof. Since Stuart had left with his family, Mariah got to have dinner with her family after all— and she savored every moment of it. Her sisters clamored to share all the minutiae of their week, from school to Christmas preparations to a new litter of kittens in the stables. Kitty was feeling better, thank heavens. Papa had confiscated Laurel's cowboy boots until she earned them back with proper, ladylike behavior—which, to Mariah's way of thinking, would take some time. Thaddeas came to lunch, too, and the contrast of the MacCallums' silent meals against the bright gas lighting and china and, most of all, the conversation of home felt conspicuous.

Not, Mariah told herself firmly, that there was anything wrong with the MacCallums' meals. But perhaps she could find a way to make them a tad more cheery . . . ?

Only Papa seemed immune to the festive atmosphere of her temporary homecoming. And even he had nodded to her and said, "Good day, Mariah Lynn," before helping her into the surrey. That he sat silent through dinner, watching her darkly from his end of the table, she simply had to accept as him being Papa.

She had, after all, gone directly against his wishes. Most fathers would not allow their daughter back at all, after being rejected for a forbidden suitor—not even for lunch!

She was enjoying her brief homecoming far too much to darken it by worrying over what she could not control.

But Papa certainly did seem to be staring at her a lot.

Mariah told her family about the MacCallums' drinking goat's milk, and how the goats would eat near about anything, and about their old, white-muzzled dog Bruce, who could not work anymore and so lived in the house, but was the best-trained dog she'd ever met. Only over dessert did Elise ask Mariah the question she'd dreaded:

"Why don't you live here anymore, Mariah?" the four-year-old demanded. "Don't you love us anymore?"

Again, she felt the weight of her father's stare.

"Of course I do! I will always love my family. I just don't . . ." Carefully, she chose her words. "I don't live here anymore, because my fiancé isn't welcome here. As my future husband, he deserves a loyalty from me that is easier for me to give by living with his family."

Elise pouted, obviously unconvinced.

Papa stood and went outside.

After lunch—and a visit to see the kittens in the stable—Mariah visited her room. Despite that she'd left only a week ago, she half-feared to find things changed. They were not. Since she'd only taken one trunk, the rest of her dresses still hung in her wardrobe and her gewgaws still filled her drawers. Now that she'd experienced life at the MacCallum homestead, she had a better idea what might come in useful. So she packed a valise full of such luxuries as more long underwear, leather gloves to protect her hands during chores, and ribbons that she could wear without drawing attention by fussing to curl her hair. She also cajoled her mother out of some of the nicest pieces from her rag bag, for making quilt squares and doll clothes. Then it occurred to Mariah that, while Mrs. MacCallum had not yet let her help prepare a dinner, perhaps she could make Christmas cookies for her hosts—and Stuart. She followed her mother downstairs to gather any special ingredients that Mrs. MacCallum might not have, or want to spare.

To her surprise, while Mariah copied the recipe, her mother sent the other girls from the kitchen. "I want to speak with Mariah alone, please," she insisted.

Sometimes when their mother demanded private time, it meant an embarrassingly personal discussion of topics ladies would prefer to avoid—such things as why women bled once a month, or where babies came from. So Mariah waited for this afternoon's topic with some wariness. Surely Mother did not think that she and Stuart . . .

That they . . .

Well, Mariah *did* know where babies came from, in theory anyway, but it sounded terribly . . . drastic. She and Stuart had done no more than kiss.

But instead, Mother simply asked, "Are you happy living with the MacCallums?"

Mariah said, "They have been marvelously hospitable."

"I'm glad to hear that. Are you happy?" Mariah's mother had odd priorities that way. Papa focused on keeping them safe, warm, fed, acceptable—the essential things, but Mother seemed to feel happiness and joy, instead of being icing on the cake, were just as important.

"I would be happier if Papa and Stuart could resolve their differences," Mariah admitted finally. Despite her longing to see better at night, to sing or laugh more often, to feel wanted—to feel useful—that one wish outweighed all the rest. "I never wanted to upset everyone so badly, Mother. You have to believe that."

"Of course I believe it. Your father knows it too."

Of that, Mariah was not so certain. "I just want to marry the man I love—and he's a good man! Stuart's honest, and hardworking, and gentle, and strong . . ." And handsome, and so very solid under her hand, and he could make her feel feverish with his intense, heavy-lidded stare—but she could not tell her mother that. "That's all any girl wants, isn't it? To marry a good man?"

Mother paused in scooping white sugar into a sack and raised her eyebrows at her oldest daughter, blue eyes amused. She was clearly feeling progressive again.

"Any normal girl," clarified Mariah hopefully. "You did, didn't you?"

"I was twenty-six when I married, darling, and almost balked then. There's nothing abnormal in wanting other things. But yes, neither is wanting a good husband wrong, either."

"But Papa's so unhappy with me now. The girls are being teased at school, I'm sure—the MacCallums, too. Stuart was threatened, even hurt because of me. While I lived here, Kitty made herself sick over it. Now that I'm with the MacCallums, Elise thinks I don't love her."

"Elise claims she isn't loved if she doesn't get an extra piece of candy," Mother warned, which made Mariah smile. Just.

"I hope that at least now everyone can accustom themselves to my choice," she finished, staring down at the piece of paper she'd been writing on.

Mother said, "And what about Mariah?"

Mariah looked up at her, confused.

"You forgot yourself," Mother prodded. "What's best for Mariah?"

Mariah sighed. "What's best for me is whatever's best for the people I love."

Mother looked unconvinced. "Be careful not to give too much power away, darling. If you believe in your decisions, the people you love, including your father and I, must find our own peace with it. If you start sacrificing Mariah this early on, you may never get her back."

"Didn't you sacrifice to marry Papa?" Though her mother rarely spoke of her youth, the girls knew she'd led a privileged life before marrying a rancher on the Wyoming frontier.

"It didn't feel like a sacrifice," said her mother now. "It rarely ever has."

And Mariah firmly said, "Neither will this. Not once I grow accustomed to it, anyway."

Maybe if she said it often enough, she could make it even more true.

As she finished writing out the cookie recipe, the clock in the parlor struck three. For Mother to drive her all the way out to the MacCallum homestead and still make it back before sundown, they would need to be leaving.

Only the thought of Stuart, waiting for her, made that thought bearable.

The back door opened and Papa stepped in, wiping his feet. "Hitched the roan mare to the buggy," he announced, carefully not looking at Mariah. "Packed the storm curtain, lest the weather turns."

Had he been in such a hurry to see her go?

"Thank you, Jacob," said Mother, putting the extra ingredients into a large flour bag for Mariah to carry back with her. "I'll go get our coats while Mariah says her good-byes."

Then Papa met Mariah's gaze, more command than offer. "I'll drive her."

It surprised her so, she barely heard her mother saying, "Why don't you do that, dear?"

Chapter Thirteen

Mariah felt nowhere near as comfortable with her father's close-mouthed silence as she had on drives past. She drew the lap-robe around her, tried not to think about the rifle under the seat, and said nothing until they'd left town—and the blatant stares of the townsfolk they passed.

Then she offered, "You'll keep on this road until just after Cut-Creek Gulch."

"I know where they live," drawled Papa.

So she said nothing again, merely watched the endless white plains stretching for what seemed like forever ahead of them, until she could hardly tell where the rolling prairie stopped and the winter-gray sky started. The buggy had just crossed the sturdy bridge over the gulch—the halfway point—when Papa asked, almost reluctantly, "You warm enough?"

"Yessir." His consideration gave Mariah the grit to attempt further conversation. "Papa?"

He grunted acknowledgment.

"I'm not sorry for loving Stuart MacCallum, Papa, but I'm sorry for disappointing you."

Remembering her conversation with her mother she thought, what would make her truly happy at this moment was for her father to say that she hadn't disappointed him.

But he chewed on the idea and finally said, "Likely you don't remember the bear cub."

It wasn't what she'd expected. "Bear cub?"

"Feller got between a black bear and her cub one spring, back when we still lived in the cabin; let her spook him into shooting her. Then he felt bad fer the cub, and roped it."

Thinking far, far back—they hadn't lived in Papa's claim cabin since she was four years old, except for the winter of the Big Die-up—Mariah did remember something about a cub. "You brought Mother and Laurel and me to see it, before you made him turn it loose," she said slowly. "Mama wanted to feed it milk, but you showed us it could already eat berries and grubs."

Papa nodded once. "You wanted that cub somethin' fierce."

She remembered that, too. The cub's roly-poly antics, its round ears and button eyes, and the way it cried "maa-aa-aa" for its dead mother had stolen her heart. Papa had let her pet it, crouching over her, guarding her from its already long, sharp claws. Its thick black fur felt somehow coarse and soft at the same time.

"I wanted it for a pet," she said. She'd cried for days after Papa let the bear go, sure that if he just saw how badly she wanted that cub, he would relent and go find it for her. But he hadn't.

"You recall why I said no, Mariah Lynn?" he prodded.

"You said that no matter how much I loved it, a bear couldn't help but be a bear, sooner or later. And that bears hurt little girls."

Papa nodded. He'd also said that if it hurt her, he reckoned he'd have to kill it, and that would be her doing for not leaving it be.

She tried not to think of the rifle under the seat, hoped Papa wasn't saying what she feared. "Why'd you think of that now, Papa?"

"A sheep farmer can't help but be a sheep farmer." No matter how much she loved him?

"Sheep farmers aren't bears," she said. "Stuart MacCallum will not suddenly turn on me."

"Bad blood with the cattlemen, even so."

"You have no right to hurt Stuart, either—or to have Hank Schmidt beat him!"

"That so?" challenged her father, handling the buggy horse with practiced ease.

"That's so," she insisted boldly. Then she thought about it. "Papa?"

He grunted again.

"I know you mean well. I love you whether you agree with me or not."

He said, "Good. Because I am dead set against this marriage."

"Because you think they'll hurt me?"

"Could be not on purpose. But they'll hurt you, one way or t'other, jest by what they are."

She could see she wouldn't change his mind, and resolved to be thankful that he'd even said this much on the topic. "That's my risk to take, isn't it? Now that I'm a woman grown?"

"Don't mean you'll have my blessing," he warned, still not looking at her.

"Yessir," said Mariah. "I realize that."

But at least he was driving her back to the MacCallum homestead himself. And when she leaned gingerly against his arm, cuddling up to his warmth under the lap blanket, Papa did not shrug her off.

It wasn't what she wanted. But it was far, far better than she'd expected.

* * *

To Mariah's supreme disappointment, Stuart was not one of the four MacCallums who stepped outside to greet her arrival. Mrs. MacCallum stood in the doorway of the cabin, beside twelve-year-old Kevin. In front of them, in the yard with old Bruce, stood Mr. MacCallum and his second-oldest son, Douglas—Stuart's herder.

Dougie's presence could only mean that Stuart had returned to his claim already. Mariah remembered his promise to come for her, were she not home by sunset, and felt confused.

"The house looks nicer from the inside," she whispered nervously to her father, as he scanned the welcome party with steely eyes.

Papa drew the roan mare to a halt. Mr. MacCallum stepped forward to help Mariah down, then collect the valise and flour sack she'd brought with her. Papa allowed it.

After that, the MacCallums simply stared at her father, and he at them.

"Mr. and Mrs. MacCallum," said Mariah, "this is my father, Jacob Garrison. Papa, these are Stuart's parents—Gavin and Margaret MacCallum—and two of his brothers. This is his partner, Douglas, and that's Kevin. And that's Bruce."

She could not tell who acknowledged the introduction first. The MacCallums and her father seemed to nod in stiff unison, as if nobody meant to be the first to lower his head.

Then Papa, focusing over the sheep farmers' heads, grudgingly said, "Obliged for your kindness to my girl."

Mariah's hosts said nothing at all. Papa had not, after all, shown their son similar kindness. But Mariah recognized the concession her father had made, to even recognize their courtesy, and felt especially proud of him as she came around the buggy to stand by his side.

"Thank you for the ride, Papa," she said. "And for talking with me."

He looked at her from under the shadow of his hat, then nodded once, curt. That was his way of saying she was welcome.

"If you're obliged," challenged Dougie, "maybe you can keep your cows off MacCallum land. They're eating our grass."

"Douglas!" Mariah protested, as surprised by his claim as by his rudeness in making it.

Papa turned slowly and drilled the boy with his intense stare. "Not likely," he drawled.

Mr. MacCallum folded his arms in front of him. "You're calling my lad a liar, then?"

"I'm sayin' your land ain't much to tempt my cattle," Papa returned. Mariah knew she had no hope of interfering now. She could only watch—watch, and feel sicker by the minute.

"You cattlemen are the ones what set the deadline," insisted Mr. MacCallum. "The least you can do is respect it."

Papa said, "You sayin' I don't?"

"We're saying that your cows—"

"Mr. MacCallum!" interrupted his wife. "Douglas! There will be no business on the Sabbath."

All three men fell silent at that, and even Papa nodded recognition of Mrs. MacCallum's argument. "Overstayed my welcome," he announced shortly. "Mariah."

"Good-bye, Papa," she said quickly, embarrassed that his first meeting with Stuart's family had so quickly degenerated into an argument—and over grass! If only Stuart had been here to help . . . but he wasn't. "I'll see you next week, at church."

He nodded at her, stoically ignored the MacCallums, and clucked to the mare. The buggy started off with a lurch, moving rapidly away in the direction of town and the mountain range beyond, leaving Mariah feeling alone and somehow exposed in its absence. Vulnerable.

Almost as if she were surrounded by . . . bears.

She firmly told herself not to be silly, pasted a determined smile to her face before she turned back to her hosts. The MacCallums had been nothing but kind.

"Did you have an enjoyable Sunday?" she asked.

"We didna make it the holiday you did," answered Stuart's mother, glancing with disapproval at Mariah's latest luggage before she went back inside.

At least Dougie picked up her flour sack, and his father her valise, before they followed.

"It's nice to see you again, Douglas," continued Mariah determinedly as she followed him in—since Dougie kept the flock while Stuart was with Mariah, she only saw him on Wednesday evenings, when he came to dine with his parents like Stuart did on Thursdays. Apparently, they alternated Sunday afternoons. "Where . . . I mean, Stuart's back at the claim, then?"

"He said to come get him if you weren't back, if that's what has your back arched," said Dougie. "He's still putting you ahead of his sheep."

Whether she deserved to be ahead of them or not?

"It shouldn't be a contest between me and the sheep," Mariah reminded him, smiling a determined hello to the other MacCallums who were seated about the main room, taking turns reading from what was likely the Bible. "I want Stuart to make a success as much as anybody."

Dougie snorted. Mr. MacCallum ignored her to go sit with his children. Mrs. MacCallum turned her back to start preparing supper, and Mariah felt more separate, more useless than ever.

Because she'd spent the day with her family, she wondered? Or because her father had driven her home?

Bad blood between the sheep men and the cattlemen, Papa had said. But surely he and the MacCallums could see each other as more than their livelihoods, if only for her sake. Someday, God willing, these two families would share grandchildren!

Sooner or later, someone had to mend their differences.

"What did you mean about Papa's cattle getting on MacCallum land?" she asked Dougie.

But Mrs. MacCallum turned sharply. "No business on the Sabbath! Mind my rules or leave my house."

Bonny, who'd been taking her turn reading aloud, fell silent.

Mariah felt slapped. Her "Yes ma'am" wobbled out of her from pure instinct.

"Yes, Ma," said Dougie, with her, and Bonny began to read again.

But as the shock of Mrs. MacCallum's reproach wore off, defensiveness crept into its place. Mariah felt in herself the most rebellious urge to choose leaving. *You don't want me here anyway, do you?* she thought darkly. At least at home, she was wanted, loved. . . .

She made herself remember Stuart. *Stuart* wanted and loved her. She was here for *him,* to spend more time with him and show loyalty to him, just as she'd explained to Elise . . . and perhaps, just perhaps, to protect him. For Stuart, she could bear anything . . . couldn't she?

At least until spring.

When Stuart saw something lying in the distance, a half-week later, he expected the worst. Instead of simply hiking out to investigate, he mounted Pooka. He wanted to be able to ride fast, if he needed—and it was easier to keep his shotgun on Pooka's saddle than to carry it.

"Stay here and guard," he warned Buster.

Pooka began to toss his head and shudder with displeasure, the nearer they rode. A closer look at the lump in the frozen grass drew a curse from Stuart's lips. "Damn."

A dead ewe, white fleece matted with blood, stared sightlessly upward at the man who'd failed to protect her.

Stuart closed his eyes, swallowed hard, then opened them and dismounted to examine this . . . this thing . . . as dispassionately as possible. No animal had done this. Someone—not something, but someone—had killed the ewe, and not here. Despite multiple cuts, including a slit throat, not enough blood stained the grass beneath the ewe, not even its snowy roots—far less blood than the cold accounted for. Besides, a corpse could not lie here for very long without attracting varmints, even in the winter.

Like several antelope before it, someone had caught one of his sheep away from the flock, killed it, cut it up so that Stuart could not even save the fleece. Then he had left it on the stony stretch of free range where he'd been grazing his flock all week.

People did not let good meat go to waste for no reason, certainly not antelope, and not even mutton. These were warnings—gory sort of "no trespassing" signs, as if the public grasslands belonged to anybody in particular, as if free range was meant to be free only to the cattlemen . . . even on the MacCallum side of the deadline.

Walking in slow circles from the dead ewe, Stuart found the U-shaped hoofprints of the horses that had left the gory remains. No great tracker, Stuart could still tell that they'd ridden away toward the southeast, and the deadline.

He thought briefly of the three Circle-T riders who'd crossed the line to deliver a beating, barely a month ago. He thought of Mariah's father who, Dougie had reported, outright denied his cattle were grazing their land. Whoever had left this particular warning obviously meant to push the sheep farther toward Montana. How could it be anybody *but* cattlemen?

Stuart glanced back toward his flock, which the dogs were tending just fine—one of the many benefits of herding domesticated sheep instead of balky, wild cattle. Making up his mind, he drew a rope from his saddle and tied the ewe's feet. A cowboy, he knew, could have made a better show of that, especially what with Pooka balking. But Stuart need not be showy to get the job done . . . whether Mariah was more used to cowboys or not.

With one last glance toward the sheep, Stuart clucked Pooka into a trot, then a canter, dragging the dead animal behind them until they reached the ravine that marked the deadline. He had to dismount in order to kick the corpse in—likely a cowboy could have done that with more style as well—but the ewe ended up in the ravine either way. It was a sorry end to all the wool and lambs he would have gotten off her over the years, much less to a sweet, dumb animal who wouldn't harm a bug. But at least when the wolves and coyotes came after it, they'd be less tempted by the close proximity of the rest of his flock.

As a bonus, thought Stuart grimly, maybe the smell of blood would spook off any straying cattle.

He returned to his flock, wondering. After what Da had told him last week about other sheep farmers receiving threats from the rancher's hired gun, Stuart little doubted that the gunman was responsible. But nobody knew who was paying him—beyond "the cattlemen."

How far would the ranchers go this time to clear the range of sheep . . . or herders?

And on top of all those questions, as Stuart reached his flock and saw another rider approaching from the direction of his father's ranch, Stuart wondered what in the name of all that was holy Mariah could be doing here.

Alone.

Everything, Mariah repeated to herself to the beat of the draft-horse's hooves, *is going to be all right.* Halfway out to Stuart's flock, the words became less a prayer and more a comfort.

It was a beautiful December day. The wind had swept away the previous night's dusting of snow until it collected in cracks and coulees and at the base of rocks, but otherwise seemed to have vanished. Frost sparkled occasionally in the dry grass. And the air smelled . . .

Fresh. Wild. Free. Full of promise.

That was the very reason Mariah had embarked on this shocking ride: promise. After over a week of uncomplaining chores, sleeping three to a bed with Stuart's sisters, and dining on mutton in respectful silence, she felt more like a foreigner at the MacCallum home than ever. In fact, she felt like a *frivolous* foreigner, purposeless and useless, despite having packed only the most serviceable of her gowns and one good church dress. And then yesterday . . .

It would turn out all right, Mariah reminded herself desperately. But she also knew, with a need that went beyond thought to instinct, that she had to see Stuart to remind herself of that. She would marry into the MacCallum family, but she would in fact marry Stuart.

So she rode the heavy-footed wagon horse across bare prairie, almost as free as the wind. She'd fashioned a simple hackamore from rope and, as the MacCallums had no spare saddles, much less a sidesaddle, she'd even straddled the beast with a leg on each side, her skirt drawn scandalously up near her knees. Nobody would see her but Stuart, and Stuart . . .

Well, it embarrassed Mariah even to know that he might catch glimpse of her stockinged legs, but it was a warm embarrassment. When she reminded herself that he would likely see them sooner or later, once they married, the December wind felt sharp against her flushed cheeks.

She recognized Stuart, on horseback, from a long way out, and not just from the white bits of cotton near him that were his sheep. Whenever she descended into a snowy gutter of the rolling grassland, she would lose sight of him, but each time she topped another rise, he would be even closer. Soon she could make out his broad shoulders and his hat, his winter coat and his horse. He drew his piebald gelding to a halt, staring at her approach, and she barely kept herself from urging the draft horse into a trot—a foolish move, bareback. Instead, she enjoyed the picture Stuart made against the frosty Wyoming range. He looked as if he owned the prairie.

Stuart would make everything all right.

But when Stuart rode forward to meet her, catching her rope bridle with one bare hand, his words of greeting were, "What can you be *thinking?*"

Chapter Fourteen

It was hardly the welcome Mariah had hoped for. "What?"

"You rode all the way out here *alone?*"

"All the way? It's barely two miles from your parents' claim!"

"Anything could have happened to you," insisted Stuart, glancing out across the prairie at his sheep. Now Mariah could see several darker shapes amidst them—two black-and-white dogs, a few goats, and what looked like . . . a burro? "Snakes, or wolves, or . . . or a blizzard."

When Stuart frowned at her, his brows leveled out in anger. Mariah usually liked how that made him look, strong and solemn.

But she knew blizzard signs as well as anyone raised in Wyoming. Wolves would not likely bother so large a horse, especially not this early in December. She ran more of a chance of finding a snake in his family's outhouse than on the winter prairie.

And Stuart took similar risks daily, without anybody scolding him.

Normally he had enough sense to have figured that out himself. So Mariah wove her fingers into the draft horse's mane and asked, "Why are you being like this? What's wrong?"

Stuart looked back at his flock and bit off a single word. "Nothing."

He wasn't . . . he wouldn't lie to her. Would he?

"What aren't you telling me?"

He sighed before he swung his attention back to her, but at least some of the tension eased from his big shoulders, and his face softened back into its usual calm—outward-slanting eyebrows and all. "Sheep business, that's all," he dismissed firmly. "No need to worry yourself about it. Unless . . ." Now a humor even warmed his solemn brown eyes. "Unless you're anxious to learn of hoof rot and such."

When she made a face at the very idea, he even smiled, and everything felt better between them again. Then he sobered and asked, "Why are you here, Mariah?" Squinting, he even echoed her question. "What's wrong?"

Being with him for the first time since Sunday made her latest run-in with Mrs. MacCallum seem petty. "Oh . . . nothing to worry you either," she admitted. "Just a little disagreement with your mother. I . . . I wanted to see you, to remember why I'm out here."

She'd *needed* to remember why she was out here, instead of happily at home being coddled and loved. She'd needed to see Stuart with a desperation usually saved for . . . for breathing. The solidity of him, sitting Pooka beside her, made everything all right.

"You rode all this way," he reminded her. "And I'll not let you ride back alone. You might as well tell me while we get the sheep back to Dougie."

His gaze slipped momentarily to those daring inches of

her stockinged calves, beneath the flounces of her skirt and her high-topped shoes, before he turned his piebald back toward the flock. But his eyes gleamed with something other than disapproval. Following, Mariah tugged the skirt as low as it would go, seated straddle. That Stuart would escort her back, on Dougie's night to go home, made her tiff with his mother seem even more trivial.

But it hadn't felt that way yesterday. Nor last night, when the memory of it kept her awake, all but trembling. Nor this morning, when what little Mrs. MacCallum said to her seemed to echo further criticisms of Mariah's upbringing. It had upset her enough that she'd risked even more criticism to flee to Stuart.

If she could not tell him, whom could she tell?

"Your mother won't let me bake Christmas cookies," she admitted, wishing she did not feel so silly as she said it.

Stuart's quick glance over his shoulder at her did nothing to contradict that feeling. "Cookies," he echoed.

"I wanted to do something nice for your family, something cheerful, so I asked to make Christmas cookies."

Worse, since she'd wanted it to be a surprise, she'd waited until she and Mrs. MacCallum were alone in the house, the children either at school or out with Emily.

Maggie MacCallum's protests still rang in Mariah's ears. *Is that all our Savior's birth means to you, Miss Garrison? Cookies?*

You canna win my children over to you with bribery.

And, *I'm sure you get cookies all you want at home, Miss, but this is* my *home.*

Mariah ducked her head, so that Stuart couldn't see when her eyes began to sting. Apparently she still felt upset after all, even in his steady presence.

"Perhaps she wanted to save her sugar for other things," Stuart suggested, after some consideration. "We're being especially careful with our supplies this winter."

For a moment, Mariah heard an implied, *unlike your family.* She rejected the thought with a hard swallow. His mother might make such an accusation, but not Stuart.

"That's why I brought the sugar from home, and white flour, too. All I needed were eggs and some baking powder." And the MacCallums had good laying hens. Eggs weren't too dear.

Stuart winced. "And Ma wouldn't accept them, is it?"

The MacCallums have never yet taken Garrison charity, and we're not starting now just because you have a taste for sweets!

"I meant it as a gift," Mariah insisted. "Not as charity." Although she was not sure at what point either wealth or charity work had become such a terrible crime.

Stuart glanced at her—then again, without even looking at her legs. He edged his gelding closer to her tall draft horse and reached out his right hand. Transferring her reins temporarily to her other hand, she reached out for him, and his fingers curled firmly around hers.

"I am sure your intentions were good," Stuart said—and somehow, just that made everything feel so much better. "I would have liked to taste your cookies."

"Perhaps I can make some at home, next Sunday," she suggested hopefully—but when his eyes flared, she said, "Or we can wait until we're married, I suppose." Just to keep the peace.

Stuart squeezed her hand, then reclaimed his to focus on his work.

Watching his competence, Mariah fell in love with him all over again.

Though sheep apparently lacked the intelligence of even cattle, they had sweet natures. She would never be allowed to ride so near to big, sharp-horned, unruly cows . . . though her sister Laurel had been known to risk it. But the woolly sheep, no larger than big dogs, seemed either content with or even ignorant of their numerous protectors. They meandered back toward their home grounds in starts and stops, like distracted children. Mariah rode peacefully beside them and Stuart both, pleased that Stuart worked them so easily that he could still chat with her.

"Does anybody even know you took Jughead?" he asked first.

"I'm no horse thief, Stuart MacCallum! I asked your father just this morning if I might go riding, and he said he wouldn't be using the horses today."

"Did you tell him you meant to ride *here* instead of just . . . about?"

She had not. Mr. MacCallum was a sweet man, far more so than his wife, but even he would likely have protested this particular outing. "No. I hope to show your parents more respect than to reject their counsel, and . . . and I would have had to reject his counsel to come see you."

Stuart shook his head, sighed—and, eyes warm, whistled at his dogs.

Beauty and Buster, his sleek border collies, moved in and out of the flock as smoothly as trout cut through river water. Sometimes they nipped at a laggard's heels until it bounced back to its brethren; sometimes they dropped low into the dead winter grass, ears alert but chin on the ground, to await further instructions from Stuart. Two goats also moved along with the flock, collar-bells tinkling out into the crisp air, eyes bright and heads high. They, Stuart explained as they rode, were there as guardians. Sheep, when eating, would keep their heads down and concentrate only on the grass, despite a coyote moving right up beside them. Goats, however, would take a bite and then watch their surroundings as they chewed. Sheep, when frightened, went completely still and silent, but goats would bleat and run. Their job was to sound the alarm should something go awry—and the burro's job was to fight away predators.

"She's very good at it," Stuart assured Mariah, and

even smiled his quiet, warm smile. "You should have seen what she did to Buster, before I had him fully trained."

"Poor Buster," commiserated Mariah. The larger of the two dogs paused and glanced in her direction, clearly aware that he was the subject of conversation. Stuart whistled sharply. With an expression that seemed almost abashed, Buster quickly resumed his herding duties.

"Do you think . . ." she ventured, wary not to win another accusation of being selfish. "Would it be all right for me to bring a cat with me, once we marry?" Her mother had always kept housecats, yet another small luxury that she'd missed these last weeks.

"Don't see why not," said Stuart, easy as that. With the sweep of an arm, he directed Beauty to go after a cluster of sheep who had fallen behind. She immediately did.

"You don't think the dogs . . . ?"

Stuart glanced at her, then whistled at the dogs. Both of them dropped to the ground, mid-task, and lay there frozen and alert—though the sheep barely noticed. Beauty and Buster practically quivered with their need to get back to their herding duties; their eyes flicked continually toward their woolly charges, but neither moved anything more than that.

Stuart whistled again, and both dogs launched back into their previous choreography.

Stuart glanced back toward her. He'd never been an expressive man, but something close to pride glowed in his close-lipped smile. "The dogs will do what I tell them," he assured her. "But you can keep the cat inside until they're used to each other, if you're worried."

She'd meant to keep the cat inside most of the time anyway. But Mariah decided not to mention that just now. Instead, she enjoyed the white-and-gray prairie, the brisk wind and, most of all, Stuart's quiet company. Halfway through the ride, he shrugged off his coat and draped it over her lap—less distraction, she supposed. He must be cold, though he still wore mittens and his MacCallum-tartan muffler against the weather. But between his coat and hers, and the heat off Jughead's back beneath her, Mariah at least, felt warm and cozy and cared for . . .

And remarkably free. After months of staying where others expected her to stay, Mariah loved the grasslands all the more because *she* had chosen to ride here herself.

When Stuart said, "This is our land," Mariah's heart beat faster at the weight of what he meant. This was Stuart's land because he had chosen it, every acre, coulee, and rise, just as she had chosen him. When they married, it would be theirs.

Looking at the winter grassland around her, she trusted both their judgments implicitly.

Stuart felt an uneasy mingling of pride and discomfort. The pride came from the fact that this was *his* claim. He had to prove it up, of course—spend the next four and a half years living off it, improving it, showing the United States government that he was no quitter. But he would do so, no matter what the cattlemen wanted. That made it his.

He'd claimed this land in his heart long before he was old enough to file on it. He chose it for the too-often-dry creek, and how it was sheltered from the worst of Wyoming's winds . . . and, perhaps, for the buffalo wallow toward the south corner, where wildflowers bloomed every spring. Even then, he'd been meeting Mariah in secret. At the time, he'd dared not dream she would yoke her life to his. But he'd still imagined her delight at the flowers.

Of course, he'd feared that someone else would claim the land first—whereas most of the young men in these parts found ways to lie about their ages, filing as young as seventeen, Stuart knew that as a sheeper he might not get away with the same thing.

As with Mariah, his land was important enough to do it properly.

So he'd waited, and either God's grace or Mariah's optimism or folks' reluctance to cross the deadline onto sheep land kept the section available. On his twenty-first birthday, Stuart claimed his quarter section of Wyoming prairie. He knew every one of the hundred and sixty acres now under his name. He'd worked this land, slept on it, dreamed of his future on it.

And now, looking at it through Mariah's eyes, the incessant bleating of sheep rattling through his head, he wondered how she could ever reconcile herself to living on a hundred and sixty acres of near nothingness.

He shouldn't have. Her face glowed as she twisted atop Jughead, taking in the rolling prairie as if she were sight-seeing. "Is that your wagon?" she asked, pointing toward the distant, curved white roof, near the haystacks he and Dougie had worked so hard to mow.

"I'll be building a proper house, by the time I've proved up," said Stuart quickly. "Maybe we could even afford a ready-made house from back East."

Mariah said, "If the wagon is good enough for you, I'm sure it's good enough for me." She smiled. "And my cat."

"Once I've sunk a proper well, I'll have a windmill," Stuart continued. "And pens . . ."

"It will be the best sheep ranch in the state," declared Mariah—then pointed. "Look! There's Dougie!"

Stuart had already seen his brother who, surprised to hear the sheep returning early, had come to see what was wrong. He would tell him about the ugly "message" they'd received in the form of a dead ewe, trade off dinner night, and take Mariah back to his father's homestead.

To his relief, both Dougie and Mariah let him, even though it meant neither hearing Dougie rant nor giving Mariah a closer look at the wagon just yet.

Stuart and Mariah rode back to his parents' home in relative silence—but it was not as easy a silence as that in which they'd ridden earlier. By time they could see his parents' white chimney smoke, if not the house itself, Mariah looked downright distressed.

"Could be . . ." Stuart reined Pooka to a stop, and Mariah followed suit. "We should walk the rest of the way in. So that . . ."

And he glanced at his duster across her lap.

"Oh!" But she nodded, and when he dismounted she let him help her off the great draft horse she'd been riding.

Stuart shrugged his coat back on, conscious of how it still held warmth from Mariah, even some of her fine, floral scent. He gathered Pooka's reins—and Jughead's rope—in his right hand, preparing to offer his left arm to Mariah . . . but hesitated.

Despite keeping her chin up, even smiling firmly, she looked somehow as unhappy as when she'd found him. Unhappiness seemed blasphemous on Mariah's pretty face.

"Are you cold?" he asked, hoping it was something that simple.

She shook her head, but he unwound the muffler from around his neck anyway. "Here," he said, looping it gently over her shoulders. "I hope it doesn't smell of . . . sheep. . . ."

To judge from Mariah's expression, she wasn't noticing any smell. To judge from her expression, he might as well have presented her with jewels or flowers. Then he realized why. It was the blue plaid muffler she'd given him from Scotland. The MacCallum colors.

Well, she would soon be a MacCallum herself—if not soon enough.

"You keep it for awhile," he insisted, embarrassed to have done something so significant without having meant to—but glad he had. "In case . . . in case you forget why you're out here."

"I won't forget again, Stuart," she assured him, eyes alight with pleasure.

And then he had to kiss her. He leaned nearer, tipped his head so his hat wouldn't hit her, and touched her soft, full lips with his own. Kissing Mariah in the frosty grass felt as right as anything he'd ever done, neither furtive nor even scandalous, despite their lack of a chaperone. His free hand found her waist. With a shuffling step he leaned against her more firmly, opened his mouth to hers . . .

He remembered her stockinged legs, so slim and curved under her skirt hem when she rode Jughead, and as their kisses deepened his breath caught in his throat—and, somehow, in the rest of him, too. He had no right. But they *were* engaged. . . .

They startled apart when a child's call floated to them on the wind. "Stuart!"

Then they smiled shyly at each other, foreheads and noses nearly touching, before glancing across the prairie to where twelve-year-old Kevin waved excitedly.

Stuart waved back, and Kevin ran off in the direction of the white column of wood smoke. He would be announcing their arrival.

Stuart took a step in the same direction, his left arm still around Mariah, perhaps too familiarly—but he stopped when, unlike the horses, she did not follow.

"We'd best get in," he reminded her.

She stood still even so, worry again darkening her face. "It *is* going to be all right, isn't it Stuart?" she asked, and the desperation in her voice worried him.

"I'll explain to my parents," he offered, though unsure he understood enough to explain it.

She shook her head, confirming it. "Not just today, not with your parents . . . everything. The sheep farmers and the cattle ranchers. *Us.* Tell me everything is going to be all right."

It pained him deeply, not to be able to promise her any such thing. She hadn't heard about the trespassing cattle, or seen the slaughtered ewe. "I canna say that," he reminded her, as gently as he could. "It's not all up to us, you know."

She ducked her head, turned into his shoulder. His answer disappointed her, he could tell.

But he would not lie. Not even to Mariah.

Especially not to Mariah.

Chapter Fifteen

Somehow, Mariah remained outwardly cheerful until the week's end. But when she learned Mr. MacCallum was taking the wagon to town on Saturday for supplies, she was willing to appear self-indulgent in order to go with him.

Mrs. MacCallum made no objections. She'd assumed an air of martyred helplessness where Mariah was concerned ever since Mariah had ridden off to see Stuart. But her look held accusations enough. Perhaps the accusations were even valid. Mariah *would* be seeing her family the very next day. But she wanted it badly enough to risk even valid censure. Even if the other MacCallum children were not allowed to go with her.

Kevin seemed particularly dismayed to be left behind. "Remember, Da," he kept saying. "A Winchester! With a tang rear sight!"

"It's not a name I'll soon be forgetting," soothed his da.

Mariah waited until she was seated beside Mr. Mac-

Callum in his wagon, driving steadily southwestward, before she asked, "Is Kevin getting a rifle for Christmas?"

Mr. MacCallum cleared his throat and said, "Not for Christmas, no."

Since he seemed unwilling to make conversation, she contented herself with counting off the familiar landmarks until she saw the red depot and Sheridan Inn in the distance and, beyond them, Sheridan itself. Home!

Until spring, she reminded herself firmly. Perhaps, she should feel guilty for not thinking of the MacCallums as her family even now. But she could not. And she felt too happy for the chance to see her own parents and sisters again to worry the subject further.

"Be back here in two hours, lass," instructed Mr. MacCallum, setting the wagon's brake in front of the Big Goose Hardware Store. "The sky's low; I dinna want a storm to catch us before we get home."

"Yessir," agreed Mariah, claiming the sack with the rejected flour and sugar from the wagon bed. "Thank you again for letting me accompany you."

He nodded, shy.

Mariah hurried several doors down to the drugstore which, she knew, boasted a telephone. But when she asked Irene, the "hello girl" to connect her to the Garrison home, Irene said nobody was answering. "Would you like me to keep trying, Mariah?"

Remembering how little time she had, Mariah declined. Not event months ago, she hadn't been the sort of girl who would walk downtown unescorted. But married women could, and she was practically married. Perhaps she could still manage a proper escort along the way.

She stopped by her brother Thad's law office, but it was locked. A block farther, she stopped at the millinery shop, run by the mother of one of her best friends from school. Charity Wills and her mother lived above the shop; it was Charity who had helped deliver Mariah's European letters to Emily MacCallum. If Charity was home for holidays from the finishing school she'd gone to back East, wouldn't they have a lot to talk about! But . . .

"Charity won't be home until next week," said Mrs. Wills, cooler than Mariah remembered her. "I will tell her you stopped in."

"Thank you." Mariah would have liked to linger, look at the beautiful new hats . . . but she did only have two hours. So she hurried on alone, her mood unsullied.

Only when she reached her tree-lined street did her cheerful step slow, her attitude falter.

The three-story house's windows seemed dark for such a cold, gray day. Though a wreath hung on the front door, no lights twinkled through the beveled panes. And no smoke came from the cook-stove's chimney—not even enough to heat the ever-present pot of coffee.

Her family's town house looked. . . . empty?

"They've gone to the ranch for the weekend," announced a quiet voice.

Mariah gasped. Then she spun, searching for the source of the voice. Only when she looked up, into an oak tree, did she recognize the wan face peeking back down at her.

"Evangeline Taylor?" she asked. "Whatever are you doing in a tree?"

The skinny girl stared downward, perhaps unable to arrive at a suitable answer, so Mariah tried another tack. "Come down from there! Proper young ladies do not sit in trees."

She remembered her sister Laurel. "Especially not other people's trees," she added.

Evangeline dropped to the walk beside her, hung her head. "I'm sorry," she said, in that low voice that seemed unwilling to claim enough volume to be properly heard. She made a sad sight, her skirt too short for her age, her stockings patched, and wisps of thin, almost colorless hair slipping from her single braid. She wore a knitted shawl against the cold, and no mittens—and brand-new shoes.

But Mariah had too much to worry about with the empty house to wonder about Evangeline's shoes. "What did you say about my family?"

"They've gone to the ranch," repeated Evangeline, daring a quick peek up through her pale lashes. "Victoria told me they would, yesterday."

"Oh. . . ." said Mariah. Her family often spent weekends at the Circle-T, returning for church Sunday morning. And they had not known she would come to town.

So why did she feel orphaned?

"I should go," whispered Evangeline, and began to turn away.

"Wait!" Realizing how rude she'd been, Mariah caught the girl's skinny arm. "It's still my home, too, and I have some things to return. Please, come with me and warm yourself."

Evangeline hesitated. "But . . . nobody's there."

"*I'm* here."

When Evangeline continued to stand there, near about cringing in the cold, Mariah slipped her hand over the girl's chapped hand and started around toward the back of the house. Evangeline followed her as docilely as a child-broke horse.

Even in a town as safe as Sheridan, her mother had a habit of locking the doors when they left for several days. "We keep a key here," she said, moving one of the stones near the back porch, and Evangeline finally said something.

"You should have told me to look away!" she cried.

Claiming the key, Mariah looked over her shoulder, surprised.

"I shouldn't know where your family keeps that," insisted Evangeline, stricken. "If something were to be stolen . . ."

"You don't mean to break in, do you?" teased Mariah, reaching the porch.

"No, but . . . please say you'll hide it somewhere else now. Please?"

"All right," agreed Mariah as the lock clicked open. "I'll hide it somewhere else. Now come in, hurry. It's cold!"

After only another moment's hesitation, Evangeline scurried into the dark kitchen.

The first thing Mariah did was turn on lights. *Ah!* She did miss good lighting. She understood the expense of kerosene and coal oil, of course. The MacCallums had good reason to limit their use of lamps. Perhaps she would need to do the same, once she and Stuart married.

But she missed it, all the same.

She put her "charity" ingredients in their proper bins, then checked the ice box—and smiled. "Would you like a sandwich? Mother left bread, and beef to slice."

"Without asking?" asked Evangeline in a whisper.

"Nobody will mind," Mariah assured her—and paused to savor that certainty. As long as she did not finish off what her mother had left, she was welcome to it, partly because her family could afford it. But partly because she was loved.

"Sit down," she invited as she made them both good, thick sandwiches. "If you're worried, I'll leave a note."

Evangeline sat.

"Why *were* you in the tree?" Mariah asked, after sitting across from the girl and setting the lunch in front of her.

Evangeline murmured something.

"Pardon?"

"You'll think I'm silly," admitted the younger girl.

"Even if I did, what would that signify? The important thing is that you feel you have a good reason. Like . . . like me choosing Stuart MacCallum to marry."

"I just . . . like being on this side of town," admitted Evangeline slowly, after chewing and swallowing a bite of sandwich. "Everything is so fine here, so clean and pretty."

Mariah considered the part of town where Evangeline likely lived, across the railroad tracks. She'd only caught glimpses of it—but it made her feel ashamed for her reservations about the MacCallums' warm homestead, no matter how useless she felt there.

"I don't think you're silly, Evangeline," she said quietly.

Evangeline's smile flickered into and then out of existence even more briefly than one of Stuart's would, but Mariah felt glad to have seen it. She felt even better when she thought to check the cookie jar—and found Christmas cookies.

After eating, she and Evangeline looked at the Christmas decorations her mother and sisters had already put up—garlands of evergreen, tied with bright red bows, and paper snowflakes pasted into the windows. Even empty of Garrisons, the house seemed filled with holiday spirit. Mariah thought to compliment Evangeline on her shoes—"My mother bought them for me," said Evangeline, awed—and talked her into accepting a spare pair of mittens.

By the time they locked up the house and headed back downtown, looking in shop windows, Mariah was in high spirits again. But then they reached the millinery.

"Look," said Mariah, pointing into the window at all the beautiful hats. "My friend Charity Wills lives there, and oh, we had such fun playing dress-up with all those hats when we were younger. She'll be home from school next week."

And Evangeline said, quietly, "Charity Wills got home from school on Monday."

It took an embarrassingly long moment for the truth to register. Mariah actually wondered, *Why would she lie to me?* before her gaze settled on Mrs. Wills, safe behind glass panes, helping a customer—and firmly ignoring the two outcasts at her window.

"Come on," she said, low, and purposefully took Evangeline's hand again.

The temperature was dropping considerably—Mariah felt even more glad for having convinced Evangeline to take the mittens—but Mr. MacCallum stood outside the store. He was not alone. Another man, his back to Mariah, was talking to him.

"—be a sight safer in Montana, is all I'm sayin'," the stranger was saying, with an eerie, mean sound to his words. "Could be you will, too."

"I'll not be leaving," said Mr. MacCallum, his voice tense. "Nor will my sons."

Then he stepped around the other gentleman to meet Mariah, without a good-day or an excuse-me. Only when the second man turned did Mariah see why.

It was Idaho Johnson, the man who'd taunted Stuart at her party. She had not recognized him, with his long coat hiding his sidearm.

Since Mr. MacCallum seemed upset, Mariah let him help her brusquely into his now-loaded wagon, then climb up himself before she dared attempt an introduction. "Mr. MacCallum, have you met Miss Evangeline Taylor? She's—"

"I know of her," said her host shortly, picking up the reins.

He knew *of* her?

She looked quickly to Evangeline, thinking perhaps she would introduce them anyway. But the Taylor girl shook her head, an imploring look in her pale eyes. Then the wagon lurched as Mr. MacCallum shook the reins, urged the team forward.

For Evangeline, Mariah would hold her tongue. All she asked Mr. MacCallum, on the long drive back, was what Mr. Johnson had been saying to him.

" 'Tis nothing for you to worry about, lass," he told her—almost as firmly as his wife might have. So she sat silently beside him on the wagon, watching the town ease slowly away from her again, and thought about Evangeline Taylor.

And she decided, as it started to snow, that she would simply ask Stuart.

By time they reached the MacCallum homestead, it was snowing fairly hard.

Stuart had never minded snowstorms so much, before. Before Mariah and the engagement, that is. Before he took on responsibility for far more than sheep.

Now, instead of being satisfied that he and Dougie had managed to herd their flock back to the wagon and safely against a cut in the land, where the beasts could huddle protected from the wind, Stuart had to worry about other things. Seemingly petty things.

He knew Mariah would not have gone out in the storm herself; surely she was as safe with his parents as she would be with hers. But when the storm stayed through all of Sunday, the wind wailing and the snow turning the night a strange kind of white, Stuart found himself worrying about not seeing her for church.

He worried about her not visiting her family—and he did not even like her family.

Compared to the physical challenge of continually checking on over four hundred snowbound Merinos, such thoughts ought not have carried such weight. But they did.

Monday never did dawn; instead, the storm continued to howl around the wagon, and Stuart's concerns continued to howl around his head. Mariah had not seemed completely happy with his parents even when she could regularly step outside—could ride away on her own. He did not want to imagine how they were wearing on each other's nerves now.

"You're making me tired," muttered Dougie, bundling up to go outside again. "I think I prefer the sheep."

The storm broke Monday night, but of course the sheep had to be seen to before Stuart could consider Mariah. . . .

Well, before be could *do* anything about Mariah.

The beasties had become little more than discolored breath holes atop drifted snow. They'd managed well enough, with plenty to drink, but the cut-bank had not offered good grazing even before their confinement against it. So Stuart and Dougie had to fork enough hay from one of their stacks to sate two days' worth of appetite.

"Go see her, for mercy's sake," said Dougie, once the sheep were eating. "You'll be no good around here until you do."

That he wanted to do just that did not surprise Stuart; the need to see Mariah felt as strong as back when they'd been meeting in secret under the bridge. His blood pounding in him, impatient to be away to her. But . . .

But the sheep.

"It's too easy to lose one, with the snow this deep." He disliked the sound of his own voice, through an old muffler of his, for saying it, but it was true enough. "Best that we both keep watch."

"Suit yourself," said Dougie with a shrug.

And Stuart did—until that afternoon when, echoing sharply across the snow-drifted prairie, he heard gunshots from the direction of his parents' homestead.

Chapter Sixteen

Like Stuart's sisters, Mariah enjoyed nothing about gunfire in "play." She did not put her fingers in her ears, as nine-year-old Caroline did. But she did stay inside to distract the youngest children while Mr. MacCallum was out teaching Kevin the finer points of using his new Winchester rifle.

This did little to improve her mood after three days of incarceration with Stuart's family.

Then Jenny, drawing pictures on the frosted windows, called, "Stuart's here!"

And Mariah had on her coat and muffler—Stuart's muffler—before Mrs. MacCallum had reached the window long enough to say, "Why is he walking?" Mariah did not wait for anyone to venture a guess before she'd rushed out into the freezing December cold to greet him, either

Stuart, looking broad and healthy beside his slimmer father as they hiked back to the homestead together, was not so rude as to rush forward himself. But he did raise a hand to greet Mariah's approach and even briefly showed his teeth in a smile, despite the cold. And when she'd floundered near enough, snow powdering her skirts and packing into the tops of her shoes, Stuart opened his arms wide. She hurled herself against his chest, almost falling the last foot or so, and he scooped her up in a great bear hug and spun her around, her knees bent and her feet etching a half-circle in the snow.

Then she ducked under his hat brim and they kissed. His face felt scratchy against hers—apparently he'd not shaved in several days—and Mariah's love for him felt bigger than the sky.

"What are you doing here?" she gasped as he set her back down. "Why are you walking—is Pooka all right? Where's Kevin?"

"Do you never button your coat, lass?" Stuart demanded back, yanking the two halves of the garment together for her while she obediently fastened the buttons with quickly numbing hands. "I'm here because I forgot about the new rifles. And I'm walking because I sent Kevin to tell Dougie not to come riding to our rescue as well."

"Our rescue?" Mariah laughed at so gallant an idea, huddling happily against him for warmth as she dug her mittens from her pockets. "What did you think we needed rescuing from—wild animals or bandits? Or Indians?"

Stuart looked down for a moment, where she could not see his expression, but Mr. MacCallum suggested, "Rival suitors, perhaps?"

That made Mariah laugh again—not just his joke, but that he'd apparently forgiven her keeping company with "that Taylor girl" enough to make it.

Not that she needed forgiveness for being seen in public with Evangeline. But apparently Stuart's parents thought she did, and . . . Oh! it all seemed so trivial and unnecessary now that Stuart was here. She refused to dwell on any of it.

At least she thought so until the three of them got inside and shed their coats, Stuart particularly hampered by the welcome of his younger siblings. Then, even as Mariah dodged little MacCallums to step nearer Stuart herself—to hold his arm, to ask him how his flock weathered the storm, to just be close to him for the first time in almost a week—his mother called him across the room. Of course Stuart went to her, bent his rather shaggy head to hers. . . .

And from the way they both glanced up toward Mariah at the same time, Stuart's brown gaze surprised and Mrs. MacCallum's caustic, Mariah did not have to be a spiritualist to guess what he was hearing. She'd certainly heard enough of it herself since her return from Sheridan.

What could you have been thinking? But they never really wanted her to answer. *Your family may tolerate ne'er-do-wells in the name of charity, but our charity begins at home.*

Righteous indignation stiffening her spine, Mariah stared right back at the both of them.

Stuart closed his eyes and, for a moment, looked very tired.

At that, Mariah made herself take a deep breath and relax her own posture. It was not fair to put him between his mother and his bride-to-be. If his mother could not honor that, at least Mariah could try to make it easier for Stuart from her own side. When Stuart opened his eyes into a wince, Mariah smiled a tiny, hopeful smile toward him.

And subtly, so quickly that she wasn't quite sure she saw it, Stuart winked at her before turning back to his mother and solemnly nodding at whatever else she said.

Mariah ducked her own head, then, lest her smile give Stuart away. But the relief that eased through her shoulders and back as she sank onto the bench by the fireplace surprised her. She hadn't thought Stuart would side with his mother . . . had she? Against her?

Then again. . . .

"Granted, Ma has strong opinions," he admitted to her, once he finally made his way back to her side. He had to add, "Get on with you, this is private," to Caroline before continuing. "But Mariah, surely you didn't go to town only to spend your time with the Taylor girl?"

Stuart wasn't sitting on the bench beside her. Instead, he'd propped one booted foot on it, so he could lean his elbow on his knee—lean over her—as he warmed himself by the fire. Mariah had to concentrate very hard not to be distracted by his thick leg or, when she looked respectfully up, his thick eyelashes as he squinted at her with just the right mixture of confusion and concern.

"I did not go looking for Evangeline," she admitted . . . then felt guilty for even admitting that, as friendless as the poor girl seemed. "But nobody else would walk with me, and when I met her, I was not about to . . . to shun her. She's Victoria's friend, after all. And have you noticed that she attends our church?"

Stuart had started to frown—but not at her. His brown eyes seemed unfocused.

"Stuart?"

When his eyes focused again, on her face, they looked pained. "Nobody else would walk with you?" he repeated—

And she realized just what she'd foolishly said.

"Oh! I didn't mean it that way, silly! My family was out at the ranch, and . . ."

But she did not sound convincing even to herself, even before she realized that she was, in fact, lying. Charity Wills would not see her because of Stuart, she felt sure. And she'd not bothered stopping to see any of her other old friends. They had begun to avoid her ever since her engagement, even before she moved in with the MacCallums.

Stuart stood, startling old Bruce awake from his nap by the fire, and strode across the room. He waved her back as she started to follow, grabbed his coat, and stepped outside. He closed the door more firmly than necessary.

Mariah saw his sisters staring at her, wide-eyed—his mother with her usual disapproval—before she pulled on her wet shoes, grabbed her coat, and followed Stuart anyway.

He stood not too far from the house, scowling out at the snowy horizon. When Mariah pulled on her coat and came to stand beside him, he dipped his gaze angrily toward her once, then sighed as he looked away and muttered, "For mercy's sake, Mariah, button your coat."

Mariah buttoned. "You're the one who kept warning me how poorly people would take to our engagement."

"It doesna mean I should like it." The words came out thick, and he scowled out at the nothingness even more fiercely.

She caught his hard arm with both of hers, hugged it. "What do I care what those people think? Obviously they aren't very good judges of character!"

His jaw tight, Stuart looked upward at the sky, trying very hard, Mariah thought, not to say or do or show more than he already had.

She could point out how *this* was why she would not shun someone like little Evangeline Taylor. Instinctively, she knew to stay silent. Then Stuart said, "If you married any other man . . ."

And his voice shook, even before he bit off his words mid-sentence.

His apparent guilt made her ache, deep inside, and she instinctively put her bare hand on his rough cheek, felt how he was gritting his teeth. "I don't want any other man, Stuart MacCallum! I want you. Don't you dare get all noble, this far down the road!"

For a long moment he did not move, and she wondered if he'd heard her. Then . . .

When he suddenly turned and yanked her against him, for a moment it frightened her. She'd had no warning, this time—he just sort of surrounded her with his body, too big and strong to be checked, and crushed her to him, and covered her mouth with his, open and needy. His kiss pressed her lips hard against her teeth, but somehow even in her surprise she didn't mind. His groan against her could have been a growl. And yes, it frightened her—for a moment.

But then she thought: Stuart. And resistance melted from her. She let her body mold against his in ways she'd not realized it could, let her head fall limply back so that he could do whatever he wanted to her, her mouth, her throat . . . anything. It was, after all, Stuart.

And once she relaxed into his strength and control, what he did to her, his tongue bold and his cheek rasping hard on hers—oh!—it felt sinful and bestial and so shockingly *good.* . . .

"Stuart!" called a voice from the house. Emily? Bonny? "Ma says that dinner's ready!"

Stuart stiffened, as if only finding his senses then. Mariah wasn't sure she'd found hers even yet. Shouldn't she feel mortified? And yet . . . when Stuart straightened and cradled her against his shoulder then, his face catching on her hair as he whispered something, Mariah only felt pleasantly dizzy—and so feverish that the snow at her feet should have melted into a puddle of hot water.

She nuzzled her face into Stuart's coat, breathed the smell of him, luxuriated in his embrace . . . finally heard what he was saying, over and over.

"I'm sorry. I'm sorry, lass. I didna mean . . . I'm so sorry."

Dazed, she tipped her face up toward his. When he lifted his own, strands of her hair still draped to his stubbled cheek until she wiped them free.

He looked stricken, and she had to ask, "Why?"

He closed his eyes then, as if in prayer, and his posture eased. Eyes closed, he kissed Mariah's forehead, then her eyelids . . .

. . . then her throat. . . .

Mariah began to feel even hotter, even more dizzy!

"Stuart Andrew MacCallum!"

At his mother's voice they bolted apart as if doused with ice water. In fact, Mariah seemed to remember her mother throwing water on a pair of cats that were behaving very rudely . . . and oh, she wished she could vanish under the snowbank!

Especially since his mother seemed to be glaring at *her* far more than at him.

"I . . . " Stuart seemed to be trying to form a sentence, low enough that it was surely meant for Mariah alone. "I never meant to hurt you, lass," he murmured.

Mariah turned back to him, just in time to see him wince at his mother's, "Inside!"

"You haven't hurt me, Stuart," she whispered back—taking a step toward the house, just to show how obedient she meant to be.

Without opening his eyes, he shook his head. "You dinna ken . . ." Then he groaned again. "You go ahead, Mariah. I'll be with you in a moment."

Something felt wrong about going without him. But she'd already disobeyed him by following him out in the first place. And he *would* be her husband . . . come spring.

So Mariah hurried meekly by his mother and sat at the table. She kept her head down even as she heard Mr. MacCallum go close the door. "It's cold, Maggie," he chided gently.

"Then he ought not be gallivanting about out there," his wife said.

Somehow even without looking, Mariah felt the woman's disapproval—and it did not bother her. Her amazement over what had just happened in Stuart's arms, how very unrestrained her normally steady, solid beau had behaved, and how very imprudently she'd responded . . .

Well, that easily distracted her from something so trivial as Mrs. MacCallum.

"He's fine, Maggie," soothed Stuart's father, and apparently he led his wife to the table, because they both sat as well. "Let us say grace."

Mariah felt downright blasphemous, listening to his solemn prayer with her heart still pounding as it did, her skin still tingling from more than the cold weather, her pulse skittering about like water on a hot skillet. She doubted even God would approve of such behavior.

Certainly her father would not!

But when the door opened and Stuart came back in, gruffly excused his tardiness and sat at the table, she could not quite suppress a smile of sheer pleasure at his return, even so.

All she could do was not look at him.

Stuart did not dare look at Mariah for half the dinner through, and even then he risked only quick, tentative glances. He'd never imagined kissing her like that—

Did that even still qualify as kissing?!

Even husbands ought not treat their wives that way, so . . . so desperate. So needy . . .

And yet he had been both. Desperate and needy. Though he had warned Mariah of what she risked in yoking her future to his, he'd never dreamed the reality of it would pierce so deeply. It hurt worse than any beating—and this was just the start. Once she married him, her entire life would be that of a sheeper's wife. Her children—their children—would face the same abuse and discrimination he'd suffered. He was doing that to her, in the meager name of love. . . .

Briefly, he'd hated himself for it.

But Mariah insisted on loving him, even so—and then Stuart had needed her love more than he needed her respect or even his own. At that moment, he'd turned to her, clung to her . . .

And somehow, his need for her had then degenerated into a blinding hunger to somehow brand her as his, irrevocably and fully, before common sense could drive him to do the right thing by ever, ever giving her up. . . .

His kiss had not been gentle. Now, peeking across the table, he noticed that her cheeks weren't just pink from cold or embarrassment. Something had scraped her jaw.

Stuart remembered that he had not shaved during the storm, and he was almost sick, right there. And yet, when Mariah finally touched his gaze with her own—timid, blushing—her predawn eyes held no accusation. They held the same love they always had. . . .

Albeit shadowed with a modest self-consciousness that pinkened her cheeks even more.

Just as well that she could distract herself by helping with the dishes, that Stuart could distract himself with Kevin's return. The twelve-year-old announced that the snow made the evening bright as afternoon, that Dougie had fed him beans for dinner, and that the Winchester was surely the best rifle ever made.

"Wait until you try yours, Stu!" the boy enthused. "You'll be glad Da bought them then!"

When they'd agreed to better arm themselves, just in case, Stuart's had been the only voice of hesitation—because of Mariah.

Now Mariah turned from his sisters at the stove and cocked her pretty head, quizzical. "You bought Stuart a Winchester, too?" she asked his father.

The way Da ducked his head belied his firm, "I did."

Stuart only stared at her, still feeling guilty for more than he could even understand, none of it involving firearms.

"Oh." Mariah turned back to drying dishes—but only for a moment. Then she let Bonny have all of the dish-towel and crossed the room, her pretty brow furrowed. "I don't understand. I thought Stuart had a rifle."

"I have a shotgun," Stuart clarified for her. "And Dougie only a sidearm."

She nodded, her brow smoothing. "And now Dougie gets the shotgun."

Kevin, far too proud, announced, "Dougie gets his own Winchester! You can't fight a war with shotguns!"

Stu said, "Whist!" But too late—Kevin had just used the worst possible word, and it hung in the room, blatant as a pig in a parlor.

"A war?" repeated Mariah carefully—and she looked to Stuart to clarify. She trusted Stuart. If he had not believed that before their behavior this evening . . .

Perhaps she trusted him too much?

"A range war," he clarified, as gently as he could. "Not that there is one," he added quickly, for his sisters' sake as well as hers.

"A range war," Mariah echoed, like a child learning new words.

"The rifles are merely a caution," assured Da. "None of it should concern you ladies."

Mariah said, still sounding simple, "A range war with whom?"

When Kevin drew breath to answer, Stuart whacked him in the stomach, just hard enough to make him catch that breath back. Kevin had never seen a true fight, after all. He did not understand what it could cost, not even with Mariah standing right there in front of him, vulnerable and confused.

Deliberately confused at that, thought Stuart. He hated to hurt her with clarification. But she was his betrothed. That made her his responsibility.

"With the ranchers, Mariah," he said. "If it came to a fight, 'twould be a fight with the cattlemen."

Chapter Seventeen

"You bought rifles to fight the cattlemen." Mariah knew very well how daft she sounded, repeating everything. But she could not sound as ludicrous as the MacCallum men. *War?* Wars were fought for independence, for freedom, for states' rights or, conversely, for abolition.

Wars were not fought over *grass.*

"Only if it comes to that," Stuart assured her mildly, as if addressing someone deathly sick or badly frightened. She was neither.

"If *what* comes to that?" she asked. When he put a steadying hand on her shoulder, brown eyes concerned, she realized this question too closely echoed the others. "Something must have happened, to compel you all to buy . . . three rifles?"

One for Kevin, one for Douglas—and one for Stuart. Her Stuart.

" 'Tis a matter for the menfolk," insisted Mr. MacCallum, while Kevin helpfully clarified, "Four. And ammunition."

The image of herself riding back from Sheridan beside Mr. MacCallum, with an armory loaded in the wagon behind her, Mariah stored away for another time.

"I don't understand," she said instead, "what could have changed? Was it—?" A horrible thought occurred to her. "Oh Stuart, is this because of what Hank Schmidt did?"

Because of her papa?

"No," said Stuart, while his mother asked, "Schmidt? Who is this Schmidt?"

Stuart closed his eyes in resignation. "Nobody, Ma."

Mrs. MacCallum glared at them both.

"Then what? There must have been a reason. If we're being careful not to waste money on lamplight, or sugar and flour, the purchase of four brand-new rifles seems rather extreme."

"Enough!" The usually soft-spoken Mr. MacCallum strode to the fireplace before facing Mariah. "Miss Garrison, this concerns me and my sons alone. We've no reason to explain ourselves to our wives, daughters, or fiancées."

Then, as if unsettled by his own sternness, he ducked his head as he added, "You and the girls had best retire, while we discuss this proper."

The others, even Emily, obediently started for the bedroom they all shared. Mariah did not. Even on a normal evening she would stay up long enough to see Stuart off. But now . . .

"It *does* concern me," she reminded Mr. MacCallum—and, lest he needed it, Stuart. "Don't forget, my father is a cattle rancher."

Mrs. MacCallum snorted, as if to imply that such transgressions were impossible to overlook. Mr. MacCallum snatched his pipe off the mantle, but did not light it. Kevin watched with wide eyes, as did Bruce the dog, whom the argument had woken.

Mariah continued watching Stuart. "It does concern me," she repeated—and for once, she understood how her spirited mother must sometimes feel. She did not *mean* to be quarrelsome. But how could she ignore something like this? "I want to understand, Stuart. Make me understand."

"Is this how you mean to let her behave?" demanded his mother.

Ignoring his mother as he gazed steadily back at Mariah—tired, it seemed extraordinarily so, but steady—Stuart said, "I do not think you want to hear these things, lass."

"If it has to do with you or my father, how could I not?"

Stuart ducked his head, dragged a hand over his face, then peeked back up at Mariah over the hand while it still covered his mouth. Only when his mother drew breath to say something else did he raise the hand, palm out, and say, "It's my affair, Ma. Mine and Mariah's. Thank you for your concern," he added, belatedly softening his voice. "But you're nae helping."

"I said from the start . . ." his mother muttered.

Stuart scowled and took Mariah by the hand. "We're going to the barn to talk," he announced and strode toward the door, her scrambling to follow. They stopped only for coats.

"Not without a chaperone," interceded his father. "Not while she lives here."

"Then send Kevin. I'll not have the two of you . . ." Stuart searched for the right word before wincing at his inability to find it. "It's not that I dinna appreciate your wisdom," he offered awkwardly. "But it's Mariah I intend to marry. It's Mariah whose da is a cattle rancher. I need to talk to her alone, without your . . ."

Criticism? thought Mariah. *Judgments? Biases?*

"Without your help," Stuart tried. "Either she and I discuss this in the barn or in the boys' bedroom." And of course the idea of them going into a bedroom together, even a boys' bedroom with little six-year-old Ian already asleep there, was out of the question.

Mr. MacCallum compromised with, "Kevin goes with you, then."

Stuart said, "As long as he keeps his tongue. You mind me, Kevin?"

Kevin nodded quickly and, proud at such responsibility—chaperoning his older brother!—hurried to grab his own coat. Mariah had already put hers on, even buttoned it.

Together, by the light of a single lantern, the three of them strode out to the barn, worn snow barely crunching beneath their boots. To Mariah, everything from the moment Kevin had said "war" seemed unreal. It was one thing to agree that the cattlemen and sheep farmers had, as her father put it, "bad blood" between them. But to speak of *war*—to buy the guns for it!

Mariah did not fear guns. But she'd feared the MacCallums' suddenly deciding they all needed new rifles, even *before* war with the cattlemen came into the discussion.

And she feared the possibility that something bad might have happened with nobody, *nobody* deigning to tell her. So after Stuart hung the lantern on its hook, and shooed Kevin off to the other side of the barn where he could watch quietly, Mariah took his soft, strong hand.

Next to her father, Stuart was the best person to be with when she felt fear.

But when he said, "It's not so extreme as Kevin made it out," a shiver of uncertainty ran through her despite his steadiness. If it were not extreme, why buy four rifles?

She did not ask that. She said, "Make me understand. Please."

Stuart drew a wooden crate closer to the light, brushed it off before letting Mariah settle onto it . . . then stood there and stared at her, wordless.

Mariah waited, even glanced toward Kevin, lying casually in the hay. He shrugged.

Finally, Stuart said, "You've known all along that the cattlemen hate the sheep farmers."

"I've known they strongly dislike sheep, yes," she admitted. "But why should that require new rifles?" She forced the harder question out. "You don't mean to shoot cattlemen, do you?"

Stuart said, "Not unless they start shooting at us first."

"Well, they won't," she said, greatly relieved.

But Stuart continued to regard her solemnly. He folded his arms, then shifted his balance and unfolded his arms, obviously uncomfortable. And his family *had* bought rifles. . . .

"You truly think they might?"

"It's happened before," said Stuart.

"Cattlemen have shot at you?"

"Not recently." But he said that so quickly, Mariah had the sudden and completely distressing sense that he'd just lied to her.

"Stuart . . . ?" she asked, desperate for him to disprove that thought.

"But when I was younger," Stuart continued, not obliging, "not long after we moved here, there was a lot of shooting against homesteaders, small ranchers, *and* sheep farmers."

Why did you just lie to me? thought Mariah, her throat constricted. But had he? She must concentrate on what he *was* telling her, not what he might not be saying.

So she asked, "Cattlemen shot at you?"

With a deep sigh, Stuart stepped closer and sank onto the box beside Mariah, took her hand in his again. "With the small ranchers, the cattle barons usually trumped up an accusation of rustling. Not ten years ago, in the Sweetwater Valley, they hanged Jim Averell and Ella Watson on false charges. And you remember the Johnson County War."

He'd used that word again. War . . .

Mariah said, slowly, "I remember that Papa made Mother take all of us on the train to Denver that week, until he telegraphed her to come home. She wouldn't tell us why. When we got back, the army had already captured the gunmen from Texas. Papa said . . ." It sounded damning, but she couldn't lie to him. "He said those men killed two rustlers."

Stuart said, "They killed two innocent homesteaders, Mariah—surrounded their cabin and gunned them down, with the governor paid to not interfere. If someone hadn't gone for help, they would've cleaned out three counties. Everyone knows it was the cattlemen who hired them."

"But . . ." But—her father wouldn't unfairly call someone a rustler. But—*everyone* couldn't know, if she did not. But—how could Stuart accuse cattle barons who'd not even stood trial?

Unwilling to argue any of that, she said, "That was Johnson County."

Stuart said, "And not a day's ride from here." And in fact, when she was very young, her parents used to drive with her to Buffalo, the county seat, several times a year for supplies.

Mariah said, "But you raise sheep! Sheep and cattle can't even use the same range!"

Stuart frowned at her then. It did not last very long—but Mariah felt certain she'd not imagined it. Stuart did not like what she'd just said, and he would not tell her why.

He looked down at their joined hands and said, "No, they don't generally accuse us of rustling. They go after our sheep. Sometimes men shoot them. Sometimes they rush the sheep off a cliff; more often the sheep bunch up, but then it's just as easy to set them afire."

Mariah bolted off the crate, even if it meant snatching her hand from Stuart's, and she held herself very tight against such pictures. "People couldn't do something so terrible as that!"

Stuart looked at her very steadily and said, "They do."

"No."

"They have."

"No!"

Stuart's tone did not falter. "They've done it to my da."

Mariah shook her head.

And Stuart said, "I've seen it."

Then Mariah could only stand, her arms wrapped about her middle, staring at him.

"When I was twelve, Da took me to check on a new herder he'd hired, and we camped there that night. We woke when six gunmen rode in and began to shoot the flock. They shot the herder, Mariah, and the dog, and they may well have shot me if my Da hadna had his rifle to chase them off. I was there, and I saw it."

Mariah wanted to shake her head but couldn't manage it. As if realizing that he'd remained seated while she stood, Stuart found his feet and came to her again, claimed her hand again. "It's real, lass."

She tipped her face up toward his, imploring him to fix it. "They really shot the dog?"

He traced some hair from her face and, for a moment, almost smiled. But it was a sad smile, and he still seemed somehow far away. "Aye. And the herder. And almost twenty sheep."

So much horror. So many questions. She settled for, "The sheriff . . . ?"

"They hid their faces under gunnysacks; he said he couldna do anything."

"Then how do you know it was cattlemen?"

Stuart bowed his head until he was able to rest it atop hers. "Oh lass . . ."

Who else would it be? he meant. And she had no suggestions. But to assume the ranchers seemed wrong—it seemed un-American!

She concentrated to manage another question. "You think it's going to happen again?"

With Stuart's face so close to hers, she saw when his eyes closed. He drew a deep breath as he straightened, patted and released her hand. He walked to the crate before turning back to her. "We do. Johnson County cost some ranchers their reputations, if little else, but that was over five years ago. Folks are forgetting, and the intimidation is starting again."

"But how?"

"Someone's hired another outside man." At her confusion, Stuart clarified, "A gunman, hired from outside the area so that nobody local need claim responsibility for his actions. The ranchers call them 'range detectives.' Johnson's trying to push back the deadline and scare us away. He's done little to take to the sheriff," he assured her, before she could ask. "As if the law would help. But cattle are being driven onto our land, challenging our claim to it. Someone even slaughtered one of my ewes and left it as a warning. Maybe things won't get any worse, but likely they will. And if they do, we mean to fight back."

Mariah slowly nodded. If someone threatened to shoot her animals, much less set them on fire, she would want to be well armed too. And yet . . .

"Stuart? Why didn't you tell me any of this."

He frowned, though more in thought than anger. After having said so uncharacteristically much, he now chose his words very carefully. "You don't much talk of the sheep, Mariah."

She waited.

"And I didna wish to worry you."

She shivered. Papa would say that someone walked over her grave. But it felt more like Stuart lying to her—again. She'd rejected the thought as almost blasphemous. But now . . .

Stuart had warned her that the townsfolk would not accept their engagement. He'd warned her about how vehemently her papa would protest. He'd even warned her about blizzards and rattlesnakes, on that beautiful afternoon when he showed her their claim, and never once had he seemed concerned with worrying her.

But with this, he had?

Perhaps he'd been right in the house, and she did not wish to know any of this. But if wishes were horses . . .

The only way out was through the truth. So she asked softly, "What else, Stuart?"

He just stared back at her. And finally, horribly, she realized why he'd kept silent.

"You think my father is involved?"

"I didna say that," he protested quickly.

"But that's why you haven't told me any of this before. You think my father hired that nasty Idaho Johnson. You think my father wants to start a range war with you!"

Stuart said nothing.

"Do you even think he's one of the men who shot your papa's herder, and sheep . . . and dog? How—how could you possibly think something so horrible about my father?"

As her voice faded, she realized she'd yelled. At Stuart. The man she loved. She wanted to apologize for forgetting herself—but not as much as she wanted him to tell her she was wrong.

To his credit, Stuart said, "Could be he's innocent. Could be the other ranchers are doing it all without his help—maybe even without his knowledge."

At least he made that effort. But Mariah felt cold, despite the barn's toasty warmth. When she reached for Stuart, he quickly met her, wrapped his arms comfortingly around her, eased her back down onto the crate. Almost on his lap, she curled against the breadth and warmth of him—and thought of her father, and felt progressively colder.

Papa's own men—his own nephew!—had hurt Stuart. On purpose.

Papa had sent Mother and all his daughters away the very week of the Johnson County War, before anything bad had happened.

Papa was a powerful man in this town. How could the

other cattlemen do something without him even *knowing* about it?

Papa had said he would rather see Stuart dead than married to her.

Mariah thought of her strong, silent father, the foundation upon which her world had rested. She thought of him not letting her have a bear cub, no matter how hard she cried, and sitting up with her or her sisters when they were sick. She remembered the big Die-Up, the worst winter Wyoming had ever known, and how in the midst of his cattle and his dreams dying in droves, Papa had silently dragged a Christmas tree into the cabin for his little daughters before going back out to face the nightmare. She thought of him standing between her and wolves, Indians, unruly men . . . of him putting her on her first horse, partnering with her for her first dance, quietly complimenting her first long dress.

And no matter how close to Stuart Mariah cuddled, she felt frozen, because no matter how likely it seemed that Papa might join a range war, she would not believe it. She *could* not.

Not even for Stuart, for whom she thought she could do anything.

She said, "It's not Papa, Stuart. I'll ask him, and he'll tell you himself."

Stuart drew a breath—then seemed to decide against whatever he'd meant to say. He just held her. But it still did not warm her.

Finally he said, "*If* something were to happen . . ."

She shook her head, but he sat back, made her meet his steady brown eyes. Unshaven like that—like a bear—he looked so very grown up. He looked big, and masculine, so . . . *other.* It did not frighten her, quite. But neither could he anchor her, like that.

"You need to think on this, Mariah Garrison," he told her steadily. "You need to think on this very hard. If it were to come to a range war, do you have it in you to choose sides?"

He did not have to ask her, *And which side would you choose?*

But that was perhaps the worst, and most important, question of all.

Mariah did as Stuart asked her, the whole rest of the week. She thought about everything he'd said—and wondered what he hadn't. Some moments, she determined that she would indeed ask her father to explain it all. Perhaps she would take Stuart with her, to hear it himself!

Other moments, she knew Papa would not deign to defend himself against such outlandish accusations—certainly not in front of a MacCallum! He would not even let Stuart into his house. Would she ask him such questions in the front yard?

Sometimes she thought Stuart must be telling the truth, that Papa had managed to deceive her, her whole life. But sometimes she remembered the sense that Stuart had lied to her—at the very least, he must be mistaken!

It left her dizzy.

On Thursday, she broke one of Mrs. MacCallum's teacups, and before she could apologize, Mrs. MacCallum said, "*We* haven't enough nice things to waste!"

As if Mariah wasted her own. As if Mariah's own mother would not have done anything to keep a guest from feeling bad about such an incident, no matter what got broken, replaceable or not. Even though Emily, and little Rose and Ian, were in the same room, Mariah blurted, "Why do you dislike me so much?"

Mrs. MacCallum said, "Your selfishness will get my boy murdered, that is why!"

And Mariah threw down her dishtowel and ran into the blessedly empty girls' bedroom, fell onto the bed she shared with Emily and Jenny, and cried for what felt like hours. First she cried at Mrs. MacCallum's cruel, baseless accusation.

Then she cried in fear that perhaps it wasn't so baseless after all.

On Saturday afternoon, Kevin went outside to shoot at empty tins. Each retort from the rifle, even muffled by a rise between the house and the boy, made Mariah cringe. So, of course, it was she Mrs. MacCallum sent to call the boy in for supper.

A strong breeze had come up, snaking veils of powdery snow over the top of the packed drifts, and young Kevin stood upwind from Mariah, his back to her. Before she reached him, she could smell gun smoke, even hear the *clang* when he hit a target. But the same wind stole her voice from her and blew it back toward the homestead. She had to follow his tracks all the way out to him, which is how she heard what he was saying, as he shot at the target. "Colonel Asa Wright!" he said, aiming.

The rifle kicked, and in the early winter dusk, a blue flame seemed to erupt from its muzzle. But the can sat untouched on its crudely formed shelf of snow.

Mariah's stride faltered. She'd spent six months in Europe with the Colonel and Mrs. Wright, as a companion to their daughter Alice. Why . . . ?

"Bill Irvine!" Again, the boy shot. Missed. Cursed.

He was pretending to shoot at local ranchers!

Mariah wanted, needed to stop him, and yet she could not seem to even draw a breath. So she had to stand there, mutely watching, as Kevin said, "Jacob Garrison!"

The rifle kicked.

The empty can flew into the air, and Kevin let out a whoop of joy at having hit his target.

Mariah wanted to crumple to her knees in the snow and be sick . . . but she still could not seem to draw breath, even for that.

And being sick would change nothing.

• • •

Stuart felt like a hypocrite. He'd begged Mariah to think—to think hard—whether she had it in her to choose sides, should it come to a range war. But he had worked himself near to exhaustion all week so as *not* to think about the same thing.

He did not dare. Knowing—loving—Mariah for four years, he knew the answer.

Even his Saturday night routine of pressing his good shirt, choosing a paper collar, and polishing his boots became a way of doing something, anything, instead of thinking on it. But when he woke in the darkness the next morning, splashed his face with near-frozen water, then shaved and dressed for church, he knew that the truth would come.

Whether he wanted it or not, he needed her answer.

As he rode toward the homestead, the sky barely the color of Mariah's eyes, Stuart saw a shadow separate from the eaves of his family's home and resolve itself into Mariah. Bundled in a coat, gloves, and muffler—their muffler—she hurried to the barn, beckoned him to follow.

Stuart had followed her to the Kissing Bridge far too often to refuse this on grounds of propriety. But he also knew, in the hollowness where he usually kept his heart, that she was not behaving so secretively in order to kiss him.

He dismounted and led Pooka into the barn, rather than leave him in the cold untended, then turned to where Mariah stood beside an empty stall.

She was twisting her mittened hands. Her face looked very white, and her eyes wide.

Then, unexpectedly, she said, "Let's marry now, Stuart. This week. Today."

The words might—*might*—have reassured him.

But the way she said them, rushed and frightened, did the opposite.

Chapter Eighteen

That, Stuart would decide later, was when the numbness started.

"Marry you," he repeated stupidly. "Today?"

"As soon as possible. We can't put it off any longer. I'm afraid . . ."

But whatever she feared, she hid by lowering her gaze to her hands and saying no more.

Stuart said, "You cannot marry me just because you're afraid."

Even without looking back at him, her shoulders stiffened in clear, petulant challenge. *Yes, I can!*

"Reverend Adams would never agree to it."

"Then . . . then we can elope." Her voice squeaked on the last word. It felt eerily like talking to some stranger, not to his Mariah—and he had no business being alone in a barn with any other woman. He had little business being alone with *her*.

Instinctively, Stuart reached for her, as if by touching her he could make her more real. She took his hands, but when he tried to pull her closer, she moved stiffly. It felt like holding someone else, too.

"Mariah, we agreed. 'Twould be unfair to our parents."

She shook her bent head, though surely not at his argument. How could an elopement of their eldest children not badly betray both families?

"And we dinna need the scandal," he reminded her.

"I don't care what people think!" Now she looked up, and her teary eyes startled him even more than her uncharacteristic claim. "I don't!"

"Of course you do, lass. If we just wait until spring . . ."

That was when he finally understood what frightened her.

If they married quickly enough, any second thoughts she had would be too late. That meant she already had second thoughts, and merely wanted to outrun them. Mariah had already decided the question he'd asked her to think on.

She just hadn't admitted it to herself yet.

"Stuart . . ." Mariah snuffled, wiping at her face with one mittened hand. "About waiting. The talk will end once we don't have an early baby. We'll just make sure not to, that's all."

What? The idea of living with her in his sheep-wagon, never more than six feet apart except when he was outside, and somehow not consummating the marriage . . .

Unimaginable. "We willna wait," he warned, his cheeks warmer than the barn merited.

Mariah nodded in a moment of foolish, beautiful victory. "Yes!"

"No! I mean . . ." Heaven help him, sooner or later they would have had to face this subject. He just hadn't expected to have to be *speaking* of it.

He could not bear to look at her as he forced the words from his mouth. "I mean, once we do marry . . . I doubt we can wait, to . . ."

He swallowed, hard, and even not looking at her he could feel her expectation.

"To risk babies," he rasped, finally. "Not and live together."

"Oh!" She realized then what he meant.

They spent a long moment, still holding hands but looking at anything but each other. Only once did Stuart peek—quickly—and see that Mariah had ducked her head again.

But she wasn't so mortified as not to argue. "But Stuart, we . . . we can . . ." Her grip twisted, tight and awkward. "That is . . . my mother says there are ways. . . ."

He either had no earthly idea what she meant, or he did not dare let his thoughts drift near a place where he might. "Ways . . . ?"

"To . . ." Now he need not look at her to know she'd averted her face, because she'd braced the top of her head against the middle of his chest.

Never had he felt so uncomfortable.

"To . . . be married . . ." she managed finally, miserably. "And not make a baby. There are ways for women to . . . make sure . . ."

Stuart closed his eyes against so fantastic a conversation—but then his eyes flew open, because with a rush of cold and noise, Mariah flew back from him as if yanked.

She *had* been yanked. His mother, come upon them together, had yanked her.

Were Stuart not already numb with mortification, this would have finished him. The most intimate, embarrassing conversation of his life had been overheard by his mother?

Only that could explain his momentary paralysis. Then Ma yanked Mariah backwards by the arm again, right out the door. "Tramp!"

And numb or not, Stuart lunged after them. "No!"

"Maggie!" Da and several of the children were pouring from the homestead to see. Worse, Mariah had fallen in the snow. Had she been pushed? Stuart's mother didn't push people! And yet—

"The girl is obscene! We raised a good boy, a clean boy, and I find them together talking obscenities and sin!"

"Enough!" Only when his own voice echoed back at him did Stuart recognize it. Only when he saw his own hand on his mother's shoulder, physically holding her back from where he'd stepped between her and Mariah, did he realize he'd been fully ready to push her, if need be.

Somewhere deep inside him, where it would never show, he began to shake then. And yet the knowledge of Mariah fallen back in the snow, her face pale, her coat bunched awkwardly on her, superceded even lost faith.

When he repeated the word lower, his throat hurt as if he'd injured it. "Enough."

Da drew his wife back. Stuart turned to Mariah, and the pain in her eyes, her shame-reddened face, lanced through his growing numbness and straight into his soul. He ignored the near-crippling pain to draw her to her feet, started to brush the snow off her coat . . .

Then he realized how inappropriate that was, to touch her hips, her legs, and stopped doing that, too. Mariah brushed herself off alone. None of his sisters, staring horrified from the stoop, came to help.

This was Stuart's fault, of course. His fault for bringing her here. His fault for pretending they could make this work. Mariah had honestly believed it, of course—but that was Mariah. She'd believed her father would accept him, too.

Stuart should have known better. He *had* known better. But God help him, he'd so wanted the mirage to be real. . . .

"We will go inside and discuss this," said Da.

Ma said, "Not. Under. My. Roof."

"Maggie, be reasonable."

"It's all right." Mariah spoke so low, Stuart almost

didn't hear her. "I don't want to go back in there. I'm finished living where I'm not wanted."

Had she felt unwanted before now? Stuart remembered something about Christmas cookies, weeks ago.

He'd known better.

After that, he let the numbness win. He owed Mariah his strength until he got her safely back to her own world—and far, far away from his. If he stayed numb, maybe . . .

Maybe he could survive the morning until then.

Huddled silently with the MacCallum children in the back of the wagon, en route to church, Mariah had never felt so dirty. Somehow worse, she'd never felt so absurd. She should have known that Stuart—steady, practical Stuart—would not sanction her fears with a rushed marriage. Perhaps she had known, but just could not bear to be the one who admitted . . .

Who finally said . . .

Perhaps she'd needed him to play the villain by speaking the words. They'd both waited so long, tried so hard, sacrificed so much! And yet, the cracks had been showing themselves for weeks now. Mariah just had not wanted to see. And after this morning . . .

Obscenities. Sin.

She wanted to draw the carriage blanket up over her head and never face another MacCallum again. The intimacies she'd ventured would sound obscene, given a public forum—and yes, many people would consider such an idea as controlling the number of one's children sinful. Her mother had thoroughly embarrassed her by discussing such things, once Mariah was old enough for long skirts. And yet surely, between a married couple . . .

Or a nearly married couple . . .

Or . . .

Mariah wanted to cover her face and smother herself. Oh, what must Stuart be thinking!

He'd been wonderful, facing down his mother and standing silent guard until the family left for church. Even now, instead of riding ahead, he rode stonily abreast of the wagon where Mariah huddled, as if daring his family to speak an ill word. But he'd said nothing since the barn.

Only once he helped her from the wagon at church did Stuart draw her aside.

"Shall I walk you home?" he asked, low. "If you dinna want to attend services . . ."

For a single, horrible moment, she misunderstood him. *Sin. Obscenities.* "I belong in church as much as anybody, Stuart MacCallum!"

He blinked, startled. Then he said, "Never doubt it," and offered his arm.

Would she have had the courage to follow his family into church otherwise? Hearing nothing of the hymns or even the sermon, Mariah wondered how she could possibly survive without Stuart's strength. She realized that she probably would have to.

And that's when the tears began to threaten, building with each unheard reading, each song. When little Elise, half of her face hidden by a big floppy bow, brazenly looked over the back of the family pew to wave at her older sister, Mariah felt something akin to panic. Too soon, she must face her own family, the family she'd shattered in order to be with Stuart, the family to whom she'd insisted . . .

. . . wrongly . . .

As the closing hymn began, she pushed to her feet and slipped out of the church, despite the attention it would draw. She'd faced so much this morning already.

Stuart caught up with her as she hurried across the snowy churchyard. He matched his stride to her own but did not, wisely, ask what was wrong.

What was *right?*

"I can't face Mother," she explained, not slowing. Her

voice sounded foolish and high. "She'll ask what's wrong, and I'll start crying, and I won't be able to talk, not even to explain, and . . . and Papa might kill someone. . . ."

And she might not even be exaggerating.

"I'll walk you home," Stuart insisted again. "Please. We . . . we must settle this, you and I."

If they said nothing, she could go home and pretend to forget about range wars or outraged mothers. She could pretend that somehow things might yet be all right, that somehow, she and Stuart could make this work. But Stuart knew better, didn't he?

She took his arm, wishing she did not need his strength so badly, and tried to blindly watch the frosted store windows instead of facing him.

Then she recognized his solemn, concerned face reflected in the windows over her own. He could see her wet eyes, her tight mouth, just fine.

"I'm sorry," said Stuart finally. "Ma behaved poorly."

Mariah gasped, even glanced momentarily at him in surprise. Stuart loved his mother. People *should* love their mother. . . . But then she'd come along.

"It must have been a shock for her," she murmured with desperate politeness.

Stuart snorted at her understatement, then looked away. "I am sorry you were unhappy there, too . . . sorry not to have seen it."

As if it were his fault. "I wasn't *continually* unhappy," Mariah protested. She'd rather liked his father, and had become tentative friends with his sisters. But . . .

But if she stopped trying to see things as they should be, instead of as they were, she had to admit that she'd fought unhappiness almost from the day she'd moved in. Never once over the last several weeks had she felt particularly bright, joyous . . . useful.

Never—except when she was with Stuart. And she wondered now if those fleeting moments of joy justified the seemingly endless days of inadequacy and stagnation.

What had Mother said? *If you start sacrificing Mariah now, you may never get her back.*

She and Stuart walked in near silence for several more blocks. Slowly, the roar and echo of unspoken truth deafened her to even the wind and the crunch of their footsteps. She kept waiting for Stuart to finally speak what they both knew, bracing herself against it. He was the one who could face harsh realities, not her. . . .

Finally, when she could barely stand the awful anticipation, she forced his hand by asking, tearily, "We aren't going to marry in the spring, are we Stuart?"

"No, Mariah." Though she'd all but made him say it, the hurt of his quiet words made her want to strike out.

"Your mother said that my selfishness would get you killed."

Stuart stopped so that she would look at him. "You must *never* think that."

His solid, scowling face began to blur before her. "You can't tell me what to do anymore," she whispered miserably.

Stuart began walking again, drawing her with him, breathing deeply. She hoped her family would take their usual route home, and not drive past them with Stuart looking so murderous and her crying.

"The beating wasna your fault either," Stuart insisted stonily. "I earned it by taking liberties with you that weren't mine to have. It was worth it, ten times over."

She began to cry then, finally, great silent sobs that convulsed her shoulders and nearly stole the strength from her legs, and Stuart drew her against him, tight. As if people would not see them. As if she still had a right to his strength.

"My only regret is hurting you," he murmured into her hair. "I'd ne'er take any of it back, except to have not hurt you."

She only cried harder. None of this was his fault. Perhaps she could not grasp the why of their disparate worlds—but she'd finally begun to recognize the power of that disparity. And yet, against all her fine intentions, she found herself tipping her head back, begging him: "Can't we make it work, Stuart? It can be all right if we try hard enough . . . can't it?"

The longing in his warm brown gaze, as he stared back down at her, gave her a fleeting hope. All he had to tell her was that everything would be all right, and she could breathe again, she could think of the future without cringing, she could . . .

She could pretend that the sheep farmers and cattle ranchers didn't hate each other, that she could somehow survive a battle between the two factions. She could pretend that she could live a happy life without the blessings of her family, that he could do the same without the approval of his. She could pretend that the next time Stuart was hurt or beaten, the fear that she'd been responsible would not destroy her. . . .

"People are staring," Stuart murmured, refusing to allow her such delusions, even now. "If we don't start walking again, they may call the law."

Mariah struggled to walk and to catch her breath, to stop her crying, all at the same time. Only when their snow-muffled footsteps took them onto the bridge—their bridge—did Stuart stop again and say the worst words of all. "I'd best go no farther. If I do . . ."

But he did not tell her what he feared he would do, otherwise.

Somehow, she made herself speak without further tears. Stuart deserved that, at least. He deserved at least a fragment of the strength from her that she'd taken from him. "Your mother will want her ring back," she said properly.

Taking off her mitten and drawing the ring from her finger was not the hardest thing she'd ever had to do. It was cold, which made the ring fit loosely anyway.

The hardest thing was unwrapping the plaid-wool muffler from her neck.

"You needn't—" began Stuart, who'd accepted even the ring with reluctance, as if he did not have every right to it.

"I'm not a MacCallum," she reminded him, her voice quavering. "You should have it. I brought it for you."

So Stuart took that, too, looked down at it in his hands. "I wish . . ." he started to say, but fell silent. Stuart had never been one for wishing, after all. That was Mariah's weakness.

She wanted to tell him she was sorry. She wanted to thank him for everything he'd been to her. Such simplistic words felt inadequate for either feeling. So instead, afraid of embarrassing herself if she stayed longer, she turned and all but ran off the bridge and away from him, around the corner to Elizabeth Street, up the walk to her home.

She belonged here, whether she'd forgotten it for awhile or not. She belonged here . . .

And Stuart MacCallum did not.

Stuart, holding the numbness to him just a little longer, slowly followed Mariah's dainty footsteps until he could see her fine, big house, around the corner. He told himself that he worried the Garrisons might not take her back. It was an excuse, of course, and a poor one.

But it let him watch her one last time as she approached the front door, as it opened, as her mother folded her into a tight embrace and drew her inside.

Then the door shut, and she was gone.

He walked back to the church, to his horse. He rode back to his parents' ugly, sprawling, sod-roofed homestead, dismounted, and went inside.

His family, at the Sunday dinner, stared with a kind of morbid expectation in the dim light. Stuart stood just inside the doorway, feeling the numbness beginning to unravel. He remembered loving these people, respecting them, caring what they thought. He suspected someday he would again. But for now . . .

He reached in his pocket and retrieved the ring, approached the table.

"Have some dinner, Stuart," offered his father. "You'll want to warm yourself."

As if he would ever feel warm again, much less here. Stuart slapped the ring onto the table in front of his mother, turned, and began to leave.

But when she said, "You'll find a better woman for it, son," he stopped.

He did not bother to turn. But he said, "I'll never touch that ring again. And if you mean to hear another civil word from me—"

"Stuart," interrupted his father—as well he should. There were lines no man should cross, no matter how provoked.

"Don't expect me for church next week," he said instead, and left. Anything else he had to tell them, he could send word with Dougie.

The numbness had just about worn off. And Stuart had a pain to face, a disappointment in himself and his world both, that he doubted a lifetime would be enough to wear away.

Chapter Nineteen

When she'd returned from her half-year in Europe, Mariah had felt as if she'd never left home—within minutes.

But after not even a month with the MacCallums, as weeks passed, she began to fear she'd lost the ability to truly go home, ever again. At least, not to the storybook life she'd once cherished. Somehow she'd lost that—her certainty that everything would turn out fine, that good prospered and bad failed, and that people who worked hard enough could earn their hearts' desire. That pragmatism was perhaps the last thing Stuart had managed to teach her.

And it still hurt nowhere near as badly as losing him.

She appreciated what she had, of course—all the more for having so nearly renounced it all. And the gaslights, warm home, and pretty clothes counted among the least of Mariah's blessing. Even the festive beauty of Christmas came and went in a meaningless blur . . .

Except that she noticed how Stuart MacCallum no longer attended church services.

No, what Mariah clung to that January were the more simple joys of hearing Elise's infectious laugh, helping cook for her family, listening to Evangeline Taylor play increasingly beautiful piano every Thursday afternoon.

She smuggled the barn-cat and her kittens into the younger girls' bedroom and savored the sight of Kitty's pinched face slowly softening to the wonder of having such clever, dainty creatures climbing over her bed, playing with her braids and stretching high to drink from her water pitcher. When Papa discovered them, Mariah enjoyed watching Elise help their mother sweet-talk him into letting the animals stay. She enjoyed knowing full well that he took as much pleasure in Kitty's rare laugh as anyone . . . and that, after all, kittens were not bear cubs.

Or sheep farmers.

Mariah savored helping her mother use her newfangled sewing machine to make quilts for the needy, taking sleigh rides out to the ranch, and spending long evenings entertaining her "Uncle" Benjamin Cooper, Papa's business partner, with his British wife and their well-behaved son. And she enjoyed realizing how little money had to do with their best blessings.

But despite those joys, it no longer felt like a storybook life because, no matter how pleasant Mariah's world, shadows seemed to lurk just beneath the surface. Elise pouted as often as she laughed, and poor Evangeline Taylor had little prospect of ever having her own piano. Kitty might never be as strong or healthy as her sisters. And as for the beautiful Circle-T Ranch, nestled alongside Goose Creek in the foothills of the Bighorn Mountains . . . *was* it so beautiful?

Mariah was almost sure bullying had nothing to do with the ranch's success. Almost.

Her father's business partner came into the ranch

kitchen late one evening as Mariah, unable to sleep, kneaded dough for the morning's biscuits. She took advantage of their unexpected privacy to ask, "Uncle Benj?"

"Well looky the night owl!" he greeted cheerfully, helping himself to some always-hot, strong coffee. A handsome man for his age, his stylish sideburns and moustache showing the only gray in his otherwise dark hair, Benjamin Cooper was as personable as Mariah's father . . . well, wasn't. Because of that, he handled most of the social responsibilities for the Circle-T.

"Do you know of someone in the area named Johnson? I believe people call him Idaho."

Uncle Benj paused, suddenly alert, coffee cup halfway to his mouth. "I know enough about the feller to know a little gal like you oughtn't, is what I know."

A few months previous, that would have dissuaded Mariah from pursuing the topic. But heartbreak had given her a certain recklessness. "Do you know if he's working for anybody?"

"Most men do, darlin'. Unless they're born wealthy." Uncle Benj grinned at that because *he,* as he liked to remind them, had been born wealthy—before the War between the States, anyhow. And he hadn't done so very badly afterward.

"Do you have any idea . . . Do you know who?"

"I haven't seen as how it was any of my business, Miss Mariah." He stared at her over his coffee cup, surprisingly sober—for him. "Now how do you figure it's any of yours?"

In for a penny . . .

"I've heard rumors that he's trying to start a range war. That he's been hired to run the sheep farmers off, or at least push back the deadline. You and Papa wouldn't let something like that happen, would you? If you knew about it, I mean?"

Still staring, Uncle Benj asked, "Why don't you ask your daddy, darlin?"

And for that, she had no good answer—except, *because I don't want to insult him.*

That, and the even more cowardly, *I'm not sure I want to know.*

By the time February arrived, Stuart had begun to hate the wagon and the claim, both. He wasn't too fond of the sheep, either. For almost as long as he'd dreamed of proving up, he'd pictured doing it with Mariah Garrison beside him. He'd always recognized the impracticality of such fantasies . . . and yet it had added something intangible, something precious to his daily work, to allow himself that little bit of a dream.

Now what did he have left but a hundred and sixty acres of frozen Wyoming plains and just over four hundred stupid sheep?

Sometimes, lying in the dark and feeling lonesome, he considered leaving the Bighorn basin entirely. Dougie could lie about his age and file on the claim, and Stuart could move far away and become something completely different. A sailor. A soldier. A coal miner.

Somebody Mariah might still love . . .

But generally he accepted that he had neither the creativity nor the drive to change his life now. Mariah had been his creativity and his drive both, and he'd let her go. Besides, Stuart's family had tended sheep for generations. He knew sheep; he was good with them. Likely, he'd work sheep until he died.

But often as not, of late, he didn't much care when that was.

First week in February, taking a turn as herder, he had a run-in that near about proved it. The day was clear, sun on snow bright as diamonds, so that he'd rubbed charcoal under his eyes to keep from going snow-blind as he watched his flock. He saw the dogs' and then the goats' heads pop up before he had any other warning of something amiss.

No sound but wind across the plains, goat bells, and the bleating of unconcerned sheep.

No movement but the circling of a hawk.

By the time he saw the rider approaching from the southwest, barely a dark speck against glowing whiteness, Stuart had mounted Pooka—complete with the Winchester scabbarded from the piebald's saddle—and ridden out to meet his visitor.

Once he got close enough to see under the lone man's hat and past another mask of charcoal eye smudges, Stuart wasn't surprised to recognize the well-armed Idaho Johnson himself. Even with his sidearm hidden by his duster, he had a rifle hanging from his saddle, and some looped rope on one side, a coiled bullwhip on the other.

Despite Mariah's optimism, Stuart had known it would come to this sooner or later.

"I reckon you must be lost, Idaho," he called onto the wind, before the gunman even reached him. "This is sheep country."

"That explains the stench," drawled Johnson. "Those damn woolly monsters of yours are stinkin' up the county, MacCallum."

Stuart said, "Not likely. County stank pretty bad when I got here."

Though when a fellow insisted on riding in from downwind . . .

Johnson just stared, the effect all the more unnerving because he'd blacked his eyes down to his weathered cheekbones, like some Sioux warrior. "So why ain't you moved on yet?" he called across the maybe ten-foot space they'd left between them.

Because nobody's had the guts to make me. At that thought, which Stuart barely bit back in time, he realized just how badly he'd taken Mariah's loss. Cowboys said obnoxious, obscene things like that; they liked to throw dust, all snort and no substance. He, however, though maybe not the shiniest coin in the pouch, was not a stupid man . . . with a few recent, painful exceptions.

He was smart enough to raise sheep over cattle or corn, anyhow. And he knew someone like Johnson not only could outshoot him, but likely reserved a seat in hell some time ago.

Just how suicidal was he feeling, to taunt the man?

Instead of daring Johnson to plug him where he sat, Stuart answered more evenly, "Because this is our side of the deadline, that's why."

"Used to be," noted the gunman, unimpressed. "But word is, the deadline's moving."

"Nobody told us it was."

Johnson said, "I'm telling you." Something about his eyes bothered Stuart, and not the blacking. They put him in mind of a fellow he'd once known with a glass eye . . .

Except Johnson had two of 'em, and they obviously worked.

"The deadline's marked by a gulch," Stuart reminded him. Gulches rarely moved.

"Not no more," Johnson insisted. "Good water in that gulch, come spring. Folks done decided to push the deadline back to where folks done started homesteading . . . maybe farther."

Stuart's was the closest homestead.

Rather than argue the obvious, Stuart narrowed his eyes—he had charcoal war paint too, after all—and asked, "What folks?"

Johnson said, "You know what's healthy for you, you'll head those hooved locusts of your'n out that way, quick-like, 'cause folks don't want this range sheep-tainted come summer."

"Without asking the people who live here?"

"Folks I'm talkin' about," noted Johnson, "don't ask."

"The cattle barons," guessed Stuart.

When the gunman smiled, it didn't reach his glassy eyes. "I'll tell 'em you were inquirin'."

Which of course did not answer the question.

"You can also tell them . . ." Stuart took a deep breath, to rein back that suicidal impulse of his again. "Tell them that the deadline stays. While you're at it, you might also want to ask for a raise. If this gets ugly, you're the one risking jail, not them."

"I got money and good lawyers on my side, MacCallum," drawled Johnson, still smiling joylessly. "What have you got?"

Maybe because the mention of lawyers reminded him of Mariah's brother—Old Man Garrison's heir—Stuart felt his own contrariness rearing up again. "Enough sheep to taint the range for cattle on both sides of the deadline, if the dogs and I decide to herd them there."

Johnson shook his head slowly. "You herd them sheep across that gulch, boy, you'd best herd your coffin right along with them, 'cause you'll be needing it."

It bothered Stuart that when he said, "We'll see about that," Johnson merely let the smile into his eyes—finally—before turning his shaggy gray mare off toward the cattle range again.

It rankled him even more that Johnson's smiling eyes, a kind of dead smile but still eerily happy, scared him as nothing else about the encounter had. Once the speck that was the gunman vanished from the white range—and no sooner—Stuart rode back to his own work, his sheep. . . .

And the rankling just got worse. Moving the deadline? Money and lawyers?

Soon Stuart and the dogs were easing the sheep back toward this week's bedding grounds, to leave them with Dougie early. For what good it would do, Stuart meant to report Johnson's open threats to the sheriff, now that the gunman had bothered to make them. Then, if the sheriff didn't care, he meant to go see a couple of cattle barons.

The sons of bitches had already cost him the woman he loved.

"Dear Miss Mariah," greeted Colonel Wright, his drawl even thicker with southern aristocracy than Benj Cooper's, "I hope my months as your guardian allow me to speak frankly?"

That he'd waited until Mariah's family was attending his son's engagement gala at the Sheridan Inn, instead of speaking to her after church all these weeks, weakened his claim of paternal concern. But unlike most of the party guests—the crème de la crème of Wyoming society, who'd wanted nothing to do with her since she'd "betrayed" them—at least the elderly gentleman was speaking at all.

"What is it, Colonel?" Mariah asked, carefully polite.

"Alden is engaged now," he admitted, as if he expected her to bemoan her loss. "And my dear Alice shall be spoken for soon. But although you have made poor decisions, and learned harsh lessons, you must not relinquish hope." He took her gloved hands in his. "Leave Sheridan, Miss Mariah. Have your mother or Lady Cooper take you to Denver, San Francisco, New York. With the blessed veil of anonymity, you may yet find a match to make your fine parents proud."

Staring at him, Mariah remembered her mother insisting that not all women need marry.

"Promise me you will consider it," the Colonel pleaded. "I shall rest easier."

So she lied and said, "I'll . . . consider it. Thank you for your concern."

He squeezed her hands once, nodded his white head—then returned to the people who were ignoring her completely, not speaking to her again for the rest of the night. So be it. Mariah knew she was here only so that her family would attend. And her family was invited so that the

Coopers would attend and the Wrights could boast of entertaining "nobility."

"If one more person curtseys," murmured Benjamin Cooper's wife to Mariah, her cultured accent undermining her repeated explanation of marrying out of any titles, "I may just order them beheaded and have it done with."

To which her husband, coming up behind her, said, "Now darlin', that's not so bad an idea. Execute a few of these waddies, and could be some new land on the market for me and Jacob to buy cheap."

"Anything for the cows, is it?" teased his wife back at him—and Mariah could hardly bear to watch the loving smile Benjamin and Alexandra Cooper shared. It made her feel . . . lost.

"I'll go check on the children," she excused herself, and fled. She had not wanted to come here, but her family insisted. Now, well into the party, the only men she'd danced with were her father, brother, Benj Cooper, and his nine-year-old son Alexander. The only women who spoke to her were her sisters, mother, "Lady" Cooper and . . .

Alice Wright? Perhaps sent by her father, Alice intercepted Mariah long enough to take her hand and say, "Why Mariah, you came." But then, turning away, she wiped her gloved hand on her skirt and whispered something to her mother about "sheep."

As Mariah stared, amazed yet again by people's cruelty, her sister Laurel passed the Wright women with uncharacteristically fond greetings, took both Alice's hands in hers and even kissed the air near Alice's cheek. Then, as she continued to Mariah's side, Laurel wiped her hands slowly down her own dress and murmured, so that only Mariah would hear, "Bitch."

Shocked, Mariah stared at her seventeen-year-old sister—such language was not tolerated in the presence of ladies, much less in their mouths! And yet, when Laurel impishly leaned in and "kiss-kissed" the air by *her* cheek, Mariah found herself fighting a smile of her own.

Failing that, she covered her mouth.

"That's the spirit," whispered Laurel. "Now do you think there are any *real* cowboys here, or were they all born with silver spoons in their mouths like that prissy Alden?" And she sauntered on, a picture of ladylike gentility.

Laurel had earned her cowboy boots back weeks ago, but Mariah knew Papa had trouble ahead of him if he truly thought to mold her into a proper lady. Maybe he would have better luck with Victoria, she thought with a sigh, hurrying on to the safety of the little ones. At least he would have no trouble with Audra. The quiet, strawberry-blonde kept Mariah and the children company, except when young Peter Connors, the banker's son, stole her away to dance.

Mariah tried to enjoy the music, tried not to remember how in love *she'd* been at fourteen . . . or the fact that she and Stuart had never danced together. Not once . . .

Then, between playing "pat-a-cake" with Elise and talking Alexander and Kitty into sharing a shy dance of their own, Mariah began to feel something different about the party. She felt . . . alert. The fine hair on the back of her neck prickled, and she felt suddenly flushed.

Looking around, she could not find a cause for that strange sensation.

"What is it, Mariah?" asked Audra, coming to her side.

Mariah met Audra's concerned gray eyes, so like her own—so like Papa's—and almost said, *something's wrong*. But then Elise tried to pick a fight with Alexander, and the moment ended. Resolving the childish tiff, Mariah did not see Victoria's approach until the fifteen-year-old appeared breathlessly at her side, face alight with her best *I-have-a-secret* expression.

"Mariah! Guess who Papa's talking to, in the hotel lobby!"

Mariah waited, impatient with such games, and Audra said, "To *whom* Papa is talking."

Victoria ignored her. "He came right in, demanding to speak with the ranchers! Of course the desk clerk said no, but he started in anyway—he got as far as the hallway. Then Papa saw him and, well, he got him back to the lobby! And now they're talking." She considered it. "Arguing, more likely."

Audra met Mariah's eyes, obviously as distressed by Victoria's presentation as whatever she might have seen. And true, it was not the sort of thing a fifteen-year-old girl should so clearly know, no matter who was involved. "Where were you, to see all this?" demanded Mariah.

"In the elevator, of course! Mr. O'Sullivan was showing me how to run it—he has such interesting stories about the people who stay here—and I stopped it between floors and . . ."

But Mariah did not hear any more because, flushing again, she suddenly realized who might have stormed into the Sheridan Inn demanding to see ranchers. . . .

Whose presence might have caused the hair at the back of her neck to prickle. . . .

And with whom her father would most certainly be arguing.

"Stuart," she whispered, and the name fit too easily in her mouth, even now.

"You guessed." Victoria looked almost disappointed.

Audra looked downright alarmed. "Mariah's sheep farmer?"

But Mariah did not care what else her sisters had to say. She was already heading for the hotel lobby, reaching the hallway just in time to see Papa's too-stiff back as he strode off, not toward the ballroom but past the fine registration desk, in the direction of the Inn's saloon.

Papa did not drink—but Mariah did not stop to worry

about that. As she reached the lobby itself, the front door was closing. No desk clerk stood behind the counter, which meant nobody to protest when Mariah hurried across the carpeted foyer and out the front door, away from the light and music, onto the verandah—

And with a rush of . . . of *completion* . . . she recognized Stuart striding down the snowy walk toward the street.

The gaslight from the street lamps threw a shadow from his hat across what little of his face was visible. His gloved hands were clenching, as if with frustration—the argument? He held his shoulders stiffly. But even from the back, she recognized every stubborn inch of Stuart.

With every anxious inch of herself, she recognized him. Not that she had any right to recognize him so quickly—or viscerally—anymore. She had no right to him at all.

She hesitated, stray snowflakes blowing onto the verandah to sting her face and neck. Perhaps the proper thing to do was to step back into the Inn and leave him be. She and Stuart were no longer . . . no longer she and Stuart, anymore. He had come looking for ranchers, not her.

Not her. . . .

Mariah's gown was no match to a Wyoming February, nor were her dancing slippers equipped for snow. And how could she bear talking to Stuart again without wanting . . . needing . . .

Without leaving herself more miserable and alone than ever—which was oh, so very miserable and alone.

But she could bear *not* speaking to him even less.

Since whatever occupied his thoughts obviously kept him from feeling any prickles or flushes from her stare, Mariah called, "Stuart?"

His back stiffened. Slowly, he turned—as solid and real as ever. Until this moment, she'd not realized how she'd begun to doubt that he was even real. And here he stood.

"Stuart?" she called again, more softly. Likely he could not even hear her, over the wind that tossed snowflakes across her face and neck, scattered them over her velvet gown.

Then Stuart was striding back to her, shrugging off his great coat as he did so, wrapping it around her even as he gained the porch, two steps at a time. "Pardon my boldness, Miss Garrison," he said, his voice especially husky, "but do you never have a coat?"

"When I do, I don't button it," she told him in a wavering voice, cherishing the sensation of his arms wrapped around her, even if it was just to hold the coat on, the sight of his dark brown eyes frowning down at her, the familiar plaid muffler he wore.

She closed her eyes and savored this one instant with Stuart with an intensity that could never be matched by the simple joys of her sisters' laughs, her mother's quilts, even kittens. And she understood, finally, why she would never feel fully able to go home to her parents again.

That wasn't where Mariah's home was anymore.

Chapter Twenty

When Stuart first saw Mariah at Alden Wright's party, he forgot Idaho Johnson's threats, the sheriff's apathy, his determination to confront those damned cattle ranchers.

Stuart even forgot to breathe. He just stood there in the hallway, snow melting off his coat onto the carpet, and stared across the room at her.

At least her arms and shoulders are covered, he thought dazedly. But he remembered, with an inner lurch, that he no longer had any say in what she covered or did not.

Then he noticed that, despite outshining every other woman in there, Mariah was not dancing. She seemed to be playing with children . . . and garnering ugly looks from other guests. So absorbed were they in eyeing her, nobody had even noticed Stuart's less-welcome approach—except for the desk clerk who'd followed him with protests and ineffectual sleeve-tugs.

"Sir," the man murmured, as if afraid some notable in

the gala beyond would hear him over the orchestra. "I must insist. This is a private party."

Stuart ignored him to glance from one of the guests to another, a completely different kind of anger building in him than that which had brought him here. He recognized the looks they were throwing, like rocks, at Mariah. He'd lived with such looks his entire life.

But he'd given her up in part so that she did not have to!

"Sir!" Tug, tug.

Stuart ached for Mariah to turn, so he could see her face. He'd not seen her in forever. . . .

Then someone noticed him after all.

One moment, Stuart stood in the hallway, watching Mariah. The next, Jacob Garrison was shouldering him bodily back into the lobby, despite his advanced age.

"You get, boy," warned the cattle baron. "Get before I kill you where you stand."

Pulling free of his harsh grasp, Stuart clearly remembered Johnson, the sheriff, and his demands to see the ranchers then. At least he had one rancher's attention. "Don't you hire folks to do your dirty work?"

"Ain't nothin' dirty against the likes of you."

Despite that Johnson had obviously thought that—and the sheriff too, though he hid it better—Garrison's admission actually disappointed Stuart. Maybe he'd been laboring under more of Mariah's hopefulness than he'd thought.

In any case, he'd come to say something.

"You and the others can make any threats you want, but the deadline stays. You won't be bullying *my* sheep off *my* range! And if you're looking for a fight—"

"I'm lookin' for a fight," agreed Garrison, steely and dangerous. When he backed away, it was with spread hands—as if to remove himself from temptation. "But it ain't about sheep. Keep clear of me, boy." He even pointed, "You been warned."

At that, the white-haired rancher strode angrily away,

past the parlor desk and toward the Inn's famous saloon, obviously for a drink.

Rather than stalk after him and pick a fight in a bar—a bar where he'd surely be outnumbered—Stuart stalked out of the Inn with its fancy music and its stench of money and deception. *Not about sheep?* Why else would the man want to kill . . .

He stopped, halfway down the walk, snow swirling lightly around him.

Mariah.

Could Garrison possibly be angry because Stuart ended the engagement with Mariah?

Ridiculous! That, if nothing else, should have won Stuart the rancher's undying gratitude. No, Garrison's threats had to be about the sheep, the deadline, the—

"Stuart?"

And in that moment, sheep and deadlines meant less than nothing.

Stuart knew that stock trailed too far from water would stampede for miles once they smelled it, no matter how far or how dangerous. The sound of his name, in that one precious voice, smelled like water on a dry range . . . and he could no more stop himself from turning and drinking in the sight of Mariah than stop a stampede.

No matter how far or how dangerous.

Her frock was dark green, trimmed with the same gold as her hair, and it looked impossibly soft to the touch—almost as soft as her. Mariah herself, though, put the dress to shame. Thinner than he remembered, but not a dram less stunning, she stood just outside the closed doors to the Inn, occasionally blinking at snow blown under the verandah roof.

Snow. For mercy's sake!

She seemed to say something else, but Stuart didn't hear. He was already giving in to his own need to protect her, to warm her . . . and maybe to wrap his arms around her one more time

Even if it was with a coat.

"Pardon my boldness, Miss Garrison," he apologized, since he had no right to do either. "But do you never have a coat?"

"When I do," said Mariah softly, tipping her head back to better see him, so that her hair spilled across his arm, so that her eyes all but glowed up at him, "I don't button it."

Stuart wanted to hold her like this forever, block out the cold and wind, take care of her . . .

"Well you're a fool not to," he grumbled, freeing one arm long enough to pull open the door, draw her into the hotel's lobby—into the music and lights and luxury, where she belonged.

He expected Mariah to challenge his right to tell her anything. Instead, she admitted, "Maybe I am." Then, to prove it, she tucked her head under his chin, leaned her cheek against his chest, and snuggled into his embrace and his coat, fully as if she belonged there.

As if the world consisted only of them, with no ranchers or fathers or society matrons to discover them at any moment.

Slowly dipping his own head to rest atop her silken curls, breathing in the rare fragrance of her, Stuart tightened his hold on her and allowed himself to briefly wonder: *Didn't it?*

Had Mariah ever been a fool, he was twice one. Impractical or not, this moment meant everything. Her father could kill him. Gunmen could slaughter every sheep he owned. And against this moment, it would mean nothing. His sense hadn't strayed so far as to not realize that at some other time, such things would matter greatly. But right now, unexpectedly holding the woman he thought lost to him forever . . .

Didn't the world consist only of them?

Maybe not. The sharp ring of a bell startled them apart, at least by several inches. The desk clerk had returned to his post and was glaring at the both of them. "This is a respectable place of business," he told them sternly. "There will be none of that!"

Stuart stepped slowly back, unwrapped his coat from Mariah's beautiful gown. They *were* respectable people, after all. They were no longer engaged, not even unofficially, for what had once seemed like good, practical reasons. Those reasons would matter greatly, too. Someday.

But not tonight. And the stricken expression on Mariah's face, as he took his coat back—that meant everything.

He'd honestly thought he could exist without her. But there was nothing practical at all about living such a shadow life either. And he was a sheep farmer in cattle country.

When had he started fearing risks?

Slowly, Stuart laid his coat on one of the lobby's horsehair sofas, followed by his hat, now wet with melted snow. "Will you dance with me, Miss Garrison?" he asked.

"I would love to dance with you, Mr. MacCallum," she whispered to him, suddenly shy.

And before he lost his nerve—before he could remember all the reasons not to—Stuart drew Mariah into his arms in a completely different, equally satisfying posture. The fingertips of his left hand easily found her spine, and whatever that green gown was fashioned from did indeed feel soft as anything—almost anything—he'd known. But the warmth of her back beneath it, that was heaven. With Mariah's gloved hand in his right, the sweep of her skirts brushing against his boots, they easily matched each other's steps, there before the iron-grill elevator.

So *this* was what dancing could be like. This was worth forgetting whatever work clothes he'd worn, whether he'd shaved or not . . . and the room full of ranchers, not twenty feet away, already willing to kill him. This was worth everything, too—and after weeks of nothingness.

Mariah said, "Stuart, I've forgotten why we thought we mustn't . . . why . . ."

The need to remember, for her, tugged at the dream like a rooster's crow. "Oh, lass . . ."

"Please don't remind me. Not just yet."

"I am having difficulty remembering myself."

She smiled, as easy to lead as a lamb to a bottle, and he spun her in a slow circle so that her curls bounced and her skirt flared gently out. "I'm glad."

"But . . ." The slow return of his senses actually hurt, like blood returning to frozen fingers. "They were solid reasons. I can remember that."

The feel of her made his whole body light. The music mesmerized him, almost as much as she did—enough to ignore their growing audience of shocked faces, the way murmuring voices began to intrude on the waltz.

"I don't care," Mariah insisted.

It hurt, to say it. It hurt, to be the strong one. "You will."

"I'll risk it." Never had she looked so determined. "I'll risk anything, Stuart. I just can't be without you anymore. Don't ask me to. *Please* don't—"

"Whist," he murmured, leaning his forehead to hers, tightening his grip on her, good sense and consequences be damned. She must not beg. She must never beg, not for something that was already hers. His pain eased with his capitulation. "I won't, lass. I willna ask it."

"Please . . ."

"I canna." The music stopped, and his feet stopped, but he stood there with his arms around her, his forehead touching hers, his eyes closed and her lavender scent, her presence, keeping him alive. "Marry me, Mariah Garrison. Foolish or nae, dinna let me lose you again. I couldna bear it. I couldna . . ."

In answer, Mariah made a consenting, mewing sound.

And the world became worth living in again.

Partly because of that, and because she was now his to protect again, Stuart made himself look up, to see why the music had not started again in the party beyond.

They were the reason.

Guests crowded the hallway, eyeing them like wolves edging toward a ewe. Stuart saw Mariah's mother pushing through the crowd, saw that Colonel Wright would reach them first.

From the other side of the lobby, toward the saloon, Jacob Garrison approached more slowly, even more dangerous.

Mariah, finally opening her eyes, whispered, "Stuart?"

He drew her closer against him. Maybe he couldn't keep her from being hurt again. But he wasn't about to give up without trying. Never again. Not without trying until his final breath. And she must never, never think he would.

So he said, "It will be all right, lass." And at Mariah's worshipful smile, he even let himself believe that maybe, just maybe, everything would.

As long as the ranchers left him alive to marry her, anyhow.

Stuart said everything would be all right, and Mariah believed him.

Whatever Papa said to him, after giving just enough orders to frighten the party guests—even the scowling Colonel Wright—back to their ballroom, at least they did not come to blows. Not even when it looked very much like it would.

And it did not keep Stuart from returning to Mariah's side as soon as Papa stalked away to fetch the surrey. Despite how her sisters had crowded around her, their voices unable to penetrate the waltz that still sang through her, Stuart drew her quickly down onto a horsehair sofa, settled into one across from her.

"I'll speak to the reverend tomorrow," he promised, leaning his elbows on his knees. *His* voice, Mariah would hear anywhere. "We'll marry as soon as we can, likely within the week."

"But not because we're afraid of changing our minds?" Even as she asked the question, she prayed it would not snap him out of this wonderful, impulsive plan.

Stuart had held her again. He'd danced with her—in the hotel lobby!

And yet . . . to marry, if he weren't quite sure . . .

"I will not change my mind," Stuart assured her, his gaze anchoring her fears as easily as that. "And I'll not ask you to live with my family again. Nor will I face down your father every time I must speak to you."

"Mariah," insisted Audra, low. "People will talk if you marry right away!"

Mariah looked at Stuart, and Stuart looked at Mariah—and then they both quickly looked at something, anything else in the polished lobby. There were after all . . . ways . . .

"It . . ." Stuart cleared his throat, sounding as uncomfortable as Mariah, her face burning, felt. "That is, talk will die down soon enough," he said.

When she dared meet his gaze again, his eyes shone with humor—very, very dark.

When Victoria, watching the road, called, "Papa's here!" Stuart helped Mariah to her feet and kissed her, right in front of her sisters and her mother and everyone. It was a sweet kiss, tender and chaste, but along with his dark eyes, it held a shiver of promise. . . .

"Will you be at church on Sunday?" she asked, clinging to his soft, sheep-farmer hands, afraid to say goodbye ever again.

"I promise," Stuart assured her.

And he was. The weather had grown too cold for him to walk her home—not and talk while he did—but after services he drew her into a corner long enough to say, "Reverend Adams will marry us Thursday afternoon. If . . . ?"

"Of course I still want to!" she insisted. "Don't . . . ?"

He ducked his head. "Part of me fears it's foolishness,"

he admitted, but before she could lose hope, he slanted his intense brown gaze upward and added, "But I'll not listen to it, if it keeps you from me. We'll have trouble, together or apart. I'd leave be together."

She hugged to his arm as tightly as was seemly in a house of God. "Your family will come . . . won't they?"

"Do you want them, then?"

"Of course! And mine . . ." She glanced toward the doorway, where Audra was widening her eyes and beckoning Mariah to hurry. Would her family attend? In the few days since the party, Papa had become as unapproachable as during Stuart and Mariah's first engagement.

"Mine, too," she said firmly, letting him help her into her coat before she followed her sisters out to the family surrey.

Everything would be all right. It had to be.

She drew her mother and father into Papa's den to tell them that she and Stuart meant to wed on Thursday, before she told her sisters. It seemed only respectful.

"Will you stand up with me, Papa?" she asked as he stared. "To give me away?"

For a long, still moment it seemed he would say nothing at all. Finally he spoke. "If you're determined to do this thing," said Papa, "I'll stand with you."

But he shrugged Mother off his arm and left the room.

The moment when Mariah most worried that perhaps, just perhaps, things would not be all right, was when she stood on her father's arm at the back of the church, waiting for the reverend to beckon her forward. Hurried as they'd been, readying her to set up housekeeping in her own home, she'd hired no music, nor had she or her sisters managed decorations.

The church looked so dark and empty!

Mr. and Mrs. MacCallum stood to one side, all nine of their remaining children—even Douglas—with them. Mariah's mother stood to the other side of the aisle, and with Thaddeas, Mariah's five sisters, Uncle Benj and his wife and son, they almost equaled the count of the MacCallums.

Nobody else had come. And the folks who were there disapproved. Was this truly the best way to start her new life?

Papa said, "You've not said vows yet, Mariah Lynn. Say the word; I'll take you home."

But the word *home* confirmed it for her.

"Thank you, Papa," she whispered back, kissing his whiskered cheek—then glanced up front, to where Stuart waited for her. "I love you. But I *am* going home."

Someone began to play piano music, and even before Mariah looked, she recognized the well-practiced piece. Evangeline Taylor had attended her wedding, too.

The minister nodded, and Papa eased Mariah forward, holding to her hand only a moment too long before he allowed her to step to Stuart's side. Then Stuart had her hand in his, instead—

And everything was going to be all right after all. With Stuart beside her in his go-to-meeting suit, his solid, familiar presence calming her nerves even as it sped her pulse, everything was going to be fine.

Everything.

Chapter Twenty-one

Reverend Adams asked, "Who gives this girl to be wed?"

For a long silent moment, Stuart expected the worst. Then Jacob Garrison rasped, "I do."

Mariah, already clutching Stuart's hand so hard that his fingers felt numb, gentled her grip in relief. Not, Stuart thought, that she would ever admit fearing her father's refusal.

After that, the wedding went by without difficulty.

So that everybody could get home before nightfall, the reverend kept the service brief. Stuart vowed himself publicly to Mariah. Mariah vowed herself publicly to Stuart. Before God, their families, and their minister, he slid the gold ring he'd bought that afternoon onto her fourth finger, making her his wife, till death do they part. *Mariah Lynn MacCallum.*

Despite all his concerns, the seeds of hope she'd planted in his life, four long years ago, had sprouted into reality—for better or for worse.

Her mother had pulled him aside before the wedding

and told him that she'd paid for meals and a room at the Inn tonight, "so you both have an evening to get used to this. It's not charity, it's a wedding gift, and it's not for you, it's for Mariah. If she decides she wants her mother, better she decides it in town than out on your homestead."

So as the families left the church—Stuart's almost silent, Mariah's hugging and kissing her as if they would never see her again—at least Stuart had someplace other than his claim to take her. That relieved him more than a little.

Whatever would happen tonight, no matter how shamefully often he'd dreamed of it, scared him some. He could only imagine how Mariah might feel. It eased him considerably to know that if he frightened or, God forbid, hurt her, she had somewhere to run. It would not be the first time a bride reacted that way. . . .

Though he had to wonder if Mariah's family would ease her back to him, like Prissy White's family had her husband—or if they'd just shoot him and have done with it.

Once the new Mr. and Mrs. MacCallum reached their room, and Stuart put down the valises he'd refused to let the bellhop take, he also appreciated that their first night as man and wife would not be in a sheep-wagon . . . no matter how sturdy a sheep-wagon it was. Even if he did fear taking a step in so elegant a chamber as this.

Not that his fine new wife didn't deserve it. And more.

Dark green carpet covered the floor to every corner of its mahogany-paneled walls A huge wardrobe stood against one wall; a carved, mirrored bureau against another. A dressing screen blocked off one corner, and two delicate chairs sat near the gabled window, on either side of a tiny, equally delicate table. "We have steam heat," explained the bellhop, who had insisted on showing them the room even without bags to carry. "The lights are electric, and you operate them over here." He switched the lamps off, then back on, just once. "And the, ahem, necessary rooms are at the end of the hallway, one for the lady and one for the gentleman."

While Mariah hurried to the window to explore their third-floor view, the bellhop nodded meaningfully at Stuart. He then grasped a handle that jutted incongruously from the center of the large wardrobe, then tugged it down just far enough to reveal that, instead of a place for clothes, he'd somehow hidden a bed in there. It embarrassed Stuart that, until that moment, he hadn't noticed the absence of the most significant piece. . . .

That is, the reason they were . . .

He nodded curt thanks to the bellhop, who said, "You folks enjoy your stay, and come down to supper anytime before nine o'clock."

Then he left. Stuart and Mariah were alone together, and for perhaps the first time, they had permission to be. *Married.* From now on, they needed nobody's permission but each other's for anything they meant to do together. The very notion of it felt as implausible to Stuart as just standing in this room did, much less watching Mariah—his wife—looking out at Sheridan.

But here he stood. And there she was.

He tried not to think of the bed behind the wardrobe.

When Mariah said, "Look, you can see the church!" he even came to stand carefully beside her, tried to admire the view himself. It was indeed fine. . . .

But not as fine as the view beside him. Somehow she'd made her hair fall into those neat ringlet curls down the back of her neck again. Against the cold from the window, her body beside him felt warm, and she smelled like spring flowers.

"My family stayed here once," she told him, "when a blizzard blew up during a party. But we stayed on the second floor. The view wasn't as nice—once the snow stopped, I mean."

He wondered if she knew where they hid the bed, then. He wondered what kind of fine places she'd stayed in

Europe. But when she turned to smile up at him, so pretty it about hurt his eyes, all he could think to say was, "Folks eat at nine o'clock at night?"

"We don't have to . . . I mean, do we?" She bit her lip, as if uncertain how much control he had over her, now that he was . . .

They were . . .

"You're hungry?" he asked, unsure of the same thing.

"I was so busy getting ready for the wedding, I didn't eat too much today," she confessed.

Surely he could at least manage to escort her down to dinner without embarrassing either of them—especially since her mother had already paid for it.

He'd managed to buy the gold ring that glittered from the warm, soft hand Mariah laid in his, though. He would buy everything else for her now, too. Surely that would be enough.

"We'll have our dinner now, then," he suggested. "Like normal folks."

"Normal married folks," she reminded him, smiling perhaps too brightly.

As if he could forget that little miracle!

Mariah enjoyed her dinner, even if she and Stuart didn't say much. She enjoyed riding back up in the elevator on his arm, too. Mr. and Mrs. Stuart MacCallum.

Truly, finally, till-death-do-they-part *married!*

Elevators usually made her nervous, but not with Stuart, solid and steady, beside her. Stuart could manage anything. Not only had he married her, he'd even lived long enough for a wedding night. Surely if Papa were going to kill Stuart, he would do it before . . .

Rather, while Mariah was still . . .

Such improper thoughts made her blush. When they got back to their room and found that someone had pulled the Murphy bed down from the wall in their absence, she blushed warmer yet. She almost wished she did not know what would happen next. She loved Stuart, of course; more than she perhaps had a right to. She enjoyed kissing and holding him. But oh . . .

There it sat. A beautifully made bed, half filling the room that they, she and Stuart, were sharing. Together. And before the night was done . . .

Mariah hoped she liked being married as much as she did kissing.

"I suppose we should . . . sit." Stuart glanced toward the chairs by the window. "And talk."

He was a solid young man from a respectable family, sheep farmers or not. His mother had raised a good, clean son. So Mariah obeyed her husband by sitting.

But she deliberately sat on the end of the bed, just to show herself that it didn't scare her. After all, she did so love kissing. . . .

When she peeked up, Stuart was staring at her—and his brown eyes had gotten darker.

"Sometimes, at my house, we sing," she told him quickly. "After dinner, I mean. Or we draw, or write letters. Papa will read the paper. But—we're each other's family now, aren't we?"

Stuart nodded. Then, taking a deep breath, he sat down beside Mariah, facing her slightly.

On the bed.

He even took her hand in his, which made her feel less . . . taut. But they sat very close. "Yes," he said. "You're my wife now. And I'm your husband. Family."

Being wife and husband seemed a great deal weightier when he said it sitting on a bed—and it had already seemed weighty.

"Sometimes we read out of a story paper," she added. "We've been reading a story about a match girl who thinks she's orphaned, and—mind you, we've only read the first two installments—but it's very good. . . ."

Stuart slipped his thick arm slowly around her, so that she could lean back if she wanted. Had there ever been a time when she'd not wanted to be in Stuart's arms?

So why was she sitting so stiffly?

"I dinna subscribe to a paper," he confessed. The touch of brogue in his voice, more than anything, hinted that he too was thinking of more than the little match girl.

"I'm sure—" When Mariah looked up at him, the movement naturally tucked her up against his side. Her . . . bodice . . . even brushed up against him, and she suddenly felt warm in her nice wedding-day dress, and confused, and impatient . . . and perhaps a little scared, at that. But Stuart was the best person to be with when she felt scared, now.

"—my family will lend me theirs, once they're finished," she assured him, leaning a little more surely into the curve of his arm, trying to breathe normally despite a strange, inner trembling. But was it so strange? She'd felt this way kissing him, once or twice. "If you don't mind me borrowing."

She meant to be happy with what he could provide her, after all. Borrowing luxuries from home—rather, from her family—hardly helped do that.

Stuart said, "That's fine."

His eyes looked almost black. He let go of her hand and wrapped his other arm around her as well, so very big . . . so very hers. He leaned closer, took a shy, sweet kiss off her lips.

The next kiss was bolder, the next more brazen yet. Mariah could not tell whose mouth opened first, who caught the other's lips with gently teasing teeth, whose tongue began to explore deeper, clumsy and needy and overwhelming. They sought and granted pleasure in unison and, unlike even during their trysts under the Kissing Bridge, they need not stop.

They weren't under a bridge, after all, but on a bed. And they were married.

She spread her hands behind his neck, filled her palms with his thick hair, his muscular shoulders, the ridge of his ribs under his shirt. He traced her spine, cupped her waist—and as he continued to kiss her, until her lips tingled and her breath rasped in her throat, one big hand slid scandalously further, onto her bottom . . .

And it stayed there!

Mariah, already flushed with the freedom of kissing Stuart all she wanted for once—for always—decided she liked the surprised jolt that hummed through her, liked that he could now touch her . . . places. It felt shockingly good, and not just where his big hand cupped her through her petticoats, but where her bosom crushed so tightly against his chest. It even felt good inside her, where Stuart could not have touched if he wanted to.

They kissed until she'd squirmed onto his lap, until her lips felt wet and swollen and she could barely breathe. And while they kissed, Stuart slowly laid the both of them, still holding to each other, down onto their sides.

On the bed.

Mariah forgot to breathe; for a moment, she even forgot to kiss him. What happened in this bed would change them forever. . . .

And she liked them so much as they were.

"Mariah . . . ?" Stuart's eyebrows leveled with concern. "You don't . . . Do you want to stop?"

But the only thing scarier than what they meant to do was the idea of not doing it, not sealing their marriage . . . not knowing. So Mariah said, "I just don't know what we're supposed to do now. Not . . . exactly."

She'd thought she felt hot before, but her blush proved her wrong.

Stuart stared at her for a long, worried moment. "Shall we get ready . . . to retire?"

Only then did it occur to her that she wasn't the only virgin on this bed. She felt glad of it. Stuart was an honorable man, and he was hers alone.

Mrs. Stuart MacCallum. For better or for worse.

But . . . but his inexperience rather scared her, too. She was so used to his competence. . . .

"All right," she agreed gamely.

Before she got up, Stuart kissed her once again, quickly. He may have been blushing, too.

Mariah changed behind the dressing screen as Stuart readied for bed in the room. Her mother had given her a new nightgown, long-sleeved white flannel in deference to the season, with little blue forget-me-nots embroidered all over it—and a sweetheart neckline. When she first saw it, Mariah had thought it was lovely, but now she wondered if Stuart would be shocked by the absence of a proper collar.

Then again, she wore no unmentionables beneath it, either, and that felt far more shocking, inside and out. Since she could do little about that—according to her basic grasp of the process—Mariah tugged at her neckline a little, hoping it at least covered her collarbone.

"I'll snuff the lights, if you like," suggested Stuart.

"Yes, please." Mariah heard him moving to the door. With a click of the electric switch, the room fell dark. She heard him going back, getting into the bed.

"It's safe now, lass," he offered.

She peeked out from behind the screen—and saw that it wasn't quite safe. Moonlight, reflecting off snow, spilled in the window from sky and ground both. She could see the little table and chairs very clearly. And in the bed . . .

Stuart wasn't completely . . . rather, totally . . .

She could make out the buttons of his union suit. But the way it molded to his chest . . . and his shoulders . . . and his arms . . .

At least he'd pulled the blankets up to his rib cage; he had one knee up, and had turned slightly toward her. She needn't deal with seeing anything under where the soft long johns clung to the curve of his ribs, yet. But its neckline barely covered *his* collarbone, either.

Despite the moonlight, his eyes looked black—and he was most certainly staring at her.

She tried to smile, to show how she trusted him, and stepped out from behind the screen. When Stuart swallowed, she saw the muscles in his chest move.

Mariah waited for . . . what? An invitation into his bed? Wasn't it *their* bed? Then Stuart swallowed again, and softly said, "You're beautiful."

And that was all the invitation she needed. As if the floor were cold instead of carpeted, she scurried across the room and into the bed, pulled the covers quickly up to her shoulders, and turned on her side to look at her husband.

Stuart, she reminded herself firmly. Her Stuart.

Wearing just the union suit, he looked even broader from this angle. Men certainly had bigger shoulders than women did. Where the neckline of his long johns pulled down she saw hair, very like the soft, springy hair that covered his forearms when he rolled up his sleeves.

She wanted to tell him he was beautiful, too, but that did not seem the right word, and she couldn't draw breath for it anyway.

Stuart squinted down at her in concentration for a moment, then turned on his side to face her, and burrowed lower in the bed, so that the blankets covered his shoulders, too. "Better?"

With his face so close, and the shadowy room around them, it was almost like when Mariah and Laurel would stay up late, whispering in their bed. Cozy, really. Mariah nodded.

Then Stuart took a deep breath, and she felt his big hand slide onto her waist—with nothing but her nightgown between it and her—and it was nothing nothing nothing like being in bed with Laurel. She'd never felt this shivery and feverish with Laurel. It was hardly an unpleasant sensation. But neither was it cozy.

"Is that all right, then?" Stuart asked, dark eyes searching hers. Mariah nodded again.

Slowly, he slid his hand around her, onto her back and up, and inched himself a little closer. His inner elbow rested on her hip and his hand cupped her shoulder. He closed his eyes, as if thinking about her shoulder for awhile, and asked, "You'll tell me if it's not all right?"

Would she have to? Mariah nodded anyway. But his eyes were closed, and when he opened them he looked very worried.

"Yes, Stuart," she whispered. "But it won't be, will it? Not all right, I mean?"

While she asked the question, his knee had just started to brush hers, solid under the covers. He quickly drew it back. "I don't know," he confessed softly.

That was not what she wanted to hear. "Oh."

Stuart drew his hand down her arm, where he could stroke her slowly, up and down, in a way that was quite comforting. "Are . . . are you scared of me, lass?"

"No!" The force of her denial startled them both—Stuart's eyes flared wider. Well, she wasn't used to whispering to him from so close yet, now was she? To prove that she wasn't scared of him, Mariah even scooted across the last few inches between them, to cuddle up against him, as she would were they standing. And fully dressed. And not in bed.

Her top half cuddled against him. Stuart blocked her bottom half with his leg.

It felt deliciously wanton, his cotton-clad knee touching her flannel-draped thigh under the very same covers.

"I could *never* be scared of you," she told him, and it was very much the truth, no matter how big he looked in bed. "Not ever. This is just . . ."

"Very new," he suggested, his gaze still caressing her, their noses almost touching. His breath had the same scent to it as his kisses, and she liked it. She also liked how he eased an arm underneath her, so that he could hold her with both arms now.

"Yes," she agreed . . . but it felt a little like lying, and he squinted at her as if he could tell, so she added. "But . . . well . . ."

Stuart waited with his usual, rocklike patience.

"Mother said it may hurt. A little. The first time. And maybe not at all. But it might."

His dark eyes widened—and suddenly did not look quite so dark. "You talked of this with your *mother?*"

"Not about us!" she assured him quickly. "Just . . . in general. She said that if Prissy White's mother had told her what to expect, perhaps things wouldn't have been such a shock that she had to run away home."

Mariah's mother had used terms like "irresponsible" and "child abuse," which seemed uncalled for since Prissy *had* been almost fifteen. But Mariah had more important things to think about. . . .

Like Stuart's big, cotton-clad arms around her, and how close and warm his chest was to her ducked head, and what they were truly talking about.

"I suppose it *would* be more of a shock to a lady," Stuart conceded quietly. "At least menfolk have generally dealt with breeding animals, so . . . um . . ."

He glanced toward the window, as if suddenly interested in the night.

Mariah laughed softly, as amused by the fact that now he seemed to know what he was talking about as by his embarrassment at the delicate topic. "Do you watch them?"

She couldn't quite see if Stuart was blushing, but she thought from the thickness in his voice that he was. "Only—it helps to know what ram has settled what ewe, and . . ."

She waited, and he frowned. "It's part of raising stock, Mariah."

"I know that!" She pushed playfully at his shoulder. His gaze fixed on her face, and she realized she was in fact touching his shoulder, with nothing between her hand and his bare skin but his union suit.

That nice, wanton feeling thrummed through her again. She left her hand where it was, admiring the heat of him, the solidity of his muscle, through the cotton.

"Does it hurt the ewes?" she asked softly.

"Not . . . not that I can tell," he murmured back, watching her eyes. Talking about sheep, Stuart didn't seem anywhere near as uncertain as he had talking about her mother—or even asking if she was all right "The ones who aren't . . . amenable . . . run away from him anyway."

Mariah laughed then. "Like Prissy White!"

Stuart tried very hard not to smile. "You're not making this any easier, lass."

Emboldened by his cheer, she slid her leg over his. "I'm not?"

"Well . . ." Since he already had both arms around her, it wasn't difficult for him to draw her closer, so that her breasts pushed up against where her forearms folded against his shoulders and her lips were in reach of his. "Not very," he admitted, and kissed her again.

It was a long, long kiss . . . bolder than usual, and very nice. Instead of just touching his shoulders, Mariah decided to slide her arms around his ribs, so she could hold him to her, too. That meant that her bosom now pressed satisfyingly against his chest, through the flannel and cotton, and even mid-kiss, Stuart seemed to like that very much. He stretched into the feel of it—

And then the rest of him pressed against her too, and she felt something hard bump against her thigh.

Not some*thing,* she quickly realized, breaking off the kiss to duck her face into his neck again. *Him!* She knew that much.

He caught his breath against her cheek. "Are you—"

"Then what do the sheep do?" she asked quickly, before he could ask if she was all right.

He kissed her cheek, then her cheekbone, then the fine hair in front of her ear. "That's nae a proper topic for conversation," he reminded her huskily.

She butted her nose into the soft spot at the base of his neck. "Stuart!"

"You're sure you want to know?" But as he asked, his lips reached her ear—and he tasted it. When she made a happy sound at how that felt, he nibbled on it.

Mariah was starting to feel far more feverish, inside and out. "Yes, please."

He sighed. But as he kissed down the side of her neck, pulling her even more firmly against all of him—even the hard parts—he murmured, "When he finds a ewe he fancies, the ram lifts a front leg against her side and he talks to her."

As he finished saying this, Stuart managed to lever himself over Mariah slightly, so that she was underneath him while he kissed around the edge of her sweetheart neckline. That meant his cheek rasped enticingly against the curve of her now aching bosom. She found herself wishing the neckline were lower, after all.

"What does he say?" she gasped.

Stuart gave up on her neckline and simply skimmed his cheek across her breasts in a way Mariah thought might very well melt her. "I don't speak sheep, lass," he murmured thickly. When he slid his knee across to the other side of her hip, to better hold himself over her, she felt the hard male part of him slide across her tummy and caught her breath in renewed surprise.

Stuart rested his cheek on her aching breasts for a moment. "Are—?"

"What's it sound like?" she gasped.

He levered himself back up over her, on his hands and knees this time, the blanket skimming off him on either side like great wings. "*What?*"

"The ram, courting the ewe."

He fell onto his side, one leg and one arm still draped possessively across her, and frowned. "Mariah Gar—"

"MacCallum," she reminded him.

Stuart stopped frowning. Then he smiled his quiet, close-mouthed smile.

"MacCallum," he corrected himself. "This is our wedding night. Why are you suddenly so interested in sheep?"

Oh. It seemed a fair question . . . but she was not sure he would like the answer. She would rather he hold her tightly against him and kiss her some more. "Well . . ."

He waited, breathing hard—but gently traced bits of hair from her face as he did. She liked that. "You don't seem so worried when you talk about sheep," she confessed.

Stuart blinked. "I'm not worried," he told her, and oh, she did want to believe that. She licked her lips, and liked how he watched her lick her lips. It made her tingle. But . . .

"But you keep asking if I'm all right," she admitted.

Stuart searched her face. "Ah. Well then . . ."

She waited some more—and while she waited, she decided to see what that tuft of hair, at the collar of his union suit, felt like on her fingertips. It felt like the hair on his arms had, too.

She wondered what other parts of him had hair.

"If anything worries me," he admitted, finally and slowly, "it's that I might hurt you. Or scare you . . ."

"You could never scare me," she reminded him. "*Never,* Stuart. I've always felt safe with you, even . . . even when we're doing something . . ."

Now he waited.

"New," she decided. "I trust you. And now you're my husband . . ."

"Oh, Mariah . . ." He began to stroke her arm again.

"I've wanted you for so long, *I'm* not sure I trust me. Not to hurt you, that is. You said yourself . . ."

"Couldn't we just not do that bit yet?" she suggested. "The bit that hurts?"

His eyes smiled at her, though still. "I'm fairly certain the bit that hurts is the main bit."

"But . . . we like kissing, too," she pointed out, though she felt cowardly for it. Prissy White's mother had told her to lie on her back and think of something pleasant, and it would all be over soon. Despite the derogatory things Mariah's mother had said about that, it did sound like the obedient thing to do.

And yet, the night and Stuart both promised so much more than obedience.

So Mariah added, "And touching. I like it when . . . when we touch each other . . ."

Stuart drew his stroking hand off her fingertips and onto the curve of her hip. And oh, she *did* like that. She liked how his eyes darkened again as he seemed to realize, caressing her hip, that she wore nothing under her nightdress.

When he spoke, it was with great difficulty. "I'm glad you like the kissing," he managed to murmur, and kissed her to prove it. This kiss lasted a long time, while Stuart's tongue tasted Mariah's lips. Something about that made her feel more like melting than ever. When she tasted Stuart's lips with *her* tongue, he moaned slightly—the sound rumbled under his ribs, which were under her hand—so perhaps he felt the same way. When they finished that kiss, he seemed to have a hard time remembering what he was saying.

"And the touching," she prompted—as an extra reminder, she unbuttoned the top button of his union suit and discovered more chest, and more hair, to explore.

Stuart nodded, with a grunt that sounded vaguely affirmative. "But Mariah, I'd be lying if I said I thought I could stay here and . . ."

"And kiss me," she whispered, kissing his chest. He tasted salty. He tasted like Stuart.

"And touch you." Stuart seemed to pant around the words, especially when he slid his hand up and tentatively touched the curve of Mariah's breast, with his hand. Despite the panting, his gaze held hers, and when she smiled, he began to explore a little more. His hand on her breast did surprising but delicious things to her whole body, especially under her nightgown.

"And . . . not . . . do the bit . . ." Stuart gave up trying to talk and kissed her, right there on her breast. Open mouthed. Mariah sighed, very very happy with how that felt.

Her whole middle seemed to be melting, even more than the rest of her, which already felt gooey as sugar candy left out in the sun. Stuart was the sun, and she was the sugar candy. . . .

"Not do the main bit?" she finished for him.

Stuart was fumbling at the buttons of her nightgown. Although she'd thought he would just, well, pull the hem up to do what needed doing, this seemed like both a wanton and wonderful idea. Mariah pushed his clumsy hands away long enough to do it herself, then lay back and let Stuart push open the flannel and kiss her and touch her in ways she'd never dreamed he would, pressing against her with more and more of his weight.

She squirmed under him, his weight felt so good. She wasn't just melting, but aching for something. She explored the hardness of his legs with her feet, and that didn't stop the ache. She ran her hands down his back, memorizing his ribs and spine through his union suit. When Stuart straightened a bit to kiss her mouth some more—his chest hair rasped her breasts and his tongue grew more daring, and she squirmed harder—she cupped his bottom. He pushed against her with the hardness that she knew was supposed to hurt, and that soothed the ache a little.

Maybe she should risk the hurting bit, after all?

Stuart sat up, straddling her, and pushed futilely at the shoulders of her nightgown, too gentle to actually tear it. "Could we . . . ?"

"Take yours off, too," she dared, shocking herself with her boldness. So he unbuttoned his union suit and pushed it off his broad shoulders and his solid arms, while Mariah shrugged her own arms and shoulders out of her nightgown. Stuart swung his weight onto one leg, stripping the rest of the way from his underwear, and Mariah wondered if she should shimmy the rest of the way from her nightgown. . . .

But then she saw Stuart naked, and forgot about everything else.

He *was* beautiful, all solid skin and muscle—and not so hairy after all. His forearms had more hair than his upper arms, and his wide shoulders were smooth. The outside of his chest wasn't hairy, but the middle of it was, all the way down from his neck to his ridged stomach to—

Despite the ache that still twisted through her, hot and anxious, Mariah felt suddenly scared of hurting again.

Stuart stared down at the naked beauty of his wife, shuddering with a barely checked need. Her golden hair spilled over the pillow, her skin dewy from their lovemaking—

And her round, tempting breasts.

He needed her. His whole being reeled with the need to take her, to bury himself in her, to have her, finally, finally, no more waiting—

Until he saw the fear in her eyes, and where she was looking. And she wasn't just his wife, but Mariah. Cursing his own lust—and how desperately he longed to slake it even now—Stuart somehow curled back onto his side again, drew up one leg to protect her from the sight. . . .

From him. No wonder wise couples probably did this clothed and under covers.

Despite a need burning through his lower back—and other places—to get on with it, Stuart cupped Mariah's beautiful face. "Whist," he managed to gasp. "Whist, lass. I am . . . trying . . ."

In fact, he'd never put more effort into anything in his life.

Mariah cuddled up against him, naked and round and soft, and his body almost finished things against the flannel skirt of her nightgown as she whispered, "Can't we kiss some more first? Just a little?"

Stuart closed his eyes to keep from embarrassing himself. He wanted . . .

Needed . . .

He opened his eyes and looked into Mariah's.

"As long as I can stand it," he groaned. But when he kissed her, his mouth and tongue mimicked what his body burned to do. . . .

That did not seem to frighten her. In fact, Mariah responded enthusiastically, held him even more tightly, arched into his touch when he reclaimed her breasts, even when he slid his hand down her back again, to parts lower. He did not mean to be obscene with her, of course, but when his fingers accidentally slipped between her legs, she felt so hot, wet . . .

His eyes burned with tears of real pain. He groaned into her hair. *Mariah,* he kept telling himself. *This is Mariah . . .*

"Stuart," she gasped, squirming against him. She even touched him softly, tentatively—there. And she did not snatch her hand away.

He grit his teeth in a desperate bid of self-control. He'd stood the pain of being beaten. Surely he could stand this.

"What do the ewes do when they're . . . amenable?"

He drew his face away from her flushed neck and looked into her eyes, but this time he wasn't about to ask if she was all right. This time, he would take it on faith. He needed her too badly. He tugged away the last of her nightgown, quickly readjusted himself between her legs to make sure . . .

Stared into her wild yet trusting gray eyes and prayed he was doing this right. . . .

As he began to press into her, wet and hot and more blissfully welcoming than heaven surely could be, Mariah gasped quietly. But God help him, he couldn't stop. Holding her with his gaze, Stuart's prayer became: *It will be all right.*

He moaned with the ecstasy of joining himself with her. But the joy of seeing Mariah smile up at him in surprised delight, arch her back with obvious pleasure, somehow equaled it. . . .

If not in such pressing ways.

Kissing her worshipfully, Stuart followed his body's need to move inside of the tight welcome that was his wife, pushing and holding her, losing himself in her, in her gasps and smiles both. Then he lost everything else, too, released his world into a final, thrusting explosion that poured into her, possessed her in every way a man could. . . .

And he didn't lose his world at all. She was it.

He hoped he did not crush her beneath him, did not hurt her. His thoughts blurred then—shudders, completion, exhaustion—until he was lying on his side again, holding Mariah perhaps too tightly against him, both of them sweated and panting great, heaving breaths. Between gasps, he kissed weakly at whatever part of her was nearest his mouth. She obligingly snuggled in and tipped her face to his, so that part would be her sweet lips.

"Oh lass," he gasped, between kisses.

"It didn't hurt!" she whispered happily. "It just . . . surprised me. Then it was wonderful."

"I love you." He'd thought he loved her more than possible, from the start. But now . . .

Now he knew he couldn't live without her. The thought frightened him, just a little. But with her safe in his arms, he couldn't worry for long.

"I love you, too," she whispered, pillowing her head more comfortably on his upper arm, playing with his chest hair. She still smelled like springtime. *His* springtime.

"Stuart," she whispered, squirming a little.

"What is it, love?" The endearment slipped so easily off his lips, he almost didn't notice.

She lowered her gaze shyly. "I'd like to do that some more. Can we?"

When her mischievous hand slid down his hip to explore the part of him that had frightened her before, the petulant expression on his usually good-natured Mariah, at what she found, made Stuart laugh out loud.

He kissed her fully, nothing held back, and felt stirrings of continued interest himself.

"Give me some time to rest, love, and I will happily oblige," Stuart promised.

And she did, exploring him so happily while she waited that it wasn't long before Stuart felt fully recovered.

And he did, this time somehow pleasing her even more, if her soft cries and shudders were any indication.

They cuddled, whispered, laughed, made love. They talked and planned and kissed slow, tired, happy kisses off each other's lips. By the next morning, Stuart believed that, with Mariah by his side, perhaps everything would be all right, after all.

Everything.

Chapter Twenty-two

February passed with snow and isolation—and Mariah loved being married. Not the least of what she loved was waking up in the frozen dark of the morning, huddled tightly against Stuart in the little bed that spanned the back of his sheep-wagon. Not only did they both somehow fit, but usually she woke to her kitten, Velvet, curled purring against her neck.

"Good morning, Mr. MacCallum," she would whisper, finding Stuart's face with hers, nuzzling him to warm her icy nose.

"Good morning, Mrs. MacCallum," Stuart would whisper back, his voice and his face equally rough. In order to kiss her, he would carefully lift the indignant kitten over to the bench that adjoined their bed, then roll over her, blankets and all. Then he would kiss her, so very thoroughly that she hardly even noticed his cold nose.

Mariah had thought Stuart an excellent kisser before they married. But he'd certainly proven the benefits of constant practice!

Sometimes, if it was early enough, they made love in the dark before starting their day. Too cold to disrobe, they found creative ways to reach hungrily under her gown or into his long johns, to push clothing just far enough aside and warm each other most enjoyably.

Afterward, when it became clear that the day would start with or without them, Stuart would take a bracing breath, slide out of bed, and lunge for the camp stove at the other end of the room. As soon as he'd stoked the fire, his teeth chattering, he would dive back under the covers with Mariah. She would squeal at the cold he brought with him. But she loved lying back against his chest, his arms wrapped tightly around her and his breath misting past her cheek, watching the sky outside their one window—heavily frosted inside and out—grow slowly gray as they waited for the stove to work its wonders.

When Stuart deemed it warm enough, he would dress, add more wood to the fire for her, wrap up against the cold, and go out to check on the animals. Mariah would put on her own coat over her flannel nightgowns—most nights she wore more than one—and her boots, to make breakfast. By the time Stuart climbed back into the wagon, bringing another armful of firewood and a burst of cold with him, she liked to have their high, narrow bed made and the little table, which slid out from under it, extended and neatly set with her good dishes.

By then, the stove nearly glowed red. Stuart would wash and shave while Mariah finished cooking breakfast, smiling when they caught each other's gaze. As they ate, they chatted of pleasant things—chores, plans, family stories. Too soon, after more kisses, Stuart headed out to check on Dougie and the sheep. With the house to herself, Mariah would wash, usually only baring one part of her at a time, before changing into a work dress—and putting her coat back on.

But what was a little cold, against such happiness?

She loved their house. Yes, it was a wagon, but such a

clever one. Not a bit of space was wasted, with drawers and compartments built into both side-benches and under the bed, too. It had a stove, of course, and a water bucket, two lamps, and the glass window. Stuart insulated the bows and canvas with tarpaper, to help keep it snug for the winter. With her kitten for company, and the constant possibility of midday visits from Stuart or her mother, her sisters-in-law, or even Stuart's reserved mother, what else could Mariah want? She finally felt needed. Useful.

Certainly her days weren't easy. Baking with a small, red-hot camp stove and limited ingredients took ingenuity. She kept a sewing needle with her for quick mends, all the time. Wash-day lasted *three* days of her week—clothes could only dry so much outside when they kept freezing, and she had little room to hang them inside. Water must be melted from snow, hauled back out to dump. And perhaps worst of all was having to use a chamber pot, since Stuart could not possibly dig an outhouse for Mariah until the ground thawed.

But chamber pots were warmer than outhouses. Clean snow made for soft wash water, once she finally carried in enough to melt. They kept store-bought soap and lamp oil, which saved work. And she had little fear of Indians, so far from the creeks, or of outlaws, so close to town. If the daytime sometimes got so dark she lit kerosene lanterns for light, or the wind shook the wagon so hard it shattered the icicle columns that had grown to the ground outside, she still knew that Stuart would be home by nightfall and that everything would be all right.

How could it not?

Especially once Stuart and her father finally learned to get along, which could not happen soon enough.

"If Stuart's not welcome for dinner, then I won't come either," she told her father evenly, after church. "I love you, and I miss you, but he's my husband."

Mother stayed silent, but waiting on Mariah's father.

Papa, who had narrowed his eyes at the word "husband," scowled off into the distance and finally said, "Your choice, Mariah Lynn."

And he turned to go get the surrey.

"My choice, to marry him, or my choice to bring him?" insisted Mariah, but Papa only raised one mittened hand to fend off the questions.

Mother smiled and said, "Go!"

But when Mariah told Stuart, he said, "I'll not break bread where I'm not wanted, lass. Go on without me. I'll be back for you by three."

"If you won't go to dinner, neither will I," she insisted. "You're my husband."

And since she wasn't saying it just to manipulate him, that was what happened.

Papa disliked Stuart all the more, to have his "invitation" thrown back in his face. Mother's suggestions, that they alternate Sundays or eat at a restaurant, met with similar protests from one or both of Mariah's menfolk. More often than not, she ended up at the MacCallum family homestead for Sunday dinners, ignoring his mother as stoically as his mother ignored her and sometimes, just sometimes, wondering why Stuart and her father could not do the same.

But she still loved being married.

March passed, with a lot more wind and a little less snow and hints of a slow-coming thaw—and Stuart loved being married. He enjoyed eating the mutton sandwiches Mariah sent with him for lunch. He enjoyed thinking about her, while he and the dogs did their best to guard the sheep from increasingly hungry predators. He enjoyed coming home to a warm, clean wagon.

And he loved the warm, clean woman who met him there.

The practical benefits of a wife—the good food, the clean and mended clothes, the brightness she brought to their home with her curtains and gewgaws—those would have seemed luxuries enough. But that it was Mariah! Through some miracle, the woman he came home to, wrapped his arms around, kissed whenever he could, was really his Mariah.

A much better housekeeper than his mother had predicted, she almost always had dinner waiting for him—though he would gladly have married her even if he'd had to do the cooking himself. Sometimes Dougie would take dinner with them, and Mariah never seemed to mind. Afterward, if they had company, they would sing or tell stories. If he and Mariah were alone, they would use the bed as a sofa and read to each other, or edit the shopping list for their next trip to town, or talk about what kind of house they wanted, when they could afford a house. Best of all was when they went from talking to kissing, kissing to touching, touching to . . .

Well, the main bit. The more weeks passed, the more they discovered pleasures that neither had ever dared imagine on their own—and they saved on kerosene doing it.

Was it sinful to so thoroughly forget himself with his own wife?

Mariah tended a calendar that forbade them, some nights. But he had agreed from the start to avoid the disgrace that talk of an early baby would raise in town—and hoped to be nearer building their house before the first one came. If that meant taking special measures for awhile, so be it. In the meantime, falling asleep with Mariah in his arms, be he physically frustrated or sated, fulfilled Stuart in ways that far surpassed his wary dreams.

Of course, the difficulties with Idaho Johnson still lingered. Since the snows prohibited most grazing, the feud stayed as frozen as the range. But Johnson had threatened Da's herders, too—and they were afraid not to honor that new deadline come spring.

It annoyed Stuart that if the herders, all bachelors, respected an unjust deadline, they left only the three MacCallum men to take the risks. Stuart hadn't cottoned to risk *before* he married. Now that he had a wife of his own, the wife of his dreams, he had far too much to lose.

But nobody was intimidating him off perfectly good grazing land—once there was grass.

Stuart already got his fill of high-handed cattle barons with Mariah's father.

Stuart finally crossed the Garrison's threshold again in late March, though he had to grit his teeth to do it. On Mariah's nineteenth birthday, she asked for *that* as her present. So he went.

Her sisters seemed friendly enough, except for Laurel. Her mother made a fine hostess. And Mariah's pleasure at her family's company, far more than the gifts they piled in front of her, made Stuart's sacrifice more than worthwhile, despite the presence of not one cattle baron but two. Smooth-talking Benj Cooper had been invited as well.

The food was better than his family's. Stuart couldn't help noticing the steam heat, the gas lighting, the kitchen pump, a stove the size of a buggy—and the indoor privy. He couldn't help noticing how faded Mariah's Sunday frock looked beside her sisters'.

Her family, he knew, sent their clothes to a Chinese laundry. . . .

When the girls went briefly upstairs, their father commanded Stuart into his den with a silent tilt of his head. Stuart suspected the older man had also noticed Mariah's degraded lifestyle.

He was right.

"I don't claim to comprehend it," announced the rancher, "but my girl seems set on you."

For a moment, he sounded downright bewildered. But

Stuart searched the man's stern, whiskered face, and figured he must have imagined it.

"Could be why she married me," Stuart suggested evenly.

"I want what's best for her, boy." *As if Stuart didn't?* "Or near as I can manage. So . . ."

For this, he wouldn't even deign to look at his son-in-law. "You've got a job on the Circle-T, if you'll take it."

"What?" Not the best answer, but Stuart honestly couldn't believe what he'd just heard.

Garrison's silence implied that Stuart had, indeed, heard him correctly.

"A job," repeated Stuart, and the rancher nodded curtly.

"On a *cattle* ranch?"

Now Garrison just narrowed his eyes, impatient with Stuart's stupidity, and waited.

Stuart didn't bother to ask, *doing what?* Surely the man realized his insult! Did he think Stuart couldn't provide for Mariah without taking wages from his father-in-law? Did he not care that Stuart was proving up his own claim, for his own land and his own business? Did he somehow believe that Stuart raised sheep merely because nobody had been generous enough to give him the chance to risk his life with big, bony, stupid cows?

Stuart hadn't closed the den door, and from the faint chattering that lilted in, Mariah and her sisters had finished whatever they'd been doing upstairs and were heading back down. For his wife's sake, Stuart did not dare utter what he really wanted to say to Old Man Garrison.

Instead he said, "Thank you, no. But if cattle ranching doesn't work out for you, I could always use another sheepherder."

Then he turned and walked out, before Garrison even had a chance to change expression, past an amused-looking Cooper—and he left as soon as possible.

Stuart loved Mariah. He would give her anything he could afford, and plenty of things he couldn't. But his self-respect, that he could not part with, even if he'd wanted to and even if she'd asked, which, being his Mariah, she did not.

But thanks in part to her father, Stuart had his fill of cattle ranchers even before springtime could revive the hostilities over the free range.

One night in late April, Stuart woke to the sense that something was different. For months of frozen cold, any sound from a coyote's yip to the kitten's mew seemed to crack across the landscape like a rifle shot. What he woke to was the unfamiliarity of . . . softness.

Not softness like Mariah's, cuddled tightly against him in the confines of their bed, or even the fur of her fool cat, curled between them. This was a softness of noise, of breath, of . . . air.

He slid out of bed, and Mariah mumbled sleepy protest. "Whist," he whispered to her, tucking the blankets up around her. He pulled on his boots and coat, cold enough all right.

But somehow, the wrappings didn't seem quite so urgent as usual.

When he stepped outside and listened to the breath of warm, dry wind, he knew why.

Chinook.

As if to confirm it, the crust of snow he stood on broke beneath him, and he fell through to his thighs. Then he laughed.

With the help of the chinook, the thaw was coming fast.

By the time Mariah woke, Stuart had been out three times, watching snow melt into slush. By the time he came in for lunch, the slush was already turning muddy in places.

By the time he got home that night, he'd slung his coat over Pooka's saddle. Mariah had banked the fire in the stove and fixed a cold dinner.

They made love naked for the first time since their wedding night.

Within days, Mariah hated the mud.

"How can you hate mud?" challenged Stuart, home for lunch. Letting Dougie herd the flock, he'd spent most of the morning hauling barrels of water in from his parents' well. Despite an earnest effort to clean up, washing his face and hands, he sat across from her otherwise muddy. The first few days it had seemed boyish. And he couldn't help it. His sheep were muddy. His dogs were muddy. His world was muddy. "Some people, aye. But mud?"

"Because it's everywhere!" she insisted.

Stuart waited, as if she had more to add. But did she need to? At night, the mud froze—but by midday, it was usually mud again. Wet, falling snow sometimes blanketed it, and the world would look clean and beautiful again. Then it would melt into more cold, sticky mud.

Mud dirtied up her once clean floor and benches and even bedclothes. After a single day, she'd given up trying to wash or sweep it away; one trip outside, to let the kitten out or dump the chamber pot, and she might as well have not made the effort. Mud soiled her petticoats and work dresses up to her knees, and this morning it had sucked a shoe right off her foot, stealing buttons in the process. Mariah had knelt in that cold, gluey mud, sifting it through her fingers, and she never did find the last two buttons.

"It's good for us," Stuart assured her, too cheerfully. "Mud brings grass."

She knew that. Her father was a rancher. But, "At the ranch, we had a mud porch."

She hadn't meant to say that, exactly. She'd certainly not meant it as an insult.

When Stuart snapped, "You're not at the ranch," it hurt anyway.

"I'm sorry," he said, almost immediately. Then, looking down, he took another bite of the same mutton stew she'd been serving for weeks. He didn't sound sorry.

"I know I'm not at the ranch," she said, as evenly as she could. "I didn't say I wanted to be."

When Stuart looked back up at her, his jaw had set and his brow furrowed in that stubborn way he had. But as he searched her face, both softened into something closer to real contrition.

"I know, love," he said solemnly, and left his meal to come around their tiny table, kneel beside her on the muddy floor. More than anything else, his calling her "love" relieved the sudden tension of their near-fight. That, and how carefully he took her hands in his. His were clean. He'd even scrubbed under the fingernails for her. "I'm sorry. I ought not have said that."

She knew she wasn't at the ranch. She was too dirty to be at the ranch. She wouldn't ever, ever eat mutton stew at the ranch. . . .

But neither would she have Stuart. Did anything else matter?

When he licked his clean thumb and wiped it tenderly across her cheek, and it came away with more mud, Mariah felt her eyes sting. "I'm sorry," she told him, though she wasn't sure what she was sorry for, except for the horrible sense of . . . of resentment that had risen so sharply between them, no matter how briefly. "I didn't mean to complain."

"Whist," he murmured, continuing to kneel solidly in front of her, to somehow steady her just by watching her eyes, his own so soft, and brown. . . .

But not brown like mud.

"Tell me about the mud porch," he urged, as if he didn't have work to do.

"You don't want to know." But she liked his asking. "Eat your stew before it gets cold."

"You're nae callin' me a liar, are you?" Before they'd married, Stuart only slipped into his parents' brogue when he forgot himself. Over the last few months, he increasingly did it on purpose, when he was feeling playful.

How could she complain about anything, when she not only had Stuart, but a Stuart who loved her so much that he sometimes let her see past his proud self-reliance to his playfulness?

"What if I did?" she teased back.

He scowled in mock threat. "I might have to throw you into the mud."

"You wouldn't!" She tried to snatch her hands free of his—but not very hard.

"I assume," he prompted, "that it's some sort of . . . porch?"

"It's a back room, right off the porch," she explained. "Nobody but guests can use the front door during mud season. We have to come in the back way, and take off their boots, so that not very much mud gets into the rest of the house."

Stuart's eyes widened. "You're family's so well off, you have an entire room for mud?"

"It's used for other things," she protested, laughing. "But not usually during mud season."

"You mean to say, you've been sheltered from the finer qualities of mud, all these years?"

"Finer qualities!"

Kissing her hands, he stood. "Take off your shoes and stockings, and I'll show you."

When she eyed him suspiciously, he scolded her again, but this time in jest. "I *do* have to go back to work soon, lass! Surely you can wait until tonight."

"Stuart!" She would never . . . Yes, she enjoyed it, very much—felt even more warm and excited, now that she understood those feelings, than she had during their trysts. But she was a lady . . .

He smiled his close-mouthed smile at her, brown eyes teasing, and took off his own boots and socks. He rolled up his pants—his legs, she'd discovered early on, were hairy too—and opened the door. "If you mean to let your fine upbringing rob you of one of the joys of springtime, that's your doing," he warned.

Almost immediately, Mariah was taking off her own shoes and stockings to follow him. When her bare feet sank deep, mud squelching up between her toes, she remembered something.

She remembered being very small, playing outside her parents' log cabin. She remembered making mud pies with baby Laurel, and carefully drawing lines of "war paint" on her mother's cheeks, and feeling loved—and happy to be finally out of the cabin. Papa, his whiskers still brown, had ridden up on a big, muddy horse. He'd leaned over and scooped her all the way up onto the saddle in front of him, and told her it would be easier for Mother to have more babies than to clean up the ones she had.

She remembered that her family hadn't always had a mud porch.

And she still felt loved—and happy to be finally out of the wagon, breathing the spring air.

"Look," Stuart urged, pointing toward the mountains. "What do you see?"

And she saw it—the faintest hint of green on the south slopes.

"*Grass!*" she told him, with such enthusiasm that he laughed.

"Aye, love. And grass means fat, healthy sheep."

She held her skirts up to keep them out of the mud as she went to him. When she saw how Stuart started watching her muddy legs, she raised her skirts even higher—over her knees. She loved how wanton she felt, when Stuart's eyes got dark like that just by looking at her.

"And fat, healthy sheep mean wool, and mutton," she guessed.

"And wool and mutton mean money," he agreed, his voice rough.

She reached him, wrapped her arms up around his shoulders, tipped her face up to his in invitation. "And money means my husband can put in the windmill he's been telling me about."

"And perhaps build you a proper house," he added.

"I have a proper house. Perhaps he can purchase his own ram. . . ."

"Mrs. MacCallum!" He narrowed his eyes in shocked amusement. "I thought I'd married myself a lady!"

Ladies, of course, did not speak of rams and breeding any more than of bulls.

Not outside of bed, anyway. And in full daylight. And in the mud!

But Mariah had the hardest time remembering to be a lady, when she had her arms around Stuart. Perhaps he'd been right. Perhaps she did not want to wait until tonight.

Not that she would say so. Not directly.

Well, not outside of bed.

But . . . as dark as Stuart's eyes were getting, she suspected he understood—and even approved. Maybe too much. Kissing each other again, they sank to their knees in the mud. When she raised a hand to Stuart's face, and he pressed his cheek into it—

He also pressed his cheek into an unintentional handful of mud.

"Oh . . . !" she whispered, trying not to laugh.

His eyes narrowed with true warning, now—and she could not possibly get away, bogged down as she was. As Stuart leaned menacingly toward her, she leaned farther back. Then she fell, and he caught her as she did, and they lay together, laughing, in the cold, wet, gluey mud.

But oh, he did have a knack for warming her up. With their mouths already open to laugh, they began to kiss. Stuart's strong arms kept Mariah from sinking further despite the weight of him. The gooey stuff glurped into her hair, slid between her fingers as she held to Stuart's shoulders—as she exalted in his kisses, his hard body over hers—and she thought perhaps she could get to like mud after all . . .

Which was when they heard the gunfire.

Chapter Twenty-three

The rifle shots—two, at first—came from the direction of the flock.

Stuart pulled Mariah to her feet, out of their muddy playground, and said, "Get my rifle."

A third shot cracked across the range. Mariah scrambled to do as she'd been told. While Stuart hurried over to his da's team, another two deliberate shots echoed across the wet range.

Saddle horses being unnecessary for hauling water, Stuart had left Pooka with Dougie. But he'd already unhitched his da's borrowed team from the buckboard before taking lunch. Now he managed to fashion a quick rope bridle despite his slimy hands. He'd mounted Jughead, bareback, by the time Mariah returned with his Winchester and his hat.

"Stuart . . . ?" she said, not as if she truly had a question to ask. More as if she wanted to beg him to stay there with her, or wanted him to tell her everything would be all right.

But sometimes things weren't all right. Stuart took his things. "Stay here," he told her.

She nodded. For the briefest moment as he stared down at Mariah—muddy and worried and more beautiful than anything he'd ever known—Stuart considered not leaving her.

For his flock?

For his brother?!

Angry at the hesitation, he rode away, wishing he had spurs on his muddy heels.

The draft horse made good time, especially once they got to the rockier part of the range, beyond Stuart's claim, where snow still packed to the north side of boulders and deep in cuts. After pulling a loaded wagon through the mire, this was easy work for the great beast.

The crack of several more rapid shots made the ride less easy for Stuart than his horse.

By the time he could see the flock, he knew this was no mere rifle practice. This was real trouble. The sheep were milling, knotting up in a senseless panic. The dogs were excited, instinctively trying to herd but without clear direction as to where; a dangerous situation. Stuart heard another shot from the direction of the gulch, then another, then another. These weren't deliberate, like the first few. These were fast and angry.

Douglas, he thought, relieved to recognize his younger brother's temper in those shots. The fool was emptying his rifle after someone. . . .

Riding closer, Stuart even caught sight of his brother, on Pooka, in the distance.

He also saw the fallen sheep that had so enraged the boy.

Three were clearly dead, two of them head-shot. One more writhed on the ground, struggling weakly for life. Red blood stained muddy gray fleece.

Fighting back fear and rage both, in favor of desperate

reason, Stuart first whistled some basic commands to the dogs—*hold them; don't go anywhere*— then dismounted and went to the struggling wether. The animal, shot in the flank, kept trying dumbly to get back up. Stuart lay his rifle on the rockiest, driest piece of ground in reach, thumbed off his suspenders and pulled his too-muddy shirt up over his head. He pressed it to where blood still oozed from the bullet hole.

The wether—one of last year's lambs, to tell by the earmark—floundered under Stuart's hand. Its dark eyes didn't understand what had happened to it.

To the southwest, in a final staccato of shots, Dougie emptied his rifle.

Still pressing on the wether's wound, hoping to slow the bleeding, Stuart looked toward the other fallen sheep. All three were ewes; two of them ready to lamb in only a few more weeks.

Ready to lamb . . .

Heavy hoofbeats—not from the gulch, but from the direction of the wagon—caught his attention, and he saw Mariah riding up on the other of Da's draft horses.

For a moment, he stared. *He'd told her to stay behind!*

But he also needed her.

"Mariah!" he yelled, and she hurried to his side, slid off the horse's bare back. He showed her what he was doing. "Hold this down. Tight."

She did, her hands sliding over his as they changed places, and Stuart scrambled over to the nearest dead ewe, felt her roundness with expert hands. Nothing.

He moved to the next—and felt faint movement.

He pulled out his knife, even as he heard Dougie riding back on Pooka. Ignoring his brother, Stuart quickly sliced open the dead ewe's stomach and removed the bloody lamb, still in its slimy sac. He cut the cord that would no longer nurture it, noticed how its movements were slowing. He had nothing left to rub it with but his cotton sleeve—long johns didn't come off so easily—but used that over his hand to clear its face of the sac as he stumbled back to Mariah.

He breathed once into the lamb's nose and mouth before kneeling beside his wife. "I need part of that shirt, love."

"Stuart!" exclaimed Dougie, dismounting at their side, rifle still in hand. "I think it was Johnson! He was shooting from behind some boulders, across the deadline!"

Tearing a piece off his muddy shirt, careful not to dislodge Mariah's hands as she fought the strength of the struggling wether, Stuart said, "Give me your shirt, Douglas."

As his brother unbuttoned the top of his comparatively clean shirt, then pulled it up over his head, Stuart did his best to clear the birth sack off the lamb, then breathed into its nose and mouth again. To his relief, it took a breath. Its black eyes winced open, and it wriggled again.

"We didn't even know he was there, until he started shooting!" Dougie continued, modestly stepping out of Mariah's line of sight as he handed his shirt to Stuart. "Then I pulled out the Winchester and started firing back. I think I scared him off!"

Stuart took the offered shirt and began to rub the lamb briskly with practiced hands, managing to dry it some. It struggled more weakly than the wether beside it. Mariah was having a hard time keeping pressure on the older sheep's wound, the way it flailed under her.

"Douglas," said Stuart, less concerned than he might once be about his brother's underwear, "help Mariah. Lass, as soon as he—yes," he continued, as Dougie, still raring to continue his tale, pressed his hands over the muddy bandage. "Here," he offered, and handed over both the lamb and the shirt to his wife. "Likely it won't survive, but if it has any hope, it *must* be kept warm. Beg pardon . . . ," he added, starting to unbutton her dress bodice just as deftly, before he'd even fully thought it out, much less asked permission. She quickly turned away from Dougie. "There," he said, turning the damp, kicking lamb against her thinner camisole, leaving smears of blood and grime on the delicate material, on her even more delicate skin, before pulling her dress bodice futilely around it. "Hold it tight against you while you take it back to the wagon. Keep rubbing it, even once it's dry. If we've any milk, mix it with molasses and water to feed it. Can you do that for me?"

"Of course I can do that!" For a blessed moment, the rage still fighting for his attention eased. There she stood, filthy, bedraggled, and half-dressed, flinching from neither the immodesty nor the horror of the afternoon and taking orders as if he could ask anything of her at all.

That possibility frightened him in totally different ways than everything else.

"Have you got a needle on you?" he asked, instead of kissing her.

"It's . . . here . . ."

Stuart held the lamb to her front for her while she produced a sewing needle from her cuff. Then Stuart did kiss her.

"Thank you, love." Then he turned back to Dougie, wiped off his knife, and set about trying to get the bullet out of the wounded sheep. He heard Mariah riding away; knew that somehow, unassisted, she'd mounted a great draft horse with a newborn lamb in her arms.

How he'd won her, he might never be sure.

"I went after him, of course," Dougie continued, using his full weight to hold the wether still while Stuart worked. "I would have chased him no matter how far he went—maybe back to whoever hired him!—except for the gulch. It's flooded almost to its banks, Stu! It would be death to cross it. Not that I didn't think of trying."

"Not on my horse, I hope," muttered Stuart, concentrating on his bloody task. He used his finger to probe the wound for the bullet. He didn't know if he was helping—but he had to try.

"I thought of it," insisted Dougie, almost unseated off the upset sheep. "Whoa, boy!"

That, and the sound of Da and Kevin riding and hallooing from the northeast, waving at them with raised rifles, gave Stuart an idea. "Bite his ear."

"What?"

"It's something cowboys do to quiet an unbroken horse they mean to ride. Try it!"

He felt his brother's amazement and ignored it. He had no intention of telling Douglas that he'd learned that little tidbit from his wife, the rancher's daughter; nor what pleasant ear-nibbling had led to her telling him. He just readied his knife to ease out the bullet.

Dougie, already using his body and his legs to hold the wether down, leaned closer to its thrashing head and, after getting knocked in the jaw, he bit its ear. Whether from shock or outrage, the animal stopped its bleating and simply lay and panted.

This had the double benefit of calming the sheep and shutting Dougie up.

At least until Da and Kevin reached them.

Stuart got the bullet out, poured canteen water over the wound and sewed it shut with a hair from Pooka's tail, bandaging it tightly with strips of Dougie's shirt. He used the rest of his brother's shirt to bind the animal's feet. Da, shaking his head at the carnage, went quietly about the cruel task of skinning the dead sheep, so that Stuart and Dougie would have something to show for their investment. He might manage some mutton off the head-shot animal, as well.

"Leave one to take to the sheriff," instructed Stuart. "Leave the ewe."

His father nodded. They both knew he meant the one

with her belly still swollen from the lamb that would never be born.

Kevin wanted to stay and listen to Dougie's tales of bravery, instead of starting to unknot the rest of the still milling flock, but Stuart told him to work or leave, so the boy went to work.

"It was Johnson, Da," insisted Dougie. "I'd swear it was Johnson."

"You saw him?" asked the older sheepman.

But there, some of Dougie's bravado faltered. "Only from the back," he admitted.

Noting the blood on his hands, the corpses beside him, Stuart felt his grasp on mere efficiency wavering under rage. "Could you identify the horse?"

"It was too far away, and across a flooded gulch besides." So they had nothing to truly report to the law, at all—except an unidentified gunman off their property shooting four sheep.

"I think I scared him off," announced Dougie—again.

Stuart said, "You didna scare anybody off."

"You weren't here!" Douglas reminded him. "You were home wooing your bride—"

Had he noticed the odd mud patterns on their clothes? Stuart glared him into silence. "I heard the gunfire. Five careful, planned shots. He shot four of our sheep in five tries, from . . . how far away do you think that boulder is?" From where he kneeled, beside the fallen wether, he could barely see the rock amidst the snow-patched land across the gulch. "And he stopped well before you started firing wild," Stuart added.

"I was trying to protect our sheep. Your sheep!"

"You didn't even tell the dogs what to do when you went after him," Stuart reminded him, angrier by the moment. "You know what excited dogs can do, left on their own with the sheep! Even Kevin knows! What if they pushed the flock into the floodwaters?"

His dogs were smart—but they were just dogs, animals with a need for herding sheep that could overwhelm any instinct, whether they knew where to drive the animals or not.

"What would you have done?" demanded Dougie, having heard enough. "You know so much more than me; you're such a better herder. What would you have done differently?"

Stuart knew what he would like to have done differently. He would like to have caught a sign, some hint, that a rider had come within shooting distance of their range. Surely if they stayed alert, he or the dogs could have noticed a flurry of upset birds, heard a faint whicker from the horse, something! He would like to have measured the return fire more carefully. He would like to have given the dogs the commands they needed to guard the flock during the excitement. He would like to realize that of course the gulch would be impassible before deserting the sheep.

But of course, Stuart couldn't know if he would have done any of it.

"I would have been here," he suggested solemnly, and lifted the injured wether. "I'm taking this one to Mariah; I'll be back for the dead ewe."

Appeased, Douglas nodded.

"I'll go with you to the sheriff, lad," said his father. "Not that it'll do us much good."

Likely it would do them no good whatsoever. But Stuart honestly knew no other options, except to do nothing. And that was no option at all.

While Mariah was still tending the baby lamb, Stuart brought the injured wether to her, told her he was going to see the sheriff, put on clean clothes and left again.

She looked around her lovely little home, muddied and bloodied and now housing livestock that was clearly not housetrained, and felt too numb to cry. She'd tried so hard to make this place a nice home for Stuart. For her and Stuart both . . .

"No," she told herself firmly, looking for some last piece of clean material—a sheet or a towel—on which to wipe her face. In desperation, she chose the curtain. "It's all right."

Just saying that helped a great deal.

Someday soon, the mud would dry, the wether would heal, the lamb would grow, and she could clean everything again. Stuart was safe, thank God—and Dougie, and the dogs—and Sheriff Ward would find whoever had done this awful thing and arrest him. Everything would be all right. In the meantime, she had to focus on what she *could* do.

And to Mariah's surprise, she could do a great deal.

While cuddling the lamb to her chest, she found the remedy box her mother had sent with her to her new home. Then, setting the newborn back into the box she'd made for it by the stove, she checked under the poor wether's bandages. After carefully trimming the thick, curly, dirty wool away from the area surrounding its wound, she used a small flask of medicinal liquor to clean it—oh, he did kick at that!—and made a poultice to draw out any sickness. Then she wrapped it with fresh bandages, made from her sheet instead of Stuart's muddy, torn shirt, gave him water to drink in a cooking pot, and turned back to her newborn lamb.

She remembered returning a lamb to Stuart, so long ago when they'd first met under the Kissing Bridge. She'd thought it darling. But this new baby, rescued from its dead mother's womb, won her heart. Far tinier than a newborn foal, it was similarly bony, with long, knobby legs and a surprisingly long tail, and long ears that it held back against its delicate head, as if suspicious of the world. As Stuart had instructed, she rubbed it briskly, though it had dried some time ago, and tempted it into sucking on a rag dipped in formula.

It tried to stand, several times, but had little luck. When she held it tight against her own warmth, like she would a real baby, it kicked at her, sometimes very hard, but she didn't mind. At least it had some fight in it.

The tight, coarse wool that covered all of it but its softer face and legs was the cleanest white she'd ever seen on a sheep, white as the winter snow. It had a wet black nose and black button eyes and long, lovely eyelashes. She thought it as darling as any kitten she'd ever seen. But Velvet, who had taken up temporary residence on the highest shelf and occasionally hissed her displeasure at these new visitors, likely would not agree.

"Maaa?" the lamb said to her, after chewing greedily on the formula-soaked rag. She had to pry its little mouth open to get the cloth back, dip it again. Good lamb. Hungry lamb.

"Mah?" she said back to it, giving it more food, and it snuggled warmly against her and wagged its tail like a puppy as it drank.

She wondered if her family would recognize her, sitting on the floor with a lamb in her lap and a grown sheep lying near the bed, her clothes likely ruined. She wasn't sure she recognized herself. But she took satisfaction in being useful. And if she tended the sheep carefully enough, concentrated on making a simple dinner despite the chaos her home had become, she barely worried about Stuart at all. Barely.

Not so much that she couldn't stand it, anyway.

But when she heard him riding back, too close to sundown, she did not hesitate to put the lamb back into its little box, near the stove for warmth, and hurry outside to meet him. Only when her feet sank into the mud, its increasingly cold wetness glooping up between her toes, did she realize she had never put her shoes back on since their play, so long ago.

"Stuart?"

Swinging easily off of Pooka, Stuart turned, stared for

a tired moment, then opened his arms to her. When she flung her arms around him, he held her extra tight. Then everything truly was all right. She did not care how filthy they were. She did not care what chores waited on them. Stuart was back, and safe, and here with her, and she could stand in his embrace forever and not care about another thing.

Too soon, he kissed her head and eased his hold on her. "I'd best see to the horse, lass," he said, almost an apology.

He sounded tired. His heavy-lidded eyes and quiet mouth seemed lax with weariness.

She kissed his raspy cheek and stepped back from him, to give him room, and he began to pull efficiently at the buckles of his saddle.

"The wether seems to be doing well," she told him. "As far as I can tell, anyway. He stood up once, but when he saw he couldn't go anywhere, he lay back down. When I touch his nose, he doesn't seem much warmer than when you brought him to me. And I've been giving him water." Which she'd regretted, once he stood up. At least she had him on sheets. "But I didn't know what else to feed him, to get his strength up."

Stuart smiled over his shoulder at her, but faintly, as if it took a great deal of effort. "Likely he's never had such coddling in his life."

"Well he deserves it. He *was* shot." She immediately regretted saying that. If Stuart wanted to talk about the shooting he would—wouldn't he?

Instead, he asked, "The bum lamb?"

"Oh, he's adorable! He's been drinking his formula and we've been talking. Not that I speak sheep. But he doesn't seem to mind."

Stuart moved the saddle onto the wagon tongue, which, braced level on a rock, made for a makeshift rail, then began to curry Pooka's back. "It's still alive?"

His tone of surprise worried her. "You thought it wouldn't be?"

"Lambing isn't for several weeks." With a last brush stroke over Pooka's side, he braced his arms across the horse's back, leaned into them and sighed. That worried her even more.

"I have coffee on the stove," she told him hopefully. "And dinner."

Stuart nodded, still bracing himself against Pooka, who looked back and snorted.

Mariah did not like asking questions that scared her. But she looked at Stuart's stiff back, felt the upset flowing off him like waves of heat off coals, and she needed to ease his upset on an even deeper level than she'd needed to mother the lamb. "Are you all right, Stuart?"

"No," he muttered, low.

"What . . . ?" She went to his side, took the curry comb from him, began to brush Pooka herself. "What did Sheriff Ward say?"

"What I expected him to say."

She hadn't realized he'd had particular expectations. She brushed the horse and waited.

"He said," clarified Stuart, "that maybe it was an accident. That maybe it was a hunter, mistaking our sheep for bighorn. That there's nothing he can do about it."

Mariah stopped currying the horse and turned to her husband. "He said *that?*"

Stuart sighed, closed his eyes. "Of course he said that, Mariah."

"He's not even going to ride out to the boulder and look for proof of who did it?"

"No, lass. He's not."

"But . . . Sheriff Ward has always seemed like such a helpful man."

When Stuart opened his eyes, for a moment, he looked at Mariah as if she were stupid. "If you have money, he's a helpful man. If you have cattle."

She reminded herself that he was upset. When she was upset about the mud, and losing buttons off her shoes, she'd said things she hadn't meant to. Of course, seeing three of his sheep murdered, Stuart might misspeak as well.

She hesitated before speaking again herself. He might not take her next suggestion well . . . but she had to ask. "Shall I ask Papa or Thaddeas to talk to him?"

She'd been right. Stuart did not take it well at all—even if all he said was, "No."

"Or . . . I could just ask Papa to look at the boulder himself. He's an excellent track—"

"I said *no,* Mariah!" Stuart took off his hat, looked angrily down at it, then at her. "You think I canna handle it myself? Is that it?"

"You know I don't think that, Stuart," she said, and went back into the wagon. It was foolish, to stand outside in the dusk and chill, giving the animals free rein of their home.

In a little while, Stuart came after her. He'd not only washed his face and hands. He'd taken off the shirt he'd worn to town and stripped the top of his long johns down, so the cotton arms dangled with his suspenders to his knees, and bathed the whole upper half of his body.

"I'm sorry, lass," he said again, wrapping her in his arms from behind as she stirred the stew on the stove. He seemed to be saying that a lot, lately. But when he held her like that with his big, bare arms, propped his chin on her shoulder, she could accept any number of apologies.

"So if the sheriff won't help us, what will we do?" she asked, still stirring the stew.

Stuart's "I don't know" sounded so forlorn, though, that she moved the stew aside and turned around into his beautiful bare chest, his loving arms, instead. She lifted her face to his, happily accepted his kisses, sank against him. And when he drew her to their bed, she lay back and welcomed him into her body as well, even more for the relief it might bring him than the pleasure it would bring her.

Chapter Twenty-four

Evangeline Taylor could not remember ever having a picnic, much less on a sheep farm. She sat quietly on a corner of the bright blanket young Mrs. MacCallum had spread near a bed of wild violets, and marveled at this latest luxury. The cool sweetness of lemonade; the delicacy of little sandwiches with their crusts cut off; these weren't what most amazed her.

Garrison and MacCallum girls alike, from those too young for school to those old enough to marry, laughed and bounded in the May sunshine like Mariah's lambs. Their lightheartedness, though fascinating to watch, awed her. She wasn't sure she even knew *how* to just . . . play. But her greatest source of amazement was that she'd been invited.

It was not as if she and Mariah, despite the delightful winter afternoon they'd spent together, were truly friends . . . were they? Mariah, across the blanket and beside her mother, was four years older, after all. And married. She politely asked after Evangeline's homework, her activities, even the weather. But Evangeline could think of nothing worthwhile to relate. Finally it occurred to her to ask after Mariah—and then she was able to sit back and listen.

Listen, and enjoy the happiness that surrounded her as surely as sunshine, softly chirring insects, and the perfume of grass and wildflowers.

"It was amazing!" Mariah told them, continuing with her tale of her last few weeks as a sheep farmer's wife. "Lambs everywhere! And they're such silly creatures. . . ."

"Oh are they?" Mrs. Garrison pushed the nose of Mariah's own lamb away from her sandwich once again.

"Pet! Behave yourself! Come here and see what I have for you. . . ." Mariah easily distracted the lamb by offering him a bottle of milk. In one bound, the lamb hopped over to her and drank greedily, wagging his stubby little tail so hard he wiggled.

"Well, of course Pet is silly," agreed Mariah, scratching fondly behind the lamb's cottony white ears. "He thinks I'm his mother—at least, that's what Stuart says. Once lambing started in earnest, Pet was too old to be adopted by any of the other ewes. But the other babies are very silly, too. Just last Sunday, something white started to chase us—and it was a lamb! Stuart says likely it fell asleep somewhere and its mother wandered away. Can you imagine a mother leaving her baby like that?"

"No," said Mrs. Garrison simply.

Evangeline could—she'd seen it happen. But she would not say so.

"Sometimes they'll stick their heads right down prairie-dog holes, and the dirt falls in and they get stuck that way until we rescue them. And you've seen how they hop about. No matter what mood I'm in, it always makes me laugh to watch them. Even Stuart smiles."

"Even Stuart?" teased her mother, briefly catching Evangeline's gaze.

Mariah ducked, blushing. "Well . . . he's been around lambs all his life. But he said that even so, spring never lasts long enough."

Little Elise ran up to the blanket with her new playmate, Rose MacCallum, by the hand. "May I have a pet lamb too?"

"No," said Mariah and her mother both, at the same time.

Mariah, thought Evangeline, managed to mention her new husband quite often. Once a woman married, her husband's interests became her own, but this seemed more than that . . . as if she just liked the sound of Stuart's name. She always seemed happy when she mentioned him

Mariah even sounded happy talking about hard work.

"Of course, it wasn't all nice. Some of the lambs died, or were abandoned—Stuart got some of the ewes without babies to adopt those. And then he and Douglas cut off every single lamb's tail! I helped, but I didn't enjoy it; I put the hot pine pitch on all that was left of their little tails. But then I could give them back to their mothers, which was better."

Evangeline supposed it would be.

"Stuart said it had to be done, to keep them clean, but I felt badly anyway. Especially . . ."

But she stopped herself. Mrs. Garrison raised her eyebrows, curious. Evangeline, sensing Mariah's embarrassment, turned to look for Victoria, giving them a moment's privacy.

"Especially the little boy lambs," murmured Mariah to her mother.

"It's the same with bull calves at branding time," whispered Mrs. Garrison. "But you know, the men aren't terribly comfortable about that either. And it does have to be done. Would you like some more lemonade, Evangeline?"

She said that last more loudly, and Evangeline turned back, shook her head.

Mariah said, "They recovered very quickly, though,

and seem happy as ever. Stuart says the hardest part will be shearing. Come Monday, other sheep ranchers will be herding their flocks to Mr.— I mean, to his father's homestead, so that they can work together shearing and dipping them. Stuart says it will take a week!" She waved a fly away. "But at least I won't be feeding all those strange men. Mother MacCallum is in charge of that, and I only have to help."

"If it's anything like roundups," said her mother, "that is a very good thing."

"How did *you* manage feeding so many men, when you first married?" asked Mariah.

Mrs. Garrison said, "I made your father hire a cook, dear."

Mariah looked as startled as Evangeline felt. "Oh!"

Evangeline took a thoughtful sip of her lukewarm lemonade. Mariah's husband, she thought, could not have hired a cook. Mariah had turned her back on money, social status, her father, even a grand house to live in a sheep-wagon.

And yet the wagon, which she'd shown off before heading out to their picnic, was clean and charming—as different from the shanty Evangeline shared with her mother as could be. Mariah had planted a vegetable garden near it, watered by bucket daily. She proudly showed off the well her husband and his brother were digging, even the outhouse they'd built "for her."

Even in lowered circumstances, Mariah had little in common with Evangeline—she still managed to be happy. And yet . . .

It made Evangeline wonder. Could *she* plant a garden outside her mother's shanty? She'd grieved when school ended and the Garrisons moved out to their ranch. Summer stretched endlessly ahead of her, with no visits to lighten her weeks. But—what if she used that extra time to somehow give her home some scrap of the Garrisons' charm?

If Mariah could do it, out on this rocky stretch of range, could Evangeline not at least try?

Then Mrs. Garrison asked, "You're happy, then?" and Mariah MacCallum said. "I have never been happier."

And Evangeline thought: Something is wrong.

Immediately she felt guilty. Who was she to second-guess a respectable woman like Mrs. Stuart MacCallum? And yet she had suspected Stuart and Mariah's relationship before anybody else. Victoria said Evangeline had "good instincts." So was something wrong?

That upset her. If Mariah could not find happiness, then how could Evangeline even hope? She decided to pay attention over the next few weeks, lest she discover what could possibly be troubling her otherwise happy . . . friend?

And in the meantime, looking shyly into her lemonade glass, she ventured to ask, "How did you start your garden?"

Dougie stated—with increasing frequency—that he'd rather Idaho Johnson leave off his slow intimidation and just come gunning for them. But Dougie's courage was that of a temperamental youth, short-fused and impatient. Stuart knew better. He understood that, as long as they kept steady, every week which passed without further assault could be used to *their* benefit as easily as to Johnson's. Every week brought opportunities to improve the claim, birth more lambs—love his wife. Every week meant another letter of protest to his congressman, his senators—even the president.

Stuart doubted anyone in power would care about the plight of the sheep farmers. But Mariah said her mother always wrote them about woman's suffrage and child labor. Stuart figured the powder keg brewing in the Bighorn Basin had to be at least as important as that.

So when spring shearing arrived, Stuart counted it as a qualified victory. Something was going to break, sooner or later. But it wasn't likely to break with dozens of armed men gathered to face it together. And it wasn't, he thought, going to stop him from selling his wool.

Besides, Stuart loved shearing. For a week, Da's usually lonely ranch—this year's gathering ground for sheep men across Sheridan County—would come alive with "wool growers."

"So you can all talk about sheep," assumed Mariah, the night before the shearing would begin. They'd camped the wagon on his da's homestead, and she was choosing which of her work dresses to wear, and with what apron.

Stuart, wearing just his pants over his union suit as he honed the blade of his shears, did not pause in his long, scraping strokes. But he noticed the way Mariah eyed the fading fabric of one dress, testing a sleeve against the inside of a pocket. If they got a good price for wool this year, she could buy dry goods to make a new one.

"It's more than talking business," he tried to explain. "It's almost a . . . kinship. For the rest of the year, the cattlemen make outcasts of us. But for a week or so, we're with our own kind."

Hanging her chosen dress, Mariah stood there in her nightgown, smoothing the fabric for a moment too long. She did not, Stuart noticed, defend the cattlemen as she normally might.

For some reason, that unsettled him, and he put his whetstone aside. "What is it?"

When she turned to him, her gray eyes looked troubled—and lighter than ever in her sun-warmed face. She'd lost weight since their marriage; her face looked slimmer and, despite her generous nightgown, he knew her body had grown leaner with the hard work she'd been doing. Sometimes he worried that she'd gotten in over her head, that he asked too much of her.

And yet she'd never seemed prettier.

"It's just . . . *I'm* not that kind, Stuart," she reminded him. "Not a fellow sheep person."

"You helped with the lambing and docking both!" Perhaps more than she should have.

"But I haven't been made an outcast," she insisted. Then, when he silently challenged that, she added, "Oh, I lost a few friends, but nobody too important. I've been so happy, I've barely noticed if anybody else avoids me. It hasn't mattered."

Except your father, he thought. That, he knew, mattered to her a great deal. But she was not lying to him. He trusted her more than that. She lied only to herself.

"What if your friends don't like me?" insisted Mariah.

Stuart put down the shears—he would just get up earlier tomorrow to finish honing them—and opened his arms to her. She came to him immediately, let him pull her onto his lap.

"How could they not, love?" he asked into her lavender-scented hair. "You're as fine a woman as they can hope to meet. And you're my wife, not just some cattleman's daughter."

She stiffened slightly in his arms. "Just some cattleman's daughter?"

"You know I didna mean it that way," he insisted quickly, kissing sunshine off her throat. "No matter whose daughter you were, you're my Mariah now. That's true enough, isn't it?"

Her hesitation bothered him even more than her faded dress. He leaned back from her. *"Isn't it?"*

The question startled her, as if her thoughts had momentarily strayed. Her mouth made an "o" of indignation. "Of course it's true! Yours now and always. You know that!"

Since he had his arms around her already, it was easy for Stuart to draw her back against him and take a kiss—a hard, deep, possessive kiss that twisted feelings up inside him.

"Aye, Mrs. MacCallum," he agreed huskily, once their

well-matched lips drowsed back from each other's. "I just wanted to make sure you knew it as well."

She leaned near his ear and whispered, "Would you like proof, Mr. MacCallum?"

"It's not necessary," he assured her in an eager whisper. "But greatly appreciated."

So she proceeded to prove it to him in the very best of ways—taking full advantage of the time that Johnson's delaying tactics bought them.

Everyone worked during shearing time. Smaller children carried cups of ginger water to the men doing the actual shearing—loud, sweaty work, full of bleating and laughing male voices and excitement. Older children, careful not to get in the shearers' way, helped carry armfuls of wool to the farmers, who tied it into bundles, then loaded the bundles into enormous sacks. The sacks went into waiting wagons, harnessed to horses half-asleep in the heat.

When Mariah got the chance she liked to watch Stuart shear. Generally, neither the sheep farmers nor their herders did that specialized work. They left it up to a band of skilled men who traveled from farm to farm, relieving the sheep of their heavy winter coats for food and pay. But as Stuart explained, he'd been one of those men for the last five years; that was in part how he'd earned enough to buy the wagon and start his own flock. "I doubt I can still shear a hundred and fifty of the beasts a day," he'd told her. "But I might yet manage an even hundred."

Which she knew meant less paid out to shearers, and more for his and Mariah's future.

Stuart, shearing, more resembled the confident man Mariah made love to at night than the awkward, solemn boy who'd first won her heart. The men worked in a large pen covered by brush for shade. As Stuart tied each animal's legs together and started shearing it, his muscles bulged beneath the clothes he'd quickly sweated through, his brown eyes often crinkled with laughter, and his smiles even showed his teeth. His camaraderie with the other shearers, most of whom he already knew, did resemble a kinship . . . had he been kin to a gregarious group of men, many of them swarthy Basques who spoke an odd language that was neither French nor Spanish.

Euskera, Stuart called it—and though he claimed not to speak it himself, she suspected him of modesty. He could certainly communicate more easily with the sheep-savvy immigrants than he ever had with his own classmates in Sheridan.

Mariah watched his interactions with the other men whenever she could. She fed Pet, and hiked back to their empty claim once a day to tend her garden. But for the most part, she helped her in-laws with the meals. Cooking for almost thirty men started before dawn. Breakfast included pancakes, fried eggs, salt pork. For lunch the men got fried mutton, mounds of potatoes, peas and beans and asparagus, bread and butter, rhubarb pies for dessert. For dinner, they had cold mutton sandwiches on freshly baked bread, pickled cucumbers, tomato relish, boiled eggs, and cake. And, twice a day, the ladies brought out thick coffee with heavy cream, and donuts.

Frying donuts in May filled the kitchen with a thick, sweet heat that made Mariah dizzy and stuck her hair in curls against her face. But it could be no worse than the work of the men outside, especially those men doing the dipping. After the sheep were shorn, these men pushed them into and along a trough of hot, rank "sheep-dip," made of tobacco and sulfur and goodness knew what, to destroy parasites.

No. Though the men's company looked more cheerful than that in the kitchen—thanks to stern Mother MacCallum—Mariah felt thankful to have one of the easier jobs. In fact, despite that only two other wives joined them for the week of shearing, she enjoyed the social occasion it became . . . and how much less alien it seemed to her than she'd feared. She savored the heady sense of making herself useful. She felt pride at the obvious respect Stuart had earned, despite his young age. She hoped that, as a sheep farmer's wife, she could make him proud, too.

The only thing that concerned her was when the sheepmen complained about the cattle ranchers—and how viciously. Not that they did not have cause for complaint!

The first night, the men started by comparing tales of their unusual losses to a cougar, the slaughtered antelope they'd found. But that quickly led to complaints about the ranchers. Idaho Johnson had called on pretty much every sheep farmer and herder in the county, always with the same warning—the cattlemen wanted them out, no matter what.

To Mariah's mounting dismay, Stuart and Dougie were not the only herders to have lost sheep to an unknown riflemen. Between them, almost thirty sheep had died in "warnings."

"Whoever shot at mine panicked 'em so, eleven scattered right off a ridge," spat a man whom Stuart called Joe.

"Rim-rocked," agreed an older man. "Ain't nothing. I knew a feller lost over six hundred head that way."

That led to tales of sheep who'd been "fired," who'd been clubbed to death, who'd been stampeded by wild horses or cattle by the thousands—and townships that almost always protected the ranchers and cowboys who did it.

Of course the stories made Mariah uncomfortable. She hated to hear about the slaughter of any animals, from buffalo to wolves. But the tone in the men's voices, as they talked, upset her even more.

"Is it always the cattlemen who are behind the sheep killing?" she asked Stuart the first night, in bed. But she should not have taken so long to work up the nerve.

"Aye, lass," he managed to murmur. "Since the Indian

wars, leastwise. And the Indians . . ." he yawned, exhausted, "stole them."

But he fell asleep before she could ask more. And they rose so early the next morning, she did not want to waste the few minutes they shared with so unpleasant a topic.

The day ended that way, even so. This time, the sheep men started talking about the Wyoming Stock Growers' Association—an organization formed by the cattlemen some years back—and their fine gentleman's club in Cheyenne, where they supposedly schemed against the sheep farmers, nesters, and small-time ranchers.

Mariah had stayed at the club several times—most recently, on her way to Europe with the Wrights. It was a beautiful, three-story building. The cattlemen who congregated there followed strict rules governing profanity and ungentlemanly behavior. They had always worn suits and treated her with the utmost civility.

In fact, her "uncle" Benjamin Cooper—as charge d'affaires for the Circle-T—stayed there with his wife quite often.

For a shameful moment Mariah, serving more coffee, felt a surge of annoyance. How dare these men in their shirtsleeves, most of them sweaty and some barely able to speak English, find fault with the very gentility to which the ranchers aspired!

Then Stuart held out his coffee cup. As she stiffly filled it, he smiled his special smile for her and mouthed, "Thank you, love."

And Mariah faced the ugliness of her conceit. Stuart was one of these shirtsleeved men.

Someone said they should band together. Another suggested a wool-grower's association. Others started to predict why the Wyoming cattlemen would never allow such a thing.

Mariah felt too ashamed to hear it. She finished pouring coffee, managing smiles and "you're welcomes" to the men who thanked her. And as soon as her pot was empty, she fled to hers and Stuart's wagon.

Four other wagons, almost identical, camped near the MacCallum homestead. She only recognized hers from its placement, the curtains in the window, and the sleeping lamb tied to the wheel. *See, Mariah. You really* are *one of these people.*

How could she possibly think there was anything wrong with that? To do so was to question Stuart, still back at the dinner tables debating the dangers and strengths of organizing against the cattle ranchers. And why shouldn't he be?

Though her papa had a little too much old-time cowboy in him to enjoy the refinement of the Cheyenne Club, he'd belonged to the Wyoming Stock Grower's Association since they'd formed, the year Mariah was born. Why shouldn't the wool growers have that kind of fraternity?

And would the ranchers truly object?

Lighting a lantern, she opened a drawer and withdrew the family photograph she'd carried with her to Europe. She'd spent hours staring at the sepia-toned print. Never before had she seen anything ominous in her father's stern, unsmiling expression. That was just Papa.

The door to the wagon opened and Stuart climbed in. "Mariah? Ma says you left with nary a word, and washing to be done. What's wrong?"

For a moment, Mariah closed her eyes under the weight of too many guilts. "I'm sorry," she said, putting down the picture to face Stuart again. "I'll go help her."

But Stuart didn't move from in front of the door. "She made do without you for years," he insisted, wiping a tired hand down his face. "She'll manage tonight. What is it?"

She loved him for things like that. Stuart had insisted she entertain her mother and their sisters before the chaos of shearing started. Stuart chided her for carrying too much water to her garden alone, mourned the blisters she'd raised on her hands turning soil, clumsily helped her curl her hair for church.

How could she have thought him ignorant or vulgar, even through association? *Why?*

She could never admit such a thing to him. And yet, he had asked her a question. As her husband—her partner, her friend, her lover—he deserved an honest answer.

So she gave him part of one. "My father isn't a bad man, Stuart."

Stuart inhaled with slow understanding—then, as an afterthought, he hooked his thumbs into his suspenders to pull them down his arms. *Ah,* his attitude seemed to suggest. *That's all.* "Nobody mentioned him by name," he said. "They may not even know you're his daughter."

She wondered why he hadn't mentioned it—to keep her from being ostracized by the sheep farmers? Or was he . . .

He wasn't ashamed she was a rancher's daughter, was he?

Mariah bit her lip, wishing she knew how to keep all these awful, ugly thoughts out of her head. Even if Stuart were ashamed of her, it would serve her right.

She watched him fumble tiredly at his shirt buttons with bandaged, work-stiffened hands. Instinctively, she stepped to his side and took over for him. He smiled quiet thanks—that's how exhausted he was, to not protest her assistance—and sat, hard, on the bed so that she could pull his shirt up over his head, too. Then she started unbuttoning his pants.

"Ah, love," murmured Stuart, sinking back into the pillows. "The spirit is willing . . ."

"Don't be vulgar, Stuart MacCallum," she chided, biting back a fond smile—and blinking back guilty tears. "I just want you to rest more comfortably. There—now raise your hips . . ."

Stuart did. But he was still wearing his boots. She

couldn't get his pants off him until she took those off first.

"If you want me to rest comfortably," he yawned, "Come up here where I can hold you."

"One more boot," she insisted. She banged her elbow on the side of the wagon when she freed his second foot. *There!*

She didn't bother taking off her dress. She'd not worn a corset for months, except on Sundays—and Stuart wanted to hold her. She blew out the lamp and climbed into bed, onto him.

At first, she thought he was already asleep. When she kissed him, he did not kiss back—usually a sure sign.

"I love you, Stuart," she told him softly, confused tears stinging her eyes. Even if he did not need to hear it, she did. "Even if I love my papa too."

Stuart moved his arm up, across his cotton-clad chest in search of her. She took his hand and guided it to her waist, and he sighed with seeming contentment. He murmured something that sounded like, "Good."

But as with so much else, too much else, she could not be sure.

Chapter Twenty-five

He had, thought Stuart, been naive. He'd hoped Mariah would eventually relax her hold on past associations, could find happiness simply in being a sheep farmer's wife. His wife.

But if her upset the second night of shearing wasn't enough proof, her increased defensiveness over the next few days was.

Mariah still considered herself a rancher's daughter.

By the third night, Stuart told some of the other men about the letters he'd written. They saw even less hope in outside help than he had. "Governor Richards is a cattleman himself," Joe Allemand scoffed at dinner. "He's no better than Garrison and Cooper and all those other high-and-mighties."

Mariah slammed a platter of potato salad down in front of the sheep farmer. "Jacob Garrison is my father," she said tightly. "I won't hear you speak badly about him *or* Mr. Cooper."

The table fell silent quick enough. "Yes, ma'am," said Joe. "Begging pardon."

Conversation got awful stilted after that, though. And several of the other sheep men gave Stuart looks—half surprise, half reproach—that he would rather have missed.

When Stuart walked Mariah back to their wagon that night, she did not wait for him to admonish her. "I would have done the same thing were a bunch of cattlemen criticizing you," she defended herself softly. "You do believe that, don't you?"

Of course he believed it. Mariah thought the best of everyone—she always had—and he'd never doubted her loyalty . . . just her strength. And perhaps her discernment.

"I hope my behavior lends me less to honest criticism," he noted. Blame it on exhaustion—when she frowned up at him, confused, he clarified. "Mariah, if a man hoards free land, breaks laws, hires gunmen . . . he does open himself to a bit of criticism."

"But you can't be sure *who* has done that—if anyone! On the word of a criminal and a bully, you're willing to hear respected gentlemen slandered?"

Yes, he was, when those so-called "gentlemen" did not have his respect anyway. Even exhausted, Stuart had the wisdom to not say that.

Then, as he helped her into the wagon, Mariah added, "Governor Richards is a very nice man, too." And he wished he'd said it after all. Better that than to feel somehow deficient for not having a personal knowledge of the governor, too!

After that, the men politely held their tongue around Mariah—and increasingly around Stuart. He didn't even find out about the manifesto they meant to publish in the Sheridan newspaper, until the others had drafted it:

To the cattlemen responsible for the harassment to which our sheep and herders have been submitted: We, the undersigned wool growers of Sheridan County, give warning. Any further abuse on our range will be met with the severest repercussions.

"Each of us is going to contribute a hundred dollars from our wool income," explained Dougie, drawing Stuart aside in the shearing pens after the day's work. "So that we can hire us a good lawyer, maybe that Borah fellow who got that sheep killer in Idaho just t'other year."

Stuart had heard of that—despite the reluctance of Wyoming papers to publicize the trial, sheep farmers across the plains had cheered the rare conviction of Diamondfield Jack. And yet, Stuart felt strangely uncomfortable with the whole plan.

Maybe because he didn't live in Idaho.

"We couldn't afford Borah," he said. "The Mormons hired him, 'cause it was Mormon herders killed. Likely all the sheep men in Wyoming couldn't match that kind of money."

"Well we could always hire your brother-in-law," said Dougie, folding his dip-stained arms. "Think Thaddeas Garrison would take on his father for us?"

Stuart said, low, "You may decide with your temper, Douglas MacCallum, but I'll do nothing from pride alone. Let me think on it."

Dougie said, "Da already agreed to sign, and me too. You'd be the only one."

"Then I'd be the only one. Let me think on it."

Dougie nodded reluctantly. When Stuart asked, "Where did you mean to come up with a hundred dollars, if I don't join?" his brother even had the grace to look away.

"I thought so," said Stuart.

He pieced through the declaration's wording, more than once. No cattlemen were accused by name. Even the "harassments" were left vague enough that whoever had hired Johnson could, if willing, save face by just paying the man off and sending him on his way. The "manifesto" still made him uncomfortable—like throwing down a gauntlet. And yet . . .

Why *should* the sheep farmer always wait passively for the cattlemen to make the next move—and the next, and the next? He had no better ideas himself. Sooner or later something would break. Better that it break on their say-so than without warning. So Stuart signed.

And he did not tell Mariah anything until he did.

"You accuse them of *harassing* you?" she exclaimed that night in their wagon—and with honest surprise. If Stuart had been naive to hope she would forget her ties to cattle, perhaps he'd caught the failing from her. He'd never met a more naive woman than his wife.

"None of them personally," he reminded her.

"What if they all take it personally?" Then, more softly, she said, "No, Pet! Behave yourself!" Somehow, she saw no hypocrisy in defending the ranchers and bottle-feeding the lamb they'd orphaned at the same time.

Or else she still thought the cattlemen innocent of the shooting.

"What if they do, Mariah?" challenged Stuart. "They're all gentlemen, aren't they? So we have nothing to worry about."

She looked up at him, cuddling the wiggling lamb on her lap, and asked, "Are you angry with me?" And Stuart wasn't sure what to say. Little though he liked it, he *was* angry. But at her?

"Could be I wish you were right," he admitted finally. "Could be I don't want to see you hurt when you're proven wrong."

Mariah went back to feeding her bum lamb—but he recognized the stubborn furrow between her brows. She did not think herself wrong.

Naive.

She even asked, as over a dozen armed men left to

escort the wool wagons to the depot, why they needed so many rifles just to sell their wool.

"As long as we have them, we won't need them," Stuart assured her patiently.

But he hated to think what would happen to their biggest profits of the year if the sheep farmers indulged in the kind of blind faith that Mariah Garrison MacCallum had.

Mariah hated to think what the world would be like should Stuart's suspicions about all the ranchers—and the townsfolk who he insisted supported them—prove true. Who would *want* to live in so ugly a world as that?

And yet . . . if he were right . . .

Then she had.

The very thought made her stomach hurt, so she tried not to think it. But how could she not? Stuart seemed so certain.

Mariah even found herself "chewing the matter over," as her papa would say, at church. Colonel Wright was there, with his wife and daughter. And of course her father was there, though Uncle Benj and his family had gone to Cheyenne. Surely people who attended the same *church* would not plot against each other! But Mr. Wulfjen ran most of his cattle in Montana; Mr. Irvine in Johnson County. Why would they risk anything for Stuart's grazing range?

Much as she loved Stuart, he had to be wrong.

"Are you all right?" murmured Stuart, low, after services. "You seemed distracted."

Mariah searched his solemn face for the comfort she usually found there. "Aren't you?"

Stuart's brown eyes softened at that, and he brushed his fingers across her cheek. "It's a benefit to not putting too much faith in people, love. I needn't fear such disappointment."

She liked being called "love," but did not like his answer. She wanted to put faith in people. She would never have fallen in love with him, married him, had she not put faith in people.

Hadn't he put his faith in her?

"Mariah," he protested, from her expression alone. But the arrival of her family distracted them—her mother's quick hug and kiss, her sisters' excited reports of their week on the ranch. Victoria would be assisting Thaddeas in his law office. Laurel meant to prove up her own homestead. Audra had nearly run out of books to read. Mother thought Kitty needed spectacles.

They distracted Mariah so thoroughly that she did not notice anything amiss until they began to kiss her good-bye. Only once they left did Mariah notice Stuart, expression hard, staring past her.

"MacCallum." Her father's voice sounded more like an accusation than a greeting.

Turning, Mariah didn't dare greet him, either. She'd seen Papa stand stiff and disapproving like this before—when dealing with Stuart, in fact. His steely eyes did not even acknowledge her. They were too busy rebuking Stuart, without Papa saying a word.

"Mr. Garrison," greeted Stuart, careful to give her father basic respect—if not a bit more.

"You boys made slanderous claims, yesterday's newspaper," Papa drawled. "Can't say as I've heard tell of . . . abuse."

He made the word sound foolish, made Stuart sound foolish.

"Papa," protested Mariah, but Stuart put a hand on her shoulder and she stopped.

Reluctantly.

"What would you call someone shooting four of my sheep?" Stuart asked. "Shopkeepers denying me credit. A gunman riding out to my claim with threats?"

"Sounds like you're not too popular," Papa said. Then, as if that weren't bad enough, he added, "You're the one what owns sheep."

As if that invited trouble? Mariah couldn't stand by for that, even if Stuart was squeezing her shoulder. "Papa! You don't mean that!"

Finally, her father looked at her. It wasn't the way she remembered, with affection warming the steel gray of his eyes, softening his weathered cowboy face. In fact, she couldn't read his expression at all. "Boarded the train, Mariah Lynn," he said solemnly. "No gettin' off."

Then he touched his hat to her—not to Stuart—and turned to go drive the rest of his family back to their cattle ranch. Mariah stared after him and felt hurt. He didn't understand, she decided quickly. Given the choice between suspecting his fellow ranchers and discounting Stuart's complaints, of course he would choose the latter. She preferred the latter!

But at least she tried to understand Stuart's concerns, even when she hoped he was wrong.

Stuart said, low, "Mariah." She thought that if he said something rude about her father, no matter how justified, she would start to cry. She might start crying even without that impetus.

"What?" she asked, unable to meet his gaze.

Stuart said, "My folks are about ready to head back." After months of marriage, Mariah still rode to church in his parents' wagon. Someday, they would have their own wagon. In fact, Stuart might have been able to buy one with the hundred dollars he'd contributed to the sheep farmers' legal fund.

She took his hand and held it tight, hoping he could tell how grateful she felt for his discretion. For him. No matter how Colonel Wright, passing them as he left church, tutted his disappointment at how blatantly she'd ignored his advice for marrying "well."

Stuart squeezed her hand in return. "Let's go home," he said. And she was glad to. Really.

She only wished she didn't have to bring Stuart's continued suspicions home with them.

Stuart would never have believed even Mariah could still defend her father, not after the cattle baron's high-handed speech—*scolding*—outside of the church.

Then again, he was the one who valued reality over mere belief. In some ways, Mariah had adapted beautifully to being a sheep farmer's wife. Her garden, if not flourishing, at least survived. She had a creative way with her meals, especially with edible greens she found growing wild. She even showed a talent doctoring to Stuart, Dougie, and the sheep. She did not flinch from hard work—in fact, she took innocent pleasure in almost everything.

Maybe that had always worried him. But since shearing, Stuart found himself increasingly concerned.

Too much of Mariah's happiness stemmed from her inability to accept hard truths. She planted tomatoes, peanuts, watermelon—things that weren't likely to ripen or even grow at so high an altitude—as if certain they might yet grow for *her.* She spoke glowingly of Stuart's future, as if he might someday become a sheep baron to equal her father—did she truly realize who she'd married, or was she in love with a fantasy she'd created around him?

And she would still rather he be the victim of vicious mischief, or Johnson alone, than a united effort by the cattlemen. Stuart thought he'd resigned himself to her optimism.

But one of them had to be reasonable.

"You'd best get back to the wagon, lass," he warned several days later, when she and her bum lamb brought him lunch. Stuart was herding while Dougie took his turn at well-digging. "I don't want you so near the deadline."

"I don't look anything like a sheep," she reassured him, opening her basket and spreading the blanket on a slope, where they could comfortably keep watch on the flock. And in her faded calico dress and straw hat, tied on with a big bow under her chin, indeed she did not. "And I brought lunch for the both of us. Besides, now that the newspaper published your warning, nothing else will go wrong, will it?"

Would that it were so simple. True, the week since shearing had passed without real trouble. The day was clear, with both dogs on guard. And herding *was* quiet, lonesome work . . .

Perhaps Mariah's ranching connections were a blessing. Not even a hired gun would dare hurt a good woman, especially not the daughter of an employer, despite Garrison's words about Mariah living with her own decisions.

Stuart sat reluctantly on the blanket and accepted the sandwich she gave him. Cucumber. Who else would think of making a sandwich out of cucumbers?

"I was thinking," said Mariah, kneeling into a graceful pool of skirts beside him. "If Mr. Johnson *was* hired by a rancher, perhaps it's Alden Wright. I don't like him."

Stuart asked, "Why not?" He thought she liked everybody.

"He's . . ." Her brow furrowed as she tried to put words to so foreign a concept as suspicion. "He cares about the wrong things. Money, and appearances, and connections."

Amused, Stuart tucked a strand of sun-streaked golden hair back behind the green bow that tied her pert straw hat—the "treat" she'd chosen when they deposited their wool-draft. He'd gotten good money—from his perspective. But hers? "Everyone cares about those things, lass."

"Well yes, somewhat," she agreed, dipping her gaze at his teasing. "But Alden prioritizes them. Alice, too. Do you know, when we were in France, the Colonel spilled wine on his pants and had to buy a pair of readymades to get through the afternoon. And Alice insisted they iron out the creases, so that they wouldn't look off-the-shelf. There were little children in the street, begging for *centimes,* and the Colonel paid an extra *franc* for ironing!"

The last thing Stuart wanted to hear about was Mariah's tour of Europe. "Alden Wright is in St. Louis," he reminded her shortly, dividing his attention between her and the flock.

"He could be sending letters to Mr. Johnson," she insisted, lifting an earthenware jug from her basket. "Or telegrams."

"And risk people knowing what he's up to?" He shook his head while he chewed and swallowed a bite of cucumber sandwich. "If it came to a trial, the telegrapher or the postmaster could give witness against him."

"Against a sheep farmer?" challenged Mariah, using his own argument against him. "And here I thought the town was owned by the cattle interests."

Stuart narrowed his eyes in challenge. "And I thought you didn't believe the cattlemen were behind this in the first place."

She hugged her skirted knees and frowned. "Well . . . maybe it's the railroads."

"Johnson said it was the cattlemen to throw me off his trail?" guessed Stuart drily.

"You can't know he didn't!" she insisted.

Stuart had never told her that her father had threatened to kill him, back at the Sheridan Inn. He still didn't. It would hurt her, and he did not have it in him to hurt her, especially not on a lovely spring day like this. She wore her green-sprig calico which, faded or not, made him think of tender, growing things. In contrast to her hat, she wore no shoes, and her bare feet and ankles looked almost as tempting as the food she'd brought.

A great many herders napped during long, summer afternoons. Were Johnson not still in town, Stuart might have left the dogs on guard and moved both blanket and wife into higher grass. But he would not let her optimism seduce him.

In fact, skimming his gaze across the flock yet again, Stuart saw the goats' heads come up—and freeze. Instantly alert, he murmured, "Stay down," and stood.

At first, he saw nothing. He picked up his Winchester anyway.

"Stuart?" asked Mariah.

"It's all right," he assured her automatically—then silently cursed himself. That was what she'd wanted to hear, what he wanted to tell her. But what if it wasn't all right?

At least Mariah stayed down.

The dogs were alert now, too. Then Pooka's head came up from where he'd been grazing, and he nickered. Stuart thought he heard a horse whinny back. Then he saw horse and rider both top the rise, riding southwest as if distantly following the gulch-delineated deadline.

"A rider," he told Mariah quietly, not taking his eyes off the stranger. . . .

Until the stranger waved once. Then, squinting, Stuart recognized him. "It's that cowboy who used to follow us home from church."

"Dawson?" Before he could make her stay, Mariah stood, too. "It's Dawson!" And she stood on her toes and waved cheerfully, as if the man had been a friend to them. As if he'd not stood by and watched Stuart beaten, all those months ago.

But Mariah did not know of Dawson's involvement in that, either. Stuart hadn't realized until this afternoon how much he'd kept from his wife. Was it for her own good—or his?

Dawson waved, but kicked his roan horse into a canter and rode on.

"He's not stopping," she protested, disappointed by the very thing that had Stuart relieved. "That's not very neighborly."

"Likely he has work to do." Stuart wondered darkly just what that work might be, so near his own range. Apparently, this time, so did his wife.

"Papa's cattle don't normally come this far out . . ." She seemed to remember, then, that some of the cattle had been straying onto Stuart's side of the deadline—and Stuart's certainty that they'd been driven. Her frown certainly didn't indicate happy thoughts. "I mean . . ."

"Mariah," warned Stuart, lowering his rifle to the grass. "You knew there might be trouble when we married."

"Dawson's a nice man," Mariah insisted.

"Could be he is." Though Stuart doubted it. "But some men will do things for money that they'd not otherwise."

She said, slowly, "But Dawson works for my father."

Stuart didn't bother to say anything else. He could easily have been talking about her father in the first place. She seemed to sense that.

"Stuart," insisted Mariah, "I know you don't like my father any more than he likes you, and you've got reason. But . . . won't you even consider that he could be a good man?" A pair of butterflies darted erratically by her, but she did not seem to notice. She was too busy scowling at Stuart.

He'd kept so much from her already. "I don't know," he admitted, rather than simply denying her hopes right there. When he returned to the blanket, rifle and all, his wife didn't follow, so he added, "He's a cattle baron, Mariah. Asking me to trust a cattle baron is like . . . like asking a Union soldier to trust a Johnny Reb."

It occurred to him that if her father had fought in the Civil War—and he was of the right age—Garrison may have fought for the South, while Stuart's grandfather had defended the North. But what else could he say? He and her father already mixed like . . . like cattle and sheep. For Mariah's sake, he endured the man. Even *she* could ask no more than that, could she?

From the injured way she watched him, still not returning to the blanket, perhaps she could. "If you don't trust him even a little," she said, slowly, "it's as if you don't trust half of me."

"You know I trust you!" he scoffed.

Except perhaps when it came to seeing ugly truths.

"Mariah," he insisted. "Consider the consequences. Were I to trust your father, and you be wrong about him—I know you think you aren't, but just perhaps—it could get me killed."

Her gray eyes flashed. "That's a terrible thing to say!"

"I should hope so!"

But despite what he thought to be a remarkably astute argument, she set her jaw with increasingly familiar stubbornness. "Maybe I should go back to the wagon," she decided—to avoid arguing with him? Or just to avoid him? "Where's Pet?"

Stuart shook his head, fell tiredly back on the blanket. This too would pass, he reminded himself—which felt suspiciously like telling himself that everything would be all right. Could it be that any other possibility scared him so deeply, he just couldn't consider it?

"He ran off with some of the other lambs," he told her, staring up at the clouds. She would find her little bummer easily enough—not only did the beastie come when called, but she'd tied a bright yellow ribbon around its neck and refused to let Stu earmark it.

That was one lamb Stuart already knew would not get culled out for market in the fall . . . even if sparing it did reinforce his wife's too-hopeful outlook on the world. Likely that made him as guilty for that as her, now that Stuart thought of it. That, and so much else.

He scowled up at the clouds until it occurred to him that she'd stopped calling for Pet.

Slowly, Stuart sat up. Something felt wrong. The goats' heads had come up, and the burro's. And Mariah stood very, very still—too still—at the edge of the gulch, a yellow ribbon dangling from her hand, looking down.

Over the months, Stuart had come to know her body almost as well as his own. He could see the fear her posture now telegraphed, as surely as if she'd screamed. That she hadn't screamed, but only stared, terrified him.

Stuart grabbed his rifle and ran for her.

Chapter Twenty-six

Now Mariah understood why a sheep in trouble would stand silent and absolutely still. Ribbon dangling uselessly from her hand, she stared into the gulch, at the mountain lion crouched over the bloody lamb.

For a long, shocked moment, she could not move—could not even think.

She just *saw.* She saw the horrible, still lump of meat and wool that had once been a baby sheep. She saw the tawny animal that had killed it, all sharp low angles and slit eyes and ears pressed back against its head. It growled, a low rumble in its throat, eerily similar to how Velvet sometimes growled at Pet—but so much worse. Then it screamed at her, bloody teeth and fury. It sank back into itself, broad head lowering into its bony shoulders, muscles bunching into a pounce.

And all Mariah could think was, where was the goat?

She'd heard a bell. She'd expected a goat, probably some sheep. And now, unmoving, she stared into the slit eyes of a killer—

The crack of a rifle, beside her, snapped her out of the strange paralysis. She screamed and spun to see Stuart eject a cartridge. As beautifully solid and steady as anything Mariah had ever known, Winchester seated firmly against his shoulder, Stuart shot again.

The tinkle of a goat bell sounded from the gulch.

Mariah turned again, stared at the cougar as it struggled to its feet. At another crack of the rifle, it fell back as if kicked. Stuart shot yet again, and the cat lay still at last.

Then everything, even the goat-bell, fell silent—everything except for Stuart's hard, deep breaths. Terrified though she'd been, Mariah did not like seeing the lion die. Worse, though, was the dead lamb that bloodied the rock above it.

Finally, with great effort, she managed voice for one word. "Stuart . . . ?"

Quick as that, he had her in his arms, clutched so tightly against his warmth and strength that it should have hurt, but it didn't. It couldn't possibly hurt, especially after the sight of that dead lamb. Mariah felt the ribbon, the one she'd tied onto Pet, flutter uselessly from her numb fingers. She did not want to admit the likelihood, did not want to face it. . . .

And yet Stuart smelled like gunpowder. And she was shivering with a cold that did not match the sunny day, a cold that came from deep inside her where even she saw bad things.

"Oh, Mariah," Stuart murmured into her neck. He kissed her jaw clumsily, then cradled her cheek in one big hand to better see her, better search her face. When he pushed her new hat away and leaned his forehead against hers, closing his eyes, she realized he was shaking, too. But Stuart was never frightened! "Thank God. . . ."

Her words came out slow, clumsy. "I couldn't move!"

"If you had, likely he would have chased you. You did right."

"But Stuart . . ." Finally, she had to admit her true fear. "Is it Pet?"

She even tried to turn from Stuart's arms, to look again into the gulch, and Stuart protectively blocked her way. "No, love. Don't."

Instead of looking himself, he turned his attention to the flock, whistled some commands to his dogs. But when Mariah tried to go around him, to see the dead lamb, he caught her back.

"He doesn't always come when he's playing with his friends," she explained, pushing at his restraining arm. Pet was her foster lamb, her responsibility—she had to know. "So I went to find him. But he lost his ribbon, and I heard a bell, so I thought . . ."

Perhaps the dead lamb wasn't hers. "Pet," she called, just in case.

"Whist, Mariah. You canna help him."

"No," she cried, this time more in pain than summons. *"Pet!"*

Stuart pushed her gently into the grass, his rifle bumping her in the hip. He hadn't put it down yet. She felt glad he hadn't. "I'll go see," he assured her. "You stay—"

Then he squinted at something behind her. "—here," he finished, less urgently.

And something bumped Mariah in the back—and bleated.

Again she felt paralyzed, this time with hope. Stuart didn't wait for her wits to return. He dropped the rifle into the grass and scooped this lamb up with one hand, fumbled at its ears.

The baby struggled, as if offended, and bleated its protest at Mariah, fixing her with outraged, black button eyes. *Pet . . . ?*

"The ears are nae marked," said Stuart, disbelief hollowing his voice. "This one's your bum lamb, not . . ."

But he didn't have to finish. With a happy lunge, Mariah had her arms full of squirming, bleating lamb.

Her lamb! She recognized his cry, recognized his fresh, soapy smell—none of the other lambs had been washed with soap, but hers had!

Pet was all right!

Happily raising teary eyes to Stuart, she didn't understand why he looked so . . . angry? No, not angry. But for a moment, Stuart seemed almost envious.

Then he frowned to himself, shook his head, and turned to look across the gulch. "Rider," he announced, and reclaimed his rifle. "The cowboy."

Clutching Pet happily to her, Mariah saw Dawson galloping up to check on them from the other side of the gulch. "You folks all right?"

"Aye," said Stuart. "Killed a cougar."

"This far out?" Dawson knuckled his hat back from his forehead, surprised. "Middle of the day?"

"This far out," assured Stuart. Still holding her lamb, Mariah started to pay more attention to her husband again. Why would Dawson's concern anger him? "Middle of the day."

"Well I'll be dogged." The cowboy shook his head while his horse shuffled back from the smell of blood. "You sure got yourself some strange luck, MacCallum."

"Could be." But Stuart, staring into the gulch, did not bother to hide his dislike of the cowboy. "Unless it's not luck."

Something was still very wrong. But when Dawson widened his eyes at her in question, she frowned. She would not exchange silent communications behind Stuart's back.

Dawson had the sense to duck his head even as he thumbed his hat brim, easily sitting his spooky horse. "You all right, Miss Mariah?"

Stuart's head came up sharply.

"Excuse me," added the cowboy with a mischievous grin. "Mrs. MacCallum?"

"I'm fine, Dawson, thank you," Mariah called back,

before kissing Pet's head. "And my lamb is fine, too!" She tried not to think of the poor baby in the gulch.

Dawson didn't seem to know what to make of the lamb on her lap, so he looked back to Stuart. "Need some help?"

Stuart said, "Don't want to keep you from your business. You do have business this far out. Don't you?"

"Could be," said Dawson, just as cryptic. "Folks."

It was Mariah who called, again, "Thank you for checking on us!"

With a final nod, the cowboy reined his horse back from the gulch and rode away—as slowly as Stuart had walked, the first time he'd turned his back to Idaho Johnson.

Something was clearly wrong. "Stuart?"

"Not yet," he said, low.

Mariah looked around her and spotted Pet's ribbon caught on a piece of sagebrush nearby. Before she let her lamb go play, she tied his bow extra carefully around his precious little woolly neck. He bounced happily off toward the flock, safe. She still felt so grateful for that—

But it grew increasingly less important than whatever had Stuart's back arched like this. As soon as Dawson was out of earshot, she asked, "Why were you so rude? He came to help."

But Stuart, was already edging over the side of the gulch, rifle still in hand, to take a closer look at the dead mountain lion. Hearing a distant shout, Mariah saw Dougie riding toward her on Pooka. She waved reassurance—likely Mr. MacCallum would be along next—and followed her husband.

She did not like seeing Stuart stand so close to the mountain lion. She knew it was dead—could see death in the unnatural sprawl of the great beast. But . . . it was so big! Skinny, too. She could see the line of the beast's ribs, the bumps of its spine, the angles of its shoulders under dull, tawny fur. One paw, lying still by Stuart's foot, was almost as big as her husband's head.

No, she did not like seeing the two of them so close at all.

"Stay there," warned Stuart, without looking up. "It's steep."

He sounded not just angry—uncharacteristic enough, for Stuart—but furious. Mariah knew the cougar had been taking sheep for over a month now; Stuart and Dougie had found its tracks more than once. But Stuart generally took his losses to wolves, coyotes, even eagles in stride. Why not this time?

She knew her husband's posture intimately, knew when he was barely restraining himself from the cursing or tantrum a lesser man might throw.

"What is it?" she asked yet again, aching to understand. "What's wrong?"

Stuart extended one booted foot and, grunting, kicked the dead cougar over, so that it slid another foot down the side of the gulch. A goat bell tinkled cheerfully across the morbid scene—a goat bell tied securely around the dead cougar's neck.

"That's why it came out of the mountains," said Stuart.

Mariah shook her head, confused. Why would anyone tie a bell to a mountain lion?

But Stuart knew. He looked up at her, his brown eyes bright with betrayal. "The poor beast was starving. He could hunt nothing *but* sheep."

Then Mariah understood—even if she didn't want to. Once belled, the cougar couldn't stealthily approach any kind of prey except the one kind accustomed to hearing goat bells. She'd once seen some boys in town tie cans to a frightened dog's tail, and that had seemed unreasonably cruel. But *this!* "Who would do such a thing?"

And Stuart blinked up at her as if she were daft.

* * *

Seeing Mariah that close to danger was something Stuart never wanted to live through again. If he had to finally dash some of her hopes so that she could grasp the severity of what they faced from the cattlemen, he guessed that was what he had to do.

But it was still with reservations that he let her accompany him and his Da—and the dead cougar—to the sheriff's office. She hadn't seemed to believe his reports of the lawman's apathy. It was time she saw for herself.

It hadn't occurred to Stuart that Sheriff Ward might not be quite so apathetic to Stuart's wife as to Stuart. Then again, even disgraced, she was still a rancher's daughter.

"Good afternoon, Sheriff," Mariah greeted when Stuart held the door open for her, as if they were simply coming to call.

"Well howdy do, Miss Mariah." Only then did the big man glance past Mariah and add, less enthusiastically, "MacCallum. Someone using your woollybacks for target practice again? I reckon they must not have read the newspaper."

The deputy, thumbing through wanted posters in the corner, grinned.

Stuart said, "If someone shot down four cows, you'd be after them fast enough."

"Doubt I'd have to. Them cattlemen hire decent range detectives themselves." They both knew that "range detective" was just another euphemism for a hired gun like Idaho Johnson.

Stuart wondered if Mariah knew it. But she seemed annoyed by something else entirely. She looked at the grinning deputy, then at Sheriff Ward, then at the deputy again, her gaze intensifying by the moment. Then she covered her mouth and coughed delicately—and distinctly.

To Stuart's surprise, the sheriff hoisted himself to his feet. "Excuse me, ma'am. *Franklin!*"

The deputy scowled—but he stood, too.

Her status as a lady momentarily reaffirmed, Mariah's annoyance immediately eased to mere distress. "I'm sure you'll want to see what my husband has in his wagon, Sheriff," she insisted earnestly. "Someone's done something terrible!"

"Terrible, is it?" But to Stuart's surprise, Ward headed for the door at Mariah's request, stopping only to bid her "ladies first."

The deputy put down his posters and followed, leaving Stuart to bring up the rear.

Their morbid cargo would have attracted onlookers even if the dead mountain lion weren't belled. While Da told the story to Crazy Pete, the sheriff and his lackey actually had to draw a fellow or two out of the way just to take a look-see.

"Looks like you drilled yourself a panther, all right," said Ward—as if that was all Stuart had to show him. "Kinda puny, though."

"Look at its neck, Sheriff!" insisted Mariah, glancing at Stuart as if to see why he wasn't saying anything.

Stuart wasn't quite sure himself. Maybe it was because he'd gone through this with the sheriff too many times before, about the dead antelopes, the gutted ewe, Johnson's threats, even his three murdered sheep. Or maybe it was because he'd never seen Mariah act quite like this—as if she not only deserved the respect of these men, but expected them to know it.

Stuart wasn't sure he liked seeing her this way. Worse, he wasn't sure why. She did deserve their respect, after all. . . .

"Someone belled it," recognized Ward, nodding to Mariah instead of Stuart. "Well that *is* a dang dirty trick."

Her new sun hat emphasized her nod, earnestly seconding his opinion.

Since that didn't accomplish much, Stuart asked, "What do you mean to do about it?"

The sheriff snorted—so much for respect. "Critter's dead, son. What else needs doing?"

"Finding who did it?" Stuart felt Mariah watching him, and that made him uncomfortable, too.

"Well, now, that might be a touch difficult," said the sheriff, just as Stuart had expected. "Coulda been anyone belled that cat. For all I know, it could've been one of you herders, wanting to make out how you're being . . . now how did they put it, Franklin?"

"Abused and harassed," offered the deputy.

The sheriff said, "Abused and harassed."

Now Da couldn't stand it, either. "That wouldna be too smart, fixing a cougar to feed on our own stock!"

Stuart winced inwardly at the perfect opportunity that gave the lawmen to comment on the intelligence of sheep farmers.

But Mariah spoke first. "It could have killed me, Sheriff Ward!"

The sheriff actually made a noise as if he cared. But what he said was, "Now what were you doing out near them woollybacks, Miss Mariah?"

Miss Mariah. It had bothered Stuart when Dawson called her that; it all but grated on him now. He knew, then, what most bothered him about the lawmen's deference to his wife.

They were treating her as a lady *despite* her being his wife, not because of it. She'd put on stockings and shoes to come to town, and a fresh dress. It occurred to Stuart that she'd brought all of it—even the stockings—from her parents' home. With the exception of her hat, he'd not bought her clothing once since their marriage.

Left with him, she'd probably still be faded and barefoot. . . .

"I brought my husband his lunch," Mariah insisted, glancing sidelong at Stuart, a touch of confusion clouding her fine gray eyes. Did she sense his displeasure? "And while I was looking for my pet lamb, I came upon the cougar. Stuart shot before it could hurt me," she added loyally.

And he had.

But she *had* been with the sheep, to get into danger in the first place.

The sheriff said, "Well that is lucky." As if skill and alertness played no part in it at all.

On some level, Stuart recognized his resentment for the overreaction it surely was. Mariah knew him better than anybody in the world; he had nothing to prove to her. But he did his best to sound particularly calm and rational when he asked, "Can you look into who might have done this?"

He didn't even add, *you might start with men who can rope wild animals.* Someone—probably a handful of someones—had to hold the beast still long enough to tie a bell on, after all.

"Well now, son," drawled the sheriff. "As I said, that might be a touch difficult. But if I come across anything, I'll be sure to let you know."

And that was it. As usual.

Stuart felt . . . foolish. Overreactive. Paranoid.

Damn it, with a belled cat dead in his wagon, how could he feel paranoid?

But more than anything, he felt angry.

Mariah said, "You're being too modest, Sheriff. Couldn't you ask some questions?"

Ward puffed up some. "Well, I do know a few folks who tend to hear things, Miss Mariah. I'll see what—"

"*Mrs. MacCallum.*" He couldn't keep it in any longer.

Ward, Franklin, Mariah—even Da looked at Stuart with surprise. To her credit, Mariah tucked her arm under Stuart's and smiled gently at the lawmen. "Shame on me, letting you be so informal, Sheriff Ward!"

Was she flirting? Not flirting to attract romantic interest, of course—even angrier than he'd felt in a long time, Stuart would never believe that of her . . . even with men more attractive than these. But she was manipulating them with her smiles and her ladylike manners. Even that, after the day he'd had, frustrated him deeper than he ever would have expected.

Even if, this time, it didn't work.

"If I come across anything, Mrs. MacCallum," drawled Ward, "I'll let you know."

From the disrespect in his tone, he might as well have been talking to Stuart.

Or Emily. Or Bonny.

Mariah blinked, clearly taken aback, while her two allies headed back into their office with only the shortest, "Folks" by way of good-bye. It felt like watching her be snubbed by her cousin's wife all over again.

"There 'tis," sighed Da, and swung himself back into Pooka's saddle. Stuart had insisted on driving, to be closer to Mariah. Now, helping her silently into the wagon again, he wondered if that had been so wise a choice.

Her back seemed a little arched itself. And he did not feel steady enough to deal with whatever she meant to say.

All she did say, when he settled into the driver's seat beside her, was, "I wonder what Sheriff Ward intended to see, by asking questions."

Stuart released the brake. "Giddap!" Only as the wagon lurched into motion did he add, more quietly, "Nothing that would have helped us."

"You can't know that," Mariah insisted.

"I can," Stuart insisted right back. And maybe she heard something in his tone, because she did not pursue the argument.

He felt somehow that he should apologize. He loved her, after all—even annoyed with her, he loved her as much as life. Had the mountain lion hurt her or, God forbid . . .

He could not bear to imagine it, much less how it would have destroyed him.

Surely, compared to that, it was petty not to apologize for resenting her ladylike composure, for snapping at her friend the sheriff. And yet . . .

Something ugly inside him was not sorry. That ugliness resented not just her ladylike composure but the way it got her a respect that marriage to him could not. It resented being reminded that she'd been safer before she met him since—as this afternoon proved—accidents could indeed happen. It resented the fact that his sisters, who had never secretly met a boy beneath a kissing bridge, could not garner the respect she could . . . just because of who their father was.

He recognized the ugliness of those feelings, and the unfairness. Mariah had not been under that bridge alone. But recognizing it was about as much as his decency could manage, for the moment. Mariah had neither prompted nor deserved Stuart's anger. Best to hold his tongue until he could better control it.

Then she asked, hesitant, "Could we please drive by my parents' town house? As long as we're here, I'd like . . ."

She faltered to silence when Stuart slid his gaze to her. He knew what she'd meant to say, as surely as he'd predicted the sheriff's dismissal. She wanted to stop at Old Man Garrison's mansion for "a few more things." She usually did, when they came into town on a weekday.

She did not have enough room in his caravan to keep much, and so had left too many of her belongings behind when she married him. Damned if that didn't make him feel guilty, too.

"Never mind," she said, softly.

But he drove the team silently toward the tree-lined street that was named after her mother, to her family's three-story mansion, anyway. In a spring-wagon. With a dead mountain lion in back.

God forbid he feel guilty about denying her whatever it was she wanted this time, too.

"Thank you," said Mariah, when she saw what direction he'd headed.

Stuart said nothing. Not when he reined the team into Garrison's drive, around to the back of the house, and drew them to a stop. Not when Mariah kissed him on the cheek and hopped down from the wagon, hurrying over to the kitchen door—which was opened by the latest of the Garrison housekeepers.

Da, who'd never seen the Garrison place before, rode up beside Stuart as he sat waiting. Looking from the towering shade trees to the carriage house to the mansion itself, his father whistled between his teeth. "By all that's holy, lad. Could be we should've run cattle!"

Then, Stuart said something.

Too much of it, at that.

Chapter Twenty-seven

Mariah did not take very much from her room this time; it wasn't as if she had anyplace to put excess. But she did select a white shirtwaist and blue skirt to start wearing to church, since her most recent Sunday dress was fading, and a carefully wrapped vase she'd brought home from Italy. She also took the weekly story papers that her mother stacked in the pantry for her when the family finished with them. Those wouldn't take a great deal of room. She would give the ones she'd already finished to Emily MacCallum.

"Won't you take some fruit with you, dearie?" asked Mrs. Sawyer as Mariah tied her latest treasures into a bundle with a flour-sack towel. Mrs. Sawyer was taking care of Thaddeas and the house while Mariah's family spent their summer on the ranch. If the part-time housekeeper had opinions about Mariah's marriage, she kept them to herself.

Mariah considered the bowl of peaches and oranges,

imported from southern states, and her mouth watered for such a delicacy. She'd skipped lunch, after all.

But ever since the incident with Mother MacCallum and the Christmas cookies, Mariah was careful not to bring food home from her parents' house. It might reflect badly on Stuart.

So she shook her head, said thank you, and hurried back out the door before her husband or father-in-law could grow impatient.

But her husband had apparently passed impatient.

"—with the sheriff?" Stuart was asking, sounding angry. Again.

"She did have a way with her," agreed Mr. MacCallum—and Mariah realized they were talking about her.

"No," said Stuart. "Her father's money had a way with her. Did you not see it? As long as she was Miss Mariah, she could do no wrong. And why? Because Ward and his lackey looked at her, but they saw Old Man Garrison. As soon as she admitted to being Mrs. MacCallum, they treated her as badly as they do you and me."

Mr. MacCallum saw Mariah coming and cleared his throat.

"And why *would* she admit to being Mrs. MacCallum?" demanded Stuart, oblivious. "Especially since she still cannot see what a robber baron her father really—"

"Whist," insisted his father, yielding subtlety a few words too late.

"—is," finished Stuart . . . and slowly turned on the wagon seat to face her, brows flat, eyes squinting.

Clutching her bundle, Mariah stared back. She wasn't sure facing the mountain lion had stunned her so. She knew Stuart did not like how their interview with Sheriff Ward had gone—

—despite that Stuart himself had spoiled that—

—but he thought the sheriff and deputy had only been polite because of her papa's money?

He thought she didn't want people to think of her as married?

He thought her father was a robber baron?

She'd hoped it didn't really matter what he believed about her family . . . until she heard him slandering them.

Mariah's first instinct was to run back into the house and up the stairs, to lock herself in the room that she'd shared with Laurel for so many years. But she was no child—and that would mean showing Mrs. Sawyer that something was wrong. Even with the betrayal of Stuart's words crashing over her, Mariah would not do that.

After everything she'd put her family through to marry Stuart, the last thing she could do was let them think she wasn't . . .

Let them think he didn't . . .

No. She circled him and the wagon slowly, still half disbelieving what she'd heard. Then she darted into the safety of the carriage house and, past that, the stables. She'd always found comfort around horses—their warmth, their smell, their intelligence. Horses put her in mind of her father.

The robber baron.

It didn't help that one of the horses stabled here was Mariah's old mare, Buttercup. Her sisters had promised to ride the palomino regularly, after Mariah married. So why wasn't she out at the Circle-T?

Buttercup tossed her golden head, dark eyes liquid beneath a fall of corn-silk forelock, and snorted hello. She still remembered Mariah, even after all these months.

Then the horse ducked her head, rolled her eyes, and Stuart said, "Mariah . . . ?"

She walked over to Buttercup, petted her velvety nose. She wished she'd accepted the fruit after all. Poor Buttercup, neglected all these weeks while Mariah bottle-fed a lamb, might like a slice of peach.

"I did not mean for you to hear that," offered Stuart.

"That doesn't make it all right," said Mariah.

"No. I don't suppose it does."

But that had always been one of Stuart's problems—or hers. He couldn't make things all right, could he? Not always. Not like she'd hoped he could.

"My father," said Mariah, scratching behind her palomino's ear, "is no robber baron."

Stuart said nothing.

Mariah turned back to him. *"He isn't."*

Stuart stood in the doorway from the stables to the carriage house, his hands spread—still silent. That was when the hurt truly set in, infecting no one part of her, but her very being. The man before her was so very familiar. She knew those heavy-lidded eyes and outward-slanting brows, knew that faintly cleft chin and rounded jaw—and the feel and taste of his set mouth. She knew how his thick hair, the color of dark wheat, felt under her fingers. She knew those broad, set shoulders; and that thick chest; and those solid legs, planted stubbornly as he quietly waited for her to realize how blind she was being about her father.

This was Stuart, her husband, and she'd loved him almost as soon as she'd known him. . . .

But her hurt, soul-deep, came from the fear that she'd never completely known him at all.

"I am sorry, Mariah," said Stuart.

Even worse than the fear of not really knowing him was the temptation to run to him, let him hold her, beg him to lie to her some more. Because if she let herself do that, it wasn't just Stuart she wouldn't know. She'd forget herself, as well.

So despite how she ached to touch him, to let him anchor her yet again, Mariah asked, "Are you sorry for what you said, or for me hearing it?"

Stuart's brows leveled in frustration. "Both," he admitted.

She tried again. "My father is no robber baron."

Stuart thought for a moment, then said, "Could be he's not."

Could be, humoring her was a mistake. "Are you jealous of him, Stuart?"

His eyes narrowed into a darker scowl.

"My father was a respected cowboy and soldier and trail boss, too, and money had nothing to do with it. He *earned* men's respect. And he earned his fortune in cattle, the honest way, because he risked starting a ranch in the wilderness—real wilderness, not a hundred and sixty acres of rocks and sagebrush—and he stuck with it. And he's never blamed anybody, not anybody, for his setbacks. He's never blamed the Union for bankrupting Texas. He's never blamed the farmers for chasing the drovers out of Kansas. And as much as he hates sheep, I don't think I've ever heard him blame you for the overgrazed range, either. If anything sets my father apart from you, Stuart MacCallum, it's that."

She was shaking by time she finished, shaking from the words she was throwing at the man she loved. She already regretted saying them, doubly regretted her hurtful tone.

But at least they were the truth.

"Is that all?" asked Stuart, low.

And oh, she wanted it to be all, but somehow the words kept coming. "It's not fair that people don't like sheep farmers, Stuart. But that doesn't give you the right to distrust all cattlemen. That's not fair either. Have you considered that maybe people like Sheriff Ward would be more willing to help you if you were a little . . . friendlier?"

Stuart said, "Your da is nae a friendly man, and he does all right."

"And you think that's because he has money."

He scowled, said nothing at all.

Buttercup bumped Mariah's shoulder with her nose and snorted horsey breath into her hair.

"This is my horse," announced Mariah, no longer sure

what she was saying, just that she somehow, somehow had to make him understand. "Her name is Buttercup, and she's been my horse since I was twelve. She's lady-broke, and I used to ride her sidesaddle—with that sidesaddle," she added, pointing toward the wall of tack, "—all the time. Papa said to take her with me, when I went to live with your parents, and again when I married you. He said I was the only one who could sell my saddle—that's cowboy talk for giving up cattle, Stuart. Selling your saddle. But I didn't take it, or Buttercup, because I didn't want you to think expensive things like that mattered to me. But they do matter to me, Stuart, even if it's not because they're expensive. You just mattered more."

Stuart swallowed. When he released a breath, took another, his chest fell and rose with the force of it, and his voice caught. "Now I don't?"

"I didn't say that!"

He waited, his brown eyes hurt and accusing, and Mariah couldn't fight the need to go to him any longer. Even if she lost everything—her pride, her security, even herself—she could not stand here while Stuart looked at her like that.

So she went to him, hay crackling under her shoes, and she tentatively took one of his slack hands in hers. She wished he would hold her—or at least hold her hand. He did neither.

"You *still* matter more, Stuart MacCallum," she said. She looked up at him; into his familiar, sullen face; into his heavy-lidded, dark brown eyes. Her own eyes burned, and he blurred in front of her. "You have always, will always matter most of all. I just . . ."

He waited.

"I just don't understand why I have to choose," Mariah admitted, voice breaking. "I've accepted it, and I choose you, but I never understood . . ."

It wasn't until Stuart's fingers closed tightly around hers that she began to cry in earnest.

He did not pull her against him as she wished he would, as he had so often before. But he did raise his free hand to her face, traced tears off her cheeks.

"You ought not have to choose, at that," he murmured, voice thick. "Dinna cry. I never meant to make you cry . . ."

And since she hadn't meant to make him feel guilty, she just cried harder.

Stuart kissed her forehead—then squeezed her hand once more and stepped away. Panicked, Mariah swiped the back of her hand across her eyes, turned to follow him. He couldn't leave her! Not now that she'd chosen him over everything.

But he didn't leave—not through the carriage house. Instead, he walked to the stall where Buttercup stood watching them, let her sniff his hand, blew gently into her face. Then he took a bridle from the wall and slid the bit into the mare's mouth.

Mariah watched, silent, as Stuart led her mare out of her stall and began to saddle her—with Mariah's sidesaddle.

"What are you doing?" she whispered, no matter how foolish it sounded.

"Go tell the housekeeper you'll be taking her; I'll not be accused of horse theft."

"But . . ." Perhaps it should have felt like a victory. In the obvious ways, it was. She would have not just her kitten and her lamb, but her mare? *And* Stuart?

But at what price?

Something felt wrong—faintly but clearly, like a minor chord played on the piano. She'd made accusations, spoken to Stuart as no wife should speak to her husband. She'd lashed out at him for hurts he had not even caused.

This was too easy.

In the middle of competently tightening the cinch—as with so much, her husband managed to look as if he'd dealt with sidesaddles all his life—Stuart glanced over his shoulder, brows slanted in a new worry. "You are going home, aren't you?"

"*Our* home?"

He nodded, relaxing at her question. "Aye, Mariah. Our home."

The hurt flared again, that he could have doubted it. "Of course I am."

He nodded, then led the mare to her, caught Mariah in the crook of his arm, and led both ladies through the carriage house and onto the drive.

The wagon team stood sleepily, apparently grown used to their morbid load. Pooka waited, hitched to a post nearby, and Mr. MacCallum sat comfortably in the tree swing, near the pond—eating a peach.

Sitting up, he raised an eyebrow at the sight of Mariah's palomino. "What's this?"

Stuart said, "This is Mariah's horse. Once she talks to the housekeeper, I'd like you to escort her back home, please."

All Mariah's uncertainties returned. "*Why?* Where are you going?"

"I've a visit to make." Stuart put the reins in her hand and headed for the wagon.

Mariah drop-reined Buttercup and followed. "Where? Why can't I go with you?"

"Because, lass, it's someplace I need to go alone."

She grabbed his arm, hard and thick, before he reached the wagon. "Stuart?"

And he turned, drew her into his arms, and kissed her.

It was not the sort of kiss she would have expected, in front of his father. It was a hard kiss, possessing Mariah as only a husband could . . . and somehow taking what only a wife could offer. A few months ago, she might have lost all ability to stand, kissed like that. Now she wrapped her arms around him, clung to him, and kissed him back just as passionately.

He was Stuart, after all, and she loved him with everything she was. No matter what else they had to deal with—she loved him most of all.

Then Stuart straightened, set her carefully back. "Give me this, Mariah," he asked solemnly. "I have to earn my own respect, this time."

Which scared her, even through the pleasant breathlessness that lingered from his kiss. "You'll be careful?"

"Always."

"And . . . you'll come home tonight?"

Stuart nodded. "I'll come home to you."

Despite the unanswered questions between them, his eyes were very, very dark.

Evangeline Taylor lived not far from the railroad tracks, in a square shanty of cut lumber and tar paper, within a square, empty yard, surrounded by posts from what used to be a fence. She'd lived there over half her life, ever since Nell—her mother—fled the boredom of being a farm wife on a claim outside of town with an ex-miner. Not that Nell had in fact been the miner's wife. But Evangeline had vague memories of a cabin, and a burly man pretending to be her father. She even remembered flashes of a fine house before that, too—a house with polished furniture and thick carpets and too many mothers, of whom Nell had not even been her favorite.

Evangeline wasn't sure how her mother afforded even the shanty. For years, she'd feared eviction. But they'd stayed—and it fell into worse disrepair with each season and each of Nell's occasional roommates. A bottle through the front window. A chair through the back window. The fence and furniture chopped up for firewood. Evangeline despaired of ever completely escaping the stench of alcohol and urine, much less turning the place into anything like a home.

But since seeing Mariah MacCallum's sheep farm, she'd begun—tentatively—to try.

She used an old, torn dress to make curtains for the cardboard-patched windows. She planted a garden outside, and made extra trips to the well outside of the general store for water, to keep the struggling seedlings alive. Once already, she'd lost her new shoots to rabbits. But despite the setback, Evangeline thought the rabbits had been perhaps the nicest visitors the shanty had seen in some time.

She slept in a loft where the stovepipe ran through. When younger, she slept up there to stay out of sight. As she got older—after one of Nell's gentleman friends almost cornered her in the kitchen one night—she slept there because she could draw the ladder up after her. And today, she was restuffing her mattress.

Evangeline had been cutting and drying grass, or "prairie feathers," for a week now, to fill her freshly washed ticking. It smelled of summertime, and she wondered if she would, too.

Then the door to her mother's room slammed open and Nell stalked out, wearing only an untied robe. "What the hell are you doing!"

Evangeline did not risk a slap by answering. She only lifted the half-stuffed mattress slightly, so that Nell could see for herself.

"You don't have to make so much goddamn noise doing it, do you? I'm going out tonight, for God's sake!"

Evangeline obediently put down the straw and the ticking both. She hoped that if she stopped now, Nell wouldn't throw either out.

For her part, Nell stalked to the stove and poured some of the coffee Evangeline kept for her. "What the hell's gotten into you this summer anyway?"

"Ma'am?"

"Don't call me ma'am. I'm not that much older than you."

Evangeline nodded. It would do no good to tell Nell that Mrs. Garrison's daughters called *her* ma'am—when they didn't call her Mother . . . or Mama.

Nell liked to pretend she was Evangeline's older sister, anyway.

Now Nell looked closer at her daughter. "Who're you fixing that bed for, anyhow? You catting around with someone?"

Evangeline shook her head, but Nell just laughed one of her meaner laughs.

"I forgot—you're saving yourself for marriage. Take it from me, baby. If men liked wives, we wouldn't have a roof over our heads."

Evangeline said nothing. But she hoped not *all* men preferred whores to wives, even if she never got to find out—and something must have shown on her face.

"Oh, you know so much, do you?" challenged Nell. "Tell me one woman, one who keeps her husband happy."

Evangeline knew she should say nothing—it was an insult to good women to even mention them in Nell's presence. But she hated it when her mother got like this, determined to rub the world's ugliness in Evangeline's face. She hated it more with each passing year. Before she could stop herself, she said, "Mariah MacCallum."

Nell laughed. "Oh! Baby—how old are you, anyway?"

"Fifteen," whispered Evangeline, already regretting her recklessness.

"How'd you live this long and stay this stupid?"

Something must have shown on Evangeline's face again, because Nell threw her nearly empty coffee cup into the bucket by the stove. "First, MacCallum herds sheep. It can't be hard for his wife to do it better than sheep, now can it? Second, they're newlyweds. Newlyweds do it all the time whether they like it or not, especially if they're churchgoers and actually thought they had to wait. And third, even if they're the happiest couple since Adam and Eve in the Garden of Eden, I wouldn't trade places with Mariah MacCallum for all the tea in China. Life is fixing to get ugly, out in Sheepville."

The way Nell said that frightened Evangeline. Nell didn't use that tone unless she knew something bad—and relished it.

"What do you mean?"

"I mean it's never been healthy to run sheep in Wyoming, and it's about to get a lot unhealthier. Now where the hell did I leave my bottle. . . ."

Evangeline watched her mother kick through the clothes and belongings she'd left scattered in the corners, seeking a bottle that she'd surely finished the night before.

"Nell? What do you mean, unhealthier?"

"Let's just say I hear things, in my line of business. Not for me to blab." After several more kicks, Nell stopped and looked entreatingly at Evangeline. "You know, baby, if I could just find my bottle, calm my nerves a bit, I could get some more sleep before tonight. You're the one who woke me—"

She kicked over Evangeline's fresh straw. That was all right. It was just straw.

Slowly, Evangeline said, "I think I remember where Dixie left *her* bottle, when she stayed here last month."

Nell's green eyes—far prettier than Evangeline's—narrowed into dangerous slits. "Where?"

"Will you t-tell me what you heard about the MacCallums?"

Nell slapped her. The crack of it startled Evangeline even more than the blow—it never failed to. "Will you get me Dixie's goddamn bottle?"

Victoria Garrison, thought Evangeline miserably, would hold out for the information. But Evangeline did not have Victoria's grit. Instead, she had to gamble on the possibility that, if Nell cheered up, she might start talking.

It would not be the first time.

So she got up, went to the woodpile, and braved the

spiders there to dig out Dixie's bottle. She hated to do it. This was a bottle of medicine, worse than liquor.

But then she thought of Mariah MacCallum, and her smiles, and her pet lamb.

Evangeline turned and handed the bottle to her mother.

Chapter Twenty-eight

What if Mariah was right?

Stuart drove the wagon steadily to the southwest, toward the foothills and the Bighorn Range beyond, despite the late hour. He did not worry about finding his way and, as it turned out, did not need to. When he reached the road that branched west, an ironwork sign arched over it with the Circle-T symbol at its apex.

"Gee," called Stuart, easing the draft team into a right turn.

Garrison had laid claim to good land, rolling and fertile. Poplars neatly lined either side of the two-rut drive, leaves whispering in the spring breeze, and off to Stuart's right he sometimes glimpsed the heavier wood that marked this branch of the Goose Creek.

The contrast to his father's dry, rocky claim and his own settled deep in his gut. But he swallowed down the resentment of it and instead asked himself: If he'd gotten to this part of the country twenty years ago, where would he have staked claim?

The question bothered him, because it echoed the hurtful things Mariah had said. But . . .

But what if she *was* right?

Stuart did not like thinking that at all. But he disliked the danger of *not* thinking it even more.

He reminded himself that he had a belled cougar lying dead in the back of his wagon, flies already buzzing around the tarp that covered it. That was not paranoia on his part. Nor were the three dead sheep, the month before, or the stock other local sheep farmers had lost. He hadn't imagined Idaho Johnson's message "from the local cattlemen," or Old Man Garrison's threats against his life . . .

Or Garrison's claim that it wasn't about sheep?

Stuart hadn't lied to Mariah about the reception his family got when they first herded sheep into Wyoming. Before the deadline, Stuart had seen warfare that he prayed his own sons never would, much less his wife. Charred carcasses of fired sheep. The bulging eyes and stiff tongues of animals poisoned by saltpeter—which was not toxic to cattle. He would never forget the night that masked cowboys swept down onto the herder's camp, shooting sheep and dogs and humans like fish in a barrel.

The Wyoming Stock Grower's Association had backed the gunmen in the Johnson County War. Why wouldn't they support violence in Sheridan County, too? And Jacob Garrison belonged to the Wyoming Stock Grower's Association. So the question Stuart had asked himself from the start remained.

How could anyone be terrorizing this range, and Jacob Garrison not be involved?

In which case, could be Stuart did lie to Mariah about coming home tonight. He might not make it home at all. Even now, he noted riders approaching from across the pasture to his left. One was Hank Schmidt, Mariah's cousin, who'd beaten him so many months ago.

Stuart kept on driving, even once the riders flanked him. After facing how badly he and Garrison had managed to tear Mariah—*his* Mariah—in half, he could no longer respect himself without knowing, once and for all, where Garrison truly stood.

And despite the risks, and all the speculation, only one man could truly tell him that.

The medicine did cheer Nell into sharing what she knew—and now Evangeline Taylor found herself with the safety of good people in her hands. . . .

In her stupid, useless hands.

Johnson—the man folks were calling "Idaho"—hadn't liked the sheep farmer's "manifesto." He meant to ambush Stuart MacCallum's claim with a half-dozen or more men, tonight. And they weren't just gunning for sheep.

The need to do something—to do the right thing—deafened Evangeline like the rumble of a train going by at night. But what?

Nell snored in the bedroom. She would be no help, even were she conscious. Mrs. Garrison, whose winks and cookies had won a devotion Evangeline hadn't known was in her, had taken Kitty and her other daughters out of town, to see an eye doctor. Evangeline knew Mariah's father could help, but doubted he would believe the likes of her—assuming she could even manage speech in his presence. Assuming she could find his ranch, on foot, before sunset.

And then there was the younger Mr. Garrison. Mr. Thaddeas Garrison. The up-and-coming lawyer . . .

Evangeline feared going to him more than anything else.

Not that she disliked him. Since the ball at the Sheridan Inn, when he asked her to dance, Evangeline liked Thaddeas Garrison far more than she should—and therein lay the danger. She knew he'd danced with her out of charity. She knew he was a full-grown man, college-educated, who saw her as no more than a friend to his baby sister . . . if he even recognized her. And yet, it would crush something new and tender, deep inside her, if she dared approach Thaddeas Garrison and he looked at her the way his father did—

The way most respectable people in town did, the way Evangeline knew they should.

And refused to see her, refused to listen, refused to believe. How could she bear it if her reputation damaged the very people who'd been so kind to her?

Evangeline had to do something. So, deciding what Mariah or Victoria might do, she went to the sheriff's office.

Sheriff Ward—who had arrested Nell more than once—was not in. Deputy Franklin was, and the way he looked at Evangeline unsettled her.

"I know you," he said, leaning back in his chair. "You're Nell Taylor's girl, right?"

Evangeline nodded, trying not to glance at the doorway to the cells, beyond the desk. Terrible things happened back there. Nell had told her so.

But Deputy Franklin was looking at her bare legs, which had grown too long this year, and that frightened her even more. He didn't even look up from his discourteous perusal when he asked, "Somethin' I can do for you?"

Evangeline swallowed, tried to find the breath to form words. *Mariah,* she kept thinking, even as she hid one leg behind the other. *Mariah needs help.*

Then Deputy Franklin asked, "Maybe somethin' you can do for me?"

Evangeline fled the sheriff's office and the way the deputy was looking at her and the fear that nearly paralyzed her. She ran two blocks before she dared duck into an alley, to make sure he hadn't chased her. Then, panting, she raised her fisted hands to her mouth and tried not to cry at her own uselessness. Nell had not said *when* tonight Johnson and his regulators meant to ambush the MacCallums. . . .

But the afternoon sunlight was slanting sharply already. Sunset was mere hours away.

Shifting her weight from foot to foot, fighting the low whimper that tried to squeeze out of her throat, Evangeline wondered if perhaps Nell had lied. That made her feel momentarily better. Nell could be lying to her—again—or Mr. Johnson could as easily have lied to Nell. There might be no danger to Mariah at all!

But the whimper squeezed out of her throat anyway. Just as likely there *was* danger. And she was the one who'd tricked Nell into telling her. *That made whatever happened her fault.* Worse, it wouldn't happen to Evangeline. It would happen to Mariah. Her friend.

Desperate, Evangeline used her sleeve to dry her damp eyes. The important thing, Mariah had once told her, was not what other people thought about her behavior. The important thing was that *she* felt she had good reasons—for sitting in trees, marrying sheep farmers, or . . .

She'd never had better reason to act than this. So she peeked out of the alley again, then made her timid way to the law office of the esteemed Thaddeas Garrison. She could have found that office—his name printed in green and gold across the front window—with her eyes closed. But to go inside . . .

Again she found herself hesitating, trying to catch her breath, before she even touched the door. Finally, needing to think, she turned to go hide in another alley—

And bumped right into a man's chest.

The man wore a carefully pressed brown suit, with a finely buttoned vest, a silver watch fob—and cowboy boots. He smelled clean and wealthy. To Evangeline's mortification, she recognized him even before she dared raise her eyes to take in his intelligent face.

"Excuse me, Miss," said Thaddeas Garrison, helping

her catch her balance with strong hands on her shoulders. "I should look where I'm going."

As if she'd not run right into him. As if she were a respectable lady with gloves and shoes, rather than a whore's daughter with long legs and bare feet.

Now Evangeline couldn't breathe past the clamor in her head, not at all. Mariah . . .

He clearly did not recognize her. But even as he released her to her own precarious balance, started to take a step past her, Mr. Garrison paused and looked back at her, thoughtful. Now he would remember . . .

And when he remembered, he smiled. "You're Victoria's friend!"

Evangeline nodded warily, everything in her still screaming: *Mariah, Mariah, Mariah.*

"Are you here to see her? She's just inside." And he opened the door to the office, held it open for her to enter first. She stepped obediently through the doorway, into his fine, dark office.

Victoria looked up from the desk, where she was obviously handling stacks of paper. "Evangeline? Hello! How did you know I was here?" She stood, familiar and accepting and welcoming—

And Evangeline fell into her friend's surprised arms, weeping her relief. Somehow, through her tears, she managed the words, "Mariah needs help!"

At that, Thaddeas Garrison pulled out a chair for her, sat her carefully down in it, and held her hand as he crouched beside her to ask, *"How?"*

Somehow, even though it meant the insult of mentioning her mother in front of him and Victoria, Evangeline focused on his clear brown eyes and his strong, kind face—and she told him.

He listened. He believed her. He solemnly thanked her. And perhaps the biggest relief of all: Thaddeas Garrison took charge.

"We need to send a warning," he declared, standing and retrieving his hat from the rack by the door. "But we need reinforcements, too. I'll go to the ranch. Victoria, you tell Sheriff Ward what's going on, have him send word to the MacCallums. Then I want you to go back to the house—Miss Taylor, would you mind walking with her?"

Evangeline—*Miss Taylor*—nodded, so stunned that she forgot the sheriff wasn't in.

"Thank you." And he faced Victoria again. "Stay there. One of us will come get you as soon as we know anything. Understand?"

Victoria nodded.

Thaddeas nodded back once, started out the door—then turned back to Victoria. "*Stay there* Vic," he repeated, pointing at her.

"You said that," Victoria assured him. "I understand."

Thaddeas hesitated, obviously not convinced—but he did not have the time to waste. With a frustrated sigh, he vanished out the door, leaving Victoria to gather her gloves, parasol, and reticule in sudden, blessed silence.

"I understand," she repeated determinedly. "I just don't agree."

Then Evangeline remembered, gasped at her own stupidity.

"What?" demanded Victoria.

"The sheriff isn't in. Just his . . . his deputy." The memory made her scared again.

Victoria said, "You know, I don't much like that deputy."

Evangeline nodded agreement. "But your brother said—"

"Give me a moment to think," said Victoria, and started to pace.

While Evangeline waited, she looked shyly around the wonder that was Thaddeas Garrison's office; at his chair; at all his large, intimidating books; at his diploma from a college called William and Mary—and at the photograph of a young lady on his desk. A lady dressed in the height of style. A lady he must admire greatly.

Evangeline tried to like the woman in the picture. Thaddeas had smiled at her, and thanked her, and held her hand. He'd called her "Miss Taylor." That was so much more than she'd ever dreamed. . . .

"I have an idea," declared Victoria. "A very good idea."

And Evangeline began to feel frightened again.

Stuart drove toward the clapboard ranch house, a two-story, L-shaped building, white with blue shutters. He'd expected something fancier. Despite its size, and the trees around it, and all the outbuildings ranging behind it—barns, corrals, a spring house—the ranch house itself could hardly be more modest.

He drove the wagon up to the front porch, six mounted cowboys silently flanking him, and as he set the brake, he called, "Garrison!"

Instead of emerging from the house, as Stuart had expected, Garrison strolled slowly over from the corral. The cattle baron was as much a surprise as his house. This not being Sunday, the rancher wore work clothes, his chambray shirt half sweated through, his elbows stained with sawdust, his hands encased in leather work gloves. He approached stiffly, his gait showing his age as surely as did his white hair and beard. But when he raised one hand toward the windows, in silent command, he'd clearly lost none of his authority.

Waiting, Stuart noticed an old log cabin in the distance, by the creek, and a small tombstone under a tree, higher and to the left. Of course, none of this proved the man was not the robber baron Stuart had assumed him to be, any more than did Mariah's loyalty. What Mariah didn't understand was, criminals had families and histories, too.

"MacCallum," said Garrison as he stepped deliberately onto the porch, his gray eyes steely in the shadow of his

Stetson, his expression unreadable. Like his cowboys, he did not ask why Stuart was there—just waited an explanation. Maybe the fact that the sheep farmer had dared venture so deep into cattle territory stunned him as surely as it did everyone else.

It still stunned Stuart. Survival instincts developed from childhood urged him to leave, now. But Mariah's words had stunned him more, worse. For her—them—he had to know.

Stuart knew the futility of talking to Garrison. This time, he just climbed into the back of the spring wagon and, wrapping his arms around the tarp, used all his strength to lift the dead cougar, heave it over the side of the wagon—

And roll it onto the porch at Garrison's booted feet with a great, dead thud, and a residual chiming of goat bell.

"Any idea who this belongs to?" Stuart asked.

The rancher stared down at the dead cat for a long, weighted moment. Then, just as slowly, he raised his steely gaze back up to where his son-in-law stood in the wagon bed—and at last, Stuart knew.

Garrison's still-dark brow furrowed with insult, just as Stuart expected. But faintly, in gray eyes that suddenly resembled Mariah's, there echoed confusion as well.

He had not known about the belled mountain lion until now.

Which meant the range war put Mariah into more danger than Stuart had feared.

"Made yourself more enemies than I had you figured for," drawled the rancher. He pushed at the lion's big head with one booted foot, made a sound of pure disgust through his cheek at how the bell-rope had worn its scrawny neck.

Stuart said, "This one came about ten feet from losing Mariah for both of us, and I mean to find out who. It's someone low enough to hire Idaho Johnson, and it's someone who wants to get rid of the sheep."

Garrison—scowl deepening to learn Mariah had been endangered—said, "Long list."

And Stuart said maybe the bravest thing he'd managed in a long time. He said, "That's why I could use your help."

His father-in-law folded his arms in challenge, not the least bit cowed by Stuart's superior position. "Why would I help the likes of you?"

Stuart decided he still disliked the man. A lot. But Mariah had confessed to a less-than-loving relationship with Stuart's mother, too, and *they* managed to work together.

"I'm told that you're a fair and decent man," he admitted, past the bad taste in his mouth. "Even if you do hide it well."

Garrison considered that a moment longer, then made his decision. "Best come inside."

And he turned to go in, too, no more left to say in front of the help. Stuart considered, once again, that it could be a trap. Just because the rancher didn't know about the mountain lion might not mean he'd had nothing to do with the sheep killings, the threats . . .

"After you clear that carcass off my wife's porch," added Garrison, over his shoulder.

And Stuart decided to for once do what Mariah would do, and climbed down from the wagon. Mariah would expect the best from people. Stuart feared it might still get her killed—especially if her father had not hired the man threatening them.

But maybe it was a habit that could come in useful, at least now and then.

He was still wrestling the dead mountain lion back into the wagon—alone—when he heard hoofbeats approaching, fast. Stuart did not recognize the horse that galloped up the drive, orange-colored in the sunset. But he recognized the urgency to the man's speed.

"Garrison!" Stuart called, again lowering the cat onto

the porch. The name sounded better without the "mister" in front of it.

He felt almost as surprised as Thaddeas Garrison looked, swinging off the horse even as it stopped in front of the house and arriving, face-to-face, with his brother-in-law.

"MacCallum!" It didn't take the lawyer long to recover. "Thank God you're here. You can show us the way."

"The way . . ." repeated Stuart, clearly missing something. But he wasn't college-educated.

"The way to your place." And Thaddeas hurried past him and into the house, stepping over the cat without a second glance, calling back the worst possible words.

"Mariah may be in trouble."

Chapter Twenty-nine

Between her and Stuart's argument—and their incredible kiss—Mariah suspected that her father-in-law had seen a little more of his son's marriage than he would like.

They spoke little on the way home. She tried to concentrate on the beautiful weather; the afternoon sky; the joy of riding Buttercup again. But perhaps Stuart's dour pragmatism was contagious. Despite having nothing certain to worry about, Mariah remained very worried.

"Do you know where he went?" she asked her father-in-law, finally, as they rode into sight of her home. It wasn't merely a wagon anymore. She also had an outhouse, a garden, a nearly dug well, and an empty henhouse. She felt terrible for having called it "a hundred and sixty acres of rocks and sagebrush." Since they weren't farmers, what did the rocks matter? Bunch grass grew as high as a horse's belly, except where the sheep ate it as low as the nicest lawns. Wildflowers dusted the landscape with hints of gold and purple. It was a beautiful place.

"Nae, lass," Mr. MacCallum said, which did nothing to soothe her.

"Do you have any ideas?"

"With all respect—none I mean to share."

Mariah asked, "He'll be all right though, won't he?"

And her father-in-law said, "That would be up to Stuart."

Once Mr. MacCallum rode on, Mariah felt Stuart's absence too keenly to relax, despite the distraction of chores. In four months of marriage, they'd rarely been far from each other. Her confidence sank lower, along with the sun toward the Bighorn Range. Her guilt lengthened with the shadows. Where was he, that he wouldn't tell her?

She had to face that, were she as convinced of the ranchers' innocence as she'd made out, fear wouldn't be chilling her worse than the coming evening.

Mariah was weeding her garden when she heard a carriage approaching. She stood quickly, hungry for the sight of Stuart—but it was a buggy wheeling toward her, faster than any spring wagon. In fact, it was her mother's buggy.

For a horribly still moment, she felt stark anticipation of something she never wanted to hear. Then she recognized her sister Victoria driving, a white-faced Evangeline Taylor with her, and nearly choked with relief. Surely a younger sister would not be bringing bad news!

"Victoria Rose Garrison!" greeted Mariah, planting dirty hands on her hips as she strode out to meet the carriage. "Does Papa know where you two are? You've winded Rue!"

And indeed, Mother's gelding was tossing his head and breathing hard, sweated wet under his harness. But Victoria did not seem abashed—even if Evangeline did.

"You've got to come with us!" the girl insisted instead. "You have to leave here. Now."

Mariah blinked up at her. "Leave?" This was her home. She was waiting for Stuart.

And Victoria said, "Mr. Johnson is going to ambush your claim tonight."

At first, it sounded too much like something out of one of Victoria's dime novels, and Mariah was loathe to believe it. Surely Evangeline's mother made for poor hearsay. Surely even if Idaho Johnson meant them harm, he could not gather a band of a half-dozen or more local men to help. Not against her and Stuart?

But as Victoria finished her story—"You've got to come back to town where you'll be safe!" Mariah looked from one girl to the other—and she knew she had to believe them. She did not want to. But on the chance they were right . . .

She glanced at her wagon, outbuildings, lamb. If they were right, the risks of believing only the best of people could prove far too high.

"We need to bring in the sheep," she supposed, heading for the wagon. "And Dougie."

And Stuart. But much though she needed him to help, she could not summon Stuart with a gunshot—no matter how badly she wanted to. She made sure the shotgun was loaded, braced herself against the side of the wagon, and fired it once into the air, as a signal.

All three girls winced at the sharp report.

Then Mariah put down the gun and continued to piece together a clumsy start of a plan. Stuart had said that bad men like Johnson sometimes fired wagons, so . . . "Would you two take some things back to the MacCallum homestead for me, to keep them safe?"

She clambered into her small, neat home before they could even answer.

"And leave you here?" demanded Victoria, jumping from the buggy to follow her as far as the wagon's Dutch door.

"Of course 'and leave me here.' Someone has to tell Stuart, when he gets home." Please God, let it be soon. "And someone certainly has to defend the sheep."

"Thaddeas rode out to the ranch, to get Papa and reinforcements," assured Victoria. "They'll come defend the claim *for* you."

Which was good news—but this wasn't her father's or brother's claim to defend. It was Stuart's, and it was hers. Mariah would no sooner desert the land they'd worked so hard for than she would desert Stuart himself, not even on the hope of reinforcements.

"You two will take my things and tell Stuart's parents," she repeated firmly, opening a valise. Her most precious possessions did not take long to pack—her and Stuart's marriage license, Stuart's accounts and bank book, the letters they'd secreted to each other last year, and a few family photographs. Mariah caught and caged Velvet in the picnic basket. And she draped the tartan muffler over her shoulders, to keep near her until Stuart returned.

Nice clothes and Italian vases did not even signify.

"And then you're going to stay there with Mother MacCallum," she continued, carrying her treasures to Evangeline, in the buggy. She went back for her lamb.

"I understand," said Victoria.

Mariah knew her sister too well for that. "I don't care if you understand; I want you to say you'll do it."

Victoria scowled, despite the adorable sight Pet made, bouncing happily on his leash toward the buggy. "But you may need help!"

After lifting the lamb into the buggy as well, and squeezing Evangeline's hand in silent thanks, Mariah turned to her sister and hugged her. "You were brave to come warn us. But this is *our* claim, mine and Stuart's. It was my choice to marry a sheep farmer, and I cannot worry about you two on top of everything else. So the best thing you can do for me is to take the things that I care for—including yourself and Evangeline—safely back to the MacCallums. Send Stuart's father, with rifles and ammunition. *Then wait there.* Will you do that for me?"

Despite having their mother's coloring, Victoria looked surprisingly like their father for a stubborn moment. But she nodded. "I will."

"Thank you."

"Rider's coming," warned Evangeline from the buggy, and Mariah spun, hopeful.

Her hopes and shoulders sank when she saw that this wasn't Stuart, either. But she made herself say, "See? I won't be alone. Here comes Douglas."

Victoria frowned and asked the most obvious question, "But where's Stuart?"

The sun vanished behind the mountain range, and night fell on the Wyoming grasslands.

Stuart's world had condensed to one single need. He had to get home to Mariah.

Even if it meant accepting help from his in-laws to do it.

Garrison had faster horses to ride than his harness team and men anxious to ride with him. But to just stand there beside the corral, while Thaddeas smoothly roped a pony for each of them, grated Stuart's endurance raw. To delay further by saddling the beasts . . .

He wanted to swing onto the resulting mare and race away, bareback, right then. Let the damned reinforcements find their own way to his claim. Mariah needed him!

But she also needed him alive—and one sheep farmer against a half-dozen or more regulators . . . those were the kind of odds Dougie would choose. So although Stuart's pulse raced, his breath still in his chest, he managed to ease his movements around the mare long enough to slide the saddle blanket onto her back. She stood stiff, tense . . . then relaxed into the feeling.

When he spotted the cowboy Dawson across the corral, roping his own horse, Stuart even found the breath for low speech. "That one was riding deadline today," he murmured to Thaddeas, hooking stirrups over the loaned saddle. "How do we know he's not with Johnson?"

"Likely 'cause I sent him," drawled Garrison himself, arriving with rifles. He slid one into the scabbard on Thad's saddle with a firm *whoosh,* then one into Stuart's. Unwilling to waste time on an argument, Stuart did not offer to get his own from the wagon. *Mariah . . .*

Instead, every bit of him tensed as he eyed all these cowboys. "Why?"

"Heard tell there's been trouble." His father-in-law glared. "Finally."

Finally trouble? Or finally . . . At the more likely possibility, Stuart fumbled the cinch. Reading his nerves, the mare sidestepped him. "You only heard this Sunday?"

With a glare and a soothing touch to the mare's nose, Garrison moved on.

Thaddeas asked, "You think he keeps track of what's going on with the sheep farmers?"

"He owns the range, doesn't he?" Stuart went back to tightening his cinch, a little more each time the mare released a breath, holding his own breath to keep even the facade of calm.

He had to get to Mariah. . . .

"Pa just *looks* like God, MacCallum," noted his brother-in-law drily. "God talks more."

Stuart carefully let down his stirrups, and the horse barely noticed—*almost there.* "I'm one of the few folks in this town that doesn't confuse them."

Thaddeas swung into his saddle, rode his gelding in a tight circle to accustom it to his weight. "He owns half the Circle-T, is all. He'd rather leave the rest of the range be."

Could be Mariah's brother suffered from the same naiveté she did. Putting weight on the saddlehorn, Stuart tested whether his borrowed mare would stand to be mounted.

He wasn't much good to Mariah with a broken neck, either. "He's a Stock Grower."

"So are a lot of folks." Thaddeas watched Stuart mount, nodded approval. "But you don't invite a parson into a saloon and expect to do much drinking."

Ready to lead twenty heavily armed cowboys toward his own claim, Stuart guessed that had better be true. In any case, could be he had more in common with his wife than he'd thought.

He needed the explanation to be true badly enough to stop questioning it.

The sun sank behind them as they headed out. But not a man flinched from riding hell-for-leather across the darkening range, into what could be full-out war. Nor, as they neared the deadline, did they hesitate to let a sheep farmer like Stuart take the lead.

Under the drum of hoofbeats and the measured pant of horses, Stuart tried not to imagine Mariah wounded, or helpless, or at the mercy of a bastard like Johnson. If he had not married her, had not dragged her into this, she would be safe. These men had realized that, even if he had not. And now, if anything happened to her . . .

But he could not let his thoughts stray there, not and stay sane. He and the cowboys would reach the claim first, and Mariah would be all right. She *must* be all right.

If she wasn't, no amount of wealth or pride would ever absolve Stuart's selfishness.

A sharp whistle cut through the night, as they approached the gulch, and Stuart saw Garrison raise a hand, signaling them to slow down. Before Stuart had even reined in his borrowed mare, he heard it—a distant popping, like dark fireworks, through the summer night.

Gunfire.

"We canna stop!" he insisted, wild to do something. Ride. Shoot. Perhaps even kill. He'd never killed a man, but if they hurt Mariah . . .

At first glance, his father-in-law showed no concern at all—and Stuart hated him for it. Then he noted a certain brightness to the man's eyes, a tension in his set shoulders.

"You're the one what knows the area," Garrison drawled. "How *won't* they figure us to cross that gulch?"

Soldiering. Mariah had said. *Indian wars . . .*

Stuart took a shaking breath. "You've done more fighting than me," he admitted grudgingly. "We'd best figure this together."

And with a single, sharp nod, the cattle baron agreed.

"Rifle!" called Dougie MacCallum, under the barrage of gunfire.

Mariah belly-crawled to his side in the stony arroyo where they'd taken cover and handed him a loaded rifle. Then she took the Winchester he gave her and dug her hand into a box of ammunition as if grabbing a handful of candy, slid each round into the loading chamber.

She had to be careful not to burn her hand on the hot muzzle. She had to be careful not to tremble so hard that she dropped precious cartridges.

"Rifle!" called Mr. MacCallum, and Mariah crawled back to him, Stuart's old coat protecting her from the worst of the rocks, to repeat the steps.

Stuart's dark predictions had been horribly true. Mariah was caught in a range war.

Gunfire exploded to either side of her in blue flashes. Bullets sprayed her with dirt when the gunnysackers aimed too closely. And through it all, no matter how scared she was and how hard she concentrated on her job, one thing frightened her beyond all else.

Stuart had not come home.

He'd said he would. He'd promised. And Stuart did not break promises.

Compared to her fear of what it would take to detain Stuart MacCallum against his word, the night-shattering crossfire—even the bleating of frightened sheep and the awful scream of a wounded horse—seemed timeless and unreal.

One of Mr. MacCallum's herders had driven all the

sheep but a small band of older ewes eastward, onto his own land. Then he'd returned to join the MacCallum men, and Mariah, in the wash that provided the most earthen protection—and they'd waited. They'd waited for Stuart, and they'd waited for the regulators.

But the regulators got there first.

Not only did the seven riders, gunnysacks masking their faces, ford the gulch where Dougie had predicted. They even let out a shout of excitement when they saw the ewes. They rode right up, shot at the sheep—

And the MacCallum men fired back. Mariah, no shootist, took charge of keeping an extra rifle loaded. And though Stuart's coat and hat sheltered her from flying rock, their tartan could not warm her against this kind of cold. Her whole world was loud, violent, dark.

"Rifle!" shouted the Basque herder, whose name she'd forgotten. She traded weapons with him, burned her hand—blinked away tears to keep loading. Stuart had been right. Men *could* do terrible things—even to her. She only hoped her gullibility had not endangered her brothers- or father-in-law. She hoped she had not cost Stuart more than he could bear to lose, even for her.

She felt guilty for wishing Stuart here. Worse, she wished it anyway, with all her soul.

Then something about the gunfire changed, though Mariah kept frantically pushing cartridges into the Winchester's loading chamber even as she realized it. A single barrage of shots rang from behind the gunnysackers. Shooting faltered into shouts.

"MacCallums!" yelled a voice that sounded vaguely familiar. Cousin Hank? Had Papa's reinforcements arrived? Mariah kept loading rounds. "Don't shoot!"

"Whist," shushed Mr. MacCallum as his sons and herder stopped firing. "Stay down. Could be it's a trick."

Then Mariah heard the most wonderful sound in the world, so wonderful that a grateful sob burst out of her, frightening her in-laws. She heard Stuart call, "Douglas!"

Her father hadn't come—*Stuart had!* He was here, as promised. Stuart was safe.

And somehow, he'd even stopped the shooting.

Between what Stuart knew of the terrain, and what his father-in-law knew of soldiering, the gunnysackers had no chance. The cowboys led their horses carefully across one of the steepest fords on the gulch, divided into two flanks and took the gunmen wholly by surprise.

The only shots fired were to get their attention.

Better even than the sight of the regulators reaching high, empty-handed, was seeing how cleverly Da and Douglas had set in for a counter ambush. They'd clearly had advanced notice, thanks to Thaddeas.

Which meant Mariah *had* to be safe.

"Douglas!" he called again, ears ringing. "Da!"

They rose from the shelter of the wash, then, rifles in hand, blessedly uninjured. Da, Douglas, old Jules, even Kevin, and—

Stuart stared in a moment of lancing, belated terror. She *hadn't!*

Only because of his panicked hesitation did he not immediately rush forward to meet Mariah as she ran toward him. Only because of that did he glimpse movement off to his right—

Behind a rock, where nobody had been firing before, he saw a reflection of gunmetal.

Too slowly, Stuart turned, shouldered his Winchester—and realized Mariah was wearing his hat, his coat, their muffler.

Too slowly, he aimed. Too desperately slowly, he fired—not in time to beat the gunman's first shot.

A spurt of flame lit Idaho Johnson's glassy-eyed determination to kill what, in the night, *looked* like Stuart MacCallum. The gunman fell back from Stuart's shot, as surely as the mountain lion had. But the lion had not been armed. Johnson began to struggle back up—

Then jerked backward again, again, when two more rifle shots cracked into the night—Jacob and Thaddeas Garrison's.

Assured that the "range detective" had been stopped, Stuart spun back to where Mariah had fallen—and started to run. *No. No* . . . She must not be hurt, *had* to be all right . . .

And as if in answer to his prayer—their prayer—Mariah raised her head to glance in the direction of the gunman. Then she scrambled to her feet, unhurt, and rushed toward Stuart even before she had her balance.

He caught her to him, clutched her soft body tightly enough to break bones, knocked his old hat off her head as he kissed across her face, his world safe and whole again. "Oh God," he breathed—he who never took the Lord's name in vain. "Oh God, lass. What were you thinking? What in the name of holiness are you doing here?"

"I was protecting the sheep!" she exclaimed, laughing beneath his kisses.

"Hang the sheep!" And Stuart pulled her so tightly against him that she couldn't possibly speak, hid his own face in her hair so that perhaps none of her father's cowboys would see the tears burning at his eyes. Johnson had thought she was him.

She'd nearly died, mistaken for him.

When Mariah managed to wriggle enough freedom to tilt her face up to his again, no condemnation shadowed her expression. "You came!" she told him happily. "Oh, you came!"

As if she could have doubted it.

"I told you I would," he reminded her, framing her face in his hands. "I would come through hell for you. You know that."

Mariah said, "Yes, Stuart. I know that."

And he held her, and trembled, and tried to breathe. She was all he needed in the world. . . .

Even amidst shouts and gunsmoke, what a bright, fine world she made of it.

Safe in Stuart's embrace, savoring his touch and smell and warmth again, the burr of his voice and the solidity of his big arms around her, Mariah hardly noticed the rest of the world. She had no reason to. Then little snatches, voices, vaguely familiar, began to register through the blissfully isolating echo of gunfire in her head.

"This 'un needs a sawbones."

"So does the horse; likely deserves it more."

"I know you—Stinky Hal!"

"This 'un's Bucky Bolt! These boys are from the Triple-Bar, Boss! Ever one of 'em!"

The Triple-Bar, she thought vaguely, her cheek on Stuart's shoulder. *The Triple-Bar.*

Colonel Wright's ranch. But no! Colonel Wright was . . . was . . .

Not the man she'd foolishly, childishly hoped.

"Oh, Stuart," she breathed, horrified yet again by her gullibility. "You were right! It was the ranchers. . . ."

Stuart said, "Whist, love. So were you." He kissed her, softly. "It wasna all of them."

"Well I'll be!" Her own brother's voice startled Mariah further out of the prayerful stillness she'd wrapped around herself and Stuart. "You won't believe it, but this son-of-a-gun is still breathing!"

Stuart turned then, too. "Johnson?" he called to Thaddeas, over Mariah's head.

"That's the one!"

Stuart dropped his intense gaze to Mariah's, somehow confused and relieved, ashamed and happy all at the same time—and she pressed her lips gratefully to his. She would love him even if he had killed that son of a . . . gun.

But she also loved that he preferred not to.

Somehow, just that old, easy recognition of each other's thoughts, beyond their desperate embrace, embarrassed them both at the same time. They were, after all, surrounded by cowboys and brothers . . .

And fathers!

"You brought Papa?" Mariah exclaimed foolishly, only now spotting her father amidst the movement and shadows. He was tying a gunnysacker's hands together, carefully not looking in her direction. She blushed to realize that he'd seen her and Stuart holding each other like this—but joy overrode any real embarrassment. When *hadn't* she forgotten herself around Stuart MacCallum? And now . . . "Stuart, you brought Papa!"

Stuart ducked his head, self-conscious. "It was . . . mutual, lass."

"How? What did you say to him? Has he said anything to you? Will you come to dinner on Sunday now? Why did—"

"Go on," ordered Stuart gruffly, and turned her toward her father. "Go ask him yourself, and you can tell me. I've sheep to tend."

Mariah remembered the poor ewes, sacrificed as a decoy. "Oh!"

"I'll do it. Now go!"

So as Stuart stepped away from her and back to work—but not so terribly far, she made sure of that—Mariah navigated the rocky, faintly moonlit ground to her father's side.

"Papa?"

"Mariah Lynn." He tightened a knot, and the cowboy he was tying grunted in pain. "Trust you're well." As if they were meeting outside church.

"Thanks to all of you, I am," she assured him, taking his arm before he could turn to the next task. "And Victoria and Evangeline, for warning us."

Thaddeas appeared at her elbow, then. "Victoria's here? I told her to stay in town!"

Papa snorted and went back to tying up bad guys. Tightly.

"They're at the MacCallum homestead," Mariah assured her brother, giving him a much deserved hug as well—but continually peeking toward where Stuart was doctoring the sheep.

"The little . . ." Thaddeas shook his head, eyes narrowed. "I cannot wait to see how she explains herself this time."

"Best go fetch your sister home, then," suggested their father, handing the last uninjured bad guy off to Hank Schmidt. Almost under his breath he added, grudgingly, "And that Taylor girl, too, I reckon."

Mariah thought of what her father's notice would mean to Evangeline and gave him a hug, even as he took command in his usual, imperious way. "Schmidt, you and the boys take these murderin' dogs into town; give that deputy some help standin' guard so's he don't forget where he put them. Sheriff and I had best pay a call on the Colonel."

He scowled down at Mariah then, but more in his distracted, thinking way than with any real anger. He added, reluctant, "Reckon Mariah's sheep farmer will want to be there, too."

" 'Mariah's sheep farmer,' " announced Stuart, "has got livestock to tend." He even looked up from the ewe that struggled to her feet under his competent hands. "I guess I can trust you to handle it."

Papa nodded slow challenge at the return jibe. "You guess."

Mariah wanted to laugh. But there were things she should have said from the start, things left too-long unsaid. "Papa—have you ever wanted to do something you knew wasn't proper, but you did it anyway? Even once?"

Coiling what was left of his rope, Papa surprised her with a simple, "Yep."

"Well . . ." She took a deep breath. "I knew you wouldn't want me seeing Stuart, and I did it anyway. No matter how wonderfully it's turned out—and oh, it has—I owe you an apology for deceiving you. You deserved more than that. You still do. Can you forgive me?"

Her father looped the rope onto the saddlehorn of his buckskin gelding. "Yep."

And the last of the shadows that had clung to her marriage fell away, leaving her feeling free and unfettered—and perhaps a bit too confident. She dared ask, "Did whatever you did wrong turn out anywhere near as wonderful as Stuart has for me?"

Pausing, her father looked down at her for a long, quiet moment—and she realized that at some point, beneath his gruffness, the affection had returned to his steely eyes. "Ain't none of your business, Mariah Lynn."

But he almost smiled as he said it. And when he focused on someone just beyond her, and she felt Stuart's warm, heavy arms wrap around her waist from behind, Papa did not even scowl—even if the hint of a smile vanished, for the moment. Her father's smiles never did last long anyway.

"Someday," announced Mariah happily, leaning her head back into Stuart's chest, "you two are going to be great friends."

Both men spoke at the same time. "I doubt it."

Mariah laughed her delight. Stuart just held her, unforgettably *there* whether she saw him or not. And her father, shaking his head in disgust, rode off to see justice done.

When they reached their sheep-wagon, Stuart swung his wife into his arms, carried her into the wagon—to their bed—and made love to her until she forgot her own name.

But she never once forgot his.

In the hushed, naked intimacy afterward, they held each other as if they need never let go again . . . and perhaps they need not. Seen pragmatically, *everything* might not be all right.

But of the important things—far, far more was right than he'd ever dared dream.

"Your da offered me a job," he admitted, despite that it was two months after the fact. Having seen more of the men from the Garrison outfit today, he supposed that maybe, maybe, it wasn't quite the insult he'd first thought.

"He did?" Mariah's voice tickled him, reflected her incredulity. "Doing what?"

The idea was silly enough that Stuart could not say it without a smile. "Cowboying."

She laughed, and he let her. He loved her laughter . . . and her tears, and her voice, and her silence. He loved her optimism and her disillusionment, her strength and her loyalty.

He would do anything for her, should have done it months ago. "If you want me to . . ."

And Mariah stopped laughing. "You aren't serious!"

"Dougie can file on my claim, take over the flock." He propped himself up on an elbow, so that she could see just how serious he was. "You deserve more than to be made outcast, just because I'm stubborn enough to run sheep in cattle country. Surely those great ugly beasts canna be that different from sheep. . . ."

"No," decided Mariah firmly.

"No?" He felt relief, except . . . she did not mean to even discuss it?

"I'd have to divorce you and marry Dougie," she declared, almost apologetically. Their bed was too narrow for her to escape fast enough, so Stuart managed to pin her down quite easily, to capture her wrists and kiss her into submission.

"You'll nae marry Dougie," he ordered, once he had her squirming happily beneath him.

"But I don't want to have to give up that nice MacCallum muffler," she gasped. "And Kevin's too young."

"You're truly set on being married to a sheep farmer?"

Suddenly, somehow, they were not teasing. For so long, he'd feared she did not understand all she was getting into. But after tonight, she had to know the dangers, the obstacles. . . .

Mariah met his gaze with her beautiful, trusting eyes, the gray of the coming dawn. "Since the first time I met one," she whispered.

He covered her mouth with his then; kissed her so thoroughly that he almost forgot what she'd been saying. Almost.

"Thank you, love," he whispered. "Thank you for asking me to meet you under that bridge."

Remembering, Mariah's smile was the sunrise. "Since the very first time."

Epilogue

Stuart wasn't sure what to expect when he met Mariah at the Kissing Bridge, one Sunday afternoon in September. He felt glad enough for a few minutes away from her family, of course. He liked them, despite Garrison's insistence on calling him "Mariah's sheep farmer." But he did see them twice a month.

Just enough to keep track of the latest escapades of Garrison's other daughters, but not enough to get involved, which was just as he liked it. Laurel had filed on her own claim, despite being no older than Dougie, and wanted to keep it through the winter. Victoria was writing shocking editorials for the local newspaper, with the reluctant help of her friend Evangeline. Kitty's grades had improved since she started wearing spectacles. Elise was spoiled as ever, and Audra was behaving herself.

And Stuart found himself feeling increasing sympathy for the girls' father.

No, he was just as happy to step out into the quiet

autumn afternoon with the one Garrison family member who truly counted.

But it wasn't as if he and Mariah needed a bridge to kiss each other anymore.

"When you pulled on your hair," he asked now, a touch uncertain as to why she would revert to their old signal. "That meant to meet you here."

Mariah's eyes widened at his arrival, as if he'd startled her from deep thoughts. She grew more beautiful by the day. Her golden hair, pulled up as befitted a proper matron, seemed to glow with a light of its own. So did her skin. So did her eyes.

He would have thought that, after almost a year of marriage, he would no longer feel so drawn to touch her, just from looking at her, even in public.

Perhaps they might need to step under the bridge after all?

At least this time, he need not fear ambush. Idaho Johnson was in prison for life, and though Colonel Wright had managed to avoid prosecution, he'd lost his reputation, respect—and both his children's politically advantageous engagements.

Stuart tried not to take pleasure from that. Sometimes he failed. But usually he was too happy to think about it one way or the other.

"You pulled on your hair," he repeated. "Here I am."

"I can see that," said Mariah, lowering those large, fine eyes of hers, sounding unusually shy. "Thank you."

Stuart said, "You're welcome."

She was starting to worry him.

"Mariah, is something wrong?" he asked.

She lifted her healthy, happy face to him, unable to hide her smile any longer, and shook her head. "I talked to Mother, and we're both very certain that something is wonderfully right."

And something deep in Stuart's gut shifted, as subtly as a heartbeat, as dramatically as an earthquake.

* * *

Mariah would have sworn that Stuart guessed, the way his eyes flared and a smile played, ghostlike, on his usually solemn lips. But he only prompted, "Mariah . . . ?"

"You remember in July, when you got the windmill working, and the water came gushing up, and we started playing in it . . . ?" she prompted. He had to remember. Not only was the water itself precious enough to merit celebration, but it had soaked through their clothes, plastered their hair to their scalps . . . helped them forget themselves all over again.

"Aye," agreed Stuart, eyes darkening.

"We forgot to check the calendar," Mariah admitted.

He stared at her.

"I know we meant to wait awhile longer—not that there'll be a scandal, of course, but so that we could build a house first. But really, the wagon is perfectly sound, and the baby won't even be here until lambing season . . ."

Oh dear, she hadn't thought of that. Stuart would be terribly, terribly busy for lambing. But that wasn't their baby's fault!

Apparently, Stuart didn't think so either. The smile that had flirted with his lips was warming his eyes now, too. "A baby," he repeated.

Mariah nodded.

"You're certain?"

"Well . . . as certain as one can be about these things. Mother says she's suspected it for a month now."

"You've been tired," he remembered, suddenly concerned.

"Only a little—and Mother says that's normal." Not for the first time, she wished her perfect husband were a little more talkative. "You *are* happy for us, aren't you Stuart? I know we meant to wait . . ."

But from the way his beautiful brown eyes crackled down at her, with a joy he shared only with her, she supposed she had her answer. She swallowed hard, anchoring herself on the nearness of his gaze.

"Not a day goes by that I'm not happier than seems possible," he told her, low. "Now I'm twice as happy yet."

Then, to Mariah's delight, Stuart leaned down across the inches that separated them and kissed her, on the lips, right there in the open. As ever, his love warmed her like sunshine, firelight, summertime.

A peal of laughter caught their attention, and they looked to see Elise running toward them, delighted to have caught them forgetting themselves in public again. Behind her, walking more sedately, came Kitty, holding their father's hand. Behind them, Audra walked with Victoria, Thaddeas—and Evangeline Taylor, clearly saying nothing, as usual.

Papa, noticed Mariah, looked none too pleased by his oldest daughter's display.

"Do you know what else makes me happy, my love?" murmured Stuart as Mariah caught her five-year-old sister up in her arms.

"What, Stuart?" Mariah asked, and although Elise did not even know what they were discussing, she asked it too. "What, Stuart?"

Mariah wondered if she should warn Papa about this bridge, before Elise got old enough to discover it.

Stuart leaned closer, so that he could whisper in her ear—mixed with a few more kisses—"I'm happy we're married, so that your da won't shoot me down where I stand."

Mariah laughed. She could not always be sure when Stuart was joshing—but either way, they'd avoided *that* scandal, at least!

"Papa's not even armed," she reminded him, pleased when he wrapped his arms around her waist from behind, to await her sisters.

"That," predicted Stuart, "willna last long."

And since Stuart's pragmatism was far less cynical by the month, Mariah had to wonder if he was right.

Then he made her laugh again, solemn or not.

He whispered, "Have sons."

AUTHOR'S NOTE

Dear Reader:

I hope you enjoyed *Forgetting Herself*. I love the entire Garrison family, but Stuart and Mariah's heartfelt sincerity captivated me so much, I could hardly bear to turn in the manuscript!

Sheridan, Wyoming is a real and wonderful place—my brother Bert worked as a hatter there, and I loved visiting. If ever you're in the area, you can see several places on which I've based elements of the Garrison family's world: the Kendricks' Trail-End mansion (even finer than the Garrison town house), the Bradford-Brinton Memorial ranch (which Jacob's Circle-T ranch resembles), the railroad depot, the Goose Creek, and the mountains. The historic Sheridan Inn is being renovated to its original glory, and I encourage anyone who gets a chance to visit it.

I've found no evidence of range wars in Sheridan County itself. The danger that Stuart relates, however, was as real as rim-rocking, gunnysacking, and "range detectives." The Ten-Sleep massacres, the Johnson County War, and the murder of young Willie Nickell by the famous Tom Horn all took place in Wyoming. In 1905, the Wyoming Wool Growers Association was organized. I like to imagine Stuart MacCallum as having been involved.

Keep looking for my name (and the Garrisons'!) under the *Leisure* imprint. I love reader mail! Please write me at: P.O. Box 6, Euless, TX 76039 (self-addressed, stamped envelopes are always appreciated) or e-mail me at Yvaughn@aol.com.

Lair of the Wolf

Chapter Nine

Elizabeth Mayne

Lair of the Wolf also appears in these *Leisure* books:

COMPULSION by Elaine Fox
includes Chapter One by Constance O'Banyon

CINNAMON AND ROSES by Heidi Betts
includes Chapter Two by Bobbi Smith

SWEET REVENGE by Lynsay Sands
includes Chapter Three by Evelyn Rogers

TELL ME LINES by Claudia Dain
includes Chapter Four by Emily Carmichael

WHITE NIGHTS by Susan Edwards
includes Chapter Five by Martha Hix

IN TROUBLE'S ARMS by Ronda Thompson
includes Chapter Six by Deana James

THE SWORD AND THE FLAME by Patricia Phillips
includes Chapter Seven by Sharon Schulze

MANON by Melanie Jackson
includes Chapter Eight by June Lund Shiplett

On January 1, 1997, *Romance Communications*, the Romance Magazine for the 21st century made its Internet debut. One year later, it was named a Lycos Top 5% site on the Web in terms of both content and graphics!

One of *Romance Communications*' most popular features is The Romantic Relay, an original romance novel divided into twelve monthly installments, with each chapter written by a different author. Our first offering was *Lair of the Wolf*, a tale of medieval Wales, created by, in alphabetical order, celebrated authors Emily Carmichael, Debra Dier, Madeline George, Martha Hix, Deana James, Elizabeth Mayne, Constance O'Banyon, Evelyn Rogers, Sharon Schulze, June Lund Shiplett, and Bobbi Smith.

We put no restrictions on the authors, letting each pick up the tale where the previous author had left off and going forward as she wished. The authors tell us they had a lot of fun, each trying to write her successor into a corner!

Now, preserving the fun and suspense of our month-by-month installments, Leisure Books presents, in print, one chapter a month of *Lair of the Wolf*. In addition to the entire online story, the authors have added some brand-new material to their existing chapters. So if you think you've read *Lair of the Wolf* already, you may find a few surprises. Please enjoy this unique offering, watch for each new monthly installment in the back of your Leisure Books, and make sure you visit our Web site, where another romantic relay is already in progress.

Romance Communications

http://www.romcom.com

Pamela Monck, Editor-in-Chief

Mary D. Pinto, Senior Editor

S. Lee Meyer, Web Mistress

Chapter Nine
by Elizabeth Mayne

Meredyth nearly cried out as Garon hit the stones at Hanes's feet. But she had no time for tears. The moment she spied blood staining her Wolf's tunic, she was galvanized into motion.

She ran to the steps and reached for her father's armorial shield, hanging in its honored place high on the stone wall. With all her strength, she snatched the shield then hunkered down, covering Garon's limp body, protecting him as another English arrow let loose from its bow. The missile hit the shield with a force that nearly tore the protection out of her grip.

"Cease your fire, traitor!" Hanes bellowed when he saw the man fit another arrow in his bow. "In the name of the king, put down your weapon!"

Meredyth took heart. Garon's captain would protect them or die trying. She slid her arm under Garon's head, lifting it gently, kissing his brow. She could not lose him now. Not now. If he was to die, she would die with him!

Hanes's curse was followed by squeals from the kitchen area as serving women surged into the hall. The furious Welsh women joined their men in the fight against Sir Olyver and his followers.

Even Dame Allison brought the cook's heaviest wooden dough bowl down with all her might on the head of one of Sir Olyver's unfortunate men, knocking him out cold.

Confused at the sight of female warriors, one young soldier hesitated, just long enough for the cook to get her full weight behind the swing of her cast-iron pan. The youth went flying as the pan collided with him, spewing oatmeal and him all over the hearth.

"Garon!" Meredyth touched her husband cheek. He groaned and lifted his chin.

Dazed, unfocused eyes slowly opened. Garon blinked in surprise. Meredyth's pale face hovered above him. He winced as he tried to sit up. An inexplicable pain shot through his shoulder, and his arm would not move at all.

"What do you here, Merrie?" he demanded. He was amidst a battle, wasn't he? Didn't she realize this was no place for a woman?

Beyond the steps reigned bedlam. Shouts, screams, the commotion of a furious melee in full force. Garon couldn't see past Meredyth's frightened face. Had he wished her to his side? He could not answer that. His thoughts were cloudy and colored by pain.

"Sir Olyver wanted to kill you," she whispered. Then a soft breath escaped her throat.

"Aye, but I am not dead, my lady," Garon assured her, recovering his wits more quickly than he could recover his strength. "Stung, aye. Dead, nay."

"I am glad," Meredyth whispered so softly he wouldn't have believed she'd spoken at all if he hadn't seen her lips move as she formed each sweet word.

Garon stared at her, and time stood still. Had he heard her correctly? Aye, he had. He'd stake his soul on that. He wanted to kiss her, but this was no time for such. Besides, he lay in an undignified heap on the castle stairs. Still, he couldn't stop thinking of kissing her delectable lips.

From the sounds of it, all holy hell was breaking loose in the hall's confines. Why, then, could he think only of kissing his lady? She'd saved his life. Risked hers to save his. That was no reason to crave the solace of her kisses like a raw boy cut in his first quarrel with the quintain.

Meredyth brought her father's shield as close as she dared to the fletching on the arrow shaft that protruded from Garon's shoulder and bent her head to his. Sweetly, gently, she kissed him, a butterfly's kiss touching his lips. He felt so warm, so rich and full of life that her breath caught in her throat once more.

She couldn't even tear her gaze from his to attend to the confusion in the hall.

"Help me up, my lady," he said. "Let me deal with this crisis honorably. Your womenfolk are about to murder poor Sir Olyver."

"Let them," Meredyth answered. "He's a back-stabbing cur, not fit to wipe your boots."

"Be that as it may, King Edward has a modest admiration for Olyver's prowess in battle and would take unkindly to his being bludgeoned to death by the cooks and scullery maids of Glendire Castle."

"Release me at once!" Sir Olyver demanded. His dramatic voice slipped a notch toward panic as too many women and girls simultaneously assaulted him.

Meredyth sat back on the step with Garon, as the two of them looked up in surprise at this latest twist in the unusual ruckus in the Great Hall.

"When hell freezes over, Sir Olyver!" Dame Allison answered the knight's demand by clobbering him with the long-handled tin pan she used each winter night to warm Merrie's cold bed. Bertha, the alewife, lambasted him with a pastry fork, and every time he tried to lunge forward and escape their battering, the cook beat him back into the corner with a rolling pin.

Garon sat up, then looked at Meredyth with a grin on his dark face. "Remind me to charge the king for all the household pots, pans, and utensils broken in subduing the varlet." Then he laughed.

Meredyth's mouth opened in surprise. How young and boyish Garon's face looked when a smile lighted it. The flash of a Welsh red cloak drew her eyes back to the hall.

Sir Olyver tried again to gain control, but young Amy would have none of that. No sooner had her red cloak settled over Olyver's head, blinding the villain, than she yelled, "Now, ladies, to Lady Saunders' aid! Hit the English devil with everything we've got!"

The battle cry "Lady Saunders" registered squarely in Garon's ear as Meredyth moved to help him rise. Her father's armorial shield slid, unneeded now, stone steps to the hall floor, its clanging lost in the clamor of the feminine tempest unleashed upon Sir Olyver.

Garon saw that his loyal vassals were standing back, allowing Meredyth's servants free reign in their assault upon the Englishman who'd put them through so much distress. Even the seven-year-old spit boy, Benjamin, had joined the assault on the wicked knight, pelting him with rotting scraps set aside for the pigs.

The women from the kitchen had only just begun to fight, wielding their pans, spatulas, and ladles at the few men loyal to Sir Olyver.

A better or more fitting gauntlet, Garon couldn't have devised if he'd thought for a week about how to punish the curs.

Garon pulled himself together, gripped the wall, and rose to his feet. At the bottom of the stairs he saw the crest of the house of Llewellyn, an English arrow imbedded in the heart of its golden griffin.

Merrie had thrown herself and that shield across him.

He'd surely be dead if she hadn't. Still he shuddered to think what might have happened to her if she hadn't been as quick as a deer in the forest.

That arrow could have killed her.

He made to pick up the shield and restore it to its place of honor on the wall.

Bertha, the alewife, beat him to it. Her round, flushed face sobered as she stood the shield on its point. It was taller than she.

"Y'er in no shape to be picking up armor, my lord." She put her fingers to her lips and let loose a shrill whistle to quiet the tumult in the hall.

"Here now, the fight's over, ladies. Dame Allison, if you please. Our lord needs his wound tended."

"I'll get that." John Hanes took the weighty shield from the Welsh woman. He turned to Lady Meredyth, his face solemn as he looked her over, making certain she was unharmed. Then he nodded and said to her, "Ye be a foolish girl, my lady, to risk yourself in battle, but a brave girl at that. Ye have my thanks for seeing through the tricks of one man and into the heart of another."

Garon handed his sword to his page and saw that his men had moved to take Olyver into custody and lock him back in his cell in the dungeon. Castle Glendire's servants righted benches and trestles and collected their scattered pots and pans.

When there was space to move, Garon allowed Meredyth to lead him to his seat on the dais.

"Your wound must be tended and this arrow removed," Meredyth said. "I will fetch hot water."

Garon nodded distractedly, interested in the quiet way that order had been restored without command. His fingers clasped the carved knobs of old Lord Llewellyn's seat of honor as deftly cut open, Hanes his tunic to reveal the arrow in his flesh. The wound bled a bit, and Garon could feel the forged tip against the joint and the ache of swelling flesh.

Dame Allison came to the high seat, bearing her treasured casket of medicaments like a gift to a king. Meredyth returned to his side with a steaming kettle of water and clean cloths.

Garon looked to Hanes and nodded, silently signaling the soldier to deal with the arrow swiftly.

While the ladies readied their compounds and hot poultices, the English captain gripped the shaft and Garon's shoulder, and with one sure pull removed the arrow.

It was done so quickly, Garon hadn't time to cry out. He clamped his jaw rigidly, as the shock and sensation whipped through him.

A cold sweat followed swiftly on the heels of the reverberating pain, and he fixed his gaze on Meredyth's lovely face to keep his nerves steady.

As she handed Dame Allison hot cloth after hot cloth, she worried her lower lip as feverishly as he willed himself not to faint. How his weakness humbled Longshanks' Wolf! This brave, delicate princess of the House of Llewellyn could easily topple him right now were she so inclined.

Her wonderful blue eyes rose from her ministrations and met his dark gaze at long last.

"It's not so very bad, my lord," she said, forcing an encouraging smile to her lips.

With his teeth clenched, Garon flashed her a smile in return as Dame Allison finished knotting her spider's web of gauze and cloth.

Garon waved aside his concerned captain, who was hovering nearby. "See to the defenses, Hanes. Let's not have a repeat of our earlier discord. You have John Trainor under lock and key as well?"

"Nay, my lord. He's escaped," Hanes admitted. "But the castle is secure. I locked Sir Olyver in irons myself and checked them twice after. I've got the only key on my person."

"Good man." Garon stood and held his left arm out to his lady. "We will be upstairs for a time. When I come back down, I will want an accounting of those who betrayed me and fought beside Sir Olyver."

Garon turned to Meredyth. "My lady, if you will assist me, I will need help putting on a fresh tunic."

She raised her eyebrows astonished at her husband's composure after sustaining so grievous an injury, and infuriated at his stubborn, bullheaded ways. Didn't he realize he'd just had an arrow removed from his shoulder? An arrow that had missed his heart by mere inches? Was he completely without sense that he thought he could act as if nothing unusual had occurred?

She made to tell him how foolish was his plan to resume his activities so soon. Then she saw the paleness about his lips, the tightness of his brow.

Please, my wife," he said for her ears only, "do not be contrary with me now."

Meredyth swallowed her instinctive protest, laid her fingers lightly on Garon's firm forearm, and acquiesced. "As you like, my lord."

"Ah," Garon breathed with relief, "the very words I have longed to hear from my lady's lips—at last."

Watch for Chapter Ten, by Debra Dier, of Lair of the Wolf, *appearing in September 2000 in* North Star *by Amanda Harte.*